Praise for
Rain Gods

"Burke spins a tale replete with colorful prose and epic confrontations in his second novel to feature small-town Texas sheriff Hackberry Holland . . . [and a] full roster of sharply drawn lowlifes. The battle of wills and wits between Holland and Collins delivers everything Burke's fans expect."

—*Publishers Weekly*

"Crazy he may be, but Preacher is one of Burke's most inspired villains—violent and cruel, but also profoundly moralistic and self-loathing."

—*The New York Times*

"Hackberry is his own man, shaped by the unforgiving Texas soil the way [Burke's detective] Robicheaux bleeds bayou blue. . . . Burke fans will notice much that is familiar here—the lyricism, the minor key, the elegiac refrain—but the melody is new and haunting."

—*Booklist*

"Nearly every scene builds to a fine crescendo of tension."

—*Kirkus Reviews*

By James Lee Burke

Dave Robicheaux Novels

A Private Cathedral
The New Iberia Blues
Robicheaux
Light of the World
Creole Belle
The Glass Rainbow
Swan Peak
The Tin Roof Blowdown
Pegasus Descending
Crusader's Cross
Last Car to Elysian Fields
Jolie Blon's Bounce
Purple Cane Road
Sunset Limited
Cadillac Jukebox
Burning Angel
Dixie City Jam
In the Electric Mist with Confederate Dead
A Stained White Radiance
A Morning for Flamingos
Black Cherry Blues
Heaven's Prisoners
The Neon Rain

Rain Gods

James Lee Burke

Simon & Schuster Paperbacks

New York London Toronto Sydney New Delhi

Simon & Schuster Paperbacks
An Imprint of Simon & Schuster, Inc.
1230 Avenue of the Americas
New York, NY 10020

This Simon & Schuster trade paperback edition July 2021

For information about special discounts for bulk purchases, please contact Simon & Schuster Special Sales at 1-866-506-1949 or business@simonandschuster.com.

The Simon & Schuster Speakers Bureau can bring authors to your live event. For more information or to book an event, contact the Simon & Schuster Speakers Bureau at 1-866-248-3049 or visit our website at www.simonspeakers.com.

Manufactured in the United States of America

1   3   5   7   9   10   8   6   4   2

Library of Congress Cataloging-in-Publication Data is available on file.

ISBN 978-1-4391-2824-4
ISBN 978-1-9821-8343-1 (pbk)
ISBN 978-1-4391-3736-9 (ebook)

In memory of James Brown Benbow,
Dan Benbow, and Weldon Mallette

And he called to him his twelve disciples and gave them authority over unclean spirits, to cast them out, and to heal every disease and every infirmity. . . .

These twelve Jesus sent out, charging them, "Go nowhere among the Gentiles, and enter no town of the Samaritans, but go rather to the lost sheep of the house of Israel. And preach as you go, saying, 'The kingdom of heaven is at hand.'"

MATTHEW 10:1–7

Chapter 1

O<small>N THE BURNT-OUT</small> end of a July day in Southwest Texas, in a crossroads community whose only economic importance had depended on its relationship to a roach paste factory the EPA had shut down twenty years before, a young man driving a car without window glass stopped by an abandoned blue-and-white stucco filling station that had once sold Pure gas during the Depression and was now home to bats and clusters of tumbleweed. Next to the filling station was a mechanic's shed whose desiccated boards lay collapsed upon a rusted pickup truck with four flat bald tires. At the intersection a stoplight hung from a horizontal cable strung between two power poles, its plastic covers shot out by .22 rifles.

The young man entered a phone booth and wiped his face slick with the flat of his hand. His denim shirt was stiff with salt and open on his chest, his hair mowed into the scalp, GI-style. He pulled an unlabeled pint bottle from the front of his jeans and unscrewed the cap. Down the right side of his face was a swollen pink scar that was as bright and shiny as plastic and looked pasted onto the skin rather than part of it. The mescal in the bottle was yellow and thick with threadworms that seemed to light against the sunset when he tipped the neck to his mouth. Inside the booth, he could feel his heart quickening and lines of sweat running down from his armpits into the waistband of his undershorts. His index finger trembled as he punched in the numbers on the phone's console.

"What's your emergency?" a woman dispatcher asked.

The rolling countryside was the color of a browned biscuit, stretching away endlessly, the monotony of rocks and creosote brush and grit and mesquite trees interrupted only by an occasional windmill rattling in the breeze.

"Last night there was some shooting here. A lot of it," he said. "I heard it in the dark and saw the flashes."

"Shooting where?"

"By that old church. I think that's what happened. I was drinking. I saw it from down the road. It scared the doo-doo out of me."

There was a pause. "Are you drinking now, sir?"

"Not really. I mean, not much. Just a few hits of Mexican worm juice."

"Tell us where you are, and we'll send out a cruiser. Will you wait there for a cruiser to come out?"

"This doesn't have anything to do with me. A lot of wets go through here. There's oceans of trash down by the border. Dirty diapers and moldy clothes and rotted food and tennis shoes without strings in them. Why would they take the strings out of their tennis shoes?"

"Is this about illegals?"

"I said I heard somebody busting caps. That's all I'm reporting. Maybe I heard a tailgate drop. I'm sure I did. It clanked in the dark."

"Sir, where are you calling from?"

"The same place I heard all that shooting."

"Give me your name, please."

"What name they got for a guy so dumb he thinks doing the right thing is the right thing? Answer me that, please, ma'am."

He tried to slam down the receiver on the hook but missed. The phone receiver swung back and forth from the phone box as the young man with the welted pink scar on his face drove away, road dust sucking back through the glassless windows of his car.

TWENTY-FOUR HOURS LATER, at sunset, the sky turned to turquoise; then the strips of black cloud along the horizon were backlit by a red brilliance that was like the glow of a forge, as though the cooling of the day were about to be set into abeyance so the sun's heat could prevail through the night into the following dawn. Across the street from the abandoned filling station, a tall man in his seventies, wearing western-cut khakis and hand-tooled boots and an old-fashioned gun belt and a dove-colored Stetson, parked his truck in front of what appeared to be the shell of a Spanish mission. The roof had caved onto the floor, and the doors had been twisted off the hinges and carried inside and broken up and used for firewood by homeless people or teenage vandals. The only tree in the crossroads community was a giant willow; it shaded one side of the church and created a strange effect of shadow and red light on the stucco walls, as though a grass fire were approaching the structure and about to consume it.

In reality, the church had been built not by Spaniards or Mexicans but by an industrialist who had become the most hated man in America after his company security forces and members of the Colorado militia massacred eleven children and two women during a miners' strike in 1914. Later, the industrialist reinvented himself as a philanthropist and humanitarian and rehabilitated his family name by building churches around the country. But the miners did not get their union, and this particular church became a scorched cipher that few associate with the two women and eleven children who had tried to hide in a root cellar while the canvas tent above them rained ash and flame upon their heads.

The tall man was wearing a holstered blue-black white-handled revolver. Unconsciously, he removed his hat when he entered the church, waiting for his eyes to adjust to the deep shadows inside the walls. The oak flooring had been ripped up and hauled away by a contractor, and the dirt underneath was green and cool with lack of sunlight, packed down hard, humped in places, smelling of dampness and the feces of field mice. Scattered about the church's interior, glinting like gold teeth, were dozens of brass shell casings.

The tall man squatted down, his gunbelt creaking, his knees popping. He picked up a casing on the end of a ballpoint pen. It, like all the others, was .45-caliber. He cleared his throat softly and spat to one side, unable to avoid the odor that the wind had just kicked up outside. He rose to his feet and walked out the back door and gazed at a field that had been raked by a bulldozer's blade, the cinnamon-colored dirt scrolled and stenciled by the dozer's steel treads.

The tall man returned to his pickup truck and removed a leaf rake and a long-handled shovel from the bed. He walked into the field and sank the steel tip of the shovel blade with the weight of his leg and haunch and struck a rock, then reset the blade in a different spot and tried again. This time the blade went deep, all the way up to his boot sole, as though it were cutting through compacted coffee grounds rather than dirt. When he pulled the shovel free, an odor rose into his nostrils that made his throat close against the bilious surge in his stomach. He soaked a bandana from a canteen in his truck and wrapped it around the lower half of his face and knotted it behind his head. Then he walked slowly across the field, jabbing the inverted half of the rake handle into the ground. Every three or four feet, at the same depth, he felt a soft form of resistance, like a sack of feed whose burlap has rotted and split, the dry dirt rilling back into the hole each time he pulled the wood shaft from the surface. The breeze had died completely. The air was green with the sun's last light, the sky dissected by birds, the air stained by a growing stench that seemed to rise from his boots into his clothes. The tall man inverted the rake, careful not to touch the tip that he had pushed below the soil, and began scraping at a depression that a feral animal had already crosshatched with claw marks.

The tall man had many memories from his early life that he seldom shared with others. They involved images of snowy hills south of the Yalu River, and dead Chinese troops in quilted uniforms scattered randomly across the slopes, and F-80 jets flying low out of the overcast sky, strafing the perimeter to push the Chinese mortar and automatic weapons teams back out of range. The wounds on the American dead piled in the backs of the six-bys looked like roses frozen inside snow.

In his sleep, the tall man still heard bugles blowing in the hills, echoing as coldly as brass ringing on stone.

The spidery tines of the rake pulled a lock of black hair free from the dirt. The tall man, whose name was Hackberry Holland, looked down into the depression. He touched the rake at the edges of the rounded shape he had uncovered. Then, because of either a lack of compaction around the figure or the fact that it lay on top of other bodies, the soil began to slide off the person's face and ears and neck and shoulders, down into a subterranean hole, exposing the waxy opalescence of a brow, the rictus that imitated surprise, one eye lidded, the other as bold as a child's marble, a ball of dirt clenched in the figure's palm.

She was thin-boned, a toy person, her black blouse a receptacle for heat and totally inappropriate for the climate. He guessed she was not over seventeen and that she had been alive when the dirt was pushed on top of her. She was also Asian, not Hispanic as he had expected.

For the next half hour, until the light had gone from the sky, he continued to rake and dig in the field that had obviously been scraped down to the hardpan by a dozer blade, then backfilled with the overburden and tamped down and graded as smoothly as if in preparation for construction of a home.

He went back to his truck and threw the rake and shovel in the bed, then lifted his handheld radio off the passenger seat. "Maydeen, this is Sheriff Holland," he said. "I'm behind the old church at Chapala Crossing. I've uncovered the burials of nine homicide victims so far, all female. Call the feds and also call both Brewster and Terrell counties and tell them we need their assistance."

"You're breaking up. Say again? Did I read you right? You said nine homicide—"

"We've got a mass murder. The victims are all Asian, some of them hardly more than children."

"The guy who made the nine-one-one, he called a second time."

"What'd he say?"

"I don't think he just happened by the church site. I think he's dripping with guilt."

"Did you get his name?"

"He said it was Pete. No last name. Why didn't you call in? I could have sent help. You're too goddamn old for this crap, Hack."

Because at a certain age, you finally accept and trust yourself and let go of the world, he thought. But in reply, all he said was "Maydeen, would you not use that kind of language over the air, please?"

PETE FLORES NEVER quite understood why the girl lived with him. Her hair was chestnut-colored, cut short and curled on the ends, her skin clear, her blue-green eyes deep-set, which gave them a mysterious quality that intrigued men and caused them to stare at her back long after she had walked past them. At the diner where she worked, she conducted herself with a level of grace that her customers, mostly long-haul truckers, sensed and respected and were protective of. She attended classes three nights a week at a junior college in the county seat, and the previous semester had published a short story in the college literary magazine. Her name was Vikki Gaddis, and she played a big-belly J-200 Gibson that her father, a part-time country musician from Medicine Lodge, Kansas, had given her when she was twelve years old.

Her husky voice and accent were not acquired or feigned. On occasion, when she played her guitar and sang at the diner, her customers rose from their chairs and stools and applauded. She also performed sometimes at the nightclub next door, although the patrons were unsure how they should respond when she sang "Will the Circle Be Unbroken" and "Keep on the Sunny Side of Life."

She was still asleep when Pete entered the paintless frame house they rented, one that sat inside the blue shadow of a hill when the sun rose above the horizon as hot and sultry as a broken egg yolk, the light streaking across the barren land. Pete's scalp and face were pulled tight with the beginnings of a hangover, the inside of his head still filled with the sounds of the highway bar he had been in. He washed his face in the sink, the water running cool out of a faucet that drew on an aluminum cistern elevated on stilts behind the house. The hill that blocked the sunrise, almost like an act of mercy, looked made of rust and cinders and was dotted with scrub brush and mesquite trees whose root systems could barely grow deep enough to find moisture. He knew Vikki would be up soon, that she had probably waited for him last night and slept fitfully, either knowing or not knowing where he was. He wanted to fix breakfast for her, as a form of contrition or in a pretense at normalcy. He filled the coffeepot with water, and the effect of both darkness and coolness it created inside the metal was somehow a temporary balm to the pounding heat inside his head.

He smeared margarine inside a skillet and took two eggs and a piece of sliced ham from the ice chest he and Vikki used as a refrigerator. He broke the eggs in the skillet and set the ham and a slice of sourdough bread beside them and let the skillet begin to heat on the propane stove. The smell of the breakfast he wanted to cook for Vikki rose into his face, and he rushed out the back door into the yard so he would not retch on his clothes.

He held on to the sides of a horse tank, his stomach empty now, his back shaking, a pressure band tightening across his scalp, his breath an insult to the air and the freshness of the morning. He thought he heard the thropping downdraft of gunships and the great clanking weight of an armored vehicle topping a rise, its treads dripping sand, a CD of *Burn, Motherfucker, Burn* screaming over the intercom. He stared into the distant wastes, but the only living things he saw were carrion birds floating high on the wind stream, turning in slow circles as the land heated and the smell of mortality rose into the sky.

He went back inside and rinsed his mouth, then scraped Vikki's breakfast onto a plate. The eggs were burned on the edges, the yolks broken and hard and stained with black grease. He sat in a chair and hung his head between his knees, the kitchen spinning around him. Through the partially opened door of the bedroom, through the blue light and the dust stirring in the breeze, he could see her head on the pillow, her eyes closed, her lips parted with her breathing. The poverty of the surroundings into which he had taken her made him ashamed. The cracks in the linoleum were ingrained with dirt, the mismatched furniture bought at Goodwill, the walls a sickly green. Everything he touched except Vikki Gaddis was somehow an extension of his own failure.

Her eyes opened. Pete sat up straight in the chair, trying to smile, his face stiff and unnatural with the effort.

"I was fixing you breakfast, but I made a mess of it," he said.

"Where you been, hon?"

"You know, up yonder," he replied, gesturing in the direction of the highway. He waited for her to speak, but she didn't. "Why would people throw away their tennis shoes but take the shoe-strings with them?" he asked.

"What are you talking about?"

"In the places where the wets go through, there's trash and garbage everywhere. They throw away their old tennis shoes, but they take out the strings first. Why do they do that?"

She was standing up now, pulling her jeans over her panties, looking down at her fingers as she buttoned her jeans over the flatness of her stomach.

"It's 'cause they don't own much else, isn't it?" he said in answer to his own question. "Them poor people don't own nothing but the word of the coyote that takes them across. That's a miserable fate for someone, isn't it?"

"What have you got into, Pete?"

He knitted his fingers together between his thighs and squeezed them so hard he could feel the blood stop in his veins. "A guy was gonna give me three hundred bucks to drive a truck to San Antone. He said not to worry about anything in the back. He gave me a hundred up front. He said it was just a few people who needed to get to their relatives' houses. I checked the guy out. He's not a mule. Mules don't use trucks to run dope, anyway."

"You checked him out? Who did you check him out with?" she said, looking at him, her hands letting go of her clothes.

"Guys I know, guys who hang around the bar."

Her face was empty, still creased from the pillow, as she walked to the stove and poured herself a cup of coffee. She was barefoot, her skin white against the dirtiness of the linoleum. He went into the bedroom and picked up her slippers from under the bed and brought them to her. He set them down by her feet and waited for her to put them on.

"There were some men here last night," she said.

"What?" The blood drained from his cheeks, making him seem younger than even his twenty years.

"Two of them came to the door. One stayed in the car. He never turned off the motor. The one who talked had funny eyes, like they didn't go together. Who is he?"

"What did he say?"

Pete hadn't answered her question. But her heart was racing, and she answered him anyway. "That y'all had a misunderstanding. That you ran off in the dark or something. That he owes you some money. He was grinning all the time he talked. I shook his hand. He put out his hand and I shook it."

"His head looks like it has plates in it, like there's a glitter in one eye and not the other?"

"That's the one. Who is he, Pete?"

"His name is Hugo. He was in the truck cab with me for a while. He had a Thompson in a canvas bag. The ammo pan was rattling, and he took it out and looked at it and put it back in the bag. He said, 'This sweetheart of a piece belongs to the most dangerous man in Texas.'"

"He had a what in a bag?"

"A World War Two submachine gun. We were stopped in the dark. He started talking on a two-way. Some guy said, 'Shut it down. Wipe the slate clean.' I got out to take a leak, then I climbed down in an irrigation ditch and kept going."

"He squeezed my hand hard, really hard. Wait, you ran away from what?"

"Hugo hurt your hand?"

"What did I just say? Are these people dope traffickers?"

"No, a lot worse. I've got into some real shit, Vikki," he replied. "I heard gunfire in the dark. I heard people screaming inside it. They were women, maybe some of them girls."

When she didn't answer, when her face went blank as though she were looking at someone she didn't know, he tried to examine her hand. But she went to the kitchen screen, her back to him, her arms folded across her chest, an unrelieved sadness in her eyes as she stared at the harshness of the light spreading across the landscape.

Chapter 2

Nɪᴄᴋ Dᴏʟᴀɴ's sᴋɪɴ joint was halfway between Austin and San Antonio, a three-story refurbished Victorian home with fresh white paint on it, set back in oak trees and pines, the balcony and windows strung with Christmas-tree lights that stayed up year-round. From the highway, it looked like a festive place, the gravel parking lot well lit, the small Mexican restaurant next door joined to the main building by a covered walkway, indicating to passersby that Nick wasn't selling just tits and ass, that this was a gentleman's place, that women were welcome, even families, if they were road-tired and wanted a fine meal at a reasonable price.

Nick had given up his floating casino in New Orleans and had left the city of his birth because he didn't like trouble with the vestiges of the old Mob or paying off every politician in the state who knew how to turn up his palm, including the governor, who was now in a federal prison. Nick didn't argue with the world or the venal nature of men or the iniquity that most of them seemed born in. His contention was with the world's hypocrisy. He sold people what they wanted, whether it was gambling or booze, ass on the half shell, or the freedom to fulfill all their fantasies inside a safe environment, one where they would never be held accountable for the secret desires they hid from others. But whenever a groundswell of moral outrage began to crest on the horizon, Nick knew who was about to get smacked flat on the beach.

However, he had another problem besides the hypocrisy of others: He had been screwed at birth, given a dumpy fat boy's body to live inside, one with flaccid arms and a short neck and duck feet, and bad eyesight on top of it, so that he had to wear thick, round glasses that made him look like a goldfish staring out of a bowl.

He dressed in elevator shoes, sport coats that had padded shoulders, and expensive and tasteful jewelry; he paid a minimum of seventy-five dollars for his shirts and ties. His twin daughters went to private school and took piano, ballet, and riding lessons; his son was about to become a freshman at the University of Texas. His wife played bridge at the country club, worked out every day at a gym, and did not want to hear details about the sources of Nick's income. She also paid her own bills from money she made in the stock and bond market. Most of the romance in their marriage had disappeared long ago, but she didn't nag and was a good mother, and by anyone's measure, she would be considered a person of good character, so who was Nick to complain? You played the cards you got dealt, duck feet or not.

Nick didn't argue or contend with the nature of the world. He was boisterous and assumed the role of the diffident fool if he had to. He didn't put moves on his girls and didn't deceive himself about the nature of their loyalties. Born-again Christians were always talking about "honesty." Nick's "honest" view of himself and his relationship to the world was as follows: He was an overweight, short, balding, late-middle-aged man who knew his limits and kept his boundaries. He lived in a Puritan nation that was obsessed with sex and endlessly tittering about it, like kids just discovering their twangers in the YMCA swimming pool. If anyone doubted that fact, he told himself, they should click on their television sets during family hours and check out the crap their children were watching.

According to Nick, the only true sin in this country was financial failure. Respectability you bought with your checkbook. *That* was cynicism? The Kennedy family earned their fortune during Prohibition selling Bibles? Poor guys ran the United States Senate? A lot of American presidents graduated from city colleges in Blow Me, Idaho?

But right now Nick had a problem that never should have come into his life, that he had done nothing to deserve, that his years of abuse at the hands of schoolyard bullies in the Ninth Ward of Orleans Parish should have preempted as payment for any sins he had ever committed. The problem had just walked into the club and taken a seat at the bar, ordering a glass of carbonated water and ice with cherry juice, eyeballing the girls up on the poles, the skin of his face like a leather mask, his lips thick, always suppressing a grin, the inside of his head constructed of bones that didn't seem to fit right. The problem's name was Hugo Cistranos, and he scared the living shit out of Nick Dolan.

If Nick could just walk out of the front of the club into the safety of his office, past the tables full of college boys and divorced working stiffs and upscale suits pretending they were visiting the club for a lark. He could call somebody, cut a deal, apologize, offer some kind of restitution, just get on the phone and do it, whatever it took. That was what businessmen did when confronted with insurmountable problems. They talked on the phone. He wasn't responsible for the deeds of a maniac. In fact, he wasn't even sure what the maniac had done.

That was it. If you didn't know what the sick fuck had actually done, how could you be blamed for it? Nick wasn't a player in this, only a business guy trying to divert the competition after they had threatened to drive under his escort services in Houston and Dallas, where 40 percent of his cash flow originated.

Just walk into the office, he told himself. Ignore the way Hugo's eyes bored into the side of his face, his neck, his back, peeling off his clothes and skin, picking the few specks of his dignity off his soul. Ignore the proprietary manner, the smirk that silently indicated Hugo owned Nick and knew his thoughts and his weaknesses and could reach out whenever he wished and expose the frightened little fat boy who'd had his lunch money taken from him by the black kids in the schoolyard.

The memory of those days in the Ninth Ward caused a surge of heat to bloom in Nick's chest, a flicker of martial energy that made him close one hand in a fist, surprising him at the potential that might lie inside the fat boy's body. He turned and looked Hugo full in the face. Then, with his eyelids stitched to his forehead, Nick approached him, his lighted cigarette held away from his sport coat, his mouth drying up, his heart threading with weevil worms. The girls up on the poles, their bodies sprayed with glitter, their faces pancakelike with foundation, became smoke-wreathed animations whose names he had never known, whose lives had nothing to do with his own, even though every one of them courted his favor and always called him Nick in the same tone they would use when addressing a protective uncle. Nick Dolan was on his own.

He rested his right hand on the bar but did not sit down, the ash from his cigarette falling on his slacks. Hugo grinned, his eyes following the trail of smoke from Nick's cigarette down to the yellow nicotine stain layered between his index and middle finger. "You still smoke three decks a day?" Hugo said.

"I'm starting to wear a patch," Nick said, holding his eyes on Hugo's, wondering if he had just lied or told the truth and sounded small and foolish and plaint, regardless.

"Marlboros will put you in a box. The chemicals alone."

"Everybody dies."

"The chemicals hide the smell of the nicotine so you won't be thinking about the damage it's doing to your organs. Spots on the lungs, spots on the liver, all that. It goes on in your sleep and you don't even know it."

"I'm about to go home. You want to see me about something?"

"Yeah, you could call it something. Want to go in your office?"

"The cleaning woman is vacuuming in there."

"Makes sense to me. Nothing like running a vacuum cleaner in a nightclub during peak hours. Tell me the name of the cleaning service so I don't call them up by mistake. I'll walk outside with you. You ought to see the sky. Dry lightning is leaping all over the clouds. Have your smoke out in the fresh air."

"My wife is waiting dinner on me."

"That's funny, since you're notorious for always closing the joint yourself and counting every penny in the till."

"There a second meaning in that?"

Hugo drank from his carbonated water and chewed a cherry on the back of his teeth, his expression thoughtful. "No, there's no second meaning there, Nicholas." His tongue was bright red. He wiped his mouth with a paper napkin and looked at the smear of color on it. "I hired some extra personnel that I need your advice about. A kid that's proving to be a pain in the ass." He leaned forward and squeezed Nick's shoulder, his face suffused with warmth and intimacy. "I think it's gonna rain. You'll like the fresh smell in the air. It'll get all that nicotine out of your clothes."

Outside, the air was as Hugo had described it, scented with the possibility of a thunderstorm and the smell of watermelons in a field on the far side of live oaks at the back of Nick's property. Nick walked in front of Hugo into a space between a Buick and Hugo's big black SUV. Hugo propped one arm on the fender of his vehicle, blocking Nick's view of the club. He wore a sport shirt and pleated white slacks and shined Italian shoes. In the electric glow from the overhead lamps, his propped forearm was taut and pale and wrapped with green veins.

"Artie Rooney is light nine chippies," Hugo said.

"I don't know anything about this," Nick said.

Hugo scratched the back of his neck. His hair was ash-blond, streaked with red, like iodine, gelled and combed straight back so that his high forehead had a polished look resembling the prow of a ship. "'Wipe the slate clean.' What do those words mean to you, Nicholas?"

"It's Nick."

"This question still stands, Nick."

"They mean 'forget it.' The words mean 'pull the plug.' They don't mean go apeshit."

"Let me see if I got your vision of things straight. We kidnap Rooney's Thai whores, put at least one of his coyotes in a hole, then turn a bunch of hysterical slopes loose on a dirt road so I can either ride the needle or spend the next forty years in a federal facility?"

"What's that you said about a coyote?"

Nick felt something blink in his mind, a dysfunctional shutter snapping open and closing, a malfunction in his brain or in his subconscious, an impaired mechanism that for a lifetime had not stopped him from speaking or given him the right words to say until it was too late, leaving him vulnerable and alone and at the mercy of his adversaries. Why had he asked a question? Why had he just exposed himself to more knowledge of what Hugo had done on a dark road to a truckload of helpless Asian women, maybe girls as well? Nick felt as though his ectoplasm were draining through the soles of his shoes.

"I'm at a loss on this, Hugo. I got no idea what we're talking about here," he said, his eyes sliding off Hugo's face, his words like wet ash in his throat.

Hugo looked away and pulled on an earlobe. His mouth was compressed, his mirth leaking from his nose like air escaping a rubber seal. "You're all the same," he said.

"Who's the 'you'?"

"Monkey see no evil. You hire others to do it for you. You owe me ninety large, Nicholas, ten grand for each unit I had to take off Artie's hands and dispose of. You also owe me seven grand for transportation costs. You owe me another five large for employee expenses. The vig is a point and a half a week."

"*Vig?* What vig? Are you out of your mind?"

"Then there's this other issue, a kid I hired out of a wino bar."

"What kid?"

"Pete Rumdum. What difference does it make? He got off the leash."

"No, I'm not part of this. Let me by."

"It gets a little more complicated. I've been to the rathole he lives in. A girl was there. She saw me. So now she's a factor. Do I have your attention?"

Nick was stepping backward, shaking his head, trying to remove himself from the closed space that seemed to be crushing the light out of his eyes. "I'm going home. I've known Artie Rooney for years. I can work this out. He's a businessman."

Hugo took out his pocket comb and ran it through his hair with one hand. "Artie Rooney offered me his old Caddy to put you on a crash diet. Enforced total abstinence. Fifteen to twenty pounds a day weight loss guaranteed. Inside your own box, get it? Know why he doesn't like you, Nicholas? Because he's a real mick and not a fraud who changes his name from Dolinski to Dolan. I'll drop by tomorrow to get my cash. I want it in fifties, no consecutive numbers on the bills."

The words were going too fast. "Why'd you turn Artie Rooney down on the hit?" Nick said, because he had to say something.

"I already got a Caddy."

Two minutes later, when Nick walked back into his nightclub, the pounding music of the four-piece band was not nearly as loud as the thundering of Nick's heart and the rasping of his lungs as he tried to suck oxygen past the cigarette he held in his mouth.

"Nick, your face is white. You get some bad news?" the bartender said.

"Everything is great," Nick replied.

When he sat on the bar stool, his head reeling, his duck feet were so swollen with hypertension that he thought his shoes would burst their laces.

BEFORE HE FINALLY went to bed, Hackberry Holland had gone into the shower stall as his only salutary refuge from his experience behind the church, washing his hair, scrubbing his skin until it was red, holding his face in the hot water as long as he could stand it. But the odor of disinterred bodies had followed him into his sleep, trailing with him through the next day into the following twilight, into the onset of darkness, the hills flickering with electricity, the horn of an eighteen-wheeler blowing far down the highway like a bugle from a forgotten war.

Federal agents had done most of the work at the murder scene, setting up a field mortuary and flood lamps and satellite communications that probably involved Mexican authorities as well as their own departmental supervisors in D.C. They were polite to him, respectful in their perfunctory fashion, but it was obvious they thought of him as a curiosity if not simply a bystander or witness. At dawn, when all the exhumed bodies had been bagged and removed and the agents were wrapping up the site, a man in a suit, with white hair and threadlike blue and red capillaries in his cheeks, approached Hackberry and shook hands in farewell, his smile forced, as though he was preparing to ask a question that was not intended to offend.

"I understand you were an attorney for the ACLU," he said.

"At one time, many years ago."

"Quite a change in career choices."

"Not really."

"I didn't tell you something. One of our agents found some bones that have been in the ground a long time."

"Maybe they're Indian," Hack said.

"They're not that old."

"Maybe the shooter has used this site before. The dozer was brought in on a truck. It went out the same way. Maybe this is a very organized guy."

But the FBI agent in charge of the exhumation, whose name was Ethan Riser, was not listening. "Why did you stay out here digging up all these bodies by yourself? Why didn't you call in sooner?" he said.

"I was a POW during the Korean War. I was at Pak's Palace, plus a couple of other places."

The agent nodded, then said, "Forgive me if I don't make the connection."

"There were miles of refugees on the roadways, almost all of them headed south. The columns were infiltrated by North Korean soldiers in civilian clothes. Sometimes our F-80s were ordered to kill everybody on the road. We had to dig their graves. I don't think that story ever got reported."

"You're saying you don't trust us?" the agent said, still smiling.

"No, sir, I wouldn't dream of saying that."

The agent stared at the long roll of the countryside, the mesquite leaves lifting like green lace in the breeze. "It must be like living on moonscape out here," he said.

Hackberry did not reply and walked back to his truck, pain from an old back injury spreading into the lower regions of his spine.

* * *

IN THE LATE 1960s, he had tried to help a Hispanic friend from the service who had been beaten into a pile of bloody rags on a United Farm Workers picket line and charged with assaulting a law officer. At the time Hackberry was four fingers into a bottle of Jack Daniel's by midafternoon every day of the week. He was also a candidate for Congress and deep in the throes of political ambition and his own cynicism, both of which poorly masked the guilt and depression and self-loathing he had brought back with him from a POW camp located in a place the North Koreans called No Name Valley.

At the jail where his friend would eventually be murdered, Hackberry met Rie Velásquez, who was also a United Farm Workers organizer, and he was never the same again. He had thought he could walk away from his friend's death and from his meeting with the girl named Rie. But he was wrong on both counts. His first encounter with her was immediately antagonistic, and not because of her ideals or her in-your-face attitude. It was her lack of fear that bothered him, and her indifference to the opinions of others, even to her own fate. Worse, she conveyed the impression that she was willing to accept him if he didn't ask her to take him or his politics seriously.

She was intelligent and university-educated and stunning in appearance. He manufactured every reason possible to see her, dropping by her union headquarters, offering her a ride, all the while trying to marginalize her radicalism and dismiss and hold at bay her leftist frame of reference, as though accepting any part of it would be like pulling a thread on a sweater, in this instance unraveling his own belief system. But he never confronted the issue at hand, namely that the working poor she represented had a legitimate cause and that they were being terrorized by both growers and police officers because they wanted to form a union.

Hackberry Holland's political conversion did not take place at a union meeting or at Mass inside a sympathetic Catholic church, or involve seeing a blinding light on the road to Damascus. An irritable lawman accomplished the radicalization of Hackberry Holland by swinging a blackjack across his head and then trying to kick him to death. When Hackberry awoke on the concrete floor of a county lockup, his head inches from a perforated drain cover streaked with urine, he no longer doubted the efficacy of revolutionaries standing at the jailhouse door to sign up new members for their cause.

Rie had died of uterine cancer ten years ago, and their twin sons had left Texas, one for a position as an oncologist at the Mayo in Phoenix, the other as a boat skipper in the Florida Keys. Hackberry sold the ranch on the Guadalupe River where they had raised the children, and moved down by the border. If he'd been asked why he had given up the green place he loved for an existence in a dust-blown wasteland and a low-paying electoral office in a county seat whose streets and sidewalks and buildings were spiderwebbed with heat cracks, Hackberry would have had no explanation, or at least not one he would discuss with others.

The truth was, he could not rise in the morning from his bed surrounded by the things she had touched, the wind blowing the curtains, pressurizing the emptiness of the house, stressing the joists and studs and crossbeams and plaster walls against one another, filling the house with a level of silence that was like someone clapping cupped palms violently on his eardrums. He could not wake to these things and Rie's absence and the absence of his children, whom he still saw in his mind's eye as little boys, without concluding that a terrible theft had been perpetrated upon him and that it had left a lesion in his heart that would never heal.

A Baptist preacher had asked Hackberry if he was angry at God for his loss.

"God didn't invent death," Hackberry answered.

"Then who did?"

"Cancer is a disease produced by the Industrial Age."

"I think you're an angry man, Hack. I think you need to let go of it. I think you need to celebrate your wife's life and not mourn over what you cain't change."

I think you ought to keep your own counsel, Hackberry thought. But he did not say the words aloud.

Now, in the blue glow of early dawn and the fading of the stars in the sky, he tried to eat breakfast on his gallery and not think about the dreams he'd had just before waking. No, "dreams" wasn't the right word. Dreams had sequence and movement and voices inside them. All Hackberry could remember before opening his eyes into the starkness of his bedroom was the severity of the wounds in the bodies of the nine women and girls he had found buried by a bulldozer behind the church. How many people were aware of what a .45-caliber round could do to human tissue and bone? How many had ever seen what a .45 machine-gun burst could do to a person's face or brain cavity or breasts or rib cage?

There was a breeze out of the south, and even though his St. Augustine grass was dry and stiff, it had a pale greenish aura in the early dawn, and the flowers in his gardens were varied and bright with dew. He didn't want to think about the victims buried behind the church. No, that wasn't correct, either. He didn't want to think about the terror and the helplessness they had experienced before they were lined up and murdered. He didn't want to brood on these things because he had experienced them himself when he had been forced to stand with his fellow POWs on a snowy stretch of ground in zero-degree weather and wait for a Chinese prison guard to fire his burp gun point-blank into their chests and faces. But because of the mercurial nature of their executioner's bloodlust, Hackberry was spared and made to watch while others died, and sometimes he wished he had been left among the dead rather than the quick.

He believed that looking into the eyes of one's executioner in the last seconds of one's life was perhaps the worst fate that could befall a human being. That parting glimpse into the face of evil destroyed not only hope but any degree of faith in our fellow man that we might possess. He did not want to contend with those good souls who chose to believe we all descend from the same nuclear family, our poor, naked, bumbling ancestors back in Eden who, through pride or curiosity, transgressed by eating forbidden fruit. But he had long ago concluded that certain kinds of experiences at the hands of our fellow man were proof enough that we did not all descend from the same tree.

Or at least these were the thoughts that Hackberry's sleep often presented to him at first light, as foolish as they might seem.

He drank the coffee from his cup, covered his plate with a sheet of waxed paper, and set it inside his icebox. As he backed out of the driveway in his pickup truck and headed down the two-lane county road, he did not hear the telephone ringing inside his house.

He drove into town, parked behind the combination jail and office that served as his departmental headquarters, and entered the back door. His chief deputy, Pam Tibbs, was already at her desk, wearing jeans and cowboy boots and a short-sleeve khaki shirt and a gun belt, her face without expression. Her hair was thick and mahogany in color, curly at the tips, with a bit of gray that she didn't dye. Her most enigmatic quality lay in her eyes. They could brighten suddenly with goodwill or warmth or intense thought, but no one could be quite sure which. She had been a patrolwoman in Abilene and Galveston and had joined the department four years ago in order to be near her mother, who had been in a local hospice. Pam had a night-school degree from the University of Houston, but she spoke little of her background or her private life and gave others the sense they should not intrude upon it. Hackberry's recent promotion of her to chief deputy had not necessarily been welcomed by all of her colleagues.

"Good morning," Hackberry said.

Pam held her eyes on his without replying.

"Something wrong?" he said.

"An Immigration and Customs Enforcement guy by the name of Clawson just left. His business card is on your desk."

"What does he want?"

"Probably your ass."

"Pardon?"

"He wants to know why you didn't call in for help when you found the bodies," she replied.

"He asked you that?"

"He seems to think I'm the departmental snitch."

"What'd you tell him?"

"To take a walk."

Hackberry started toward his office. Through the window he could see the flag straightening on the metal pole in the yard, the sun behind clouds that offered no rain, dust gusting down a broken street lined by stucco and stone buildings that had been constructed no later than the 1920s.

"I heard him talking on his cell outside," Pam said at his back.

When he turned around, her eyes were fixed on his, one tooth biting down on the corner of her lip.

"Will you just say it, please?"

"The guy's a prick," she replied.

"I don't know who's worse, you or Maydeen. Will y'all stop using that kind of language while you're on the job?"

"I heard him talking outside on his cell. I think they know the identity of the witness who called in the shots fired. They think you know his identity, too. They think you're protecting him."

"Why would I protect a nine-one-one caller?"

"You have a cousin name of William Robert Holland?"

"What about him?"

"I heard Clawson use the name, that's all. I got the impression Holland might be your relative, that maybe he knows the nine-one-one caller. I was hearing only half of the conversation."

"Don't go anywhere," Hackberry said. He went into his office and found the Immigration and Customs Enforcement agent's business card centered squarely in the middle of his desk blotter. A cell phone number was written across the top; the area code was 713, Houston. He punched in the number on his desk phone.

"Clawson," a man's voice said.

"This is Sheriff Holland. I'm sorry I missed you this morning. What can I help you with?"

"I tried your home, but your message machine wasn't on."

"It doesn't always work. What is it you want to know?"

"A significant lapse of time occurred between your discovery of the bodies out by the church and your call to your dispatcher. Can you clear me up on that?"

"I'm not quite sure what the question is."

"You wanted to dig them up by yourself?"

"We're short on manpower."

"Are you related to a former Texas Ranger by the name of—"

"Billy Bob Holland, yeah, I am. He's an attorney. So am I, although I don't practice anymore."

"That's interesting. We need to have a chat, Sheriff Holland. I don't like getting to a crime scene hours after local law enforcement has tracked it up from one end to the other."

"Why is ICE involved in a homicide investigation?" Hackberry asked. He could hear the chain rattling on the flagpole, a trash can clattering drily on a curbstone. "Do you have the identity of the nine-one-one caller?"

"I'm not at liberty to discuss that right now."

"Excuse me, sir, but I have the impression that you consider a conversation a monologue in which other people answer your questions. Don't come bird-dogging my deputies again."

"What did you say?"

Hackberry replaced the receiver in the phone cradle. He walked back into the outer office. Pam Tibbs looked up from her paperwork, a slice of sunlight cutting her face. Her eyes were a deep brown, bright, fixed on his, waiting.

"You drive," he said.

THE AIR WAS muggy and warm when she parked the cruiser in the abandoned Pure filling station across from the stucco shell of the old church. Hackberry got out on the passenger side and looked at the phone booth on the perimeter of the concrete. The clear plastic panels were sprayed and scratched with graffiti, the phone box itself unbolted and removed. The sun had gone behind a cloud, and the hills had turned as dark as a bruise.

"The feds took the box?" Pam said.

"They'll dust it and all the coins inside and keep us out of the loop at the same time."

"Who owns the land behind the church?"

"A consortium in Delaware. They bought it from the roach paste people after the Superfund cleaned it up. I don't think they're players, though."

"Where'd the killers get the dozer to bury the bodies? They had to have some familiarity with the area. There were no prints on the shell casings?"

"Nope."

"Why would anyone kill all these women? What kind of bastard would do this?"

"Somebody who looks like your postman."

The sun came out of the clouds and flooded the landscape with a jittering light. Her brow was moist with perspiration, her skin browned and grainy. There were thin white lines at the corners of her eyes. For some reason, at that moment, she looked older than her years. "I don't buy that stuff."

"What stuff?"

"That mass killers live in our midst without ever being noticed, that they're just normal-looking people who have a screw torqued too tight in the back of their heads. I think they have neon warning signs hung all over them. People choose not to see what's at the end of their noses."

Hackberry watched the side of her face. There was no expression on it. But in moments like these, when Pam Tibbs's speech would rise slightly in intensity, a heated strand of wire threaded through her words, he would remain silent, his eyes deferential. "Ready?" he said.

"Yes, sir," she said.

They fitted on polyethylene gloves and began walking down opposite sides of the road, searching through the grass and scattered gravel and empty snuff containers and desiccated paper litter and broken glass and discarded rubbers and beer cans and whiskey and wine bottles. A quarter mile from the phone booth, they traded sides of the road and retraced their steps back to the booth, then continued on for two hundred yards in the opposite direction. Pam Tibbs descended into a grassy depression and picked up a clear flat-sided bottle that had no label. She hooked one finger through the bottle's lip and shook it gently. "The worm is still inside," she said.

"Have you seen that shape of bottle before?" he asked.

"Out at Ouzel Flagler's place. Ouzel always tries to keep it simple. No tax stamps or labels to create undue paperwork," she replied. She dropped the bottle in a large Ziploc bag.

* * *

OUZEL FLAGLER RAN an unlicensed bar in a plank shed next to the 1920s brick bungalow he and his wife lived in. The bungalow had settled on one side and cracked through the center, which caused the big windows on either side of the porch to stare out at the road like a cross-eyed man. Behind the house was a wide arroyo, outcroppings of yellow rock jutting from the eroded slopes. The arroyo bled into a flat plain that shimmered with heat, backdropped in the distance by purple mountains. Ouzel's acreage was dotted with junked construction equipment and old trucks that he hauled from other places and neither sold nor maintained. Why he collected acres of junk rusting into the creosote brush was anybody's guess.

His longhorns were rheumy-eyed and spavined, their ribs as pronounced as wagon spokes, their nostrils and ears and anuses auraed with gnats. Deer and coyotes got tangled in the collapsed and broken fence wire that surrounded his cedar posts. His mescal probably came from Mexico, right up the arroyo behind his house, but no one was sure, and no one cared. Ouzel's mescal was cheap and could knock the shoes off a horse, and no one, at least in the last few years, had died from it.

The crystal meth transported through his property was another matter. People who were sympathetic with Ouzel believed he had made a deal with the devil when he'd gotten into the sale of illegal mescal; they believed his new business partners were stone killers and that they had drawn Ouzel deep into the belly of the beast. But it was Ouzel's burden to carry and certainly not theirs.

He peered out of the screen door on the shed. He was wearing an incongruous white dress shirt with puffed sleeves and patriotic tie and pressed slacks. But Ouzel's affectations were poor compensation for his pot stomach and narrow shoulders and the purple chains of vascular knots from Buerger's disease in his neck and upper chest that gave him the appearance of a carrion bird humped grotesquely on a perch.

The dust drifted off the sheriff's cruiser and crusted on the screen. Ouzel stepped outside, forcing a smile on his face, hoping to talk in the sunlight and wind, not inside, where he had not yet cleaned up last night's bottles.

"Need your help, Ouzel," Hackberry said.

"Yes, sir, anything I can do," Ouzel replied, looking innocuously at the mescal bottle the sheriff held up inside a Ziploc bag.

"I can probably lift some prints off this and run them through AFIS and end up with diddly-squat for my trouble. Or you can just tell me if a guy named Pete bought some mescal from you. Or I can lift the prints and find out that both your and Pete's prints are on the bottle, which means I'll have to come back here and talk with you about the implications of lying to an officer of the law in a homicide investigation."

"Y'all want a soda or something?" Ouzel asked.

"The worm in that bottle is still moist, so I doubt it was in the ditch more than a couple of days. Both of us know this bottle came from your bar. Help me on this, Ouzel. What we're talking about here is a lot more weight than you're ready to deal with."

"Those Asian women at Chapala Crossing? That's why you come out here?"

"Some of them were girls. They were machine-gunned, then buried by a bulldozer. At least one of them may have still been alive."

Ouzel's stare broke. "They were alive?"

"What happened to your hand?" Hackberry said.

"This?" Ouzel said. He touched the tape and gauze wound around his wrist and fingers. "Kid at the market slammed the car door on it."

"What's his name?" Pam said.

"Ma'am?"

"My nephew works at the IGA. You're saying maybe my nephew crushed your fingers and didn't tell anybody about it?"

"It was in Alpine."

A heavy woman in a sundress that barely covered her huge dugs came out the back door, looked at the cruiser, and went back inside.

"Have the feds been here?" Hackberry said.

"No, sir, no feds."

"But somebody else was here, weren't they?" Hackberry said.

"No, sir, just neighborly people dropping by, that sort of thing. Nobody is bothering me."

"Those men will kill both you and your wife. If you've met them, you know what I say is true."

Ouzel gazed at his property and at all the paint-blistered road graders and dozers and front-end loaders and farm tractors and chemical tankers leaking fluid into his land. "It's a mess out here, ain't it?" he said.

"Who's Pete?" Hackberry asked.

"I sold a pint of mescal to a kid name of Pete Flores. He's part Mexican, I think. He said he was in Iraq. He come in one day with no shirt on. My wife went and got him a shirt of mine."

"You have a dress code?" Pam said.

"You meet up with him, take a look at his back. Get you a barf bag when you do it, too."

"Where's he live?" Hackberry asked.

"Don't know and don't care."

"Tell me who hurt your hand."

"It's going to be a hot, windy one, Sheriff, with little likelihood of rain. Wish it wasn't that way, but some things here'bouts don't ever change."

"You'd better hope we don't have to come back out here," Pam said.

Hackberry and Pam got back in the cruiser. Ouzel started to walk away, then heard Hackberry roll down the window on the passenger side of the cruiser. "Is any of the equipment on your property operational?" Hackberry asked.

"No, sir."

"Can you tell me why you keep all this junk here?"

Ouzel scratched his cheek. "With some places, I guess anything is an improvement."

Chapter
3

Vikki Gaddis called the diner at the truck stop on her cell and told her boss she couldn't work that night and in fact was quitting, and could she please get her wages, maybe in cash, because she would be en route to El Paso, which was a lie, when the banks opened in the morning.

The owner, Junior Vogel, lifted the receiver from his ear and held the sound piece so it caught the full volume of noise from the counter and tables and jukebox and cooks dinging the bell at the serving window as they clattered plateloads of food onto the Formica surface for the waitresses to pick up. "You'll make at least fifty bucks in tips. Cut me some slack here, Vikki."

"I'm packing. I'll be in at eleven. Junior?"

"*What?*"

"Cash, okay? It's important."

"You're letting me down, kid." He hung up, not angrily, but he hung up just the same, knowing that for the next three hours, she would worry about the manner in which she was paid or worry that he would be gone when she got there.

Now it was 10:51 as she drove down the two-lane state

highway toward the truck stop, the wind rushing at her through the glassless windows, the road grit stinging her face as the car body shook on its frame. The floor of the car was almost ankle-deep in trash—Styrofoam food containers, paper cups, oily rags, a can of wasp spray, a caulking gun, old newspaper black with footprints. Six weeks ago one of Pete's army friends, a peyote-soaked Indian from the Pima rez in Arizona, had given him the car for forty dollars, a six-pack of Diet Coke, and a pocketknife. The car tags were valid, the battery good, the engine hitting on at least six of the eight cylinders.

Pete had said he would trade up and buy a good used car for Vikki as soon as he got a job roughnecking on a platform out in the Gulf of Mexico. Except he'd had two other offshore jobs, and in both instances the company oversight personnel decided that a man whose back looked like red alligator hide and who screamed in his sleep probably wasn't cut out for communal living.

She had turned from the county road onto the state highway five miles back. Then a solitary vehicle had either followed her onto the state highway or come out of nowhere and remained behind her for at least the last six or seven minutes. She was driving only forty-five miles an hour because of the airflow through the windows, and the vehicle tracking behind her should have passed by this time. She accelerated up to fifty-five, then sixty, the low, humped hills dotted with dark brush speeding by. The pair of headlights, one slightly higher than the other, grew small and smaller in the rearview mirror, then disappeared into a glow behind the silhouette of a hill.

She could smell the nocturnal odor of the desert, like the smell of damp flowers crushed inside the pages of an old book. She could see the slick surface of a dried-out riverbed, the mud shining under the moon, the green plant life along the banks bending in the breeze. She had spent the first thirteen years of her life in the red-butte country of southwestern Kansas, but she loved Texas and its music and its people, whether others denigrated it or not, and she loved Pete, whether others looked upon him as a sad and doomed product of war or not, and finally, she loved the life she believed they could have together if only her love could prove greater than all the forces that seemed determined to destroy it.

When she had thoughts such as these, she wondered if she wasn't grandiose and vain and driven by pride and ego. She wondered if the black wind scented by the desert and speckled with road grit wasn't a warning about the nature of self-deception. Wasn't the greatest vanity perhaps the belief that one's love could change the fate of another, particularly the fate of an innocent and kind Texas boy who had made himself party to a mass murder?

The images those last words conjured up in her mind made her want to weep.

A brilliant glare appeared in the rearview mirror. A vehicle with its high beams on was coming hard up the state two-lane now, swinging wide on a curve across the yellow stripe. The reflected glare was like a white flame in her eyes. A Trans Am passed her, blowing road heat and exhaust and dust through her windows. The Trans Am's windows were up, but for just an instant she saw the humped shapes of two men in the front seat, the driver wearing a top hat. Neither of them seemed to look at her. In fact, the man in the passenger seat seemed to keep his face deliberately averted. In the distance she could see the truck stop strung with lights, the run-down nightclub next door, a couple of eighteen-wheelers parked by the diesel pumps, their cabs lit. She realized she had stopped breathing when the Trans Am accelerated toward her back bumper. She let out her breath, her heart shrinking back into a cold place at the bottom of her chest.

Then the car with the uneven headlights was behind her

again. But this time she was not going to be frightened. She took her foot off the accelerator and watched the speedometer needle drag down to fifty-five, fifty, then forty-five, thirty-eight. The car behind her pulled out to pass, its engine laboring. When it went by her, she saw a solitary man behind the wheel. His windows were half open, which meant his air conditioner was off and he was saving every teaspoon of gasoline possible, just as she was.

Pete had gotten a ride to Marathon, where he hoped to talk a distant cousin into selling him a used car off his car lot on credit. If the cousin refused, Vikki was to meet Pete in Marathon regardless, and they would lose themselves in a city, maybe Houston or Dallas. Or maybe head for Colorado or Montana. Everything they owned was in the trunk or on the backseat of the car, tape-wrapped or held together with twine. On top of all the boxes in the backseat was her J-200 sunburst Gibson.

The cell phone chimed on the seat. She opened it and placed the receiver against her ear. "Where are you?" she said.

"At the lot. We got us a Toyota with a hundred grand on it. The tires are good, and it doesn't have any oil smoke coming out of it. You got your paycheck?"

"I'm almost at the diner." She paused. Up ahead, the Trans Am was pulling in to the nightclub. A square of light from the truck stop slid off the face and shoulder of the man in the passenger seat. "Did any of those guys at the church have an orange or red beard?"

"No," Pete said. "Wait a minute. I'm not sure. One guy in the dark had a beard. Why?"

"Some guys just pulled in to the beer joint. The driver is wearing a hat like the Mad Hatter's." Her tires began crunching across the gravel in the parking lot. "They're staring at me. *Think*, Pete. Did you see a guy with an orange beard?"

"Get away from them."

"I have to get paid. We don't have any money," she said, her irritability and frustration rising.

"Screw the money. Junior can mail it to us. We'll make out."

"On what?" she said. When there was no answer, she glanced at the cell phone's screen. She had lost service.

Just ahead of her, the man driving the car with lopsided headlights parked by the entrance to the diner and went inside. He was thin and of medium height and wore an old suit coat, even though it was summer.

She parked next to his car, a beat-up Nissan, and turned off the engine. The men in the Trans Am had gotten out and were stretching and yawning in front of the nightclub. It had been a dance hall in the 1940s, and colored lights from inside shone through a window cut in the shape of a champagne glass over the entranceway. A tattered canvas canopy extended out from the door over a series of limestone slabs, on either side of which were two huge ceramic pots planted with Spanish daggers. A lone palm tree, as dark and motionless as a cutout, was silhouetted against a pink and green neon cowgirl holding a guitar, one booted foot raised. In the distance, behind the club, was a geological fault where the land seemed to collapse and dissolve into darkness, flat and enormous and breathtaking, as if an inland sea had evaporated overnight and left its depths as beveled and smooth as damp clay.

If Pete had not taken a job from men no one in his right mind would trust. If Pete had only had faith in what the two of them could do together if they tried.

The man with the orange beard wore a denim shirt scissored off at the armpits. His upper arms were meaty and sunburned, and one arm had a blue anchor tattooed inside a circle of red and blue stars. He twisted the cap off a beer bottle and toasted Vikki with it before he drank. He removed the bottle from his mouth and lifted up his shirt with two fingers and blotted his lips. "Little breezy in that car of yours, isn't it?" he said.

"I've got your license number. I'm going to leave it inside with my boss," she said.

"You got no problem with me," he replied, smiling.

She headed for the front door of the diner, an empty coffee thermos hooked through one finger.

"Come have a drink with us," he said at her back.

Junior was behind the cash register when she came in, his face as lined and woebegone as a prune, his sideburns razor-etched and flared on his cheeks. He was talking to the driver of the Nissan. "My delivery man didn't come today, so I'm down on my milk. Sorry, but I cain't sell you none."

"Where's the next store?" the driver of the Nissan said. His hair was scalped on the sides and long and combed straight back on top.

"Back in town," Junior said.

"It's closed. It's after eleven."

"Why didn't you buy it before closing time?"

"We had a carton in the ice chest at the Super 8. But it must have spoiled. Mister, my baby girl is three months old. What am I going to do?"

Junior blew out his breath. He went into the kitchen and returned with a half-gallon carton of whole milk and set it on the counter.

"How much is it?" the driver of the Nissan asked.

"Two bucks."

The driver of the Nissan put a single bill on the glass countertop and began counting pennies, nickels, and dimes on top of it. He exhausted the coins in one pocket and began searching in the other.

"Forget it," Junior said.

"I got to pay you for it."

"You a Christian?"

"Yes, sir."

"Put it in the plate."

"God bless you, sir."

Junior nodded, his mouth a tight line. He watched the man go out the door into the lot, then turned his attention to Vikki. "Next," he said.

"I'm sorry to quit on you without notice. I know you've got your hands full," she said.

"It's that boy, isn't it?"

"I need my money, Junior."

He glanced at some penciled numbers on a scrap of paper by the register. "You got a hundred and eighty-three dollars and four cents coming. You're gonna have to take a check, though. I need it for the IRS and four other agencies I pay on your behalf."

"Can't you stop acting like a shit?"

He raised his eyebrows, then exhaled out his nose. He shoved a receipt book toward her and opened the cash register. "I saw that guy with the beard trying to come on to you out there," he said as he counted out her money.

"You know him?"

"No."

"He's probably drunk." She started to say something else. She looked over her shoulder. She could see the Trans Am next to the nightclub. The two men were not in it and not in the parking lot, either.

Junior handed her the bills and silver he had counted out of the drawer and added ten dollars to it. "You had that coming out of the tip jar. Take care of yourself, kid."

She lifted her thermos. "You mind?"

"Why ask me?"

She went behind the counter and opened the coffee spigot above her thermos and filled it with scalding coffee. She closed and opened her eyes, suddenly realizing how tired she was.

She used the restroom and went back outside. The man with

the orange beard was sitting in the passenger seat of his vehicle, eating Mexican food from a Styrofoam container with a small plastic fork, the car door hanging open, his feet on the gravel. The driver of the vehicle was nowhere in sight, but the engine was running, a clutch of keys vibrating in the ignition.

"I was on a destroyer escort in Fort Lauderdale three days ago," the man with the orange beard said. "I've been around the world four times backward. That means I've been around the world eight times. What do you think of that? You ever been around the world?"

"*I* have," Junior said from the door of the diner. "Want to tell me about your travels? I was middleweight champion of the Pacific fleet. You a tomato can?"

"A what?"

"A bleeder. Keep bothering my waitress like that and see what happens."

Vikki got into her vehicle and turned around in the lot but had to wait for an eighteen-wheeler to get past before she could drive back onto the highway. In her rearview mirror, she saw the man in the top hat come out of the nightclub and get in the Trans Am. He wore jeans and suspenders and a white T-shirt, and his torso was too long for his legs. The man with the beard closed his car door and tossed the Styrofoam container and the uneaten food out the window.

Vikki pressed the accelerator to the floor, the safe electric glow of the truck stop and diner disappearing behind her. A newspaper flew off the asphalt like a bird with giant wings and whipped through the front window and wrapped itself on the crown of the passenger seat before spinning in a vortex inside the car. She slapped the tangle of pages down with one hand and tried to see who was behind her. There were several sets of headlights in her rearview mirror now, and she couldn't tell if any of them belonged to the man with the orange beard.

A truck passed her, then an open convertible with a teenage girl sitting on top of the backseat, her arms outspread in the wind, her chin lifted, her blouse flattening on her breasts, as though the stars and the bloom of the desert and the warm nocturnal loveliness of the moment had been created especially for her.

When Vikki rounded the next curve, the headlights of the vehicle behind her reflected off a hillside and she clearly saw the Trans Am, riding low and sleek on good tires, the engine powerful and loud and steady. She mashed on the gas, but her vehicle did not accelerate. Instead, the pistons misfired, and a balloon of black oil smoke exploded out of the exhaust pipe. She felt as though she were in a bad dream in which she knew she had to run from an enemy but her legs were knee-deep in mud.

What a fool she had been. Why hadn't she confronted the two men in front of Junior and dealt with them in front of the diner, even called the cops if she had to?

She flipped open her cell phone on her thigh, trying with her thumb to punch in the diner's number. Up ahead, she saw the Nissan parked on the side of the road, the hatch open, the father of the three-month-old baby girl on his knees, pushing a jack under the rear bumper.

She slowed and pulled in behind him. He stared up into her high beams, his face white, distorted, his eyes watering, his narrow head and long nose and greased hair like those of a man who was out of sync with his own era, a man for whom loss was a given and ineptitude a way of life. She left the parking lights on and cut the engine.

The Trans Am streaked past her, the bearded passenger giving her a double thumbs-up, his friend in the top hat bent hard over the wheel.

But the driver of the Nissan was concentrated on Vikki, still looking up at her, blinking, his eyes straining in the darkness. "Who are you?" he said.

"I saw you at the diner. You needed milk for your little girl. Are you all right?"

She was standing directly over him. He had spread a handkerchief on the gravel to kneel on but had not taken off his coat. He had just placed the jack under the rear of the car frame, but neither of the back tires appeared to be flat.

"I think I got a bubble in my tire. I could hear it slapping. They do that sometimes when they're fixing to blow," he said. He got to his feet, brushing at one knee. "Problem is, I forgot I don't have a spare." Because of the grease in his hair, it looked wet-combed and shiny on his collar, as though he had just emerged from a fresh shower. There were soft lumps in his facial skin, similar in size to the bites of horseflies. He glanced over his shoulder at the empty road. In the distance, a pair of high beams bounced off a hillside into the sky. "We're at the Super 8 in town. My wife probably thinks I got kidnapped. My sister's husband has a shoe store in Del Rio. I'm supposed to go to work for him day after tomorrow."

He waited for her to speak. The stars were smoky, like dry ice evaporating on black velvet, the wind starting to gust through an arroyo behind her. She thought she could smell night-blooming flowers, water braiding along the edge of a bleached riverbed, an alluvial fan of damp sand cut by the hoofprints and the clawed feet of animals.

"Ma'am?" he said.

She couldn't concentrate. What was he asking her? "Do you want a ride to your motel?" she said.

"Maybe I can make it. It was you I was worried about."

"Pardon?"

"I got the sense those fellows in the Trans Am were hassling you. You know those fellows? That was them that roared on by, wasn't it?"

"I don't know who they are. Do you want a ride?"

What had he just said? He had asked about the two men in the Trans Am, but he had been looking at her, not them, when they passed. He seemed to be thinking now, with an expression like that of a fool humorously considering his alternatives at someone else's expense. The headlights that had silhouetted a hill in the distance disappeared, and the outline of the hill dissolved into the darkness. "I can limp in with this tire as it is, I guess. But it's kind of you to stop. You're mighty attractive. Not many women traveling alone would stop on the road at night to help a man in distress."

"I hope your new job works out all right for you," she said. She turned and walked toward her vehicle. She could feel the skin on her back twitching. Then she heard a sound that didn't belong in the situation, that didn't fit with everything the driver had told her.

He had opened a cell phone and was talking into it. She got in her vehicle and turned the key in the ignition. The engine caught for perhaps two seconds, then coughed and died. She turned the ignition again, pumping the accelerator. The stench of gasoline from a flooded carburetor rose into her face. She turned off the ignition so she would not run down the battery. She placed her hands on the steering wheel and kept them absolutely still, making her face devoid of all expression so he could read nothing in it. He approached her window, dropping the cell phone in his coat pocket, reaching with his other hand for something stuck in the back of his belt.

She unscrewed the plastic drinking cup from the top of her thermos, then unscrewed the cap and rubber plug on the thermal insert and began pouring coffee into the cup, her heart seizing up as his silhouette filled her window.

"People call me Preacher," he said.

"Yes?"

"Everybody has got to have a name. Preacher is mine. Step

out here with me, ma'am. We have to get going pretty quick," he said.

"In your dreams," she said.

"I promise I'll do everything for you I can. Arguing about it won't help. Everybody gets to the barn. But for you maybe that won't necessarily have to happen tonight. You're a kind woman. I'm not forgetting that."

She threw the coffee at him. But he saw it coming and stepped away quickly, raising one arm in front of his face. In his other hand, he held an unblued titanium revolver, one with black rubber grips. It was not much larger than his palm.

"I cain't blame you. But it's time for you to get yourself in the trunk of my automobile. I've never struck a woman. I don't want you to be the first," he said.

She stared straight ahead, trying to think. What was it she was not seeing or remembering? Something that lay at the tips of her fingers, something that was like a piece of magic, something that God or a higher power or a dead Indian shaman out in the desert had already put at her disposal if only she could just remember what it was.

"I have nothing you want," she said.

"You dealt the hand, woman. It's your misfortune and none of my own," he said, pulling open her door. "Now you slide yourself off that car seat and come along with me. Nothing is ever as bad as you think."

Amid the litter on the floor, she felt the coldness of a metal cylinder touch her bare ankle. She reached down with her right hand and picked up the can of wasp spray, one that the manufacturer guaranteed could be fired steadily into a nest from twenty feet away. Vikki stuck the spout directly into the Nissan driver's face and pressed down the plastic button on the applicator.

A jet of foaming lead-gray viscous liquid struck his mouth and nose and both of his eyes. He screamed and began wiping at his eyes and face with his coat sleeves, spinning around, off balance, all the while trying to hold on to his pistol and open his eyes wide enough to see where she was. She got out of the car and fired the spray into his face again, backing away from him as she did, spraying the back of his head, hitting him again when he tried to turn with her. He slammed against her vehicle and rolled on the ground, thrashing his feet, dropping the revolver in the grass.

She tried to get back inside her vehicle, but he was on his hands and knees, grabbing at her ankles, his eyes blistered almost shut. She fell backward and felt her forearm come down hard on the revolver. She picked it up, gathering its cool hardness into her palm, and staggered to her feet. But he came at her again, tackling her around one leg, striking at her genitalia with one fist.

She pointed the revolver downward. It was a Smith & Wesson Airweight .38 that held five rounds. She was amazed at how light yet solid and comforting it felt in her hand. She aimed at the back of his calf and pulled the trigger. The frame bucked in her hand, and fire flew from the muzzle. She saw the cloth in his trousers jump and even smoke for a second. Then it seemed as though his entire pants leg was darkening with his blood.

But the man who called himself Preacher wasn't through. He made a grinding sound down in his throat, as though both eating his pain and energizing himself, and threw his weight against her, locking his arms around her knees. She fell in the grass and struck at his head with the revolver, lacerating his scalp, to no avail. Then she screwed the muzzle into his ear. "You want your brains on your shirt?" she said.

He didn't let go. She lowered the revolver and aimed at the top of his shoe but couldn't position her finger adequately to pull against the trigger's tension. She worked her thumb over the hammer, cocked it back, and squeezed the trigger against the guard. The barrel made a second loud pop, and a jet of blood exploded from the bottom of his shoe. He sat up on his haunches and grabbed his foot with both hands, his jaw dropping open, his face the pained red of a boiled crab.

She got into her vehicle and turned the ignition. This time the engine caught, and she dropped the transmission into low and began easing back onto the highway.

"My father was a Medicine Lodge police officer and taught me how to shoot when I was ten years old. Next time you won't get off so easy, bubba," she said.

She flung the .38 through the passenger window into the darkness and rolled across his cell phone, crushing it into pieces. Then she pushed the accelerator to the floor, a cloud of blue-black oil smoke ballooning behind her.

Chapter
4

NOBODY COULD BE this unlucky, Nick Dolan told himself. He had taken his wife and daughters and son with him to their vacation house on the Comal River, outside New Braunfels, hoping to buy time so he could figure out a way to get both Hugo Cistranos and Artie Rooney off his back—in particular Hugo, whom Nick had stiffed for the thousands he claimed Nick owed him.

His vacation home was built of white stucco and had a blue-tile roof and a courtyard with a wishing well and lime and orange trees, and terraced gardens and stone steps that descended to the riverbank. The river had a soap-rock bottom that was free of silt and was green and cold and fed by springs even in August, and pooled with shadows from the giant trees that grew along the bank. Maybe he could enjoy a few days away from problems he did not create, that no one could blame him for, and this trouble would just blow over. Why shouldn't it? Nick Dolan had never deliberately hurt anybody.

But when he looked out his window and saw a man with a shaved, waxed head stepping out of a government car, he knew the cosmic plot to make his life miserable was still in full-throttle, turbo-prop overdrive and the Fates were about to special-deliver another fuck-you message to Nick no matter where he went.

The government man must have been at least six-four, his shoulders like concrete inside his white shirt, his forehead knurled, his eyes luminous pools behind octagon-shaped rimless glasses, eyes that Nick could only associate with space aliens.

The government man was already holding up his ID when Nick opened the door. "Isaac Clawson, Immigration and Customs Enforcement. You Nick Dolan?" he said.

"No, I just look like him and happen to live at this address," Nick answered.

"I need a few minutes of your time."

"For what?"

The sun was hot and bright on the St. Augustine grass, the air glistening with humidity. Isaac Clawson touched at the sweat on his forehead with the back of his wrist. In his other hand he clutched a flat, zippered portfolio, the fingers of his huge hand spread on it like banana peels. "You want to do something for your country, sir? Or would you like me to ratchet up the procedure a couple of notches, maybe introduce you to our grand-jury subpoena process?"

"What, I didn't pay into workman's comp for the guy who cuts my lawn?"

Clawson's eyes stayed riveted on Nick's. The man's physicality seemed to exude heat and repressed violence, a whiff of testosterone, an astringent tinge of deodorant. The formality and tie and white shirt and big octagon-shaped glasses seemed to Nick a poor disguise for a man who was probably at heart a bone breaker.

"My kids are playing Ping-Pong in the game room. My wife is making lunch. We talk in my office, right?" Nick said.

There was a beat. "That's fine," Clawson said.

They walked through a foyer into an attached cottage that

served as Nick's office. Down on the river, Nick could see a chain of floaters on inflated inner tubes headed toward a rapids. Nick sat in a deep leather swivel chair behind his desk, gazing abstractedly at the sets of mail-order books he had bought in order to fill the wall shelves. Clawson sat down in front of him, his elongated torso as straight as a broomstick. Nick could feel the tension in his chest rising into his throat.

"You know Arthur Rooney?" Clawson asked.

"Everybody in New Orleans knew Artie Rooney. He used to run a detective agency. People in the graveyard knew Artie Rooney. That's 'cause he put them there."

"Does Rooney use Thai whores?"

"How would I know?"

"Because you're in the same business."

"I own a nightclub. I'm a partner in some escort services. If the government doesn't like that, change the law."

"I got a short wick with people like you, Mr. Dolan," Clawson said, unzipping the portfolio. "Take a look at these. They really don't do justice to the subject, though. You can't put the smell of decomposition in a photograph."

"I don't want to look at them."

"Yeah, you do," Clawson said, rising from his chair, placing eight eight-by-ten black-and-white blowups in two rows across Nick's desktop. "The shooter or shooters used forty-five-caliber ammunition. This girl here looks like she's about fifteen. Check out the girl who caught one in the mouth. How old are your daughters?"

"This doesn't have anything to do with me."

"Maybe. Or maybe it does. But you're a pimp, Mr. Dolan, just like Arthur Rooney. You sell disease, and you promote drug addiction and pornography. You're a parasite that should be scrubbed off the planet with steel wool."

"You can't talk to me like that."

"The hell I can't."

Nick wiped the photos off his desk onto the floor. "Get out. Take your pictures with you."

"They're yours. We have plenty more. The FBI is interviewing your strippers. I'd better not hear a story that doesn't coincide with what you've told me."

"They're doing what? You're ICE. What are you doing here? I don't smuggle people into the country. I'm not a terrorist. What's with you?"

Clawson zipped up his empty portfolio and looked around him. "You got you a nice place here. It reminds me of a Mexican restaurant in Santa Fe where I used to eat."

After Clawson was gone, Nick sat numbly in his swivel chair, his ears booming like kettledrums. Then he went into his wife's bathroom and ate one of her nitroglycerin pills, sure that his heart was about to fail.

WHEN HIS WIFE called him to lunch, he scooped up the photos the ICE agent had left, stuffed them into a manila envelope, and buried them in a desk drawer. At the table in the sunroom, he picked at his food and tried not to let his worry and fear and gloom show in his face.

His wife's grandparents had been Russian Jews from the southern Siberian plain, and she and their son and the fifteen-year-old twins still had the beautiful black hair and dark skin and hint of Asian features that had defined the grandmother even in her seventies. Nick kept looking at his daughters, seeing not their faces but the faces of the exhumed women and girls in the photos, smeared lipstick on one girl's mouth, grains of dirt still in her hair.

"You don't like the tuna?" Esther, his wife, said.

"The what?" he replied stupidly.

"The food you're chewing like it's wet cardboard," she said.

"It's good. I got a toothache is all."

"Who was that guy?" Jesse, his son, asked. He was a skinny, pale boy, his arms flaccid, his ribs as visible as corset stays. His IQ was 160. In the high school yearbook, the only entries under his picture were "Planning Committee, Senior Prom" and "President of the Chess Club." There had been three other members of the chess club.

"Which guy?" Nick said.

"The one who looks like an upended penis," Jesse said.

"You're not too old for a smack," Esther said.

"He's a gentleman from Immigration. He wanted to know about some of my Hispanic employees at the restaurant," Nick said.

"Did you pick up the inner tubes?" Ruth, one of the twins, asked.

Nick stared blankly into space. "I forgot."

"You promised you'd go down the rapids with us," Kate, the other twin, said.

"The water is still high. There's a whirlpool on the far end. I've seen it. It's deep right where there's that big cut under the bank. I think we should wait."

Both girls looked dourly at their food. He could feel his wife's eyes on the side of his face. But his daughters' disappointment and his wife's implicit disapproval were not what bothered him. He knew his broken promise would result in only one conclusion: The twins would go down the rapids anyway, with high school boys who were too old for them and would gladly provide the inner tubes and the hands-on guidance. In his mind, he already saw the whirlpool waiting for his girls, white froth spinning atop its dark vortex.

"I'll get the tubes," Nick said. "Eat your food slowly so you don't get cramps."

He went back to his office and locked the door. What was he going to do? He couldn't even think of a way to safely dispose of the photographs, at least not in the daylight. ICE had his name, Hugo Cistranos was circling him like a shark, and his conscience was pulsing like an infected gland. He couldn't think of one person on earth he could call upon for help.

He sat at his desk, his face in his hands. How long would it be before Hugo Cistranos was at his door, demanding his money, implying Nick was a coward, making remarks about his nicotine habit, his weight, his bad eyesight, his inability to deal with the catastrophe his careless words "Wipe the slate clean" had created?

To sit and wait for misfortune to befall him was insane. He had heard over and over about people "surrendering" control during times of adversity. Screw that. He thumbed through his Rolodex and punched a number into his desk phone.

"How'd you get this number?" a voice with a New Orleans accent said.

"You gave it to me, Artie."

"Then fuck me."

"Hugo Cistranos says you offered him your Caddy to clip me."

"He's lying. I value my Caddy. It's a collectible."

"Hugo is lots of things, but a liar isn't one of them."

"You should know. Hugo is your employee, not mine. I don't hire psychopaths."

"I'm not guilty of what you think."

"Yeah? What might that be? What might you be guilty of, Nicholas?"

Nick could hear the telephone wires humming in the silence.

"You don't want to say? I don't think there's a tap on my line. If you can't wash your sins with your old podna Artie Rooney, who can you trust, Nicholas?"

"It's Nick. You told Hugo my family name was Dolinski?"

"It's not?"

"Yeah, it is, because my grandfather had to change it so him and his family didn't end up in a soap dish. They had to change it so the anti-Semite Irish cocksuckers in Roosevelt's State Department wouldn't shut them out of the country."

"That's a heartbreaking story, Nick. Maybe you could sell it as one of those docudramas? Didn't your grandfather used to sell shoestrings door-to-door along Magazine?"

"That's right, with Tennessee Williams. They also ran a soup kitchen together in the Quarter. His name is in a couple of books about Tennessee Williams."

Nick could hear Artie laughing. "Your grandfather and a world-famous country singer sold soup to winos? Famous, rich guys do that a lot," Artie said. "When you're in Houston or Big D, drop around. Life is no fun without you. By the way, tell Hugo he owes me. For that matter, so do you."

The line went dead.

NICK DETERMINED THAT his angst and funk would not control the rest of his day. He rented huge fat inner tubes in town, big enough to float a piano on. He stopped by the bakery and bought a carrot cake glazed with white icing and scrolled with chains of pink and green flowers. He packed a half-gallon of peach ice cream in dry ice. He put on a pair of beach sandals and scarlet rayon boxing trunks that hung to his knees, and walked his children down to the riverside and ran a long nylon cord through all the tubes, lacing them together so they would not become separated as they floated downstream toward the rapids.

Nick was first in the chain, ensconced in his tube, his skin fishbelly white, wraparound black Ray-Bans on his face. The shade trees slid by overhead, the sunlight spangling in their leaves. He laid his neck on the rubber, its warm petrochemical smell somehow comforting, the current tickling his spine, his wrists trailing in the water. Up ahead was a partial dam that channeled the current through a narrow opening. He could hear the sound of the rapids growing in volume and intensity and feel the tug of the river redirecting his course.

Suddenly, he and his children were sliding with the waves through the gap, rocketing through white water and geysers of foam, their own happy screams joining those of the other floaters, the sun overhead as blinding as an arc welder's torch.

The whirlpool by the deep cut under the embankment disappeared behind them, powerless to reach out and draw Nick's family into its maw.

They dragged their tubes out on the shoals and paid a kid with a truck to drive them upstream so they could refloat the river. They stayed in the water until sunset, whipping through the rapids like old pros. At the end of the day, Nick was glowing with sunburn, his hair and oversize boxing trunks gritty with sand, his heart swelling with pride in himself and in his children and the things he owned and the good life he had been able to provide for his family.

They ate the cake and peach ice cream on a blanket next to the river while the sun burned away to a tiny spark inside rain clouds in the west. He could smell the odor of charcoal lighter and meat fires on the breeze, and see Japanese lanterns strung through his neighbor's trees, and hear music from a lawn party someone was hosting on the opposite side of the river. The summer light was trapped high in the sky, as though nature had set its own rules into abeyance. Somehow the season had become eternal, and somehow all of Nick's concerns with mortality had been emptied from his life.

He walked his children back up the stone steps to his house, then went into his office, removed the manila folder of photographs from his desk, and picked up a can of charcoal lighter and a book of matches from beside his barbecue pit. When he returned to the riverbank, the sky was purple, the sky filled with birds that seemed to have no place to land, and he thought he smelled gas in the trees. The surface of the river seemed thicker, its depths colder. The blue-green lawn of the house across the water was now littered with beer cups and paper plates, the band still playing, like a radio someone had forgotten to turn off.

The sunburn on his face and under his armpits ached miserably. He pulled the photos from the envelope, rolled them into a cone, and squirted charcoal lighter along their sides and edges. When he struck a paper match and touched it to the fluid, the fire crawled quickly up the cone to his fingers. He tried to separate the photos and keep them burning without dropping them or injuring his hand. Instead, they spilled into the grass, the faces of all the women and girls staring up at him, the heat blackening the paper in the center, curling the photos' edges, dissolving hair and tissue and eyes and teeth inside a chemical flame.

The odor of burned hair on the backs of his hands rose into his face, and in his head he saw an oven in southwest Poland, its iron door yawning open, and inside the oven he saw the barest puff of wind crumble the remains of his daughters into ash.

A HISPANIC MAN had called in a 911 on an injured or drunk man stumbling around by the side of the state highway in the dark.

"Is this man a hitchhiker?" the dispatcher asked.

"No, he's by a car. He's falling down."

"Has he been struck by a vehicle?"

"How do I know? He ain't in good shape, that's for sure. He's trying to get in the car. There he goes again."

"Goes where?"

"On the ground. I take that back. He's up again and crawling inside, Jesus, a truck just went roaring by. The guy's gonna get mashed."

"Give me your location again."

The caller gave the number on a mile marker. But evidently, in the poor light, he read the numerals wrong, and the deputy who was dispatched to the scene found only an empty stretch of highway, tumbleweed bouncing across the center stripe.

AFTER HACKBERRY HOLLAND had gotten the name of Pete Flores from Ouzel Flagler, he'd called the electric cooperative and been told a P. J. Flores was a member of the co-op and could be found up a dirt road fifteen miles from the county seat, living in a house where the electricity was scheduled to be cut off in three days for nonpayment of service.

It was 7:31 A.M. when Hackberry and Pam Tibbs drove up a pebble road to a grassless parcel of land where a frame house sat in the shadow of a hill, its front door open, the curtains blowing inside the screens. There were no vehicles out back or in the dirt yard. A crow sat on top of the cistern. It flapped its wings and lifted into the sky when Hackberry and Pam Tibbs stepped up on the gallery.

"It's Sheriff Holland," Hackberry called through the screen. "I need to talk to Pete Flores. Step out on the gallery, please."

No answer.

Hackberry went through the door first. The wind seemed to fill the inside of the house in a way that reminded him of his own home after his wife had died, as though a terrible theft had just occurred for which there was no redress except silence. He walked deeper into the house, his boots loud on the plank floors. A half-eaten cheese sandwich lay on a plate on top of the kitchen table. Dry crumbs were scattered on the plate. A faucet dripped into an unwashed pan in the sink. A garbage sack, double-bagged and taped, rested on the back screen porch, as though someone had planned to carry it down to the Dumpster on the road or to bury it and had been interrupted.

The medicine cabinet and the bedroom closet were empty, coat hangers strewn on the floor. The toilet paper had been removed from the spindle. Hackberry looked through the front screen and saw a small Hispanic boy on a bicycle in the yard. The boy was not more than ten or eleven, and he was staring at the pump shotgun affixed to the cruiser's dashboard. The bicycle the boy rode was old and had fat tires and was too big for a boy his size.

"You know where Pete Flores is?" Hackberry asked, stepping out on the gallery.

"He ain't home?" the boy said.

"Afraid not."

The boy didn't speak. He got back on the bike, his face empty.

"I'm Sheriff Holland. Pete's helping me with a little matter. Do you know where he might be?"

"No, sir. Miss Vikki ain't home, either?"

"No, nobody is here right now."

"Then how come you're in their house?"

Hackberry sat down on the steps and removed his hat. He straightened the felt in the crown. He lifted his face into the sunlight that was breaking over the hill. "What's your name?"

"Bernabe Segura."

"Pete might be in some trouble, Bernabe. What's Miss Vikki's last name?"

"Gaddis."

"Do you know where I could find her?"

The little boy's face was clouded, as though he were looking at an image buried behind his eyes.

"Are you listening, Bernabe?"

"There were some men here last night. They had flashlights. They went inside the house."

"So you came here to check on Pete?"

"We were gonna hunt for arrowheads today."

"You shouldn't have come here by yourself. Where's your father?"

"I don't have one." Bernabe tapped on his handlebars. "Pete give me this bike."

"Where can I find Miss Vikki, Bernabe?"

JUNIOR VOGEL LEANED on the counter. "I knew it," he said.

"Knew what?" Hackberry said.

Junior picked up a towel from the counter, wiped his hands with it, and threw it in the direction of a yellow plastic container filled with soiled towels and aprons. "It's that damn kid she's been mixed up with. Pete Flores. What'd he do?"

"Nothing I know of. We just need some information from him."

"Who you kidding? When that boy isn't drunk, he's hungover. I knew she was in trouble when she left the diner. I should have done something about it."

"I'm not sure I follow you."

"She came in for her check. But two or three things were going on at the same time. Like a bad omen or something. I don't know how to put it. A guy wanted to buy milk for his baby. Then a couple of guys in a Trans Am started coming on to her. I didn't sort it out at the time."

Pam Tibbs looked at the side of Hackberry's face, then at Junior and back at Hackberry. "We don't have any idea what you're talking about, sir. Can you take the pralines out of your mouth?" she said.

"This guy said he was staying at the Super 8 and needed milk for his three-month-old baby girl. I asked him why he didn't go to the convenience store. He said it was after eleven and the store was closed. So I got him a half-gallon out of my refrigerator and told him to give me two bucks for it. But he didn't have the two bucks. How can a guy be out looking for milk and driving across Texas with his family when he doesn't even have two bucks in his pocket?

"While I'm dealing with this guy, these two characters in a Trans Am are hassling Vikki. I don't have trouble in my place, but suddenly, I got it all at one time, you follow me now? Drunks and hard cases don't mess with my employees, Vikki in particular. Everybody knows that. 'Orchestrated,' that was the word I was looking for. It was like it was all orchestrated."

"You get a license number on any of these guys?" Hackberry said.

"No."

Hackberry placed his business card on the glass counter. "Call us if you hear from Vikki or if you see any of these guys again," he said.

"What's happened to Vikki? You ain't told me squat," Junior said.

"We don't know where she is. As far as we know, you're the last person to have seen her," Hackberry said.

Junior Vogel let out his breath, the heel of his hand pressed to his head. "I looked out the window and the guy with the milk was ahead of her. The two creeps in the Trans Am got some gas and followed in the same direction. I watched it happen and didn't do anything."

THE SKY WAS gray with dust as they drove back down the state highway toward town, Pam Tibbs behind the wheel.

"I talked to my cousin Billy Bob Holland," Hackberry said. "He's a former Texas Ranger and practices law in western Montana. He's known Pete Flores since he was a little boy. He says

Pete was the best little boy he ever knew. He also says he was the smartest."

"These days it's not hard for a good kid to get in trouble."

"Billy Bob says he'd bet his life this boy is innocent of any wrongdoing, at least of the kind we're talking about."

"My father was in Vietnam. He was psychotic when he came home. He hanged himself in a jail cell." Pam's eyes were straight ahead, her hands in the ten-two position on the steering wheel, her expression as empty as a wood carving.

"Pull on the shoulder," Hackberry said.

"What for?"

"That road bull is waving at us," he replied.

The inmates were from a contract prison and wore orange jumpsuits. They were strung out in a long line on the swale, picking up litter and stuffing it into vinyl bags they tied and left on the shoulder. A green bus with steel mesh on the windows was parked up ahead. So was a flatbed diesel truck with a horse trailer anchored to the back bumper. One mounted gunbull was at the back and another at the head of the line working along the road. An unarmed man in a gray uniform with red piping on the collar and pockets stood on the swale, waiting for the cruiser. He wore yellow-tinted aviator shades and an elegant white straw cowboy hat. His uniform was flecked with chaff blowing off the hardpan. His neck and face were deeply lined, like the skin on a turtle. Neither Hackberry nor Pam Tibbs knew him.

"What's going on, Cap?" Hackberry said, getting out of the cruiser.

"See that Hispanic boy over yonder with Gothic-letter tats all over him?" A polished brass tag on the captain's pocket said RICKER.

"Yes, sir?" Hack said.

"He killed a bar owner with a knife 'cause the bar owner wouldn't return the money this kid lost in the rubber machine.

Guess what he just found back there in the rocks? I almost downloaded in my britches when he handed it to me."

"What'd he find?" Hackberry said.

The captain removed a stainless-steel revolver from his pants pocket. "It's an Airweight thirty-eight, a five-rounder. Two caps already popped. Don't worry. The hammer is sitting on a spent casing."

Hackberry removed a ballpoint from his shirt pocket and put it through the trigger guard and removed the revolver from Ricker's hand. Pam Tibbs got a Ziploc bag from the cruiser and placed the revolver inside it.

"I shouldn't have handled it?" Ricker said.

"You did all the right things. I appreciate your waving us down," Hackberry said.

"That ain't all of it. Better take a look over here," Ricker said. He walked ahead and pointed at a grassy spot where, during the rainy season, water ran off the road into the swale. "I suspect somebody is a pint or two down right now."

Over a wide area, the grass was stippled with blood, and in places the blood had pooled and dried on top of the dirt. Pam Tibbs squatted down and looked at the grass and the broken blades and the depressions in it and the areas where the blood smears had taken on the characteristics of a body drag. She stood up and walked back toward the cruiser, in the direction of the truck stop and diner, and squatted down again. "I'd say there were two vehicles here, Sheriff," she said. "My guess is the victim was shot about here, close to vehicle one, then was dragged, or dragged himself, on up to vehicle two. But why would the shooter throw away the weapon?"

"Maybe it wasn't his. Or rather, it wasn't hers," Hackberry said.

"You want to print me and that Hispanic boy to exclude us when you dust the gun?" Ricker said.

"Yep. And we need to wrap the crime scene. Some feds will probably be talking to you later."

"What the hell the feds want with me?"

"You heard about all those Asian women who were murdered?"

"That's what this is about? I got enough grief, Sheriff."

"That makes two of us. Welcome to the New American Empire, Cap."

Chapter 5

A s HE LAY in a bed with a view of a chicken yard, a railed pen with six goats inside it, and a bladeless, rusted slip of a windmill strung with dead brush blown from a field of weeds, the man whose nickname was Preacher could not get the woman out of his mind, nor the scent of her fear and sweat and perfume while he wrestled with her on the ground, nor the expression on her face when she fired the .38 round through the top of his foot, exploding a jet of blood from the sole of his shoe. Her expression hadn't been one of shock or pity, as Preacher would have expected; it had been one of triumph.

No, that wasn't it, either. What he had seen in her face was loathing and disgust. She had fried his eyes with wasp spray, taken his weapon, shot him at close quarters, crushed his cell phone with her tire, and left him to bleed out like a piece of roadkill. She had also taken the time to call him bubba and inform him he had gotten off easy. She had done all this to a man considered by some, in terms of potential, to be one notch below the scourge of God.

The sheaf of bandages and tape on his calf smelled of

medicinal salve and dried blood, but the pain pills he had eaten
and the veterinarian's injection had numbed the nerves down to
the ankle. The plaster cast on his foot was another matter. It felt
like wet cement on his skin, and the heat and sweat and friction
it generated turned his wound into an aching misery. Twenty
minutes ago, the electric power had failed and the fan on the
table by his bed had died. Now he could feel the heat and humidity intensifying in the walls, the tin roof expanding, pinging
like a banjo string.

"Put some more ice on my foot," he said to Jesus, the Hispanic
man who owned the house.

"It melted."

"Did you call the power company?"

"We don't got a phone, boss. When it gets hot like this, we
got brownouts. After the day gets cooler, the electricity goes
back on."

Preacher pressed the back of his head into the pillow and
stared at the ceiling. The room was sweltering, and he could smell
a growing stench from inside the hospital gown he had worn for
two days. When he closed his eyes, he saw the girl's face again,
and it filled him with both desire and resentment for the sexual
passion she excited in him. Hugo had brought him his .45 auto.
It was a 1911 model—simple in design, always dependable, effective in ways most people couldn't imagine. Preacher ran his
hand along the bottom of his mattress and felt the hardness of
the .45's frame. He thought of the girl, her deep-set eyes and her
chestnut hair that was curled at the tips, and the way her tongue
and teeth looked when she opened her mouth. He held the last
image in his mind for a long time. "Tell your wife to get a sponge
and wash me," he said.

"I can bathe you."

"I look like a *maricón* to you?" Preacher said, grinning.

"I'll ask her, boss."

"Don't ask. Tell her. Hugo paid you enough money, didn't he? For you and your family and the veterinarian who left me with all this pain? Y'all got paid plenty, didn't you, Jesus? Or do you need more?"

"It's *bastante*."

"Hugo gave you *bastante* to take care of the gringo. '*Bastante*' means 'enough,' doesn't it? How should I take that? Enough to do what? Sell me out? Maybe tell your priest about me?" Preacher's eyes became hazy and amused.

Jesus's hair was as black and shiny as paint, barbered like a matador's, his skin pale, his hands small and his features frail, like those of a consumptive Spanish poet. He was not over thirty, but his daughter was at least ten and his overweight wife could have been his mother. Go figure, Preacher thought.

THAT EVENING THE power was back on, but Preacher could not shake either his funk or his misgivings about his environment and his caretakers. "Your name is a form of irreverence," he said to Jesus.

"Is a what?"

"Try to speak in complete sentences. Don't leave the subject out of your sentences. 'Is' is a verb, not a noun. Your parents gave you the Lord's name, but you take money to hide a gringo and break the laws of your country."

"I got to do what I got to do, boss."

"Take me outside. Don't put me downwind of those goats, either."

Jesus set up the collapsible wheelchair by the bedside and worked Preacher into the seat, then wheeled him out the front door into the lee of the house, Preacher's .45 resting on his lap. The view to the south was magnificent. The sky was lavender, the desert wastes bound not by earthy borders but by the arbitrary definitions of light and shadow. Few people would have found such a vista spiritually comforting, but Preacher did. The dry riverbeds were prehistoric, the flumes strewn with rocks the color of wizened apples and plums and apricots. Preacher saw wood that rain and wind and heat had carved and reshaped and hardened into bleached objects that could be mistaken for dinosaur bone. The desert was immutable, as encompassing as a deity, serene in its own magnitude, stretching into the past all the way back to Eden, a testimony to the predictability and design in all creation, a mistress beckoning to those who were unafraid to enter and conquer and use her.

"You ever hear of Herbert Spencer?" Preacher said.

"Who?" Jesus said.

"That's what I thought. Ever hear of Charles Darwin?"

"*Claro que sí.*"

"It was Herbert Spencer who understood how society worked, not Darwin. Darwin wasn't a sociologist or philosopher. Can you relate to that?"

"Whatever you say, boss."

"Why are you grinning?"

"I thought you was making a joke."

"You think I need you to agree with me?"

"No, boss."

"Because if you did, that would be an insult. But you're not that kind of man, right?"

Jesus lowered his head and folded his arms, his face drawn with fatigue and his inability to deal with Preacher's convoluted rhetoric. A purple haze was settling on the mesas and vast wasteland that lay to the south, the dust rising off the hardpan, the creosote brush darkening inside the gloom. Not far away, Jesus saw a coyote digging hard into a gopher's burrow, flinging the dirt backward with its nails, darting its muzzle into the hole.

"You got any family, people who can help take care of you, boss?" Jesus said.

It was a question he shouldn't have asked. Preacher lifted his head the way a fish might when feeding on the surface of a lake. There was an unexpected and unreadable bead of light in his eyes, like a damp kitchen match flaring on the striker. "I look like a man with no family?"

"I thought maybe there was somebody you wanted me to call."

"A man inseminates a woman. The woman squeezes the kid out of her womb. So now we've got a father and a mother and a child. That's a family. You're saying I'm different somehow?"

"I didn't mean nothing, boss."

"Go back inside."

"When it's cool, the mosquitoes come out. They'll pick you up and carry you off, boss."

Preacher's expression seemed to go out of joint.

"I got you, boss. When you're ready to eat, my little girl made some soup and tortillas special for you," Jesus said.

Jesus went through the back door, not speaking until he was well inside the house. Preacher watched the coyote dip a gopher out of the hole and run heavily and stiff-necked across the hardpan, the gopher flopping from its jaws. Jesus's wife came to the window and stared at Preacher's silhouette, her fist pressed to her mouth. Her husband pulled her away and closed the curtain, even though the house was superheated by the propane cooking stove in the kitchen.

In the morning a windburned man with an orange beard and blue tats on his upper arms delivered a compact car for Preacher's use and then left with a companion in a second vehicle. Jesus's little girl brought Preacher his lunch to him on a tray. She set it on his lap but did not go away.

"My pants are on the chair. Take a half dollar out of the pocket," he said.

The girl took two quarters from his trousers and closed her palm on them. Her face was oval and brown, like that of her mother, her hair dark brown, a blue ribbon tied in it. "You ain't got no family?" she asked.

"You ask too many questions for a person your age. Somebody should give you a grammar book, too."

"I'm sorry you was shot."

Preacher's eyes lifted from the girl's face to the kitchen, where Jesus and his wife were washing dishes in a pan of greasy water, their backs to Preacher. "I was in a car accident. Nobody shot me," he said.

She touched the cast with the ends of her fingers. "We got ice now. I'll put it on your foot," she said.

So Jesus had opened his mouth in front of his wife and daughter, Preacher thought. So the little girl could tell all her friends a gringo with two bullet holes in him was paying money to stay at their house.

What to do? he asked himself, staring at the ceiling.

Late that afternoon he had a feverish dream. He was firing a Thompson submachine gun, the stock and cylindrical magazine turned sideways so the recoil would jerk the barrel horizontally rather than upward, directing the angle of fire parallel to the ground rather than above the shapes he saw in the darkness.

He awoke abruptly into the warm yellow glare of the room and wasn't sure where he was. He could hear flies buzzing and a goat's bell tinkling and smell the odor of water that had gone sour in a cattle pond. He picked up a damp cloth from a bowl on his nightstand and wiped his face with it. He sat on the side of the mattress, the blood draining down into his foot, waiting for the images in his dream to leave his mind.

Through the kitchen doorway he could see Jesus and his wife and little girl eating at their kitchen table. They were eating tortillas they'd rolled pickled vegetables inside, their faces leaning over their bowls, crumbs falling from their mouths. They made him think of Indians from an earlier era eating inside a cave.

Why'd Jesus have to blab in front of the kid? Preacher wondered. Maybe he plans to blab to a much wider audience anyway, maybe to the *jefe* and his khaki-clad half-breed dirtbags down at the jail.

Preacher could feel the coldness of the .45's frame protruding from under the mattress. His crutches were propped against a wood chair in the corner. Through the window he could see the tan compact Hugo had ordered delivered for his use.

The veterinarian was coming back that evening. The veterinarian and Jesus and his wife and the little girl would all be in the house at one time.

This crap was on Hugo Cistranos, not him, Preacher thought. Just like the gig behind the stucco church. It was Hugo who'd blown it. Preacher hadn't invented how the world worked. The coyote's ability to dig the gopher out of its burrow was hardwired into the coyote's brain. A hundred-million-year-old floodplain disappearing into infinity contained only one form of meaningful artifact: the mineralized bones of all the mammals, reptiles, and birds that had done whatever was necessary in order to survive. If anyone doubted that, he needed only to sink the steel bucket on a backhoe into one of those ancient riverbeds that looked like calcified putty in the sunset.

Jesus brought Preacher his supper at dusk.

"What time is the vet going to be here?" Preacher asked.

"No is vet. *Es médico,* boss. He gonna be here soon."

"Answer the question: When will he be here?"

"Maybe fifteen minutes. You like the food okay?"

"Hand me my crutches."

"You getting up?"

Preacher's upturned face looked like the edge of a hatchet.

"I'll get them, boss," Jesus said.

Jesus's wife had hand-washed Preacher's trousers and shirt and socks and underwear, replaced his coins and keys and pocket-knife in the pockets, and hung them neatly on the wood chair by the wall. Preacher worked his way to the chair, gathered up his clothes, and sat back down on his mattress. Then he slowly dressed himself, keeping his mind empty of the events that would take place in the house within the next few minutes.

He had not tucked in his shirt, allowing it to hang outside his trousers. Through the front window, he saw the veterinarian's paint-skinned truck clattering over the ruts in the road, churning a cloud of fine white dust in the air. Preacher slid the .45 from under his mattress and pushed it inside the back of his belt, then pulled his shirt over the grips. The veterinarian parked in back and cut the engine, just as the rooster tail of dust from his truck broke across the front of the house and drifted through the screens. Preacher lifted himself onto his crutches and began working his way toward the kitchen, where Jesus and his wife and little girl sat at the table, waiting for the veterinarian, who clutched a sweating six-pack of Coca-Cola.

The veterinarian was unshaved and wore a frayed suit coat that was too tight on him and a tie with stains on it and a white shirt missing a button at the navel. He suffered from myopia, which caused him to squint and to furrow his brow, and as a consequence the villagers looked upon him as a studious and educated man worthy of respect.

"You look very good in your clean clothes, señor. Do you not want me to change your bandages? I brought you more sedatives to help you sleep," the veterinarian said to Preacher.

The veterinarian was framed against the screen door, the late red sun creating a nimbus around his uncut hair and the stubble on his jowls.

Preacher steadied his weight and eased his right hand from

the grip on the crutch. He moved his hand behind him slowly, so as not to lose his balance, his knuckles touching the heaviness of the .45 stuck down in his belt. "I don't think I'll need anything tonight," he said.

They all stared at him in the silence, the bare lightbulb overhead splintering into yellow needles, reducing the differences in their lives to pools of shadow at their feet. *Now, now, now,* Preacher heard a voice in his head saying.

"Rosa made you some peanut-butter cookies," Jesus said.

Was that the little girl's name or the name of the wife? "Say again?"

"My little girl made you a present, boss."

"I'm diabetic. I cain't eat sugar."

"You want to sit down? You look like you're hurting, boss."

Preacher's right hand opened and closed behind his back. He sucked in slightly on his bottom lip. "How far up the dirt road to the highway?"

"Ten minutes, no more."

Preacher swallowed drily and slid his palm over the grips of the .45. Then his stare broke, and he felt a line of tension like a fissure divide the skin of his face in half. He pulled his wallet from his back pocket and labored on the crutches to the kitchen table. He splayed open the wallet and began counting a series of bills onto the table. "There's eleven hundred dollars here," he said. "You educate that little girl with it, you buy her decent clothes, you get her teeth fixed, you send her to a doctor and not to some damn quack, you buy her good food, and you burn a candle at your church in thanks you got a little girl like this. You understand me?"

"You don't got to tell me those things, boss."

"And you get her a grammar book, too, plus one for yourself."

Preacher worked his wallet into his pocket and thumped

across the floor on his crutches and out the screen into the yard, under a purple and bloodred sky that seemed filled with the cawing of carrion birds.

He fell behind the wheel of the Honda and started the engine. Jesus came out the back screen of his house, a can of Coca-Cola in his hand.

"Some guys just don't know how to leave it alone," Preacher said under his breath.

"Boss, can you talk to Rosa? She's crying."

"About *what*?"

"She heard you talking in your sleep. She thinks you're going to hell."

"You just don't get it, do you?"

"Get what, boss?"

"It's right yonder, all around us, in the haze of the evening. We're already there," Preacher said, gesturing at the darkening plain.

"You one unusual gringo, boss."

WHEN HACKBERRY HOLLAND woke inside a blue dawn on Saturday morning, he looked through his bedroom window and saw the FBI agent Ethan Riser in his backyard, admiring Hack's flower beds. The FBI agent's hair was as thick and white as cotton, the capillaries in his jaws like pieces of blue and red thread. The iridescent spray from Hackberry's automatic sprinklers had already stained Riser's pale suit, but his concentration on the flower beds seemed so intense he was hardly aware of it.

Hackberry dressed in a pair of khakis and a T-shirt and walked barefoot onto the back porch. There were poplar trees planted as a windbreak at the bottom of his property, and inside the shadows they made on the grass he could see a doe and her fawn watching him, their eyes brown and moist inside the gloom.

"You guys get up early in the morning, don't you?" he said to the FBI agent.

"I work Sundays, too. Me and the pope."

"What do you need, sir?"

"Can I buy you breakfast?"

"No, but you can come inside."

While the agent sat at his kitchen table, Hackberry started the coffeemaker and broke a half-dozen eggs in a huge skillet and set two pork chops in the skillet with them. "You like cereal?" he said.

"No, thanks."

At the stove, Hackberry poured a bowlful of Rice Krispies, then added cold milk and started eating them while the eggs and meat cooked. Ethan Riser rested his chin on his thumb and knuckle and stared into space, trying not to look at his watch or show impatience. His eyes were ice-blue, unblinking, marked by neither guile nor doubt. He cleared his throat slightly. "My father was a botanist and a Shakespearean actor," he said. "In his gardens he grew every kind of flower Shakespeare mentions in his work. He was also a student of Voltaire and believed he could tend his own garden and separate himself from the rest of the world. For that reason, he was a tragic man."

"What did you want to tell me, sir?" Hackberry said, setting his cereal bowl in the sink.

"There were two sets of prints on the Airweight thirty-eight the road gang supervisor gave you. We matched one set to the prints of Vikki Gaddis we took from her house. The other set we matched through the California driver's license database. They belong to a fellow by the name of Jack Collins. He has no criminal record. But we've heard about him. His nickname is Preacher. Excuse me, are you listening?"

"I will be as soon as I have some coffee."

"I see."

"You take sugar or milk?" Hackberry said.

Ethan Riser folded his arms and looked out the window at the deer among the poplar trees. "Whatever you have is fine," he said.

"Go ahead," Hackberry said.

"Thank you. They call him Preacher because he thinks he may be the left hand of God, the giver of death." Ethan Riser waited, his agitation beginning to show. "You're not impressed?"

"Did you ever know a sociopath who didn't think he was of cosmic importance? What did this guy do before he became the left hand of God?"

"He was a pest exterminator."

Hackberry began pouring coffee into two cups and tried to hide his expression.

"You think it's funny?" Riser said.

"Me?"

"You said you were at Pak's Palace. I did some research. That was a brick factory where Major Pak hung up GIs on the rafters and beat them with clubs for hours. You were one of them?"

"So what if I was or wasn't? It happened. Most of those guys didn't come back." Hackberry scraped the eggs and meat out of the skillet onto a platter. Then he set the platter on top of the table. He set it down harder than he intended.

"We hear this guy Preacher is a gun for hire across the border. We hear he doesn't take prisoners. It's a free-fire zone down there. More people are being killed in Coahuila and Nuevo León than in Iraq, did you know that?"

"As long as it doesn't happen in my county, I'm not interested."

"You'd better be. Maybe Collins has already killed Pete Flores and the Gaddis girl. If he's true to his reputation, he'll be back and brush his footprints out of the sand. You hearing me on this, Sheriff?"

Hackberry blew on his coffee and drank from it. "My grandfather was a Texas Ranger. He knocked John Wesley Hardin out of his saddle and pistol-whipped him and put him in jail."

"What's that mean?"

"Mess with the wrong people and you'll get a shitpile of grief, is what it means."

Ethan Riser studied him, just short of being impolite. "I heard you were a hardhead. I heard you think you can live inside your own zip code."

"Your food's getting cold. Better eat up."

"Here's the rest of it. After nine-eleven, Immigration and Naturalization merged with Customs and became ICE. They're one of the most effective and successful law enforcement agencies we have under Homeland Security. The great majority of their agents are professional and good at what they do. But there's one guy hereabouts who is off the leash and off the wall."

"This guy Clawson?"

"That's right, Isaac Clawson. Years ago two serial predators were working out of northern Oklahoma. They made forays up into Kansas, the home of Toto and Dorothy and the yellow brick road. I won't describe what they did to most of their victims because you're trying to eat your breakfast. Clawson's daughter worked nights at a convenience store. These guys kidnapped both her and her fiancé from the store and locked them in the trunk of a car. Out of pure meanness, they set fire to the car and burned them alive."

"You're telling me Clawson's a cowboy?"

"I'll put it this way: He likes to work alone."

Hackberry had set down his knife and fork. He gazed out the back door at the poplar trees. The sky was dark, and dust was blowing out of a field, the tips of the poplars bending in the wind.

"You okay, Sheriff?"

"Sure, why not?"

"You were a corpsman at the Chosin?"

"Yep."

"The country owes men and women like you a big debt."

"Not to me they don't," Hackberry said.

"I had to come here this morning."

"I know you did."

Ethan Riser got up to leave, then paused at the door. "Love your flowers," he said.

Hackberry nodded and didn't reply.

He wrapped the uneaten pork chops in foil and placed them in the icebox, then put on a gray sweat-ringed felt hat and in the backyard scraped the eggs off the platter for his bird dog and two barn cats that didn't have names and a possum that lived under the house. He went back in the kitchen and took a sack of corn out of the icebox and walked down to the poplar trees and scattered the corn in the grass for the doe and her fawn. The grass was tall and green in the lee of the trees, channeled with the wind blowing out of the south. Hackberry squatted down and watched the deer eat, his face blanketed with shadow, his eyes like those of a man staring into a dead fire.

Chapter 6

NICK DOLAN FELT he might have dodged a bolt of lightning. Hugo Cistranos had not shown up at the club or followed him to his vacation home on the Comal River. Maybe Hugo was all gas and flash and Afghan hash and would just disappear. Maybe Hugo would be consumed by his own evil, like a candle flame cupping and dying inside its own wax. Maybe Nick would finally get a break from the cosmic powers that had kept him running on a hamster wheel for most of his life.

Just outside the city limits of San Antonio, Nick lived in a neighborhood of eight-thousand-to-ten-thousand-square-feet homes, many of them built of stone, the yards cordoned off by thick green hedges, the sidewalks tree-shaded. The zoning code was strict, and trucks, trailers, mobile homes, and even specially outfitted vehicles to transport the handicapped could not be parked on the streets or in driveways overnight. But Nick cared less about the upscale, quasi-bucolic quality of his neighborhood than he did about the latticework enclosure and patio he had built with his own labor behind his house.

The palm trees that towered overhead had come from Florida,

their root balls wrapped in wet burlap, the excavations they were dropped into sprinkled with dead bait fish and bat guano. The grapevine that wound through the latticework had been transplanted from his grandfather's old home in New Orleans. The flagstones had been discovered during the construction of an overpass and brought by a friendly contractor to Nick's house, four of them chiseled with a seventeenth-century Spanish coat of arms. His hedges flowered in spring and bloomed until December. In the center of his patio were a glass-topped bamboo table and bamboo chairs, all of it shaded by Hong Kong orchid trees rooted inside redwood barrels that had been sawed in half.

In the cooling of the day, Nick loved to sit at the table in fresh white tennis togs, a glass of gin and tonic and cracked ice in his hand, an orange slice inserted on the lip of the glass, and read a book, a best seller whose title he could drop in a conversation. The breeze was up tonight, the lavender sky flickering with heat lightning, the freshly clipped ends of the flowers in his hedge like thousands of pink and purple eyes couched among the leaves. Nick had smoked only nineteen cigarettes that day, a record. He had many things to be thankful for. Maybe he even had a future.

Inside the fragrance of his enclosure, he felt himself drowsing off, the weight of his book pulling itself from his hand.

His head jerked up, his eyes opening suddenly. He rubbed the sleep out of his face and wondered if he was having a bad dream. Hugo Cistranos was standing above him, grinning, his forearms thick and scrolled with veins, as though he had been wrist-curling a barbell. "Looks like you got quite a sunburn on the river," he said.

"How'd you get in my yard?"

"Through the hedge."

"Are you nuts coming here like this?"

Nick's scalp constricted. He had just done it again, admitting guilt and complicity about things he hadn't done, indicating he and Hugo had a relationship of some kind, one based on shared experience.

"Didn't want to embarrass you at the club. Didn't want to ring the bell and disturb your family. What's a guy to do, Nicholas? We've got mucho shit-o to work through here."

"I don't owe you any money."

"Okay, you owe it to my subcontractors. Put it any way you want. The vig is running as we speak. My chief subcontractor is Preacher Jack Collins. He's a religious fanatic who did the hands-on work behind the church. Nobody knows what goes on inside his head, and nobody asks. I just delivered him his Honda and paid his medical expenses. Those services are all on your tab, too, Nicholas."

"I don't use that name."

"No problemo, Nick-o. Know why I had to pay Preacher's medical expenses? Because this broad here put two holes in him."

Hugo placed a four-by-five color photograph on the glass tabletop. Nick stared down at the face of a girl with recessed eyes, her chestnut hair curled at the tips. "Ever see this cutie?" Hugo asked.

Nick's scalp constricted again. "No," he replied.

"How about this kid?" Hugo said, placing another photo next to the girl's. A soldier in a United States Army dress uniform, an American flag on a staff as a backdrop, stared up at Nick.

"I never saw this person, either," Nick said, studiously not letting his eyes drift back to the girl's photograph.

"You said that pretty quick. Take another look."

"I don't know who they are. Why are you showing these pictures to me?"

"Those are two kids who can bring a lot of people down. They have to go off the board, Nick. People got to get paid, too, Nick. That means I'm about to be your new business partner, Nick. I've got the papers right here. Twenty-five percent of the club and the

82 JAMES LEE BURKE

Mexican restaurant and no claim on anything else. It's a bargain, little buddy."

"Screw you, Hugo," Nick said, his face dilating with the recklessness of his own rhetoric.

Hugo opened a manila folder and sorted through a half-inch of documents, as though giving them final approval, then closed the folder and set it on the table. "Relax, finish your drink and have a smoke, talk it over with your wife. There's no rush." He looked at his wristwatch. "I'll send a driver for the papers, say, tomorrow afternoon, around three. Okay, little buddy?"

NICK HAD HOPED he would never see the girl named Vikki Gaddis again. His nonnegotiable rules for himself as the operator of a skin joint and as the geographically removed owner of escort services in Dallas and Houston had always remained the same: You paid your taxes, and you protected your girls and never personally exploited them.

Nick's rules had preempted conflicts with the IRS and purchased for him an appreciable degree of respect from his employees. About eighteen months back, he had run a want ad in the San Antonio newspapers for musicians to play in the Mexican restaurant he had just built next to his strip club. Five days later, when he was out in the parking lot on a scalding afternoon, Vikki Gaddis had driven off the highway in a shitbox leaking smoke from every rusted crack in the car body. At first he thought she was looking for a job up on the pole, then he realized she hadn't seen the ad but had been told he needed a folksinger.

"You're confused," Nick said. "I'm opening a Mexican restaurant. I need some entertainment for people while they're eating dinner. Mexican stuff."

He saw the disappointment in her eyes, a vague hint of desperation around her mouth. Her face was damp and shiny in the heat. Heavy trucks, their engines hammering, were passing on the highway, their air brakes hissing. Nick touched at his nose with the back of his wrist. "Why don't you come on in the restaurant and let's talk a minute?" he said.

Nick had already hired a five-piece mariachi band, one complete with sombreros and brocaded vaquero costumes, beerbellied, mustached guys with brass horns that could crack the tiles on the roof, and he had no need of an Anglo folksinger. As he and the girl walked out of the sun's glare into the air-conditioned coolness of the restaurant, the girl swinging her guitar case against her hip, he knew that an adulterer had always lived inside him.

She wore white shorts and a pale blue blouse and sandals, and when she sat down in front of his desk, she leaned over a little too far and he wondered if he wasn't being played.

"You sing Spanish songs?" he said.

"No, I do a lot of the Carter Family pieces. Their music made a comeback when Johnny Cash married June. Then the interest died again. They created a style of picking that's called 'hammering on and pulling off.' "

Nick was clueless, his mouth hanging open in a half-smile. "You sing like Johnny Cash?"

"No, the Carters were a big influence on other people, like Woody Guthrie. Here, I'll show you," she said. She unsnapped her guitar case and removed a sunburst Gibson from it. The case was lined with purplish-pink velvet, and it glowed with a virginal light that only added to Nick's confused thoughts about both the girl and the web of desire and need he was walking into.

She fitted a pick on her thumb and began singing a song about flowers covered with emerald dew and a lover betrayed and left to pine in a place that was older than time. When she chorded the guitar, the whiteness of her palm curved around the neck, and she depressed a bass string just before striking it, then released it, creating a sliding note that resonated inside the sound hole. Nick was mesmerized by her voice, the way she lifted her chin when she sang, the muscles working in her throat.

"That's beautiful," he said. "You say these Carter guys were an influence on Woody Herman?"

"Not exactly," she replied.

"I already got a band, but maybe come back in a couple of weeks. If it doesn't work out with them—"

"You have an opening for a food server?" she asked, putting away her guitar.

"I got two more than I need. I had to hire the cook's sisters, or she was gonna walk on me."

The girl snapped the locks on her case and raised her eyes to his. "Thanks, you've been real nice," she said.

An image was forming in his mind that turned his loins to water. "Look, I got a place next door. Slap my face if you want. The money's good, the girls working for me don't have to do anything they don't want to, I throw drunks and profane guys out. I try to keep it a gentlemen's club even if some bums get in sometimes. I could use a—"

"What are you saying?"

"That I got an opening or two. That maybe you're in a tight spot and I can help you out till you find a singing job."

"I'm not a dancer," she said.

"Yeah, I knew that," he said, his face small and tight and burning. "I was just letting you know my situation. I only got so many resources. I got kids of my own." He was stuttering, and his hands were shaking under the desk, his words nonsensical even to himself.

She was getting up, reaching for the handle on her guitar case, the back of one gold thigh streaked with a band of light.

"Ms. Gaddis—"

"Just call me Vikki."

"I thought maybe I was doing a good deed. I didn't mean to offend you."

"I think you're a nice man. I enjoyed meeting you," she said. She smiled at him, and in that moment, in order to be twenty-five again, Nick would have run his fingers one at a time through a Skilsaw.

Now, as he sat amid trellises and latticework that were green and thick with grapevine grown by his grandfather, an honest and decent man who had sold shoestrings from door to door, he tried to convince himself the girl in the photo was not Vikki Gaddis. But it was, and he knew it, and he knew her face would live in his sleep the rest of his life if Hugo killed her. And what about the soldier? Nick had recognized the elongated blue and silver combat infantryman badge on his chest. Nick could feel tears welling in his eyes but couldn't decide if they were for himself or for the Thai women machine-gunned by somebody named Preacher Collins or for Vikki Gaddis and her boyfriend.

He lay down in the middle of his lawn, his arms and legs spread in the shape of a giant X, a weight as heavy as a blacksmith's anvil crushing his chest.

WHEN HACKBERRY LOOKED out his office window and saw a silver car with a mirror wax job coming hard up the street, blowing dust and newspaper into the air, the sun bouncing off the windshield like the brassy flash of a heliograph, he knew that either a drunk or an outsider who couldn't read speed limit signs or government trouble was about to arrive in the middle of his afternoon, free curbside delivery.

The man who got out of the car was as tall as Hackberry, his starched white shirt form-fitting on his athletic frame, his shaved and polished head gleaming under an afternoon sun that looked like a yellow flame. A dark-skinned man with a haircut like a nineteenth-century Apache's sat hunched over in the backseat, both arms pulled down between his legs, as though he were trying to clutch his ankles. The dark-skinned man's eyes were slits, his lips purple with either snuff or bruises, the back of his neck pocked with acne scars.

Hackberry put on a straw hat and stepped outside into the shade of the sandstone building that served as his office and the jail. The man with the shaved head held up his ID. The lidless intensity in his eyes and the tautness in his facial muscles made Hackberry think of a banjo string wound tightly on a wood peg, the tension climbing into a tremolo. The man said, "Isaac Clawson, ICE. I'm glad you're in your office. I don't like to chase a local official around in his own county."

"Why is Danny Boy Lorca on a D-ring?"

"You know him?" Clawson said.

"I just used his name to you, sir."

"What I mean is, do you know anything about him?"

"About once a month he walks from the beer joint down to the jail and sleeps it off. He lets himself in and out."

"He's the drinking buddy of Pete Flores. He says he doesn't know where Flores is."

"Let's have a talk with him," Hackberry said. He opened the back door of the sedan and leaned inside. The smell of urine welled into his face. There was a skinned place on Danny Boy's right temple, like a piece of fruit that had been rubbed on a carrot grater. There was a dark area in his wash-faded jeans, as though a wet towel had been pressed into his groin.

"Have you seen Pete Flores around?" Hackberry said.

"Maybe two weeks back."

"Y'all were drinking a little mescal together?"

"He was eating in Junior's diner on the four-lane. That's where his girlfriend works at."

"We think some guys are trying to hurt him, Danny. You'd be doing Pete a big favor if you helped us find him."

"I ain't seen him since what I just told you." Danny Boy's eyes slid off Hackberry's and fastened on Clawson's, then came back again.

Hackberry straightened up and closed the door. "I think he's telling the truth," he said.

"You psychic with these guys?"

"With him I am. He doesn't have any reason to lie."

Clawson took off his large octagonal glasses and wiped them with a Kleenex, staring down the street, a deep wrinkle between his eyes. "Can we go inside?"

"It's full of cigarette smoke. What'd you do to Danny Boy?"

"I didn't do anything to him. He's drunk. He fell down. When I picked him up, he started to swing on me. But I didn't do anything to him." Clawson opened the back door and used a handcuff key to free Danny Boy from the D-ring inset in the floor, then wrapped his fingers under Danny Boy's arm and pulled him from the backseat. "Get going," he said.

"You want me to hang around, Sheriff?" Danny Boy said.

"Did I tell you to get out of here?" Clawson said. He pushed Danny Boy, then kicked him in the butt.

"Whoa," Hackberry said.

"Whoa what?" Clawson said.

"You need to dial it down, Mr. Clawson."

"It's Agent Clawson."

Hackberry was breathing through his nose. He saw Pam Tibbs at the office window. He turned to Danny Boy. "Go down to Grogan's and put a couple on my tab," he said. "The operational word is 'couple,' Danny."

"I don't need a drink. I'm gonna get something to eat and go back to my place. If I hear anything on Pete, I'll tell you," Danny Boy said.

Hackberry turned and started back toward his office, ignoring Clawson's presence. He could hear the flag popping in the breeze and the flag chain tinkling against the metal pole.

"We're not done," Clawson said. "Last night somebody made two nine-one-one calls from a pay phone outside San Antonio. I'll play you part of it."

He removed a small recorder from his pants pocket and clicked it on. The voice on the recording sounded like that of a drunk man or someone with a speech defect. "Tell the FBI there's a whack out on a girl name of Vikki Gaddis. They're gonna kill her and a soldier. It's about those Thai women that got murdered." Clawson clicked off the recorder. "Know the voice?" he said.

"No," Hackberry said.

"I think the caller had a pencil clenched between his teeth and was loaded on top of it. Can you detect an accent?"

"I'd say he's not from around here."

"Here's another piece of information: One of our forensic guys went the extra mile on the postmortem of the Thai females. They had China white in their stomachs, balloons full of it, the purest I've ever seen. Some of the balloons had ruptured in the women's stomachs prior to mortality. I wonder if you stumbled into a storage area rather than a graveyard."

"Stumbled?"

"English lit wasn't my strong suit. You want to be serious here or not?"

"I don't buy that the place behind the church was a storage area. That makes no sense."

"Then what does?"

"I've been told of your personal loss, sir. I think I can appreciate the level of anger you must have to deal with. But you're not going to verbally abuse or put your foot on anybody in this county again. We're done here."

"Where do you get off talking about my personal life? Where do you get off talking about my daughter, you sonofabitch?"

Just then the dispatcher Maydeen stepped outside and lit a cigarette. She wore a deputy's uniform and had fat arms and big breasts and wide hips, and her lipstick looked like a flattened rose on her mouth. "Hack doesn't let us smoke in the building," she said, smiling from ear to ear as she inhaled deep into her lungs.

PREACHER JACK COLLINS paid the cabdriver the fare from the airstrip to the office-and-condo building that faced Galveston Bay. But rather than go immediately into the building, he paused on his crutches and stared across Seawall Boulevard at the waves folding on the beach, each wave rilling with sand and yellowed vegetation and dead shellfish and seaweed matted with clusters of tiny crabs and Portuguese men-of-war whose tentacles could wrap around a horse's leg and sting it to its knees.

There was a storm breaking on the southern horizon like a great cloud of green gas forked with lightning that made no sound. The air had turned the color of tarnished brass as the barometer had dropped, and Preacher could taste the salt in the wind and smell the shrimp that had been caught inside the waves and left stranded on the sand among the ruptured blue air sacs of the jellyfish. The humidity was as bright as spun glass, and within a minute's time it glazed his forearms and face and was turned into a cool burn by the wind, not unlike a lover's tongue moving across the skin.

Preacher entered a glass door painted with the words RED-STONE SECURITY SERVICE. A receptionist looked up from her desk and smiled pleasantly at him. "Tell Mr. Rooney Jack is here to see him," he said.

"Do you have an appointment, sir?"

"What time is it?"

The receptionist glanced at a large grandfather clock, one whose face was inset with Roman numerals. "It's four-forty-seven," she said.

"That's the time of my appointment with Mr. Rooney. You can tell him that."

Her hand moved toward the phone uncertainly, then stopped.

"That was just my poor joke. Ma'am, these crutches aren't getting any more comfortable," Preacher said.

"Just a moment." She lifted the phone receiver and pushed a button. "Mr. Rooney, Jack is here to see you." There was a beat. "He didn't give it." Another beat, this one longer. "Sir, what's your last name?"

"My full name is Jack Collins, no middle initial."

After the receptionist relayed the information, there was a silence in the room almost as loud as the waves bursting against the beach. Then she replaced the receiver in the cradle. Whatever thoughts she was thinking were locked behind her eyes. "Mr. Rooney says to go on up. The elevator is to your left."

"He tell you to call somebody?" Preacher asked.

"I'm not sure I know what you mean, sir."

"You did your job, ma'am. Don't worry about it. But I'd better not hear that elevator come up behind me with the wrong person in it," Preacher said.

The receptionist stared straight ahead for perhaps three seconds, picked up her purse, and went out the front door, her dress switching back and forth across her calves.

When Preacher stepped out of the elevator, he saw a man in a beige suit and pink western shirt sitting in a swivel chair behind a huge desk, framed against a glass wall that looked out onto the bay. On the desk was a big clear plastic jar of green-and-blue candy sticks, each striped stick wrapped in cellophane. His hips swelled out at the beltline and gave the sense that he was melting in his swivel chair. He had sandy hair and a small Irish mouth that was downturned at the corners. His skin was dusted with liver spots, some of them dark, almost purple around the edges, as though his soul exuded sickness through his pores. "Help you?" he said.

"Maybe."

Down on the beach, swimmers were getting out of the water, dragging their inner tubes with them, a lifeguard standing in his elevated chair, blowing a whistle, pointing his finger at a triangular fin whizzing through a swell at incredible speed.

"Can I sit down?" Preacher said.

"Yes, sir, go right ahead," Arthur Rooney said.

"Should I call you Artie or Mr. Rooney?"

"Whatever you want."

"Hugo Cistranos work for you?"

"He did. When I had an investigative agency in New Orleans. But not now."

"I think he does."

"Sir?"

"Do I need to speak louder?"

"Hugo Cistranos is not with me any longer. That's what I'm saying to you. What's the issue, Mr. Collins?" Artie Rooney cleared his throat as though the last word had caught in his larynx.

"You know who I am?"

"I've heard of you. Nickname is Preacher, right?"

"Yes, sir, some do call me that with regularity, friends and such."

"We just moved into this office. How'd you know I was here?"

"Made a couple of calls. Know that song 'I Get Around' by the Beach Boys? I get around, albeit on crutches. A woman put a couple of holes in me."

"Sorry to hear about that."

"Some other people and I got stuck with a piece of wet work.

Supposedly, it was initiated by a little fellow who runs a skin joint for middle-aged titty babies. Supposedly, this little fellow doesn't want to come up with the money to pay his tab. His name is Nick Dolan. Know who I'm talking about?"

"I've known Nick for thirty-five years. He had a floating casino in New Orleans."

Preacher chewed on a hangnail and removed a piece of skin from his tongue. "I got to thinking about this little fellow, the one with the titty-baby joint about halfway between Austin and San Antone. Why would a fellow like that have a bunch of Asian women shot to death?"

Artie Rooney had crossed one leg over his knee and propped one hand stiffly on the edge of his desk, his stomach swelling over his belt. "You're talking about that big slaughter down by the border? I'm not up on that, Mr. Collins. To be frank, I'm a little lost here."

"I'm not a mister, so don't call me that again."

"I didn't mean to be impolite or insult you."

"What makes you think you have the power to offend me?"

"Pardon?"

"You have a hearing problem? Why is it you think you're so important I care about your opinion of me?"

Rooney's eyes drifted to the elevator door.

"I wouldn't expect the cav'ry if I were you," Preacher said.

Rooney picked up his phone and pushed a button. After a few seconds, he replaced the receiver without speaking into it and leaned back in his chair. He rested his elbow on the arm of the chair, his chin on his thumb and forefinger, his pulse beating visibly in his throat. There was a bloodless white rim around the edge of his nostrils, as though he were breathing refrigerated air. "What'd you do with my secretary?"

"A little Mexican girl across the river said I might have to go to hell. You want me to tell you what I did?"

"To the girl? You did something to a little girl is what you're telling me?" Rooney's hand seemed to flutter at his mouth, then he lowered it to his lap.

"I think you worked some kind of scam on this Dolan fellow. I'm not sure what it is, exactly, but it's got your shit-prints on it. You owe me a lot of money, Mr. Rooney. If I'm going to hell, if I'm already there, in fact, how much you reckon my soul is worth? Don't put your hand on that phone again. You owe me a half million dollars."

"I owe you *what*?"

"I've got a gift. I can always tell a coward. I can always tell a liar, too. I think you're both."

"What are you doing? Stay away from me."

Out on the beach, a mother up to her hips in the water was scooping her child from a wave, running with it up the incline, her dress ballooning around her, her face filled with panic.

"Don't get up. If you get up, that's going to make it a whole lot worse," Preacher said.

"What are you doing with that? For God's sakes, man."

"My soul is going to be in the flames because of you. You invoke God's name now? Put your hand on the blotter and shut your eyes."

"I'll get you the money."

"Right now, in your heart, you believe what you're saying. But soon as I'm gone, your words will be ashes in the wind. Spread your fingers and press down real hard. Do it. Do it now. Or I'll rake this across your face and then across your throat."

With his eyes tightly shut, Artie Rooney obeyed the man who loomed above him on crutches. Then Preacher Jack Collins laid the edge of his barber's razor across Rooney's little finger and mashed down on the back of the razor with both hands.

Chapter 7

Nɪᴄᴋ ʜᴀᴅ ʜᴇᴀʀᴅ of blackouts but was never quite sure what constituted one. How could somebody walk around doing things and have no memory of his deeds? To Nick, the terms "blackout" and "copout" seemed very similar.

But after Hugo Cistranos had left Nick's backyard, telling him he had until three o'clock the next afternoon to sign over 25 percent of his strip joint and restaurant, Nick had gone downstairs to the game room, bolted the door so the children wouldn't see him, and gotten sloshed to the eyes.

When he woke in the morning on the floor, sick and trembling and smelling of his own visceral odors, he remembered watching a cartoon show around midnight and fumbling with a deadbolt. Had he been sleepwalking? He stood at the bottom of the stairwell and stared up the stairs. The door was still locked. Thank God neither his wife nor the children had seen him drunk. Nick didn't believe a father or husband could behave worse than one who was dissolute in front of his wife and children.

Then he saw his car keys on the Ping-Pong table and began to experience flashes of clarity inside his head, like shards of a mirror reconstructing themselves behind his eyes, each one containing an image that grew larger and larger and filled him with terror: Nick driving a car, Nick in a phone booth, Nick talking to an emergency dispatcher, headlights swerving in front of his windshield, car horns blowing angrily.

Had he gone somewhere to make a 911 call? He went upstairs to shower and shave and put on fresh clothes. His wife and children were gone, and in the silence he could hear the wind rattling the dry fronds of his palm trees against the eaves. From the bathroom window, the sunlight trapped inside his swimming pool wobbled and refracted like the blue-white flame of an acetylene torch. The entire exterior world seemed superheated, sharpedged, a garden of cactuses and thorn bushes, scented not with flowers but with tar pots and diesel fumes.

What had he done last night?

Dropped the dime on Hugo? Dropped the dime on himself?

He sat at his breakfast table, eating aspirin and vitamin B, washing it down with orange juice straight out of the carton, his forehead oily with perspiration. He went into his office, hoping to find relief in the deep, cool ambience and solitude of his bookshelves and mahogany furniture and the dark drapes on the windows and the carpet that sank an inch under his feet. A bright red digital 11 was blinking on his message machine for his dedicated phone-and-fax line. The first message was from his wife, Esther: "We're at the mall. I let you sleep. We have to talk. Did you go out in the middle of the night? What the hell is wrong with you?"

The other messages were from the restaurant and the club:

"Cheyenne says she's not going on the pole the same time as Farina. I can't deal with these bitches, Nick. Are you coming in?"

"Uncle Charley's Meats just delivered us seventy pounds of spoiled chicken. That's the second time this week. They say the problem is ours. They off-loaded on the dock, and we didn't carry it in. I can't put it in the box, and it's smelling up the whole kitchen."

"Me again. They were pulling each other's hair in the dressing room."

"The code guy was here. He says we have to put a third sink in. He says he found a dead mouse in the dishwasher drain, too."

"Nick, there were a couple of guys in here last night I had trouble with. One guy had navy tats and a beard like a fire alarm. He said he was gonna be working for us. I kicked them out, but they said they'd be back. I thought maybe you needed a heads-up. Who is this asshole?"

"Hey, it's me. There's some flake on top of the toilet tank in the women's can. I had Rabbit clean the shitters spotless early this morning. Farina was in there ten minutes ago. When she came out, she looked like she'd packed dry ice up her nose. Nick, babysitting crazy whores is not in my curriculum vitae. She wants your home number. You want me to give it to her? I can't process these kinds of problems."

Nick held down the delete button and erased every message on the machine, played and unplayed alike.

It was seventeen minutes to one o'clock. Hugo's driver would be at the house at three P.M. to pick up the signed documents that would make Hugo Cistranos his business partner. The 25 percent ownership ceded to Hugo would of course be only the first step in the cannibalization of everything Nick owned. Nick sat in the darkness, his ears filled with a sound like wind blowing in a tunnel.

He had never confessed to anyone the fear he had felt in the schoolyard in the Ninth Ward. The black kids who took his lunch money from him, who shoved him down on the asphalt, seemed to target him and no one else as though they recognized both difference and weakness in him that they exorcised in themselves by degrading and forcing him to go hungry through the lunch hour and the rest of the afternoon, somehow freeing themselves of their own burden.

But why Nick? Because he was a Jew? Because his grandfather had adopted an Irish name? Because his parents took him to temple in a neighborhood full of simpletons who would later believe *The Passion of the Christ* was solid evidence that his people were guilty of deicide?

Maybe.

Or maybe they smelled fear on his skin the way a barracuda smells blood issuing from a wounded grouper.

Fear, the acronym for "fuck everything and run," he thought sadly. That had been the history of his young life. And still was.

He punched his wife's cell phone number into the console on his desk.

"Nick?" her voice said through the speakerphone.

"Where are you?" he said.

"Still at the mall. We're about to have lunch."

"Drop the kids at the country club and come home. We'll pick them up later."

"What is it? Don't lie to me, either."

"I need to show you where some things are."

"What things? What are you talking about?"

"Come home, Esther."

After he hung up, he wondered if his need was as naked as it sounded. He sat in a deep, stuffed leather chair and rested his forehead on his fingertips. It had been raining the night he met Esther twenty-three years ago. She was waiting for the streetcar under the steel colonnade at the corner of Canal and St. Charles Avenue, in front of the Pearl, where she worked as a night cashier after studying all day in the practical nursing program at UNO. There were raindrops in her hair, and in the neon glow of the restaurant's windows, she made him think of a multicolored star in a constellation.

"There's a storm blowing off Lake Pontchartrain. You shouldn't be out here," he had said to her.

"Who are you?" she replied.

"I'm Nick Dolan. You heard of me?"

"Yeah, you're a gangster."

"No, I'm not. I'm a gambler. I run a cardroom for Didoni Giacano."

"That's what I said. You're a gangster."

"I like 'white-collar criminal' better. Will you accept a ride from a white-collar criminal?"

She had on too much lipstick, and when she twisted her mouth into a button and fixed her eyes speculatively on Nick's, his heart swelled in a way that made him take a deep breath.

"I live Uptown, just off Prytania, not far from the movie theater," she said.

"That's what I thought. You are definitely an Uptown lady," he said. Then he remembered his car was in the shop and he had taken a cab to work. "I don't exactly have my car with me. I'll call a cab. Could I borrow a dime? I don't have any coins."

It was 1:26 P.M. when Nick heard Esther pull into the driveway and unlock the front door. "Where are you?" she called.

"In the office."

"Why are you sitting in the dark?" she said.

"Did you lock the front?"

"I don't remember. Did you go somewhere last night? Did you get into some trouble? I looked at the car. There're no dents in it."

"Sit down."

"Is that a gun?" she said, her voice rising.

"I keep it in the desk. Esther, sit down. Please. Just listen to me. Everything we own is in this file case. It's all alphabetized. We have a half-dozen equity accounts at Vanguard, tax-free stuff at Sit Mutuals, and two offshore accounts in the Cayman Islands. All the treasury bonds are short-term. Interest rates are in the dumps right now, but by next year gas prices will drive bonds down and rates up, and there'll be some good buys out there."

"I think you're having a nervous breakdown."

He got up from his chair and took both of her hands in his. "Sit down and listen to me like you've never listened before. No, no, don't talk, just listen, Esther."

She sat on the big square dark red leather footstool by the leather chair and watched his face. He sat back down, leaning forward, his gaze fixed on her shoes, his hands still clasping hers.

"I got involved with some evil men," he said. "Not just low-lifes but guys that got no parameters."

"Which guys?"

"One was a button man for the Giacanos. His name is Hugo Cistranos. He used to work for Artie Rooney. He's for hire, on the edge of things. Hugo is kind of like a virus. Money has got germs on it. You do business, sometimes you pick up germs."

"What's this guy got to do with the restaurant or the night-club?"

"Hugo did something really bad, something I didn't think even Hugo would do."

"What does that have to do with you?" she said, cutting him off, maybe too conveniently, maybe still not wanting to know how many pies Nick had a finger in.

"I tell you about it, you become a party to it. Hugo says it's on me. He says I ordered him to do it. He's trying to blackmail us. He might kill me, Esther."

She was breathing faster, as though his words were using up the oxygen in the room. "This man Hugo is claiming he killed somebody on your orders?"

"More than one."

"More than—"

"I have to deal with it this afternoon, Esther. By three o'clock."

"Someone may kill you?"

"Maybe."

"They'll have to kill me, too."

"No, this is the wrong way to think. You have to take the children to the river. Hugo has no reason to hurt you or them. We mustn't give him any reason to do that."

"Why does he want to kill you if he wants to blackmail you?"

"Because I'm not going to pay him anything."

"What else are you planning, Nick?"

"I'm not sure."

"I see it in your face. That's why you have the gun."

"Go to the river with the children."

"They'll have to walk in my blood to hurt our family. You understand that?" she said.

AT THREE P.M. sharp, Nick walked out to the curb and waited. His neighborhood was marbled with shadows from the rain clouds that had moved across the sun. A blue Chrysler came around the corner and approached him slowly, the tires clicking with gravel embedded in the treads, like the nails on a feral animal, the driver's face obscured by a dark green reflection of trees on the windshield. The Chrysler pulled to the curb, and the driver, a man with a wild orange beard, put down the passenger window. "Howdy," he said.

"I tried to call Hugo and save you a trip, but he's not answering his cell," Nick said. "You got another number for him?"

"I'm supposed to be picking up some signed contracts," the driver said, ignoring the question. His teeth were wide-set, his complexion florid, like that of a man with perpetual sunburn, his wrists relaxed on the crosspiece of the steering wheel. He wore shined needle-point boots and a long-sleeve print shirt tucked inside beltless white golf slacks; the hair on his chest grew onto the ironed-back lapels of his shirt. "No signed contracts, huh?"

"No signed contracts," Nick said.

The driver looked into space, then opened his cell phone and dialed a number. "It's Liam. He wants to talk to you. No, he doesn't have them. He didn't say why. He's standing right here in front of his house. That's where I am now. Hugo, talk to the guy."

The driver leaned over and handed Nick the cell phone through the window, smiling, as though the two of them were friends and had mutual interests. Nick put the cell phone to his ear and walked into his yard between two lime trees bursting with fruit. He could feel the humidity and heat rising from the St. Augustine grass into his face. He could hear a bumblebee buzzing close to his head. "I haven't said no to your offer, but I need a sit-down before I finalize anything."

"It's not an offer, Nicholas. 'Offer' is the wrong word."

"You used the name of this guy Preacher. He's the guy who's supposed to give me cold sweats, right? If he's a factor, he should be there, too."

"Be where?"

"At the sit-down. I want to meet him."

"If you meet Jack Collins, it'll be about two seconds before you become worm food."

"You're saying you can't control this guy? I'm supposed to give you twenty-five percent of two businesses so I can be safe from a guy you can't control?"

"You're not giving me anything. You owe me over a hundred thou. I owe that to other people. If you don't pay the vig, the vig falls on me. I don't pay other people's vig, Nick."

"Was your driver at my club last night?"

"How would I know?"

"A guy answering his description got thrown out. He was shooting off his mouth with my manager. He claimed he was going to be working there. You want the sit-down or not? You called this guy Collins a religious nut. If I get to him first, I'll tell him that."

There was a long pause. "Maybe your wife gave you a blow job this morning and convinced you you're not a pitiful putz. The truth is otherwise, Nick. You're still a pitiful putz. But I'll call Preacher. And I'll also have those transfers of title rewritten. Forget twenty-five percent. The new partnership will be fifty-fifty. Give me some shit and it will go to sixty-forty. Guess who will get the forty."

Hugo hung up.

"Got everything worked out?" the driver of the Chrysler said through the window.

PETE AND VIKKI got exactly sixteen miles up a dark highway when the car Pete's cousin had sold him on credit dropped the crankshaft on the asphalt, sparks grinding under the frame as the car slid sideways into soil that exploded around them like soft chalk.

When Pete called, the cousin told him the car came with no guarantees and the cousin's car lot did not have a complaint window for people with buyer's remorse. He also indicated he and his wife were leaving with the kids early in the morning for a week of rest and relaxation in Orlando.

Vikki and Pete removed two suitcases and Vikki's guitar and a bag of groceries from the car and stood by the roadside, thumbs out. A tractor-trailer rimmed with lights roared past them, then a mobile home and a prison bus and a gas-guzzler packed with Mexican drunks, the top half of the car cut off with an acetylene torch. The next vehicle was an ambulance, followed by a sheriff's cruiser, both of them with sirens on.

Two minutes later, a second cruiser appeared far down the road, its flasher rippling, its siren off. It came steadily out of the south, a bank of low mountains behind it, the stars vaporous and hot against a blue-black sky. The cruiser seemed to slow, perhaps to forty or forty-five miles per hour, gliding past them, the driver holding a microphone to his mouth, his face turned fully on them.

"He's calling us in," Pete said.

"Maybe he's sending a wrecker," Vikki said.

"No, he's bad news." Pete widened his eyes and wiped at his mouth. "I told you, he's stopping."

The cruiser pulled to the right shoulder and remained stationary, its front wheels cut back toward the center stripe, the interior light on.

"What's he doing?" Vikki said.

"He's probably got a description of us on his clipboard. Yep, here he comes."

They stared numbly into the cruiser's approaching headlights, their eyes watering, their hearts beating. The air seemed clotted with dust and bugs and gnats, the roadway still warm from the sunset, smelling of oil and rubber. Then, for no apparent reason, the cruiser made a U-turn and headed north again, its weight sinking on the back springs.

"He'll be back. We have to get off the highway," Pete said.

They crossed to the other side of the asphalt and began walking, glancing back over their shoulders, their abandoned car with all their household possessions dropping behind them into the darkness. A half hour later, a black man wearing strap overalls with no shirt stopped and said he was headed to his home, seventy miles southwest. "That's pert' exactly where we're going," Pete said.

They paid a week's advance rent, twenty dollars per day, at a motel on a stretch of side road that resembled a Hollywood re-creation of Highway 66 during the 1950s: a pink plaster-of-Paris archway over the road, painted with roses; a diner shaped like an Airstream trailer with a tin facsimile of a rocket on top; a circular building made to look like a bulging cheeseburger with service windows; a drive-in movie theater and a miniature golf course blown with trash and tumbleweed, the empty marquee patterned with birdshot; a red-green-and-purple neon war bonnet high up on the log facade of a beer joint and steak house; three Cadillac car bodies buried seemingly nose-first in the earth, their fins slicing the wind.

"This is a pretty neat place, if you ask me," Pete said, sitting on the side of the bed, looking through the side window at the landscape. He was barefoot and shirtless, and in the soft light of morning, the skin along his shoulder and one side of his back had the texture of lamp-shade material that has been wrinkled by intense heat.

"Pete, what are we going to do? We don't have a car, we're almost broke, and cops are probably looking for us all over Texas," Vikki said.

"We've done all right so far, haven't we?" Pete began talking about his friend Billy Bob Holland, a former Texas Ranger who had a law practice in western Montana. "Billy Bob will he'p us out. When I was little, my mother used to bring home men, usually late at night. Most of them were pretty worthless. This one guy was more worthless than all the rest put together and then some. One night he smacked both me and my mom around. When Billy Bob found out about it, he rode his horse into the beer joint and threw a rope on the guy and drug him out the front door into the parking lot. Then he kicked him into next week."

"Your lawyer friend can't help a fugitive. All he can do is surrender you."

"Billy Bob wouldn't do that."

"We have to get your disability check."

"That's kind of a problem, isn't it?" Pete stood up and propped one arm against the wall, gazing out the window, his upper torso shaped like a V. "That check should have come yesterday. It's just sitting there in the box. The government always gets it there on the same date."

"I can ask Junior to get it and send it to us," she said.

"Junior doesn't quite look upon me as a member of his fan club."

Vikki was sitting at the small desk by the television set. She stared emptily at the decrepit state of their room—the water-stained wallpaper, the air-conditioning unit that rattled in the window frame, the bedspread that she feared to touch, the shower stall blooming with mold. "There's another way," she said.

"To turn ourselves in?"

"We haven't done anything wrong."

"I tried it already. That one won't flush," he said.

"You tried to turn us in?"

"I called a government eight hundred number. They switched me around to a bunch of different offices and finally to a guy with Immigration and Customs. He said his name was Clawson."

"Why didn't you tell me?"

"It didn't go too well. He said he wanted to meet me, like somehow all this was between him and me and we were buds or something. He had a voice like a robot. You know what's going on when people talk like robots? They don't want you to know what they're thinking."

"What'd you tell him, Pete?"

"That I was by the church when the shooting started. I told him the guy who was paying me three hundred dollars to drive the truck was named Hugo. I told him I feel like a damn coward for running away while all those women were being killed. He said I needed to come in and make a statement and I'd be protected. Then he said, 'Is Ms. Gaddis with you? We can he'p her, too.'

"I said, 'She's not a part of this.' He says, 'We know about the characters at the truck stop, Pete. We think they either killed her or she put a hole in one of them. Maybe she's dead and lying unburied someplace. You need to do the right thing, soldier.' "

Pete sat back down on the bed and began drawing his shirt

up one arm, the network of muscles in his back tightening like whipcord.

"What'd you say?"

"I told him to kiss my ass. When people try to make you feel guilty, it's because they want to install dials on you. It also means they're gonna sell you down the river the first chance they get."

"Can the FBI trace a cell phone call?" she asked.

"They can locate the tower it bounces off of. Why?"

"I'm going to call Junior."

"I think that's a bad idea. Junior makes a lot of noise, but Junior looks after Junior."

"You only get thirty percent disability. It's hardly enough to pay the rent. What are we supposed to do? This all started in a bar where you were drinking with idiots who soak their brains in mescal. For three hundred dollars, you put our lives in the hands of people who are morally insane."

She saw the injury in his face. She turned away, her eyes closed, tears squeezing onto her eyelashes. Then, in her inability to control even the tear ducts in her face, she began hammering the tops of her thighs with her fists.

THAT AFTERNOON, WHILE Pete slept, Vikki walked down the road and used the pay phone to call Junior collect at the diner. She told him about the disability check and about their financial desperation. She also told him that the man Junior had sold milk to had tried to kidnap and possibly kill her.

"Maybe that's more information than I need to know," he said.

"Are you serious? That guy was in your diner. A guy with an orange beard was there, too. I think he was part of it."

"The check's at the mailbox in front of that shack y'all were living in?" Junior said.

"You know where we were living. Stop pretending."

"The sheriff was here. So were some federal people. They thought maybe you were dead."

"I'm not."

"Did you shoot that guy who came here to buy milk?"

"Are you going to help us or not?"

"Isn't this called aiding and abetting or something?"

"You are really pissing me off, Junior."

"Give me your address."

She hesitated.

"Think I'm gonna turn you in?" he said.

She gave him the address of the motel, the name of the town, and the zip code. With each word she spoke, she felt like she was taking off a piece of armor.

After she hung up, she went to the bar and asked the bartender for a glass of water. The combination steak house and beer joint was a spacious place, cool and dark, with big electric floor fans humming away, the heads of stuffed animals mounted on the debarked and polished log walls. "I put some ice and a lime slice in it," the bartender said.

"Thank you," she replied.

"You look kind of tuckered out. You visiting here'bouts?"

She gulped from the iced drink and blew out her breath. "No, I'm a Hollywood actress on location. You need a waitress?"

PAM TIBBS WALKED from the dispatcher's cage into Hackberry's office, tapping with one knuckle on the doorjamb as she entered.

"What is it?" Hackberry said, looking up from some photos in a manila folder.

"There's a disturbance at Junior's diner."

"Send Felix or R.C."

"The disturbance is with that ICE agent, Clawson."

Hackberry made a sucking sound with his teeth.

"I'll take it," Pam said.

"No, you won't."

"Are those the photos of the Thai women?" she said. When he didn't answer, she said, "Why are you looking at those, Hack? Say a prayer for those poor women and stop sticking pins in yourself."

"Some of them are wearing dark clothes. Some of them are wearing what were probably the best clothes they owned. They weren't dressed for hot country. They thought they were going somewhere else. Nothing at that crime scene makes sense."

Pam Tibbs gazed at the street and at the shadows of clouds moving across the cinder-block and stucco buildings and broken sidewalks. She heard Hackberry getting up from his chair.

"Is Clawson still at the diner?" he asked.

"What do you think?" she replied.

It took them only ten minutes to get to the diner, the flasher bar rippling, the siren off. Isaac Clawson's motor-pool vehicle was parked between the diner and the nightclub next door, both rear doors open. Junior was handcuffed in the backseat, wrists behind him, while Clawson stood outside the vehicle, talking into a cell phone.

"Hack?" she said.

"Would you give it a rest?"

She pulled up behind Clawson's vehicle and turned off the engine. But she didn't open the door. "That guy called you a sonofabitch. He'll never do that in my presence again," she said.

Hackberry put his hat back on and got out on the gravel and walked toward Isaac Clawson. To the south, he could see heat waves rippling off the hardpan, dust devils spinning in the wind, the distant ridge of mountains etched against an immaculate blue sky. He wore a long-sleeve cotton shirt snap-buttoned at the wrists, which was his custom at the office, regardless of the season, and he felt loops of moisture already forming under his armpits.

"What's the problem?" he said to the ICE agent.

"There is no problem," Clawson replied.

"How about it, Junior?" Hackberry said.

Junior wore white trousers and a white T-shirt and still had a kitchen apron on. The sideburns trimmed in a flare on his cheeks were sparkling with sweat. "He thinks I know where Vikki Gaddis is."

"Do you?" Hackberry asked.

"I run a diner. I don't monitor the lives of kids who cain't stay out of trouble."

"Everybody tells me you had more than an employer's interest in Vikki," Clawson said. "She's broke and on the run and has no family. I think you're the first person she would come to for help. You want to see her dead? The best way to accomplish that is to keep stonewalling us."

"I don't like your sexual suggestions. I'm a family man. You watch your mouth," Junior said.

"Could I speak to you a moment, Agent Clawson?" Hackberry said.

"What you can do is butt out," Clawson replied.

"How about a little professional courtesy?" Pam Tibbs said.

Clawson looked at her as though noticing her for the first time. "Excuse me?"

"Our department is working in cooperation with yours, right?" she said.

"And?" Clawson said.

Pam looked away and hooked her thumbs in her gun belt, her mouth a tight seam, her eyes neutral. Hackberry walked into the shade, removing his hat, blotting his forehead on his sleeve. Clawson brushed at his nose, then followed. "All right, say it," he said.

"You taking Junior in?" Hackberry said.

"I think he's lying. What would you do?"

"I'd give him the benefit of the doubt, at least for the time being."

"Benefit of the doubt? You found nine dead women and girls in your county, and you're giving a man who may be an accomplice to fugitive flight the benefit of the doubt? It's going to take me a minute or two to process that."

"Humiliating a man like Junior Vogel in front of his customers and employees is not going to get you what you want. Back off a little bit. I'll come back and talk to him later. Or you can come back and we'll talk to him together. He's not a bad guy."

"You seem to have a long history in the art of compromise, Sheriff Holland. I accessed your file at the Department of Veterans Affairs."

"Really? Why would you do that, sir?"

"You were a POW in North Korea. You gave information to the enemy. You were put in one of the progressive camps for POWs who cooperated with the enemy."

"That's a lie."

"It is? I had a different impression."

"I spent six weeks in a hole in the ground in wintertime under a sewer grate that was manufactured in Ohio. I knew its place of origin because I could see the lettering embossed on the iron surface. I could see the lettering because every evening a couple of guards urinated through the grate and washed the lettering clean of mud. I spent those weeks under the grate with only a steel pot to relieve myself in. I also saw my best friends machine-gunned to death and their bodies thrown into an open latrine. However, I don't know if the material you found at the VA contained those particular details. Did you come across that kind of detail in your research, sir?"

Clawson looked at his watch. "I've had about all of this I can take," he said. "It's against my better judgment, but I'm going to kick your man loose. I'll be back. You can count on it."

"Turn around, you pompous motherfucker," Pam Tibbs said.

"Say that again?" Clawson said.

"You learn some manners or you're going to wish you were cleaning chamber pots in Afghanistan," Pam said.

Hackberry put on his hat and walked away, forming a pocket of air in one jaw.

ACROSS THE HIGHWAY, at an open-air watermelon stand, a man wearing black jeans and unpolished black hobnailed boots and wideband suspenders and a Grateful Dead T-shirt, the fabric washed so many times it was ash-gray, sat at a plank table in ninety-six-degree shade, the wind popping the canvas tarp above his head. A top hat rested crown-down beside him on the bench. He carved the meat out of his watermelon rind with his pocketknife and slipped each chunk off the back of the blade into his mouth, watching the scene by the side of Isaac Clawson's vehicle play itself out.

When the people across the highway had gone their separate ways, he put on his hat and walked away from the watermelon stand to use his cell phone. His swollen lats and long upper torso and short legs gave him the appearance of a tree stump. A moment later, he returned to the table, wadded up his melon rinds in damp newspaper, and stuffed the newspaper and the rinds in a trash barrel. A cloud of blackflies swarmed out of the barrel into his face, but he seemed to give them little notice, as though perhaps they were old friends.

Chapter 8

THE SALOON WAS old, built in the nineteenth century, the original stamped-tin ceiling still in place, the long railed bar where John Wesley Hardin and Wild Bill Longley drank still in use. Preacher Jack Collins sat in the back against a wall, behind the pool table, under a wood-bladed fan. Through a side window he could see a clump of banana trees, their fronds beaded with drops of moisture that looked as heavy and bright as mercury. He watched the waiter bring his food from a service window behind the bar. Then he shook ketchup and salt and pepper and Louisiana hot sauce on the fried beef patty and the instant mashed potatoes and the canned string beans that constituted his lunch.

He raised his eyes slightly when the front door opened and Hugo Cistranos entered the saloon and walked out of the brilliant noonday glare toward Preacher's table. But Preacher's expression was impassive and showed no recognition of the events taking place around him, not even the arrival of his food at the table or the fact that Hugo had stopped at the bar and ordered two draft beers and was now setting them on the table.

"Hot out there," Hugo said, sitting down, sipping at his beer, pushing the second glass toward Preacher.

"I don't drink," Preacher said.

"Sorry, I forgot."

Preacher continued eating and did not ask Hugo if he wanted to order.

"You eat here a lot?" Hugo said.

"When they have the special."

"That's the special you're eating now?"

"No."

Hugo didn't try to sort it out. He looked at the empty pool table under a cone of light, the racked cues, a hard disk of pool chalk on a table, the cracked red vinyl in the booths, a wall calendar with a picture of the Alamo on it that was three years out of date, the day drinkers humped morosely over their beer glasses at the bar. "You're an unusual kind of guy, Jack."

Preacher set his knife on the edge of his plate and let his eyes rove over Hugo's face.

"What I mean is, I'm glad you're willing to work with me on this problem I'm having with Nick Dolan," Hugo said.

"I didn't say I would."

"Nobody wants you to do anything you don't want to, least of all me."

"A sit-down with the owner of a skin joint?"

"Dolan wants to meet you. You're the man, Jack."

"I have a hole in my foot and one in my calf. I'm a gimp. Sitting down with a gimp is going to make him pay the money he owes you? You cain't handle that yourself?"

"We're gonna take fifty percent of his nightclub and his restaurant. Ten percent of it will be yours, Jack. That's for the late payment I owed you. Later, we'll talk about the escort services Nick owns in Dallas and Houston. Five minutes after we sit down, his signature is going to be on that reapportionment of title. He's a sawed-off fat little Jew putting on a show for his wife. Believe me, you'll make him shit his pants. Let's face it, you know how to give a guy the heebie-jeebies, Jack."

Hugo salted his beer and drank from the foam. He wore a Rolex and a pressed sport shirt with a diamond design on it. His hair had just been barbered, and his cheeks were glowing with aftershave. He did not seem to notice the tightness around Preacher's mouth.

"Where's the sit-down?" Preacher asked.

"A quiet restaurant somewhere. Maybe in the park. Who cares?"

Preacher cut a piece of meat and speared string beans onto the tines of his fork and rolled the meat and string beans in his mashed potatoes. Then he set down the fork without eating from it and looked at the row of men drinking at the bar, slumped on their stools, their silhouettes like warped clothespins on a line.

"He plans to pop both of us," Preacher said.

"Nicholas Dolan? He'll probably have to wear adult diapers for the sit-down."

"You got him scared, and you want him even more scared?"

"With Nick Dolan, it's not a big challenge."

"Why do cops use soft-nose ammunition?" Preacher asked.

"How should I know?"

"Because a wounded or scared enemy is the worst enemy you can have. The man who kills you is the one who'll rip your throat out before you know he has his hand on you. The girl who blinded me with wasp spray and pumped two holes in me? Would you say that story speaks for itself?"

"Thought I'd let you in on a good deal, Jack. But everything I say seems to be the wrong choice."

"We're going to talk to Dolan, all right. But not when he's expecting it, and not because you want to take control of his business interests. We'll talk to Dolan because you screwed things up. I think you and Arthur Rooney have been running a scam of some kind."

"Scam? Me and Arthur? That's great." Hugo shook his head and sipped from his beer, his eyes lowered, his lashes long like a girl's.

"I paid him a visit," Preacher said.

A smile flickered on Hugo's face, the skin whitening around the edges of his mouth. "No kidding?"

"He's got a new office there in Galveston, right on the water. You haven't talked to him?" Preacher picked up his fork and slipped the combination of meat and string beans and potatoes into his mouth.

"I broke off my connections with Artie a long time ago. He's a welcher and a pimp, just like Dolan."

"I got the impression maybe you weren't 'jacking the Asian women for Dolan. You just let Dolan think that way so you could blackmail him and take over his businesses. It was yours and Rooney's gig from the jump."

"Jack, I'm trying to get your money to you. What do I have to do to win your faith? You're really hurting my feelings here."

"What time does Dolan close his nightclub?"

"Around two A.M."

"Take a nap. You look tired," Preacher said. He started to eat again, but his food had gone cold, and he pushed his plate away. He picked up his crutches and began getting to his feet.

"What did Artie tell you? Give me a chance to defend myself," Hugo said.

"Mr. Rooney was trying to find his finger on the floor. He didn't have a lot to say at the time. Pick me up at one-fifteen A.M."

PETE FLORES DID not dream every night, or at least he did not have dreams every night that he could remember. Regardless, each dawn he was possessed by the feeling he had been the sole spectator in a movie theater where he had been forced to watch a film whose content he could not control and whose images would reappear later, in the full light of day, as unexpectedly as a windowpane exploding without cause.

The participants in the film he was forced to watch were people he had known and others who were little more than ciphers behind a window, bearded perhaps, their heads wrapped with checkered cloths, cutouts that appeared like a tic on the edge of his vision and then disappeared behind a wall that was all at once just a wall, behind which a family might have been sitting down to a meal.

Pete had read that the unconscious mind retains a memory of the birth experience—the exit from the womb, the delivering hands that pull it into a blinding light, the terror when it discovers it cannot breathe of its own accord, then the slap of life that allows oxygen to surge into its lungs.

In Pete's film, all of those things happened. Except the breech was the turret in an armored vehicle, the delivering hands those of a dust-powdered sergeant with a First Cav patch on his sleeve who pulled Pete from an inferno that was roasting him alive. Once more on the street, the sergeant leaned down, clasping Pete's hand, trying to drag him away from the vehicle.

But even as broken pieces of stone were cutting into Pete's buttocks and back, and machine-gun belts were exploding inside his vehicle, he knew his and the sergeant's ordeal was not over. The hajji in the window looked like he had burlap wrapped around the bottom half of his face. In his hands was an AK-47 with two jungle-clipped banana magazines protruding from the stock. The hajji hosed the street, lifting the stock above his head to get a better angle, the muzzle jerking wildly, whanging rounds off the vehicle, hitting the sergeant in at least three places, collapsing him on top of Pete, his hand still clasped inside Pete's.

When Pete woke from the dream the third day in the motel, the room was cold from the air conditioner, blue in the false dawn, quiet inside the hush of the desert. Vikki was still asleep, the sheet and bedspread pulled up to her cheek. He sat on the side of the bed, trying to focus on where he was, shivering in his skivvies, his hands clamped between his knees. He stared through the blinds at a distant brown mountain framed against a lavender sky. The mountain made him think of an extinct volcano, devoid of heat, dead to the touch, a geological formation that was solid and predictable and harmless. Gradually, the images of a third-world street strewn with chunks of yellow and gray stone and raw garbage and dead dogs and an armored vehicle funneling curds of black smoke faded from his vision and the room became the place where he was.

Rather than touch her skin and wake her, he held the corner of Vikki's pajama top between the ends of his fingers. He watched the way the air conditioner moved the hair on the back of her neck, the way she breathed through her mouth, the way color pooled in her cheeks while she was sleeping, as though the warmth of her heart were silently spreading its heat throughout her body.

He did not want to drink. Or at least he did not want to drink that day. He shaved and brushed his teeth and combed his hair in the bathroom with the door closed behind him. He dressed in a clean pair of jeans and a cotton print shirt and slipped on his boots and put on his straw hat and carried his thermos down to the café at the traffic light.

He put four teaspoons of sugar in his coffee and ate an order of toast spread with six plastic containers of jelly. A Corona beer sign on the wall showed a Latin woman in a sombrero and a Spanish blouse reclining on a settee inside an Edenic garden, marble columns rising beside her, a purple mountain capped with snow in the background. Down the counter, a two-hundred-pound Mexican woman with a rear like a washtub was bent over the cooler, loading beer a bottle at a time, turning her face to one side, then the other, each time she lowered a bottle inside. She wiped her hands on a dish towel and removed Pete's dirty plate from the counter and set it in a sink of greasy water.

"Those bottles pop on you sometimes?" he asked.

"If the delivery man leaves them in the sun or if they get shook up in the case, they will. It hasn't happened to me, though. You want more coffee?"

"No, thanks."

"There's no charge for a warm-up."

"Yes, ma'am, I'll take some. Thank you."

"You put a lot of sugar in there, huh?"

"Sometimes."

"You want me to fill your thermos?"

He'd forgotten he had brought it with him, even though it stood right by his elbow. "Thanks, I'm good," he said.

She tore a ticket off a pad and put it facedown by his cup. When she walked away, he felt strangely alone, as though a script had been pulled preemptively from his hands. He could hear the bottles clinking inside the cooler as she resumed her work. He paid the cashier for his coffee and toast, and gazed out the front door at the sun lighting the landscape, breaking over arid mountains that seemed transported from Central Asia and affixed to the southern rim of the United States.

He walked back to the service counter. "It's gonna be a hot one. I might need one of those singles with lunch," he said.

"I don't have any cold ones," the Mexican woman said.

"I'll put it on top of the air conditioner at the motel," he said. "Fact is, better give me a couple."

She put two wet bottles in a paper bag and handed them to him. The top of Pete's shirt was unbuttoned, and the woman's eyes drifted to the shriveled tissue on his shoulder. "You was in Iraq?"

"I was in Afghanistan, but only three weeks in Iraq."

"My son died in Iraq."

"I'm sorry."

"It's six-thirty in the morning," she said, looking at the bottles in his hand.

"Yes, ma'am, it is."

She started to speak again but instead turned back to her work, her eyes veiled.

He walked back to the motel and stopped by the desk. Outside, he heard an eighteen-wheeler shifting gears at the traffic light, metal grinding. "We got any mail?" he said to the clerk.

"No, sir," the clerk said.

"What time does the mailman come?"

"Same time as yesterday, 'bout ten."

"Guess I'll check by later," Pete said.

"Yes, sir, he'll sure be here by ten."

"Somebody else couldn't have misplaced it, stuck it in the wrong box or something?"

"Anything I find with y'all's name on it, I promise I'll bring it to your room."

"It'll be from a man named Junior Vogel."

"Yes, sir, I got it."

Outside, Pete stood in the shadow of the motel and looked at the breathtaking sweep of the landscape, the red and orange and yellow coloration in the rocks, the gnarled trees and scrub brush whose root systems had to grow through slag to find moisture. He slapped a mosquito on the back of his neck and looked at it. The mosquito had been fat with blood and had left a smear on his palm the size of a dime. Pete wiped the blood on his jeans and began walking down the two-lane road that looked like a displaced piece of old Highway 66. He walked past the miniature golf course and angled through the abandoned drive-in theater, passing through the rows of iron poles that had no speakers on them, row after row of them, their function used up and forgotten, surrounded by the sounds of wind and tumbleweed blowing through their midst.

He walked for perhaps twenty minutes, up a long sloping grade to a plateau on which three table sandstone rocks were set like browned biscuits one on top of another. He climbed the rocks and sat down, his legs hanging in space, and placed the bag with the two bottles of beer in it by his side. He watched a half-dozen buzzards turning in the sky, the feathers in their extended wings fluttering on the warm current of air rising from the hardpan. Down below, he watched an armadillo work its way toward its burrow amid the creosote brush, the weight of its armored shell swaying awkwardly above its tiny feet.

He reached into his pocket and took out his Swiss Army knife. With his thumb and index finger, he pulled out the abbreviated blade that served as both a screwdriver and a bottle opener. He peeled the wet paper off the beer bottles and set one sweating with moisture and spangled with amber sunlight on the rock. He held the other in his left hand and fitted the opener on the cap. Below, the armadillo went into its burrow only to reappear with two babies beside it, all three of them peering out at the glare.

"What are you guys up to?" Pete asked.

No answer.

He uncapped the bottle and let the cap tinkle down the side of the rocks onto the sand. He felt the foam rise over the lip of the bottle and slide down his fingers and the back of his hand and his wrist. He looked back over his shoulder and could make out the screen of the drive-in movie and, farther down the street, the steak house and beer joint where Vikki had used another last name and taken a job as a waitress, the money under the table. He wiped his mouth with his hand and could taste the salt in his sweat.

At the foot of the table rocks, the polished bronze beer cap seemed to glow hotter and hotter against the grayness of the sand. It was the only piece of litter as far as he could see. He climbed down from the rocks, his beer bottle in one hand, picked up the cap, and thumbed it into his pocket. The armadillos stared up at him, their eyes as intense and unrelenting as black pinheads.

"Are you guys friendlies or Republican Guard? Identify yourself or get shot."

Still no response.

Pete reached for the bottle of beer on top of the rocks, then approached the burrow. The adult armadillo and both babies scurried back inside.

"I tell you what," he said, squatting down, a bottle in each hand. "Anybody that can live out here in this heat probably needs a couple of brews a lot worse than I do. These are on me, fellows."

He poured the first beer down the hole, then popped off the cap on the second one and did the same, the foam running in long fingers down the burrow's incline. "You guys all right in there?" he asked, twisting his head sideways to see inside the burrow. "I'll take that as an affirmative. Roger that and keep your steel pots on and your butts down."

He shook the last drops out of both bottles, stuck the empties in his pockets, and hiked back to town, telling himself that perhaps he had just walked through a door into a new day, maybe even a new life.

At ten A.M. exactly, he went down to the motel office just as the mailman was leaving. "Did you have anything for Gaddis or Flores?" he said.

The mailman grinned awkwardly. "I'm not supposed to say. There was a bunch of mail for the motel this morning. Ask inside."

Pete opened the door and closed it behind him, an electronic *ding* going off in back somewhere. The clerk came through a curtained doorway. "How you doing?" he said.

"I'm not sure."

"Sorry, I didn't see nothing in there for y'all."

"It's got to be here."

"I looked, believe me."

"Look again."

"It's not there. I wish it was, but it's not." The clerk studied Pete's face. "Your rent is paid up for four more nights. It cain't be all that bad, can it?"

THAT NIGHT VIKKI took her sunburst Gibson to work with her and played and sang three songs with the band. The next morning there was no mail addressed to her or Pete at the motel office. Pete used the pay phone at the steak house to call Junior Vogel at his home.

"You promised Vikki you were gonna pick up my check and send it to us," he said.

"I don't know what you're talking about."

"You damn liar, what'd you do with my check? You just left it in the box? Tell me."

"Don't call here again," Junior said, and hung up.

AT TWO A.M. Nick Dolan watched his remaining patrons leave the club. He used to wonder where they went after hours of drinking and viewing half-naked women perform inches away from their grasp. Did their fantasies cause them to rise throbbing and hard in the morning, unsated, vaguely ashamed, perhaps angry at the source of their dependency and desperation, perhaps ready to try an excursion into the dark side?

Was there a connection between what he did and violence against women? A female street person had been raped and beaten by two men six blocks from his club, fifteen minutes after closing time. The culprits were never caught.

But eventually, out of his own ennui with the subject, Nick had stopped thinking about his patrons or worrying about their deeds past or present, in the same way a butcher does not think about the origins and history of the gutted and frozen white shapes hanging from meat hooks in his subzero locker. Nick's favorite admonition to himself remained intact and unchallenged: *Nick Dolan didn't invent the world.*

Nick drank a glass of milk at the bar while his girls and barmaids and bartenders and bouncers and janitors said good night and one by one went outside to their cars and their private lives, which he suspected were little different from anyone else's, except for the narcotics his girls often relied upon.

He locked the back door, set the alarm, and locked the front door as he went out. He paused in front of the club and surveyed the parking lot, the occasional car passing on the four-lane, the great star-strewn bowl of sky overhead. The wind was balmy blowing through the trees, the clouds moonlit; there was even a promise of rain in the air. The .25 auto he had taken from his desk rested comfortably in his trousers pocket. The only vehicle in the parking lot was his. For some reason the night struck him as more like spring than late summer, a time of new beginnings, a season of tropical showers and farmers' markets and baseball training camps and a carpet of bluebonnets and Indian paintbrush just over the rise on the highway.

But for Nick, spring was special for another reason: No matter how jaded he had become, spring still reminded him of his youthful innocence and the innocence his children had shared with him.

He thought of the great green willow tree bending over the Comal River behind his property, and the way his children had loved to swim through its leafy tendrils, hanging on to a branch just at the edge of the current, challenging Nick to dive in with them, their faces full of respect and affection for the father who kept them safe from the world.

If only Nick could undo the fate of the Thai women. What did the voice of Yahweh say? "I am the alpha and omega. I am the beginning and the end. I am He who maketh all things new." But Nick doubted that the nine women and girls whose mouths had been packed with dirt would give him absolution so easily.

He walked across the parking lot to his car, watching the tops of the trees bend in the wind, the moon like silver plate behind a cloud, his thoughts a tangled web he couldn't sort out. Behind him, he heard an engine roar to life and tires ripping through gravel down to a harder surface. Before he could turn around, Hugo's SUV was abreast of him, Hugo in the passenger seat, a kid in a top hat behind the wheel.

"Get in, Nick. Eat breakfast with us," Hugo said, rolling down the window.

A man Nick didn't know sat in the backseat, a pair of crutches propped next to him.

"No, thanks," Nick replied.

"You need to hop in with us, you really do," Hugo said, getting out of the vehicle and opening the back door.

The man who sat in back against the far door was watching Nick intently now. His hair was greased, the part a neat gray line through the scalp, the way an actor from the 1940s might wear his hair. His head was narrow, his nose long, his mouth small and compressed. A newspaper was folded neatly in his lap; his right hand rested just inside the fold. "I'd appreciate you talking to me," the man said.

The wind had dropped, and the rustling sounds in the trees had stopped. The air seemed close, humid, like damp wool on the skin. Nick could hear his pulse beating in his ears.

"Mr. Dolan, do not place your hand in your pocket," the man said.

"You're the one they call Preacher?" Nick asked.

"Some people do."

"I don't owe you any money."

"Who said you did?"

"Hugo."

"That's Hugo, not me. What are you carrying in your pocket, Mr. Dolan?"

"Nothing."

"Don't lie."

"What?"

"Don't be disingenuous, either."

"I don't know what that word means."

"You'll either talk to me now, or you'll see me or Bobby Lee later."

"Who's Bobby Lee?"

"That's Bobby Lee there," Preacher said, indicating the driver. "He may be a descendant of the general. You told Hugo you wanted to meet me. Don't demean yourself by pretending you didn't."

Nick could hear a brass band marching through his head. "So now I've met you. I'm satisfied. I'm going home now."

"I'm afraid not," Preacher said.

Nick felt as though a garrote were tightening around his chest, squeezing the blood from his heart. *Face it now, when Esther and the kids aren't with you,* a voice inside him said.

"You say something?" Preacher asked.

"Yeah, I have friends. Some of them are cops. They come here sometimes. They eat free at my restaurant."

"So where does that leave us?"

Nick didn't have an answer. In fact, he couldn't keep track of anything he had said. "I'm not a criminal. I don't belong in this."

"Maybe we can be friends. But you have to talk to me first," Preacher said.

Nick set his jaw and stepped inside the SUV, then heard the door slam behind him. The kid in the top hat floored the SUV onto the service road. The surge of power in the engine caused Nick to sway against the seat and lose control of the safety strap he was trying to snap into place. Preacher continued to look at him, his hazel eyes curious, like someone studying a gerbil in a wire cage. Nick's hand brushed the stiff outline of the .25 auto in his side pocket.

Preacher knocked on his cast with his knuckles. "I got careless," he said.

"Yeah?" Nick said. "Careless about what?"

"I underestimated a young woman. She looked like a schoolgirl, but she taught me a lesson in humility," Preacher said. "Why'd you want to meet me?"

"Y'all are trying to take over my businesses."

"I look like a restaurateur or the operator of a strip joint?"

"There's worse things."

Preacher watched the countryside sweeping by. He closed his eyes as though temporarily resting them. A moment later, he reopened them and leaned forward, perhaps studying a landmark. He scratched his cheek with one finger and studied Nick again. Then he seemed to make a decision about something and tapped on the back of the driver's seat. "The road on the left," he said. "Go through the cattle guard and follow the dirt track. You'll see a barn and a pond and a clapboard house. The house will be empty. If you see a car or any lights on, turn around."

"You got it, Jack," the driver said.

"What's going on?" Nick said.

"You wanted a sit-down, you got your sit-down," Hugo said from the front passenger seat.

"Take the pistol out of your pocket with two fingers and put it on the seat," Preacher said. Half of his right hand remained inside the fold of the newspaper on his lap. His mouth was slightly parted, his eyes unblinking, his nose tilted down.

"I don't have a gun. But if I did, I wouldn't give it to you."

"You're not a listener?" Preacher said.

"Yeah, I am, or I wouldn't be here."

"You were planning to shoot both me and Hugo if you could catch us unawares. You treated me with disrespect. You treated me as though I'm an ignorant man."

"I never saw you before. How could I disrespect you?" Nick replied, avoiding Preacher's initial premise.

Preacher sucked on a tooth. "You attached to your family, Mr. Dolan?"

"What do you think?"

"Answer my question."

"I have a good family. I work hard to provide for them. That's why I don't need this kind of shit."

"You true to your vows?"

"This is nuts."

"I believe you're a family man. I believe you planned to take out me and Hugo even if you had to eat a bullet. You'd eat a bullet for your family, wouldn't you?"

Nick felt he was being led into a trap, but he didn't know how. Preacher saw the confusion in his face.

"That makes you a dangerous man," Preacher said. "You've put me in a bad spot. You shouldn't have done that. You shouldn't have patronized me, either."

Nick, with his heart sinking, saw the driver's eyes look at him in the rearview mirror. The tips of his fingers inched away from the outline of the .25 to the edge of his pocket. He glanced at Preacher's right hand, partially inserted inside the folded newspaper. The paper was turned at an angle, pointed directly at Nick's rib cage.

The SUV turned off the service road and passed through a break in a row of slash pines and thumped across a cattle guard onto farmland spiked with weeds and cedar fence posts that had no wire on them. Nick could see moonlight glowing on a pond, and beyond the pond, a darkened house with cattle standing in the yard. He folded his arms on his chest, burying his hands in his armpits to stop them from shaking. The driver, Bobby Lee, looked at Nick in the mirror again, a dent in each of his cheeks, as though he were sucking the saliva out of his mouth.

"I knew it'd come to this," Nick said.

"I don't follow you," Preacher said.

"I knew one of you bastards would eventually blindside me. You're all the same—black pukes from the Desire, Italian punks from Uptown. Now it's an Irish psychopath who's a hump for Hugo Cistranos. None of y'all got talent or brains of your own. Every one of you is a pack animal, always figuring out a way to steal what another man has worked for."

"Do you believe this guy?" the driver said to Hugo.

"I don't steal, Mr. Dolan," Preacher said. "But you do. You steal and market the innocence of young women. You create a venue that makes money off the lust of depraved men. You're a festering sore in the eyes of God, did you know that, Mr. Dolan? For that matter, you're an abomination in the eyes of your own race."

"Judaism isn't a race, it's a religion. That's what I'm talking about. All of you are ignorant. That's your common denominator."

Bobby Lee had already cut the headlights and was slowing to a stop by the pond. The open end of the newspaper in Preacher's lap was still pointed at Nick's side. Nick thought he was going to be sick. Hugo pulled open the back door and ran his hand along Nick's legs. His face was so close that Nick could feel Hugo's breath on his skin. Hugo slipped the .25 auto from Nick's pocket and aimed it at the pond.

"This is a nice piece," he said. He released the magazine and worked the slide. "Afraid to carry one in the chamber, Nicholas?"

"It wouldn't have done me any good," Nick said.

"Want to show him?" Hugo said to Preacher.

"Show me what?" Nick said.

Preacher tossed the newspaper to the floor and got out on the other side of the vehicle, pulling his crutches after him. The newspaper had fallen open on the floor. There was nothing inside it.

"Tough luck, Nicholas," Hugo said. "How's it feel to lose to a guy holding a handful of nothing?"

"Bobby Lee, open up the back. Hugo, give me his piece," Preacher said.

"I can take care of this," Hugo said.

"Like you did behind that church?"

"Take it easy, Jack," Hugo said.

"I said give me the piece."

Nick could feel a wave of nausea permeate the entirety of his metabolism, as though he had been systemically poisoned and all his blood had settled in his stomach and every muscle in him had turned flaccid and pliant. For just a moment he saw himself through the eyes of his tormentors—a small, pitiful fat man whose skin had become as gray as cardboard and whose hair glowed with sweat, a little man whose corpulence gave off the vinegary stink of fear.

"Walk with me," Preacher said.

"No," Nick said.

"Yes," Bobby Lee said, pressing a .45 hard between Nick's shoulder blades, screwing it into the softness of his muscles.

The cows in the yard of the farmhouse had strung shiny green lines of feces around the pond. In the moonlight Nick could see the cows watching him, their eyes luminous, their heads haloed with gnats. An unmilked cow, its swollen udder straining like a veined balloon, bawled with its discomfort.

"Go toward the house, Mr. Dolan," Preacher said.

"It ends here, doesn't it?" Nick said.

But no one spoke in reply. He heard Hugo doing something in the luggage area of the SUV, shaking out a couple of large vinyl garbage bags and spreading them on the carpet.

"My family won't know what happened to me," Nick said. "They'll think I deserted them."

"Shut up," Bobby Lee said.

"Don't talk to him that way," Preacher said.

"He keeps sassing you, Jack."

"Mr. Dolan is a brave man. Don't treat him as less. That's far enough, Mr. Dolan."

Nick felt the skin on his face shrink, the backs of his legs begin to tremble uncontrollably, his sphincter start to give way. In the distance he could see a bank of poplars at the edge of an unplowed field, wind flowing through Johnson grass that had turned yellow with drought, the brief tracings of a star falling across the sky. How did he, a kid from New Orleans, end up here, in this remote, godforsaken piece of fallow land in South Texas? He closed his eyes and for just a second saw his wife standing under the colonnade at the corner of St. Charles and Canal, raindrops in her hair, the milky whiteness of her complexion backlit by the old iron green-painted streetcar that stood motionless on the tracks.

"Esther," he heard himself whisper.

He waited for the gunshot that would ricochet a .25-caliber round back and forth inside his brainpan. Instead, all he heard was the cow bawling in the dark.

"What did you say?" Preacher asked.

"He didn't say anything," Bobby Lee said.

"Be quiet. What did you say, Mr. Dolan?"

"I said Esther, the name of my wife, a woman who will never know what happened to her husband, you cocksucker."

Nick could hear the tin roof on the farmhouse lift and clatter in the wind.

"What's wrong, Jack?" Bobby Lee said.

"You swear to God that's your wife's name?" Preacher said.

"I wouldn't cheapen her name by swearing to a man like you about it."

"Don't let him talk to you like that, Jack."

Nick could hear Preacher breathing through his nose.

"Give me his piece. I'll do it," Bobby Lee said.

"Bring the vehicle around," Preacher said.

"What are you doing?" Bobby Lee asked. He was taller than Preacher, and his top hat was silhouetted against the moon, giving him the appearance of even greater height.

"I'm doing nothing."

"Nothing?"

"We leave this man alone."

"I don't get it."

"Esther told King Xerxes if he killed her people, he'd have to kill her, too. That's how she became the handmaiden of God. You don't know that?"

"No, and I don't waste my time on that biblical claptrap, either."

"That's because you're uneducated. Your ignorance isn't your fault."

"Jack, this guy knows too much."

"You don't like what I'm doing?" Preacher said.

"This is a wrong move, man."

Nick could hear the wind and a sound like grasshoppers thudding against the side of the farmhouse. Then Bobby Lee said, "All right, to hell with it."

Nick heard Bobby Lee's footsteps going away, then the voices of Bobby Lee and Hugo merging together by the SUV. Preacher inched forward on his crutches until Nick could smell the grease in his hair.

"You take care of your wife," Preacher said. "You take care of your kids. You never come near me again. Understood?"

But Nick's mouth was trembling so bad, from either fear or release from it, that he couldn't speak.

Preacher threw Nick's .25 auto into the pond, the rings from the splash spreading outward, rippling through the cattails. As Preacher worked his way back toward the SUV, his shoulders were pushed up by his crutches, close to his neck, as if he were a scarecrow whose sticks had collapsed. Nick stared dumbly at his three abductors as though they were caught forever inside a black-and-white still taken from a 1940s noir movie—the giver of death in silhouette, stumping his way across the baked earth, Hugo and Bobby Lee looking at Nick with faces that seemed aware that a new and dangerously complex presence had just come aborning in their lives.

Chapter
9

JUNIOR VOGEL HAD told his cook he was going to have lunch with his wife. But he did not show up at his house, nor did he come home that evening. Junior was a temperate man, a member of the Kiwanis, a deacon in his church, and was not given to erratic behavior. That night his wife called 911. By dawn his wife was convinced he had been abducted.

At 7:16 A.M. a trucker carrying a load of baled hay reported what he thought was a wrecked vehicle at the bottom of a steep arroyo, just off a two-lane road eight miles south of Junior's house. The guardrail on the road shoulder was broken, and the mesquite growing out of the rocks on the other side had been bark-skinned or stripped of leaves by the vehicle's descent.

Hackberry Holland and Pam Tibbs parked the cruiser in a turnout and threaded their way down the arroyo, slag and gravel sliding from under their boots, the dust rising into their faces. The wrecked pickup truck looked like it had rolled, crumpling the cab's roof, blowing out the windshield, coming to rest on a wash bed of dry rocks coated with butterflies trying to find moisture.

The driver was still behind the wheel. The airbags had not inflated.

Hackberry worked his way between a boulder and the driver's door. The driver was round-shouldered and slumped forward, his un-cut hair extending over his collar. From the back, he looked as though he had fallen asleep. The morning was still cool, and the pickup was in shadow, but the odor that had collected inside the cab was already eye-watering.

Pam came around the front of the vehicle from the other side, pulling on polyethylene gloves, staring past the dashboard and the shards of glass that sparkled on top of it. Junior Vogel's eyes seemed to stare at the dashboard, too, except they contained no expression, and his brow was tilted forward as though he were involved with a final introspective thought. A blowfly crawled across one of his flared sideburns.

"The airbags are turned off. Junior had grandchildren, didn't he?" Pam said.

"Yep."

"Think he fell asleep at the wheel?" she said.

"Could be. But he went missing in the middle of the day."

Pam looked up the side of the arroyo at the broken guardrail. "There's no curve up there, either. Maybe he dropped a tie-rod."

"The turnoff to his place is almost ten miles back. What was he doing down here?" Hackberry said.

Above them, an ambulance pulled to the side of the road. Two paramedics got out and looked down from the guardrail, their faces small and round against a blue sky.

"The driver is dead. There're no passengers. Give us a few minutes, will you, fellows?" Hackberry called up.

"Yes, sir," one of them said.

Holding his breath and a wadded-up handkerchief to his mouth, Hackberry reached inside the vehicle to turn off the ignition. Except it was already turned off. A rabbit's foot dangled from the key chain.

"Look at this, Hack," Pam said. She was standing behind the vehicle now. "There's a big dent in the bumper. There's no dust on the dent at all. The rest of the bumper is filmed with dried mud."

"You think somebody plowed into the back of Junior and put him through the rail?" Hackberry said.

"Junior was a master at passive-aggressive behavior," she replied. "Two weeks after he was put in charge of the picnic committee at his church, half the congregation was ready to convert to Islam."

"The ignition key is turned off," Hackberry said. He had stepped back from the cab but was still holding the handkerchief to his mouth.

"It looks to me like he probably died of a broken neck," Pam said. "He could have stayed conscious long enough to turn off the key to prevent a fire. I would if I was in his situation."

"No, this one is hinky," Hackberry said. He took a breath of clean air, then opened the door. "There're glass splinters all over his shirtfront but almost none on the seat belt." He used his index finger to feel inside the mechanism that automatically rolled up the safety belt when the driver released the latch on the buckle. "There's glass inside the slit. This belt was released, then pulled back out again."

"Somebody took Junior out of the truck and put him back in it?"

Hackberry went to the rear of the pickup and looked at the damaged bumper. He cleared his throat, spat to one side, and waited for the breeze to clear the air around him. "We thought Junior might know where Vikki Gaddis is," he said. "Maybe somebody else came to the same conclusion."

"Somebody ran him off the road and beat it out of him and then broke his neck?" Pam said.

"Maybe that's why Junior went by his house without turning off. He didn't want to put his wife in danger."

A skein of small rocks trickled down the arroyo. Pam looked up at the empty space in the guardrail. "There's R.C. and Felix and the coroner. What do you want to do?"

"We treat it as a homicide."

Hackberry walked to the far side of the pickup, opened the passenger door, looked inside, and searched behind the seat. The glove box hung open, but nothing inside it seemed disturbed. Then he saw the bright rectangular wedge mark where a screwdriver had been inserted to snap the tongue on the lock.

Why would someone need a screwdriver to open a glove box if the key was hanging in the ignition?

Hackberry tried the ignition key on the glove box, but it wouldn't turn in the lock.

He walked farther up the arroyo and mounted a flat rock that gave him an overview of the truck and the path of its descent from the guardrail. The two deputies who had just arrived, R. C. Bevins and Felix Chavez, were helping the coroner climb down the incline. Hackberry squatted on his haunches and pushed his hat back on his head, his knees popping, the butt of his holstered .45 revolver cutting into his rib cage. A breeze puffed through the bottom of the arroyo, and a cloud of black butterflies lifted off the wash bed. The sun was already a red ball rising over the hills, but the arroyo was still in shadow, the stone cool to the touch, the riparian desert ambience almost beautiful.

Maybe that was the history of the earth, he thought. Its surface was traversed by pain, inhumanity, and mass murder, but the scars were as transient and meaningless to the eye as blowing sand. The most poignant expression of our suffering—the voices of the dying—had no more longevity than an echo disappearing over the edge of an infinite plain. How could millions of years trail off into both silence and invisibility?

He stood up and thumbed his shirt tight inside his trousers. Down below, not twenty feet away, a beige envelope lay in a tangle of driftwood that reminded him of elk horns piled on the edge of a hunter's camp. He climbed down from the rock he was standing on and picked up the envelope. It had a cellophane window in it and had been torn open raggedly on one side, destroying most of the return address. It was empty, but enough of the printing remained in the upper-left-hand corner to identify its origins.

"What'd you find?" Pam asked.

"An envelope from the Department of Veterans Affairs."

"You think it's from Junior's glove box?"

"That's my guess. The valet key was in the ignition, but the key to the glove box wasn't."

Pam inserted her thumbs in her gun belt, her elbows sticking straight out from her sides. Then she scratched her forearm, her eyes gazing back at the wrecked pickup. "Junior went out to Pete and Vikki's place and got Pete's disability check for him. But he didn't forward it," she said, more to herself than the sheriff. "Why not?"

"Probably cold feet."

"Or the fact he could be a mean-spirited, self-righteous bastard when he wanted to," she said.

"How about it, Sheriff?" one of the paramedics shouted from above.

"Come on down," he replied, just as the sun broke above the rim of the arroyo and lit its sharp surfaces with a glare that burned the shade away within seconds.

FIVE HOURS LATER, Darl Wingate, the coroner, came into Hackberry's office. He had been a career forensic pathologist with the army before retiring. Regardless of the skill or knowledge he had acquired in his own field, he seemed to apply none of it to his own life. He smoked, ate poorly, drank too much, had terrible relationships with women, and appeared to make a religion out of cynicism and callousness. Hackberry often wondered if Darl's profligate attitude toward both morality and his own health was manufactured, or if indeed he wasn't one of those whose experience in the world had caused him to believe in nothing.

"Did y'all find a tooth in the vehicle?" Darl said.

"No, we didn't."

Darl had pulled up a chair and was sitting on the far side of the desk. He had a face like a parody of a stage character's, with a cleft in the chin and a tiny mustache, the cheeks slightly hollowed by either age or a sickness he disclosed to no one. Hackberry smelled a mint on his breath and wondered what time that morning Darl had poured his first drink.

"Vogel had a gaping hole where a molar should have been. It wasn't broken off. There were deep bruises inside the lips," Darl said.

"He was tortured?"

"Have you eaten lunch?"

"No."

"How much do you want to hear before you eat?"

"Get to it, will you, Darl?"

"There was a lot of penile and testicular damage. It was probably done with a metal instrument. Probably the same pliers somebody used on his mouth. Cause of death was a coronary."

"His neck wasn't broken?"

"It was broken, all right, but he was already dead when that happened."

"You're sure about all this?"

Darl fitted a cigarette into a gold holder, then put it and the holder away, as though remembering Hackberry's proscription against smoking in the building. "Maybe he pulled his own tooth," he said. "Or maybe the steering wheel hit him in the face and cut him inside the mouth but not outside. Or maybe his genitals were remodeled by the airbag that didn't inflate. You want to know what I really think?"

"Go ahead."

"That whatever information this poor guy had, he begged to give it up unless his wick went out first. I hope that's what happened. I hope he sank down in a big well of blackness. I got to have a smoke. I'll be outside."

"I need to make a phone call. Go to lunch with me."

"I already ate."

"Go to lunch with me anyway," Hackberry said.

After Darl had gone outside, Hackberry called the FBI agent Ethan Riser. "I've got a problem of conscience here. I'm going to lay it off on you, and you can do whatever you want with it," he said.

"What's this big problem?" Riser said.

"Junior Vogel was probably run off the road yesterday and tortured to death. Your man from ICE, this character Clawson, wanted to put him in custody, but I talked him out of it."

"Clawson was talking with Vogel?"

"You didn't know?"

"I don't always have an opportunity to talk with Clawson directly."

Hackberry wondered at the amazing amount of latitude bureaucratic language could create for its practitioners. "I think Junior had Pete Flores's disability check in his possession," he said. "I think he was probably going to forward it to Pete. We should have been on top of that check, you guys as well as me and my department."

"We were."

"Sir?"

"Clawson had another agent on it. They messed up."

"You sure that's all there is to it?" Hackberry said.

"Want to explain that?"

"I think your man Clawson has serious psychiatric problems. I don't think he should have a badge."

"He's not *our* man."

"Nice talking to you, sir," Hackberry said, and eased the receiver back into the phone cradle.

PREACHER JACK COLLINS had once read that the neurological and optical wiring of horses created two screens inside their heads and allowed them to simultaneously monitor two broad and separate visions of their surroundings. To Preacher, this did not seem a remarkable step in the evolution of a species.

For him, there had always been two screens inside his head: one that people walked onto and off of and that he looked at or ignored as he chose; on the other, the one on which he was a participant, there were dials and buttons that allowed him to reverse or change the flow of traffic, or to distort or smudge out images that didn't belong there.

He had a dark gift, but it was a gift nonetheless, and he had been convinced since adolescence that his role in the world was preordained and it was not his province to question the unseen hand that had shaped his soul before he was conceived.

A floor fan in the back of the saloon fluttered his trouser cuff and cooled the skin around the edges of his cast. From where he sat with a white mug of black coffee hooked on his index finger, the long boxcar-like structure of the saloon was almost like a study in man's journey from the womb to the last page on his calendar. The early sunlight shone on the outside windows with the kind of delivery-room electric glare that blinded the newborn. The saloon had been a dance hall once, and the checkerboard floor was still in place, walked upon by hundreds if not thousands of people who never looked down at their feet and saw the mathematical design in their lives.

The only light source in the building that never changed shape was the brilliant yellow cone created by the tin-shaded bulb over the pool table. It lit the mahogany rails and leather pockets and green felt of the table and swallowed the arms and necks and shoulders of the players who bent over it. Preacher wondered if any of them, their buttocks arched tightly against their jeans, their genitalia touching the wood, the right arm tensed to drive the cue like a spear into a white ball, ever saw themselves as fools leaning into their own coffins.

The waiter brought Preacher his refill in a metal pot painted blue and flecked with white specks. The waiter left the pot on the table alongside a saucer with six sugar cubes on it. The two screens in Preacher's head were muted now, as they often were at sunrise, and in moments like these, he wondered if the silence was part of a larger design or an indication of divine abandonment.

In Elijah's search to hear the voice of God, he had awakened to find that during the night an angel had provided him a jug of water and a cake cooked on a hot stone. But the voice of Yahweh was not to be found in an earthquake or the wind or even inside a fire. That's what the scripture said. The voice would speak in a whisper at the entrance to a cave, one that Preacher would enter when it was time.

But how would he recognize it? How would he know it was not just the wind blowing through a hole in the earth?

The fire-exit door opened suddenly, causing Preacher's hand to jerk, spilling his coffee. Bobby Lee stood framed against the sunlight in the alleyway, wearing bradded orange work pants and a white T-shirt and a top hat, his wideband suspenders notched into his deltoids, his jaw unshaved.

"Didn't mean to give you a start," Bobby Lee said, wiping his nose with the heel of his hand, surveying the saloon's interior. "What a dump. You actually eat in this place?"

"Don't you ever come up behind me like that again," Preacher said.

"Little touchy this morning?"

Preacher cleaned the coffee off his hand with a paper napkin. "Put some money in the jukebox," he said.

"What do you want to hear?"

"I look like I care what's on that jukebox?"

Bobby Lee got change from the bartender and fed the jukebox with eight quarters, then sat down across from Preacher.

"Tell me," Preacher said.

"It got messy. We had to chase the guy and run him off the road."

"Go on."

Bobby Lee shrugged. "The guy didn't want to give it up. Liam explained the choices the guy had. I guess the guy didn't believe what Liam told him."

"Can you take the crackers out of your mouth?"

"The guy died. I think he had a heart attack." Bobby Lee saw Preacher's eyes narrow. "It's on him, Jack. He wouldn't cooperate."

Preacher picked up a sugar cube and plunked it into his coffee, his eyes never leaving Bobby Lee's.

"I thought you were diabetic," Bobby Lee said.

"You thought wrong. Finish what you were saying."

Bobby Lee's gaze seemed to turn inward, as though he were searching his memory, wondering if he was mistaken or if Preacher was lying to him. Then his gaze came into focus again. "The guy said something about a Siesta motel in a town by the border. It was hard to understand what he was saying."

"He didn't speak the same language as you and Liam?" Preacher said.

"You know, what Liam was doing."

"Doing what?"

"Jack, you sent us to get information. We pushed the guy's truck through a guardrail in broad daylight. We had to park the car up the road and climb down into a canyon. We had a few minutes to work the situation and cover our ass and extract ourselves."

"Extract yourself?"

"Is there an echo in here? The problem is not me and Liam."

There was a beat. "Then who's the problem?" Preacher said.

"You're worried about this girl identifying you, but you let the Jewish guy slide. In the meantime, none of us have got paid. Not me, not Liam, not Hugo, and not you. Does that make sense to you?"

"Tell me, why would the Jewish man want all those women killed? He's a procurer. Procurers don't kill their women," Preacher said.

The first song ended on the jukebox. Bobby Lee waited for the next song to begin before he spoke again. "I didn't know what you and Hugo were gonna do behind the church. I think you made a mistake, Jack. But don't blame me for it. I just want to get paid. I think I'm gonna go back to Florida and take some more interior design courses at Miami-Dade. With one more semester, I can get an associate of arts degree."

Preacher's eyes roved over Bobby Lee's face and seemed to reach inside his head and search his thoughts.

"Why you staring at me like that?" Bobby Lee asked.

"No reason."

"I'm gonna be frank here. Hugo and I think you're slipping, like maybe you should get some counseling or something."

"What did you do with the restaurant owner?"

"Before or after?" Bobby Lee saw the heat rising in Preacher's face. "Liam broke his neck, and we strapped him back in his truck. Nobody saw us. It'll go down as an accident."

"Did you take anything from the truck?"

"No," Bobby Lee said, shaking his head, his eyes flat.

"You don't think a coroner will know the man's neck was broken after he was dead, that his body was moved?"

Bobby Lee put a matchstick in his mouth, then removed it and looked back at the jukebox. He folded his hands on top of the table and studied his fingers. His facial skin had the texture of boiled pig hide.

"You wanted to tell me something else?" Preacher asked.

"Yeah, when we gonna get paid?" Bobby Lee replied.

"What did you take from that man's vehicle?"

"What?"

Preacher removed his hand from his coffee cup and lifted one finger. "I've been your friend, Bobby Lee, but I cain't abide a liar. Give careful thought to your next statement."

The side of Bobby Lee's face twitched as though a doodlebug were crawling across it.

SATURDAY MORNING, HACKBERRY was planting rosebushes in the shade of his house, setting the root balls in deep holes he had dug out of coffee grounds and compost and black dirt, when he saw Pam Tibbs's car turn off the state road and come through the wood arch that spanned his driveway. She had been on duty all night and was still in uniform, and he assumed she was on her way to her house, where she lived with three cats, a twenty-year-old quarter horse, and a screened-in aviary full of injured birds.

When she got out of her car, she had a bag of charcoal in one hand and a plastic bag packed with picnic food hanging from the other. "It's late for planting roses, isn't it?" she said.

"At my age, everything is late," Hackberry said.

"I've got some sausage links and potato salad and beans and slaw and buns, if you'd like to have an early lunch," she replied.

He stood up and took off his straw hat and blotted his forehead on his sleeve. "Something happen last night I should know about?"

"We busted a Mexican with tar and three grand in cash on him. I think he might be a mule working for Ouzel Flagler. That's the third one we arrested this month."

At the rear of the house was a paintless picnic table with an umbrella set in the center of it. She put the charcoal and the food on the table and slipped the flats of her hands in her back pockets and looked at Hackberry's barn and poplar trees and vegetable garden bursting with Big Boy tomatoes. Her handcuffs were drawn through the back of her belt, the tip of a braided blackjack protruding from her side pocket. He waited for her to continue, but she didn't.

"Let's have it, Pam," he said.

"Isaac Clawson was at the office an hour ago. He wants to track as much pig flop into your life as he can, Hack."

"Who cares?"

"You're too nice. People blindside you."

"You're going to protect me?"

She turned around and fixed her eyes on him. "Maybe somebody should."

He pressed a dent out of the crown of his hat with his thumb and replaced it on his head, a smile at the corner of his mouth, one eye a little more narrow than the other. "You got a cold drink in that bag?"

"Yes, sir," she replied.

He cracked open the Coca-Cola she'd brought and took a long swallow. It was ice-cold and hurt his throat, but he continued to swallow, his gaze directed at two blue jays in his mulberry tree. He could feel Pam's eyes on the side of his face. He lowered the bottle from his mouth. "You're a good lady," he said.

Her face seemed to go soft in the shade, like a flower in late afternoon. Then he heard a voice, one as clear as the sound of the birds in the trees: *Don't say any more.*

She folded her arms across her breasts. "You got any charcoal lighter?" she said.

"Inside the toolshed," he replied.

The moment had passed, the way a kitchen match can flare and burn and die inside one's chest. He went back to work in his garden, and Pam started a fire in his grill and covered the picnic table with a cloth and began laying out sausage links and buns and paper plates and plastic forks.

Twenty minutes later, Isaac Clawson's government car came up the driveway. Hackberry walked to the gate, rolling up the cuff on one sleeve, touching his sunglasses in his pocket, not looking directly at Clawson, his expression neutral, his back turned to Pam. Clawson's rimless octagonal glasses were wobbling with light, his shaved head polished and gleaming, the cranial indentations ridged with bone. His eyes shifted off Hackberry's face and focused on Pam, who was turning sausages on the grill inside a patch of shade.

"You work at home sometimes?" he said to Hackberry.

"What's the nature of your errand, sir?" Hackberry said.

"Errand?"

"Want to join us in a hot dog?"

"No, I want a man in custody for the murder of Junior Vogel." With two fingers, Clawson pulled a color photo out of his shirt pocket. "You know this guy?"

The photo had not been taken in a booking room and looked like one used for employee identification. The man in the photo had wide-set eyes, an upper lip that was too close to the nose, and a full orange beard, one that a nautical man might wear.

"Who is he?" Hackberry asked.

"His name is Liam Eriksson. Yesterday he and a woman tried to cash Pete Flores's disability check at an auto-title loan place in

San Antonio. They'd both been drinking. When the clerk went in back with the check, they took off. The surveillance camera got them both on tape. We got Eriksson's thumbprint off the counter. Eriksson had gotten a library card with Flores's name on it."

"How much was the check for?"

"Three hundred and fifty-six bucks."

"He linked himself to incriminating evidence from a homicide scene for three hundred and fifty-six dollars?"

"Who said any of these guys are smart? There're just more of them than there are of us. You haven't made a press release indicating Vogel's death was a homicide?"

"Not yet."

"What does his family know?"

"That others 'may' have been involved in his death."

"Let's keep it that way. Eriksson is a frequenter of prostitutes. Maybe he's still with the woman who was on the surveillance tape. If we can find the woman, we'll probably find him, unless he knows he's been ID'd in a homicide investigation."

"Who's the woman?"

"The clerk said he didn't know her. The surveillance camera only got the back of her head."

"Where'd you get the photo of Eriksson?"

"He worked as a contract security man in Iraq. He was suspected of firing arbitrarily into the automobiles of civilians. There was a video of his work on CNN. Cars were veering out of their lane and crashing into other cars. His company got him out of the country before he was charged."

"I'll have to share some of this with Junior's wife."

"Why?"

"Because they have a right to know," Hackberry said.

"What about the rights and safety of the citizenry?"

"You know what the Catholic theological definition of a lie is? To deny others access to knowledge to which they're entitled."

"I think this place is an open-air mental asylum."

"Can I have the photo of Eriksson? Or at least a copy of it?"

"Maybe later."

"Later?"

Hackberry heard Pam's footsteps behind him on the St. Augustine grass.

"Why don't you haul your ass down the road?" she said to Clawson.

"Take it easy," Hackberry said.

Clawson removed his glasses, polished them with a Kleenex, and put them back on, crinkling his nose. "Can you tell me why you bear me such animosity?" he asked Pam.

"When your daughter and her fiancé were abducted and murdered, she was working as a night clerk at a convenience store," Pam said. "You didn't know the risk exposure for a woman working nights at a convenience store? You weren't making enough money to provide a better situation for her? Is everyone else supposed to pay the price for your guilt, Agent Clawson? If that's the case, it's a real drag."

Clawson's face had gone white. "Don't you dare talk about my daughter," he said.

"Then you stop hiding behind her, you miserable fuck."

"Sheriff, you get this crazy bitch out of my face."

"No, you hold on a minute," Hackberry replied.

But it was too late. Hackberry saw Pam Tibbs pull her blackjack from her pocket, letting the spring-mounted, leather-weighted end dip away from her wrist, tightening her fingers on the leather-braided wood handle, stepping toward Clawson all in one motion. Before Hackberry could knock her arm down, she whipped the blackjack across the side of Clawson's head, snapping her wrist into the swing, slashing open his scalp, slinging a red stripe down his white shirt.

His glasses fell from his face, cracking on a flagstone. His eyes were wide with shock, out of focus, his mouth open in a great round O. He raised his forearm to ward off the second blow, but she caught him on the elbow, then behind the ear. His knees buckled, and he grabbed the gate to keep from going all the way down.

Hackberry locked his arms around Pam, pinning her hands at her sides, lifting her into the air, carrying her backward deeper into the yard. She fought with him, kicking the heels of her boots into his shins, pulling at his wrists to force him to unclasp his hands, butting her head into his face.

Clawson propped one hand against the fender of his car and held himself erect, struggling to get a handkerchief out of his pocket to stop the blood that ran in strings down his forehead and into his eyebrows. Hackberry carried Pam to the back of the house, her feet still off the ground, the smell of her hair and body heat rising into his face.

"You stop it, Pam. I'll throw you in the horse tank. I swear to God I'll do it," he said.

They were back in the shade, the wind rustling through the mulberry tree, the lawn suddenly cool and smelling of the damp soil he had turned over with a spading fork at sunrise. He felt the stiffness go out of her back and her hands relax on top of his.

"You finished?" he said.

She didn't answer.

"Did you hear me?"

"I'm done. Let me go," she said.

He set her down and put his hands on her shoulders, turning her toward him. "You just dropped both of us in the cook pot," he said.

"I'm sorry."

"Go in the house. I'm going to try to square it."

"Not on my account."

"Pam, this is one time you shut up and do what I say."

She closed and opened her eyes as though awakening from a dream. Then she walked to the table and sat down on the bench and propped her hands on her knees and stared into space, her hair tousling in the breeze.

Hackberry went inside, took a first-aid kit and a handful of dish towels from a kitchen closet, and went back out front. Clawson was sitting in the passenger seat of his car, the door open, his feet on the gravel driveway; he was talking into a cell phone. The handkerchief wadded up in his left hand was almost entirely red. He closed the cell phone and dropped it on the seat.

"Did you call for the paramedics?" Hackberry said.

"No, I called my wife. I'm supposed to meet her in Houston tonight."

"I'll take you to emergency receiving."

"You were a navy corpsman, Sheriff. Do what you need to do. This didn't happen. I slipped on the metal stairs at the motel."

Hackberry waited for him to go on.

"You heard me," Clawson said.

"That's the way you want it?"

"We take down the guys who killed those Asian women and Junior Vogel. Nothing gets in the way of that objective. You tell your deputy what I said."

"No, you tell her."

"Bring her out here," Clawson said.

"You don't take her to task."

Clawson cleared his throat and pressed his handkerchief to a deep cut that was bleeding through his eyebrow. "No problem."

"Let's take a look at your head, partner," Hackberry said.

Chapter 10

NICK DOLAN SWALLOWED a tranquilizer and a half glass of water, took Esther into his office, and closed the door behind him. With the dark velvet drapes closed and the air-conditioning set to almost freezing levels, there was an insularity about his office that made Nick feel not only isolated and safe but outside of time and place, as though he could rewind the video and erase all the mistakes he had made in his journey from the schoolyard playground in the Lower Ninth Ward to the day he bought into an escort service and the attendant association with people like Hugo Cistranos.

He told Esther everything that had happened during his abduction—the ride in the SUV down the highway to the empty farmhouse, Preacher Jack Collins sitting next to him, the New Orleans button man Hugo Cistranos and the strange kid in a top hat sitting in front, the moon wobbling under the surface of a pond whose banks glistened with green cow scat. Then he told Esther how the man called Preacher had spared him at the last moment because of her name.

"He thinks I'm somebody out of the Bible?" she said.

"Who knows what crazy people think?" Nick said.

"There's something you're leaving out. Something you're not talking about."

"No, that's it. That's everything that happened."

"Stop lying. What did these men do in your name?"

"They didn't do it in my name. I never told them to do what they did."

"You make me want to hit you, to beat my fists bloody on you."

"They killed nine women from Thailand. They were prostitutes. They were being smuggled across the border by Artie Rooney. They machine-gunned them and buried them with a bulldozer."

"My God, Nick," she said, her voice breaking in her throat.

"I didn't have anything to do with this, Esther."

"Yes, you did." Then she said it again. "Yes, you did."

"Hugo was supposed to deliver the women to Houston. That's all it was."

"All it was? Listen to yourself. What were you doing with people who smuggle prostitutes into the country?"

"We've got a half-interest in a couple of escort agencies. It's legal. They're hostesses. Maybe some other stuff goes on, but it's between adults, it's a free country. It's just business."

"You've been running escort services?" When he didn't reply, she said, "Nick, what have you done to us?" She was weeping quietly in the leather chair now, her long hair hanging in her face. Her discomposure and fear and disbelief, and the black skein of her hair separating her from the rest of the world, made him think of the women lined up in front of Preacher's machine gun, and his lips began to tremble.

"You want me to fix you a drink?" he said.

"Don't say anything to me. Don't touch me. Don't come near me."

He was standing over her, his fingers extended inches from the crown of her head. "I didn't want anybody hurt, Esther. I thought maybe I'd get even with Artie for a lot of the things he did to me when I was a kid. It was dumb."

But she wasn't hearing him. Her head was bent forward, her face completely obscured, her back shaking inside her blouse. He took a box of Kleenex from his desk and set it on her lap, but it fell from her knees without her ever noticing it was there. He stood in the darkened coldness of his office, the jet of frigid air from the wall duct touching his bald pate, his stomach sagging over his belt, the smell of nicotine rife on his fingers when he rubbed his hand across his mouth. If he had ever felt smaller in his life, he could not remember the instance.

"I'm sorry," he said, and started to walk away.

"What do these gangsters plan to do now?"

"There was a witness, a soldier who was in Iraq. Him and his girlfriend could be witnesses against Hugo and the kid in the top hat and this guy Preacher."

"They're going to kill them?"

"Yeah, if they find them, that's what they'll do."

"That can't happen, Nick," she said, raising her head.

"I called the FBI when I was drunk. It didn't do any good. You want me to go to prison? You think that will stop it? These guys will kill those kids anyway."

She stared into space, her eyes cavernous. Through the floor, she and Nick could hear the children turning somersaults on the living room carpet, sending a *thud* down through the walls into the foundation of the house. "We can't have this on our souls," she said.

THE MOTEL WAS a leftover from the 1950s, a utilitarian structure checkerboarded with huge red and beige plastic squares, the metal-railed upstairs walkways not unlike those in penitentiaries, all of it located in a neighborhood of warehouses and bankrupt businesses and joyless bars that could afford no more than a single neon sign over the door.

The swimming pool stayed covered with a plastic tarp year-round, and the apron of grass around the building was yellow and stiff, the fronds of the palm trees rattling drily in the wind. On the upside of things, hookers did not operate on its premises, nor did drug dealers cook meth in the rooms. The sodium halide lamps in the parking lot protected the cars of the guests from roving bands of thieves. The rates were cheap. Arguably, there were worse rental lodgings in San Antonio. But there was one undeniable characteristic about the motel and the surrounding neighborhood that would not go away: The rectangularity of line and the absence of people gave one the sense that he was standing inside a stage set, one that had been created for the professional sojourner.

Preacher sat in a stuffed chair in the dark, staring at the television set. The screen was filled with static, the volume turned up full blast on white noise. But the images on the screen inside Preacher's head had nothing to do with the television set in his room. Inside Preacher's head, the year was 1954. A little boy sat in the corner of a boxcar parked permanently on a siding in the middle of the Texas-Oklahoma Panhandle. It was winter, and the wind was gray with grit and dust, and it chapped the cheeks and lips and dried out the hands and caused the skin to split around the thumbnails. A blanket draped over a rope divided the boxcar in half. On the other side of the blanket, Edna Collins was going at it with a dark-skinned gandy dancer while two more waited outside, their hands stuffed in their canvas coat pockets, their slouch hats pulled low over their ears as protection against the wind.

Preacher's motel windows were hung with red curtains, and

the lamps in the parking lot seemed to etch them with fire. He heard footsteps on the steel stairway, then a shadow crossed his window and someone tapped tentatively on the jalousie.

"What do you want?" Preacher said, his eyes still fixed on the television screen.

"My name is Mona Drexel, Preacher. We met once," a voice replied.

"I don't remember the name."

"Liam is like a client of mine."

He turned his head slowly and looked at her shadow on the frosted glass. "Liam who?"

"Eriksson."

"Come in," he said.

He smelled the cigarette odor on her clothes as soon as she entered the room. Against the outside light, her hair possessed the frizzy outline and color of cotton candy. The foundation on her face made Preacher think of an unfinished clay sculpture, the lines collapsing under the jaw, the mouth a bit crooked, the eye shadow and rouge both sad and embarrassing to look at.

"Can I sit down?" she said.

"You're in, aren't you?"

"I heard that maybe people are looking for Liam because of this government check he took into one of these car-title loan places. I didn't want to have my name mixed up in this, because I'm not really involved or a close friend of his. See, we had a few drinks, and he had this check, and he wanted to party some more, so I went along with him, but it kind of hit the fan for some reason, and Liam said we ought to get out of there, and he thought you were gonna be pissed off, but that was all over my head and not really my business. I just wanted to clear this up and make sure nobody has a misunderstanding. Since we'd already met, I didn't think you'd mind me coming by to answer any questions you might have."

"Why should I have questions for you?"

"A couple of people told me this is what I should do. I didn't mean to bother you during your program."

Then she looked at the empty screen. She was sitting on the edge of the bed, out of breath and holding her hands in her lap, unsure of what she should say next. She placed one foot on the top of the other as a little girl might, chewing her lip.

"I don't like touching the bedspreads in motels," she said, half smiling. "There's every kind of DNA in the world imaginable on them, not that I mean this place is any worse than any other, it's just the way all motels are, with unclean people using everything and not caring that other people are gonna use it later."

The side of Preacher's face was immobile, the eye that she could see like a marble pushed into tallow. "Mona Drexel is my stage name," she said. "My real name is Margaret, but I started using Mona when I was onstage in Dallas. Believe it or not, it was a club Jack Ruby once owned, but you can call me whatever you want."

"Where's Liam now?"

"That's why I'm here. I don't know. Maybe I can find out. I just don't want to hurt anybody or have anybody think I'm working against them. See, I'm *for* people, I'm not *against* anybody. There's a big difference. I just want everybody to know that."

"I can see that," he said.

"Can you turn down the volume on the television?" she said.

"Do you know what I do for a living?"

"No."

"Who told you I was staying at this motel?"

"Liam said you use it sometimes when you're in town. That noise is really loud."

"That's what Liam told you, did he?"

"Yes," she said. "I mean, yes, sir, he just mentioned it in passing."

"Do you know where Liam got the government check?"

"No, he didn't tell me. I don't talk with clients about their personal business."

"That's a good way to be."

"It is, isn't it?" she said, crossing her leg on her knee, her mouth jerking as though she wanted to smile. She watched Preacher's face in the white glow of the television screen. His eyes never blinked; not one muscle in his face moved. Her own expression went dead.

"I have clients that become friends," she said. "After they're friends, they're not clients again. Then I have friends that are always friends. They never become clients. They're friends from the first time I meet them, know what I mean?"

"No, I don't," he replied.

"I can be a friend to somebody. I have to make a living, but I believe in having friends and helping them out." She lowered her eyes. "I mean, we could be friends if you want."

"You remind me of someone," he said, looking at her directly for the first time.

"Who?" she asked, the word turning to a rusty clot in her throat.

He stared at her in a way no one had ever stared at her in her life. She felt the blood drain from her head and heart into her stomach.

"Somebody who never should have been allowed around small children," he said. "Do you have children?"

"I did. A little boy. But he died."

"It's better that some people don't live. They should be taken before their souls are forfeit. That means some of us have to help them in ways they don't like, in ways that seem truly awful at the time." Preacher reached out into the darkness and pulled a straight chair closer to him. On it were his wallet, a small automatic, an extra magazine, and a barber's razor.

"Sir, what are you planning to do?" she said.

"You understood what I said." He smiled. His statement was not a question but a compliment.

"Liam wanted to party. He had the check. I went with him." Her breath was tangling in her chest, the room starting to go out of focus. "I have a mother in Amarillo. My son is buried in the Baptist cemetery there. I was gonna call her today. She's hard of hearing, but if I shout, she knows it's me. She's seventy-nine and cain't see real good, either. We still talk to each other. She doesn't know what I do for a living."

Preacher was holding something in his hand, but she couldn't bring herself to look at it. She went on, "If you let me walk out the door, you'll never see me again. I'll never tell anyone what we talked about. I'll never see Liam again, either."

"I know you won't," he said in an almost kindly fashion.

"Please, sir, don't."

"Come closer."

"I don't want to."

"You need to, Mona. We don't choose the moment of our births or the hour of our deaths. There are few junctures in life when we actually make decisions that mean anything. The real challenge is in accepting our fate."

"*Please*," she said. "Please, please, please."

"Get on your knees if you want. It's all right. But don't beg. No matter what else you do in this world, don't beg."

"Not in the face, sir. Please."

She was on her knees, her eyes welling with tears. She felt his hand grasp hers and lift her arm into the air, turning up the paleness of her wrist and the green veins in it. The static-filled storm on the television screen seemed to invade her head and blind her eyes and pierce her eardrums. Her fingernails bit into her palm. She had heard stories of people who did it in a warm bathtub and supposedly felt no pain and just went to sleep as the water turned red around them. She wondered if it would be like that. Then she felt his thumb dig into her palm and peel back her fingers.

"What are you doing?" she said.

"You go into the brightness of the sun. You go inside its whiteness and let it consume you, and when you come out on the other side, you've become pure spirit and you never have to be afraid again."

She tried to pull her hand from his, but he held on to it.

"Did you hear me?" he said.

"Yes, sir," she said.

He placed five hundred-dollar bills across her palm and folded her fingers on them. "The Greyhound for Los Angeles leaves in the morning. In no time you'll be in Albuquerque, and you'll see what I mean. You'll go west into the sun across a beautiful countryside, a place that's just like the world was on the day Yahweh created light. The person you were when you walked into this room won't exist anymore."

When she got to the bottom of the stairs, she lost a shoe. But she did not stop to pick it up.

DURING THE RIDE to the car-title loan office in San Antonio, Hackberry did not speak again of Pam's attack on the ICE agent Isaac Clawson. They were in his pickup truck, and the undulating countryside was speeding by rapidly, the chalklike hills layered with sedimentary rock where the highway cut through them, the sun a dust-veiled orange wafer by late afternoon.

Finally, she said, "You don't want to know why I hit Clawson?"

You attacked him with a blackjack because you're full of rage, he thought. But that was not what he said. "As long as it doesn't happen again, it's not my concern."

"My father started having psychotic episodes when I was about eight or nine and we were living up in the Panhandle," she said. "He'd look out on a field of green wheat and see men in black pajamas and conical straw hats coming through elephant grass. He went into a treatment program at the naval hospital in Houston, and my mother stayed there to visit him. She put me in the care of a family friend, a policeman everybody trusted."

"Sure you want to talk about this?" he said, steering around a silver-plated gas tanker, his yellow-tinted aviator shades hiding the expression in his eyes.

"That bastard raped me. I told a teacher at school. I told a minister. They lectured me. They said the cop was a fine man and I shouldn't make up stories about him. They said my father was mentally ill and I was imagining things because of my father's illness."

"Where's this guy today?"

"I've tried to find him, but I think he died."

"I used to dream about a Chinese guard named Sergeant Kwong. The day I informed on two fellow prisoners, I discovered I was the eighth man to do so. My fingernails were yellow talons, and my beard was matted with the fish heads I licked out of my food bowl. My clothes and boots were caked with my own feces. I used to think that Kwong and his commanding officer, a man by the name of Ding, had not only broken me physically but had stolen my soul. But I realized that in truth, they'd probably lost their own soul, if they ever had one, and at a certain point I had no control over what I did or what they did to me."

"You don't dream about it anymore?"

He looked through the windshield at the dust and smoke from wildfires, and the way the hills went out of focus inside the heat waves bouncing off them, and for just a second he thought he heard bugles echoing out of a valley that had no name.

"No, I don't dream very much anymore," he said.

She looked out the side window and watched the countryside go by.

THE LOAN OFFICE was located on a corner where three streets that had once been cow trails intersected and formed a kind of financial center for people who possessed little of value to others, except perhaps their desperation.

Next to the loan office was a bail bonds office. Next to the bail bonds office was a pawnshop. Down the street was a saloon with a railed and mirrored bar, a kitchen that served food, and a clientele to whom the pawnshop, the bondsman, and the car-title loan office were as indispensable as the air they breathed. Few of them cared, or for that matter even knew, that John Wesley Hardin and Wild Bill Longley had been regulars at the saloon.

Hackberry parked in the alley behind the loan office and entered through the side door, removing his hat, waiting until the clerk was free before he went to the counter. Hispanic and Anglo working people were sitting at school desks filling out forms; a woman in glasses oversaw them as she might retarded people. Hackberry opened his badge holder on the counter and placed the photo of Liam Eriksson beside it. "Know this fellow?" he said to the clerk.

"Yes, sir, the FBI was in here about him. I'm the one called up the cops on him," the clerk said. "He brought in a stolen check."

"There was a woman with him?"

"Yes, sir, but I wasn't paying her that much mind. He's the one had the check."

"You don't know who the woman was?"

"No, sir," the clerk replied. He had neat black hair and a mustache and a deep tan and wore gray slacks and a blue dress shirt and a striped tie.

"You work here long?"

"Yes, sir, almost five years."

"Get a lot of United States Treasury checks in here?"

"Some."

"But not many," Hackberry said.

"No, sir, not a lot."

"Never saw the woman before?"

"Not that I recall. I mean, I'm pretty certain on that."

"Pretty certain you don't know her or pretty certain you don't recall?"

"A mess of folks come in."

"This fellow Eriksson and the lady were drunk?"

The clerk looked blankly at Hackberry.

"Eriksson is the real name of the man who was impersonating Pete Flores. He and the woman were drunk?"

"Pretty marinated," the clerk said, starting to smile for the first time.

"For ID, Eriksson had a library card?"

"Yes, sir, that was the extent of it."

"Why'd you take the check in back?"

"To run it by my manager."

"After five years here, you had to consult with your manager? You didn't know the check was stolen, one brought in by a drunk with a library card? You had to ask your manager? That's what you're telling me?"

"It's like I said."

"There's no reason Eriksson would have a history with a business like yours. That means the woman probably brought him here. I also think she's probably a hooker and a shill and brings her customers here with regularity. I think you're lying through your teeth, bub."

"Maybe I've seen her once or twice," the clerk said, his eyes shifting off Hackberry's face.

"What's her name?"

"She goes by 'Mona,' I think."

Hackberry pulled at his earlobe. "Where does Mona live?"

"Probably any place a guy has a bottle and two glasses and a few bucks. I don't know where she lives. She's not a bad person. Why don't you give her a break?"

"Tell that to the guy Liam Eriksson tortured to death," Hackberry said.

The clerk threw up his hands. "Am I in the shitter?"

"Could be," Hackberry said. "I'll be giving it some thought."

HACKBERRY AND PAM began their search for the woman named Mona in a backward pattern, starting up the street through a series of low-bottom bars where no one seemed to possess any memory for either faces or names. Then they reversed direction and went block by block through a district of secondhand stores, and missions that sheltered the homeless, and bars with darkened interiors, where, like prisons, time was not measured in terms of the external world and the patrons did not have to make comparisons.

Hackberry didn't know if the cause was the smell of the alcohol or the dissolute and wan expression on the faces of the twenty-four-hour drinkers at the bar when he opened the front door of a saloon, but he soon found himself revisiting his long courtship with Jack Daniel's, like a compulsive man picking up pieces of glass with his fingertips.

Actually, "courtship" wasn't the appropriate word. Hackberry's experience with charcoal-filtered whiskey had been a love affair as intense as any sexual relationship he'd ever had. He'd dreamed about it, awakened with a thirst for it in the morning, and turned the first drink of the day into a religious ritual, bruising a sprig of mint inside the glass, staining the shaved ice with three fingers of Jack, adding a half teaspoon of sugar, then setting the glass in the freezer for twenty minutes while he pretended that whiskey had no control over his life. The first sip made him close his eyes with a sense of both release and visceral serenity that he could associate only with the rush and sense of peace that a morphine drip had purchased for him in a naval hospital.

"Not much luck, huh, kemosabe?" Pam said as they entered a saloon that was defined by an old checkerboard dance floor and a long railed bar with a big yellowed mahogany-framed mirror behind it.

"What'd you call me?" Hackberry asked.

"It's just a joke. Remember the Lone Ranger and his sidekick, Tonto? Tonto was always calling the Lone Ranger 'kemosabe.' "

"That's what Rie, my second wife, used to call me."

"Oh," Pam replied, clearly not knowing what else to say.

Hackberry opened his badge holder and placed the photo of Liam Eriksson on the bar for the bartender to look at. "Ever see this guy in here?" he said.

The bartender wore a short-sleeve tropical print shirt. His big forearms were wrapped with a soft pad of hair, and just above his wrist was a green and red tattoo of the Marine Corps globe and anchor. "No, cain't say I've ever seen him."

"Know a gal by the name of Mona, maybe a working girl?"

"What's she look like?"

"Middle-aged, reddish hair, five feet three or four."

The bartender propped his arms on the bar and stared at the painted-over front window. He shook his head. "Cain't say as I remember anyone specific like that."

"I noticed your tattoo," Hackberry said.

"You were in the Corps?"

"I was a navy corpsman attached to the First Marine Division."

"In Korea?"

"Yes, sir, I was."

"You made the Chosin or the Punch Bowl?"

"I was at the Chosin Reservoir the third week of November, 1950."

The bartender raised his eyebrows, then looked at the painted-over window again. "What's the beef on this gal Mona?"

"No beef at all. We just need some information."

"There's a woman who lives at the Brazos Hotel about five blocks toward downtown. She's a hooker, but more of a juicer than a hooker. Her dance card is pretty used up. Maybe she's your gal. Y'all want a drink? It's on me."

"How about carbonated water on ice?" Pam said.

"Make that two," Hackberry said.

Neither Hackberry nor Pam noticed a solitary man sitting at a back table, deep in the gloom behind the pool table. The man was holding up a newspaper, appearing to study it in the poor light that filtered through an alleyway window. His crutches were propped on a chair, out of sight. He did not lower his newspaper until Hackberry and Pam had left the saloon.

THE BRAZOS HOTEL was made of red sandstone, built in the 1880s, and seemed to rise like a forgotten reminder of lost Victorian elegance in the midst of twenty-first-century urban decay. The lobby contained potted palms, a threadbare carpet, furniture from a secondhand store, a telephone switchboard with disconnected terminals jacked into the holes, and an ancient registration desk backdropped by pigeonholes with room keys and mail in them.

A short-necked, heavyset Mexican woman was behind the desk, a big smile on her face when she talked. Hackberry showed her the photo of Liam Eriksson.

"Yeah, I seen him. Not for a few days, but I seen him here a couple of times, sitting in the lobby or going up the stairs. The elevator don't always work, so he'd take the stairs."

"Did he rent a room here?" Hackberry asked.

"No, he was here to see his girlfriend."

"Mona?" Hackberry said.

"That's right, Mona Drexel. You know her?"

"I've been looking for her. Is she in now?"

"You a sheriff, huh? How come you don't have a gun?"

"I don't want to scare people. Which room is Ms. Drexel in?"

"Her room is one-twenty-nine. But I haven't seen her in a couple of days. See, the key is in her box. She always leaves her key when she goes out, 'cause sometimes maybe she drinks a little too much and loses it."

"Could I have the key, please?"

"Are you supposed to do that, go in somebody's room when they ain't there?"

"If you give us permission, it's okay," Hackberry said.

"You sure?"

"She could be sick in there and need help."

"I'll open it for you," the Mexican woman said.

The three of them took the elevator upstairs. When the Mexican woman inserted the key in the door and started to turn it, Hackberry put his hand on hers. "We'll take it from here," he said, his voice almost a whisper.

Before the woman could respond, Pam fitted her hands on the woman's shoulders and moved her away from the door. "It's okay," she said, slipping a revolver from under her shirt. "We appreciate what you've done. Just stay back."

Hackberry turned the key and pushed the door open, staying slightly behind the jamb.

The room had been vacated, the closet cleaned out, the drawers in the dresser hanging open and empty. Pam stood in the middle of the room and bit on a thumbnail. She put her revolver back inside the clip-on holster on her belt and pulled her shirt over the handles. "What a waste of time," she said.

Hackberry went into the bathroom and came back out. In the shadows between a small writing table and the bed, he saw a wastebasket crammed full of newspaper and fast-food wrappers and soiled paper towels. He picked up the can and dumped it on the bedspread. Used Q-tips and balls of hair and dust and wads of Kleenex fell out on the bedspread with the other trash. After Hackberry sorted it all out, he washed his hands in the bathroom. When he came out, Pam was standing over the writing desk, studying the cover of a *Time* magazine she had positioned under the desk lamp.

"This was stuck under the pillow. Take a look," she said.

The magazine was two months old, and on the mailing label was the name and address of a beauty parlor. At least a half-dozen phone numbers were inked on the cover. Pam tapped her finger on a notation at the bottom of the cover, one that someone had circled twice for emphasis. "'PJC, Traveler's Rest two-oh-nine,'" she read aloud.

"Preacher Jack Collins," Hackberry said.

"The one and only. Maybe we've got the sonofabitch," she said.

She dialed information and asked for both the phone number and the street address of a Traveler's Rest motel. She wrote both down in her notebook and hung up. "It's not more than two miles away," she said.

"Good work, Pam. Let's go," he said.

"What about Clawson?"

"What about him?"

"We're supposed to coordinate, right?"

Hackberry didn't reply.

"Right, Hack?" she said.

"I'm not totally confident about Clawson."

"After you get all over my case about this guy, you suddenly have reservations?"

"One of his colleagues told me Clawson works alone. I took that to mean he operates under a black flag. We don't do business that way."

"The guy could have ruined my career and sent me to jail on top of it. If you're going to stiff him now, I won't be party to it."

Hackberry opened his cell phone and punched in Clawson's number. "It's Sheriff Holland," he said. "We think we've got Jack Collins located. We just got lucky. A bartender knew the woman Eriksson was with at the car-title place. We're at her hotel now. It looks like she's blown town." Hackberry gave Clawson the room number and the address of the motel where he thought Preacher Jack Collins might be staying.

"You're fairly certain he's there?" Clawson said.

"No, not at all. We found a notation on a magazine cover. There's no telling how long ago it was written there."

"I'm on the River Walk," Clawson said. "I thought I had a lead on Eriksson, but it didn't work out. I'll need to arrange backup. Don't do anything till I get back to you."

Hackberry closed the cell phone and looked at Pam.

"*What?*" she said.

"We're not supposed to do anything until he calls us back." He stared at her, his eyes not quite focused.

"Finish your thought," she said.

"Remind me not to take your advice anymore."

"Anything else?"

"Screw Clawson. We bust Jack Collins," he said.

ISAAC CLAWSON PARKED his car a half block from the Traveler's Rest motel, put on a rain hat and coat, covering the butt of his holstered semiautomatic, and walked the rest of the way. It was almost dusk, and the wind was blowing in the streets, scouring dust into the sky. He heard the rumble of thunder just as a solitary raindrop struck his face. The decrease in barometric pressure and the sudden cooling of the day and the raindrop that he wiped on his hand and looked at seemed so unusual and unexpected after a week of triple-digit heat that he wondered if somehow the change in weather signaled a change in his life.

But that was a foolish way to think, he told himself. The great change in his life had come irrevocably in the night when two sheriff's deputies had appeared at the door of his suburban home, removing their hats, and tried to tell him in euphemistic language that a young woman thought to be his daughter had been left locked with her fiancé inside the trunk of a burning automobile. From that moment on, Isaac knew the events of his future life might be modifiers of his mood or his worldview or the degree of anger he woke with in the false dawn, but nothing would ever give him back the happiness he had once taken for granted.

In fact, if there was any release from that night back in Tulsa, it came to him only when he canceled the ticket of someone he could associate in his mind with the two degenerates who had murdered his daughter.

He looked at his watch. It was 7:19, and the street lamps had come on in the motel parking lot. A rain shower was sweeping across the city, the clouds pierced with columns of sunlight, the air smelling of wet flowers and trees and the odor that rain makes when it touches warm concrete in summer.

He glanced up at the lavender hue of the heavens and opened his mouth and felt a raindrop hit his tongue. What a foolish thing to do, like a kid discovering spring, he thought, taking himself to task again.

The motel clerk was a rail of a man, dressed like a cowboy, in a black shirt with roses sewn on it and gray trousers with stripes, the cuffs tucked inside Mexican stovepipes stenciled with red and green flower petals. He wore a flesh-colored Band-Aid at the corner of one eye.

Clawson started to reach for his ID and instead rested his hand on the counter. "Got a nonsmoking room for two?" he asked.

"Need a king or a pair of queens?"

"My wife and I would like two-oh-nine if it's available. We stayed there the night our son graduated from college."

The adhesive on the clerk's Band-Aid was loose, and he pressed it back tight against the skin with the back of his wrist. He looked at his computer screen. "That one is occupied. I could put you in two-oh-six."

"Let me ask my wife. We're kind of sentimental about our boy's graduation."

"I know what you mean," the clerk said.

"You hurt your eye?"

"Yeah, put a stick in it. Not too smart, I guess."

After Isaac Clawson went back outside, the clerk looked in the mirror. The Band-Aid on his face had come almost completely loose, exposing a pair of tattooed blue teardrops at the corner of his eye. He flattened the Band-Aid into place once more and picked up the telephone, punching in only three digits.

Clawson picked up a free shopper's guide from a newspaper box and held it over his head as he walked into the motel parking lot, as though going to his automobile to confer with his wife. Then he cut around the far side of the motel and entered an outdoor breezeway in the center of the building and mounted the stairs. The clouds were purple in the west, the sun like a yellow rose buried inside them, the sky streaked with rain. In weather like this, his father used to say the devil was beating his wife. Why was Isaac having thoughts like these now, about his boyhood, about his family? Why did a great change in his life seem to be at hand?

*   *   *

THERE HAD BEEN an eight-vehicle pileup by an intersection of I-35 and I-10, a chemical tanker jackknifing and sloshing its load across six lanes of traffic. Hackberry had clamped his magnetized portable flasher on the roof of his truck cab and was trying to thread his way along the road's shoulder to an exit by a shopping center. He handed his cell phone to Pam. "Try Clawson again," he said.

She got Clawson's voice mail. She closed the cell phone but kept it in her lap. "Want to call the locals for backup?" she asked.

"For Clawson?"

She thought about it. "No, I guess he wouldn't appreciate that too much."

"Hang on," Hackberry said.

He swung across the swale, bouncing hard through the bottom, spinning grass and dirt off the rear tires as he powered up the far side. He went the wrong way on the road shoulder, then cut across another swale onto an entrance to I-10 that was free of congestion, the truck slamming down on the springs. Pam kept one hand fastened on the dashboard.

"You all right?" Hackberry said.

"What do you think Clawson plans to do if he gets to Collins before we do?" she asked.

"Maybe he already has a team backing him up. See if you can get hold of Ethan Riser. His number is in my contacts."

"Who?"

"The FBI agent."

Pam tried Riser's number, but the call went directly into voice mail. She left a message.

"Sorry for lecturing you about Clawson. I didn't think he'd try to use us," Pam said.

"Reach behind the seat and get my pistol, will you?"

It and its holster and its belt with loops for cartridges were wrapped inside a brown paper bag. Pam slipped the bag free of the gun and the belt that was wound around the holster and set them on the carpet by the console. The pistol was a customized remake of a frontier double-action .45 revolver. It was charcoal blue with white handles and a brass trigger guard and a seven-and-a-half-inch barrel. Its balance was perfect, its accuracy and lethality at forty yards not up for debate.

"You've never fired it on the job, have you?" she said.

"Who told you that?"

"No one."

He looked at her.

"I just knew," she said.

They were on an elevated expressway, roaring past a neighborhood of warehouses and alleyways with clumps of banana trees in them and houses with dirt yards. Against a rainy, sunlit, mauve-colored sky that made Hackberry think of the Orient, he could see a three-story building with a neon sign on the roof that read Traveler's Rest.

WHEN ISAAC CLAWSON reached the second floor, he realized the numbers on the room doors were going to be a challenge. The numbering was not sequential; some of the rooms were set in an alcove, inside the breezeway, and some of the rooms did not have any numbers at all. Down the walkway, a cleaning cart was parked against the handrail. A Hispanic maid sat on a bench by the cart, humped forward in a cleaning smock of some kind, eating a sandwich, a scarf knotted under her chin, the mist from the rain blowing in her face.

The palm fronds by the pool were thrashing in the wind, twisting against the trunks. Clawson passed room 206, the room that had been offered to him by the clerk, and saw that the next room had no number and the one after that was 213 and the one after that was 215. He realized that for whatever reason, odd numbers were on one side of the breezeway and even numbers on the other.

Except for 206.

"Where's two-oh-nine?" he said to the cleaning person, whose mouth was full of cheese and bread.

"Siento mucho, señor, pero no hablo inglés."

Then why not learn some inglés if you're going to live in this country? he said to himself.

He went in the other direction, going past the breezeway into an area of even numbers. At the far end of the building, with his hand pushed back inside his coat, his thumb hooked on the holstered butt of his semiautomatic, he paused and looked out over the city. Somewhere out there in the fading light was the Alamo, where he and his wife had taken their daughter when she was nine. He had not tried to explain to her the actuality of the events that had occurred there, the thousands of Mexican soldiers charging the walls on the thirteenth day of the siege, the desperation of the 118 men and boys inside who knew this was their last morning on earth, the screams of the wounded who were bayoneted to death in the chapel. Why should a child be exposed to the cruelty that had characterized much of human history? Hadn't men like Bowie and Crockett and Travis died so children like his daughter could be safe? At least that was what Clawson had wanted to believe.

How could he have known at the time that his child's death would be a far worse one than any experienced by the Texans inside the mission? Clawson could feel his eyes watering. He hated himself for his emotions, because his remorse for not having taken better care of his daughter had always paralyzed him and made him, too, the victim of his daughter's killers, men who had yet to be executed, who ate good food and had medical care and watched television while his daughter and her fiancé lay in a cemetery and he and his wife dwelled daily in the Garden of Gethsemane.

Theologians claimed that anger was a cancer and that hatred was one of the seven deadly sins. They were wrong, Clawson thought. Anger was an elixir that cauterized sorrow and passivity and victimhood from the metabolism; it lit fires in the belly; it provided you with that deadening of the conscience that allowed you to lock down on someone with iron sights and forget he descended from the same tree in a Mesopotamian savannah that you did.

He went back up the walkway to the central part of the building. The cleaning person was still by her cart, looking in the opposite direction. Then he discovered why he had not found room 209. The tin numerals on the door of room 206 had been affixed to the wood with three tiny nails. But the nails at the top and bottom of the numeral 6 had been removed or knocked loose from their holes by the constant slamming of the door. The 6 was actually the numeral 9, turned upside down on the remaining nail.

The curtain was drawn on the window. Clawson tried to see through the corner of the jalousie with no success. Then he realized the door was slightly ajar, perhaps not over a quarter of an inch, the locking mechanism not in place. He put his left hand on the door handle and eased his semiautomatic from the holster. Behind him, he heard the wheels of the cleaning cart begin to move stiffly on the walkway. He pushed open the door, pulling his weapon, keeping it pointed at the floor, his eyes straining into the darkness of the room.

The bed was made, the television set on, the shower drumming in the bathroom. "Immigration and Customs Enforcement," he said.

But there was no response.

He walked across the carpet, past the television screen, the light flickering on his wrist and hand and the dull black hue of his weapon. The bathroom was coated with steam, the heavy plastic curtain in the shower stall barely containing the water bouncing off its opposite side.

"Immigration and Customs Enforcement," he repeated. "Turn off the shower and place both your hands against the wall."

Again there was no response.

He gripped the edge of the curtain and ripped it back on the rod. The shower mist welled into his face.

"You shouldn't go in a man's room without a warrant," a voice said behind him. "No, no, don't move. You don't want to look at me, hoss."

Clawson stood frozen, his weapon held out by his side, the mist from the shower dampening his clothes, the back of his neck burning. But in the instant before he had been warned not to turn around, he had seen what appeared to be a hooded shape against the blowing rain, a nickel-plated pistol barrel in the figure's left hand.

"Drop your piece in the commode," the voice said.

"The cowboy at the desk dimed me?"

"You dimed yourself when you came here without backup. You're guilty of the sins of pride and arrogance, my friend. But they don't have to be your undoing. That means don't listen to the kind of thoughts you're having right now. This doesn't have to end like you think."

The grips of the semiautomatic were damp in Clawson's grasp. Moisture had beaded on his face and was running into his eyes and collar. He could hear a sound in his head that was like the roaring of the sea, like a whoosh of flame from the gas tank of a burning automobile.

BY THE TIME Hackberry turned in to the motel parking lot, the sun had disappeared completely and the thunder had grown in volume, crackling across the sky like a tin roof being peeled joist by joist off a barn.

"I can't believe this. An honest-to-God rain," Pam said.

"Try Clawson again," Hackberry said.

"Waste of time. I think he's gotten himself into a pile of shit." He gave her a look.

"You got it," she said.

He pulled in front of the motel office while she made the call. He could see a man dressed like a cowboy behind the front desk.

"No answer," Pam said.

"Well, let's see what life is like at Traveler's Rest," Hackberry said. He got out of the truck and buckled on his gun belt, the open door shielding him from view. Through the motel's front window, he saw the clerk answer the phone and then go into the back. An electronic bell rang when he and Pam entered the office.

"Be right with you," a voice in back said.

By leaning sideways, Hackberry could see the clerk standing in front of a mirror. He had just removed a Band-Aid from the corner of one eye. He rolled it up between his fingers and plunked it into a wastebasket, then peeled the paper off a fresh one and glued it against his skin, smoothing the adhesive down firmly with his thumb. He ran a comb through his hair, touched at his nostrils with one knuckle, and came back to the front desk with a smile on his face. His eyes dropped to the revolver on Hackberry's hip. "Help you?" he said.

Hackberry opened his badge holder. "Has a federal agent by the name of Isaac Clawson been here?"

"Today?"

"In the last hour."

"Federal agent? No, sir, not to my knowledge."

"Can you tell me who's staying in room two-oh-nine?"

The clerk bent to his computer, his expression earnest. "Looks like that's a gentleman who paid cash. For five days, in advance. I'll have to look up his registration card."

"Can you describe what he looks like?"

"I don't think it was me who checked him in. I don't place him offhand." The clerk touched at his nose. His eyes drifted off Hackberry's onto the parking lot and a palm tree beating in the wind. "Y'all must have brought that weather with you. We can use it," he said.

"Know a hooker by the name of Mona Drexel?"

"No, sir, we don't allow hookers in here."

"Did you see a man who has a shaved head and octagonal-shaped glasses and looks like a weight lifter?"

"Today? I don't recollect anybody like that."

"You know who Preacher Jack Collins is?"

"I know some preachers, but not one by that name."

"I hear the A.B. is for life. Is that true?"

"Sir?"

"Those blue teardrops by your eye, the ones under your Band-Aid."

"Yes, sir, I had some trouble when I was younger."

"But the Aryan Brotherhood is for life, correct?"

"No, sir, not for me, it isn't. I put all that behind me."

"You were in Huntsville?"

"Yes, sir."

"Give me the key to two-oh-nine. Don't pick up that phone while we're here. If it rings, let it ring off the wall. If you've lied to me, you'll wish you were in lockdown back at the Walls."

The clerk had to sit down when Hackberry and Pam went out of the office.

ISAAC CLAWSON HAD always subscribed to the belief that a person's life was governed by no more than two or three choices that usually seemed of little consequence at the time one made them. He had also wondered how many thoughts a man could experience in under a second, at least if his adrenaline level didn't blow his circuits first.

But was this moment in his life really one that presented him a viable choice? What was the governing principle for any lawman caught in his situation with an armed adversary? That one was easy. You never surrendered your weapon. You hung tough, you kept your enemy talking, you brassed it out, you created an electric storm of "spray-and-pray fire" no sane person would choose to walk into. If all that failed, you ate the bullet.

What were Shakespeare's words? "By my troth, I care not; we owe God a death, and let it go which way it will, he who dies this year is quit for the next." Yes, that was it. By accepting your mortality, you walked right through its shadow into the light on the far side.

But the lesson of Shakespeare and the principles Isaac Clawson had learned at Quantico and as many as five other training programs weren't entirely applicable here. If he was executed in room 209, his killer would walk free and kill again and again. In fact, there would probably be no prosecutable evidence to link Clawson's death to Preacher Jack Collins. Clawson had been acting alone, confirming his colleagues' perception that he was a driven man teetering on the edges of nervous collapse. Maybe some of his colleagues and superiors might even be glad Jack Collins had rid them of an agent no one felt at ease with.

If Isaac had just one more season to run, he could find Jack Collins and the others who had murdered the Thai women and girls and take them off the board one by one, each of them in some way payback for the death of his daughter. Even his worst detractors conceded that no one at ICE was more dedicated and successful in hunting down the traffickers in misery who were metastasizing on America's southern border.

"Last chance, hoss," the voice said behind him.

"You think you can pop a federal agent and just blow town? They'll have to pick you up with tweezers."

"Looks to me like they've done a piss-poor job of it so far."

"You're the one they call Preacher?"

"You violated the Fourth Amendment. A man's rental lodging is the same as his home. Y'all don't abide by your own Constitution. That's why you're not deserving of respect. I say y'all are hypocrites, sir. I say a pox on your house."

Isaac Clawson spun in a half-circle, swinging his semiautomatic at arm's length, the rain blowing through the door. The figure he saw standing against the wall to one side of the door seemed out of context, unrelated to the events transpiring around him. It was the cleaning woman, or what he had thought was a woman, in a head scarf and a smock, a two-barrel nickel-plated derringer aimed with her left hand, her right hand supporting herself heavily on a chair back as though she were in pain.

Isaac was sure he squeezed off a round. He must have. His finger had tightened inside the trigger guard. He had not flinched; his eyes were wide open. He should have heard the report and felt the solid kick against the heel of his hand and seen the barrel jump with the recoil, the ejected casing tinkling on the floor.

Instead, he had seen a pinpoint of brightness leap from the muzzle of the derringer. The bright circle of light made him think of fire leaking through a metal surface that had been superheated beyond its tolerance, its stress level giving way to the roaring furnace it tried to contain.

He felt a finger touch his brow, and he saw hands reaching toward him from a cool fire that somehow had been rendered harmless, as though the flames had been robbed of their heat and could have no more effect on living tissue than waving shadows could, and he knew that this time he had done something right, that he could pull his daughter and her fiancé from the burning automobile and undo the cruelty and suffering the world had visited upon them.

But as he reached for his daughter's hands, he realized his life would always be defined by inadequacy and failure. It was his daughter's hands that grasped his, not the other way around, extending out of a white radiance, slipping up higher on his wrists, seizing them with superhuman strength, pulling him into a place where resistance and rage and even the desire to make choices seemed to have dissolved into nothingness a million years ago.

Isaac's eyes were open wide when he struck the floor. Preacher Jack Collins looked at him briefly, fitted his hands on the cleaning cart, and worked his way down the walkway to the stairs at the far end of the building.

Chapter 11

NO MATTER HOW many pain pills Artie Rooney ate, the throbbing in his hand wouldn't quit. Nor could he rid himself of the well of fear that was eating its way through the bottom of his stomach. Nor could he get the name of Jack Collins out of his head. It hovered behind his eyes; he woke with it in the morning; it was in his food; it was in his coupling with his whores.

And now it was in his conversation with Hugo Cistranos, here, inside his elegant beachfront office, his helplessness as palpable as the smell of fear that rose from his armpits. He couldn't believe that only weeks ago, Jack Collins had been a name without a face, the mention of which would have caused him to yawn.

"Jack wants a half million from you?" Hugo said, slumped comfortably in a white leather chair, dressed in golf slacks and a print shirt and Roman sandals, his red-streaked hair glistening with gel.

"He blames me for the loss of his soul," Artie said.

"Jack doesn't have one. How can he blame you for losing it?"

"Because he's crazy?"

Hugo studied the backs of his hands. "You just sat there and let Jack cut off your finger? That's hard to believe, Artie."

"He was going to cut my throat. He held the razor right by my eye."

Hugo's expression became philosophical. "Yeah, I guess Jack's capable of that. Must have been terrible. How'd you explain it at the hospital?"

Artie got up from his desk, cradling his injured hand. A hurricane was building in intensity by the hour, three hundred miles southeast of Galveston. Through the enormous glass wall that fronted the beach, he could see a band of greenish cobalt along the southern horizon, and the slick leathery backs of stingrays in the swells and waves threading into yellow froth inside the wind. He wanted to put a bullet in Hugo Cistranos.

"You didn't tell anybody what happened, huh?" Hugo said. "That was probably the right choice. Must be hard accepting all this—I mean, a religious creep like that walking into your office and turning your desk into a chopping block. Gives me the willies thinking about it."

"Collins is onto us," Artie said.

"Who's this 'us' you're talking about?"

"You set up the scam, Hugo. It was your idea to kidnap the Russian's whores. You got Nick Dolan to think he was boosting the girls from me, and you got him to believe the mow-down was on him, too. From the beginning, this whole nightmare has had your name all over it."

But Hugo was already waving a finger back and forth. "Oh, no, you don't. You knew those girls' stomachs were loaded with China white, and you thought you'd rip off the Russian for both his cooze and his skag at the same time. You got greedy, Artie. I'm not taking your weight on this, my friend."

"I didn't tell you to kill them."

"When did you ever tell me *not* to kill somebody? Remember

that sex freak who creeped your house in Metairie? Why is it you never asked about him, Artie? The *Times-Picayune* did a big spread on the body parts that floated up into a picnic ground. You never made the connection?"

Artie Rooney's face had an expression on it like that of a blowfish with a hook in its mouth. Hugo took a stick of peppermint from the big clear plastic jar on Artie's desk. He gazed reflectively at the beach and the waves exploding on the tip of a jetty. "It's too bad about the whores. But they could have stayed in Thailand if they wanted. There's a gold mine in sex tours for Japanese businessmen. I'm sorry about what happened out there. But there wasn't any choice in the matter. The balloons were busting in their stomachs, and they were screaming about going to a hospital. 'Hey, guys, pump out my nine whores loaded with fifteen balloons each of uncut white heroin. While you're at it, let them tell you about the coyote we capped and buried on federal land.'"

"Oh, funny man."

"Artie, we're all sacks of fertilizer. You, me, Preacher Jack, your secretary, the families out there on the beach. You think if it was us buried by that dozer, the Asian girls would be burning incense in a Buddhist temple? They'd be shopping for makeup at Walmart."

Artie stared wanly at the Gulf and at the hurricane warning flags snapping straight out from their lanyards. Then it struck him: Hugo was talking too much, too cleverly, filling the air with words at Artie's expense in order to control the conversation. "You're scared of him," he said.

"I've worked with Preacher before. I respect his boundaries, I respect his talents."

"His boundaries? You been watching *Dr. Phil* or something? You just called Collins a religious creep. I think you're starting to rattle. I think you've had some kind of confrontation with him."

Hugo crossed his legs and untwisted the cellophane from the stick of peppermint, sucking in his cheeks thoughtfully. "Good try, no cigar. You ought to spend some time at the library, Artie, bone up on some history. Foot soldiers don't go to the wall. Officers do. Foot soldiers are always given the chance to adjust. Your bandage is leaking."

"What?"

"You're spotting your shirt. You ought to go to the hospital. What'd you do with the finger? If you put it on ice, maybe they can sew it back on."

Artie's desk phone buzzed. He picked up the receiver with his good hand. "I told you not to disturb me," he said.

"A Mr. Nick Dolan and his wife are here to see you."

"What are *they* doing here?"

The secretary didn't answer.

"Get rid of them. Tell them I'm out of town," Artie said.

"I don't think they're going away, Mr. Rooney," the secretary whispered.

Artie paused, his eyes locked on Hugo's. "Tell them to wait a minute," he said. He replaced the receiver in the cradle. "Go in my conference room and stay there."

"What for?" Hugo said.

"You ever meet Esther Dolan?"

"What about her?"

"You've energized Batgirl, you idiot."

When Nick and Esther entered the room, Artie Rooney was sitting behind his desk in a powder-blue suit and a blue-and-gold striped tie and a silk shirt that was as bright as tin, his swivel chair tilted back, his hands hanging loosely over the arms of the chair, a man in charge and at peace with the world.

"Long time, Miss Esther," Artie said, addressing her in the traditional manner that a gentleman who was a family friend would address a woman in New Orleans.

Esther didn't reply, her gaze boring into his face.

"We need to straighten out some things," Nick said.

"I'm always happy to see old friends," Artie said.

"What happened to your hand?" Nick said.

"An accident with my electric hedge clipper."

Even while he addressed Nick, Artie's attention was fixed on Esther, who wore a tight purple dress with green flowers printed on it. "Y'all sit down. I got some shrimp and a pitcher of vodka martinis in the refrigerator. You been doin' okay, Miss Esther?"

"We've tried to contact Hugo Cistranos," Esther said. "He's going to hurt a young woman and her boyfriend, an ex-soldier."

"Hugo? News to me."

"Cut the crap, Artie," Nick said.

"You came to Galveston to insult me?" Artie said.

"Nick has told me everything," Esther said. "About those gangsters working for you and how they almost killed Nick by a farmhouse. He told me about the Asian girls, too."

"You sure about what you're saying here? This has got me all confused."

"They were killed because you were smuggling them into the United States. They were peasant girls machine-gunned by one of your hired animals," Esther said.

"I'm part owner of some dating services. Maybe I'm not altogether proud of that. But I have to put food on the table like everybody else. Your husband is not innocent in this, Miss Esther. And don't be saying I murdered anybody."

"Nick just signed over all his interests in what you call 'dating services.'"

Artie looked at Nick. "I'm hearing this right? You sold out in Houston and Dallas?"

"No, I didn't sell out, I got out," Nick said.

Artie straightened in his chair and rested his arms on his desk pad. He took a pill from a tiny tin container and put it in his mouth, then swallowed it with a half-glass of water. A look of tension, of pain held carefully in place, seemed to recede back into his face. "I don't have contact with Hugo anymore. I think maybe he's in New Orleans. Maybe I'll be hanging it up here and moving back there myself."

"You going to stop that killer from hurting those kids or not?" Esther said.

"Don't be implying what you're implying, Miss Esther. You try to bring the house down, you'll find yourself standing in the living room with the roof caving on Nick's head and maybe yours, too," Artie said.

"Don't you talk to her like that," Nick said.

"Remember that time at the Prytania Theatre when we did a swirlie with your face in the commode?" Artie said.

"How about I mash your hand in your drawer?" Nick said.

"You survived in New Orleans because we allowed you to, Nick. Didoni Giacano once said your mother was probably knocked up by a yeast infection and you were not to be trusted. I told Dee-Dee his perceptions were on target but that you were also gutless and greedy, and for those reasons alone, you'd do whatever he told you, all the way to the graveyard. So in a way, I helped make your career. I think you ought to show a little gratitude."

"Dee-Dee Gee said that about my family and me?"

Artie gestured at the glass wall behind him. "See that storm building out there?" he said. "Katrina washed out most of the Ninth Ward. I hope this one changes course and hits New Orleans just like Katrina did and finishes the job. I hope you're there for it, Nick. I hope you and your people are washed off the earth. That's how I feel."

Esther leaned forward in her chair, her hands folded in her

lap, a realization growing in her face. "You deceived Nick, didn't you?" she said.

"About what?"

"The smuggling and the murder of the girls. You were using Nick somehow. That's how you set up the extortion."

"I got news for you. Your husband is a pimp. The houses you own, the cars you drive, the country club you belong to, they're all paid for by money he makes off whores. The ones you think are just college bimbos taking off their clothes at the club do lap dances and jerk off guys in the back rooms. You're a smart woman, Miss Esther. You married Mighty Mouse. Why pretend otherwise?"

She rose from her chair, her hands crimped on her purse. "My husband is a good man," she said. "I'll never allow you to hurt him. You threaten my family again, and I'll make your life awful."

"Right. Sorry you have to run," Artie said, taking another pain pill from the tin box.

"You hurt the soldier or his girlfriend, we're calling the FBI," Nick said. "I know what you can do to me, Artie. It doesn't matter. I'm not gonna have the blood of those kids on my conscience."

"How do you like that, you cheap gangster?" Esther said. "You were talking about doing swirlies on people? Think about yourself in a prison cell full of sexual degenerates. I hope you're in there a thousand years."

After they were gone, Artie opened the door to his conference room. Hugo was smoking a cigarette, gazing at the waves crashing on the beach.

"You get an earful?" Artie asked.

"Enough," Hugo replied. He mashed out his cigarette in an ashtray on the conference table. "How do you want to play it?"

"I got to tell you?"

"I'm lots of things, but omniscient isn't one of them."

"Hose everybody who needs to go. That means the soldier and his broad, that means Preacher Jack Collins, that means anybody who can dime us. That means that fat little kike and his wife and, if necessary, his kids. When I say 'hose,' I mean slick down to the tile from one end of the building to the other. I'm getting through loud and clear here?"

"No problem, Artie."

"If you're working in close?"

Hugo waited.

"Put one in Esther's mouth," Artie said. "I want her to know where it came from, too."

YEARS AGO, IN a Waycross, Georgia, public library, Bobby Lee Motree happened to see a book titled *My Grandfather Was the Only Private in the Confederate Army*. He was puzzled by the title and, flipping through the pages, tried to figure out what it meant. Then he stopped thinking about the matter altogether, in part because Bobby Lee's interest in history was confined largely to his claim that he was a descendant of perhaps the greatest military strategist in American history, a claim based on the fact that his first and second names were respectively Robert and Lee, as were those of his father, a petty thief and part-time golf caddie who was killed while sleeping on a train trestle.

Now, during a sunset that seemed somehow to be a statement about his life, he stood by his vehicle, not far from a jagged mountain whose bare slopes were turning darker and darker against the sky. The wind was hot and smelled of creosote and dust and road-patch tar that had dissolved into licorice during the day. In the distance, he saw a trio of buzzards circling high above the hardpan, their outstretched wings stenciled against a yellow sun that reminded him of light trapped behind a dirty window shade. He opened a cell phone and punched in a number.

Then he hesitated and removed his thumb from the send button. Bobby Lee wasn't feeling well. He could see torn pieces of color floating behind his eyelids, as though his power to think were deteriorating, as though his uncontrolled thoughts had become his greatest enemy.

He reached inside his SUV and drank from a can of warm soda. Was he coming down with something? No such luck. His world was coming apart. He had always admired Preacher for his professionalism and invisibility, and for the way he had become a legend, a one-man Murder, Inc., without ever going inside the system. But Preacher had gone along with Hugo on the mass mow-down of the Asians, and now he'd popped a federal agent. Somebody would have to go down for it. Hugo? That was a laugh. Preacher? Jack would eat a Gatling gun before he'd allow anyone to take him into custody. Who did that leave?

The answer wasn't one Bobby Lee liked to think about. The rest of the team consisted of him and Liam Eriksson, and Liam was already on Jack's S-list for stealing the disability check and trying to cash it while he and his hooker girlfriend were drunk. Liam and Bobby Lee were basically working stiffs, making a score here and there, putting away a few bucks for a better life, waiting for the proper time to hang it up. They weren't religious crazoids like Jack, or guys like Hugo who got off on capping people. For Liam and Bobby Lee, it was just a job. But working stiffs were disposable and replaceable. If anyone disagreed with that, he just needed to check out the audience at an ultimate-fighter match.

Bobby Lee remembered when he did his first hit, at age twenty, out on Alligator Alley between Fort Lauderdale and Naples, a five-thou whack on a Cuban who'd raped the daughter of a Mobbed-up guy from the Jersey Shore. At first Bobby Lee thought it might bother him to pop a guy he had nothing against, but it didn't. He bought the hit a couple of drinks in Lauderdale, told him he had a fishing camp in the Glades, then showed him this big grassy bay in the moonlight and parked two .22 hollow-points, *pow, pow,* that fast, behind the guy's ear, and suddenly the guy was facedown in the water, his arms outstretched, his suit coat puffed with air like he was studying the bottom of the bay, the night air throbbing with bullfrogs.

But what should Bobby Lee do now? Deep-six the brothers-in-arms stuff and blow Dodge on Preacher? That thought didn't sit well, either. If Bobby Lee was to remain a pro back in Florida, where he planned to re-enroll at Miami-Dade, doing an occasional contract job when he needed money, he had to keep his reputation intact. Also, bailing out on Preacher was a good way to ensure a lifetime of looking over his shoulder.

Bobby Lee opened his cell phone again and hit the redial button.

"Where you been?" Preacher's voice said.

"All over most of two counties."

"Think about what you just said. It's a contradiction in terms."

"What?"

"What did you find?"

"Nothing. But I got an idea."

"What do you mean, 'nothing'?"

"What I said. I couldn't find a Siesta motel. That's where the guy Junior Whatever said the girl and the soldier were staying."

"Call me back on a landline."

"Jack, the CIA isn't following us around. They pull stuff out of the air when they're after the rag heads." Bobby Lee stopped, his frustration with Preacher building. He wanted to throw the cell phone down on the asphalt and stomp it into junk. "You still pissed at Liam 'cause he tried to cash the soldier's check?"

"What do you think?"

"I say give Liam a break. The guy's out there, he's trying."

"Out where?"

This time Bobby Lee ignored Preacher's constant attempts to correct his language and somehow turn it against him. "Look, I'll call you back later. I've got a plan."

"You've been wandering around on the border for two days. That's a plan?"

"You ever know a junkie who was farther than one day away?"

"What's your point?"

"There's no difference between a junkie and a drunk. A rat goes to its hole. The soldier is a juicer and drifts in and out of A.A., at least that's the word. Hugo says he's got a pink scar on his face as thick as an earthworm. I'll find him. I guarantee it. I called the A.A. hotline and got an area schedule. You still there, Jack?"

Had the service simply gone down, or had Preacher hung up? Bobby Lee hit the speed dial, but his call went immediately to voice mail. He closed and opened his eyes, the mountain in front of him like a dark volcanic cone cooling against the evening sun.

THERE WERE FEW twelve-step groups in the area, or at least few that met more often than once a week, and the following day Pete Flores felt he was lucky to hitch a ride to one called the Sundowners that met in a fundamentalist church thirty miles down the road from the motel where he and Vikki were staying. The church house was a white-frame building with a small false bell tower on the apex of the roof and a blue neon cross mounted above the entranceway. In back were a mechanic's shed and, next to it, a cemetery whose graves were strewn with plastic flowers and jelly glasses green with dried algae. Even with the windows wide open, the air inside the building was stifling, the wood surfaces as warm to the touch as a cookstove. Pete had arrived early at the meeting, and rather than sit in the heat, he went outside and sat on the back steps and looked at the strange chemical-green coloration in the western sky, the sun still as bright as an acetylene torch on the earth's rim. The sedimentary layers of the mesalike formations were gray and yellow and pink above the dusk gathering on the desert floor. Pete felt as though he were sitting at the bottom of an enormous dried-out riparian bowl, one shaped out of potter's clay in a prehistoric time, the land giving off an almost feral odor when rain tried to restore it to life.

The man who sat down next to Pete on the step was wearing an immaculate white T-shirt and freshly pressed strap overalls. He smelled of soap and aftershave lotion, and his dark hair was boxed on the back of his neck. His thick half-moon eyebrows were neatly clipped, the cleft in his chin shiny from a fresh shave. There was a bald spot in the center of his head. When he stared southward at the desert, his mouth was a gray slit without expression or character, his eyes dulled over. He pulled a cigarette out of his pack with his lips, then shook another one loose and offered it to Pete.

"Thanks, I never took it up," Pete said.

"Good choice," the man said. He lit his cigarette and blew the smoke from the side of his mouth deferentially. "I'm new at this meet. How is it?"

"Don't know. This is my first time here, too."

"You got some sobriety in?"

"A few days, that's about it. I've got a twenty-four-hour chip."

"Twenty-four hours can be a bitch."

"You work here'bouts?" Pete asked.

"I was hauling pipe between Presidio and Fort Stockton, up to last month, anyway. I got a service-connected disability, but my boss was a pretty hard-nosed character. According to him, time in the Sandbox was for jerks."

"You were in Iraq?"

"Two tours."

"My tank got blown up in Baghdad," Pete said.

The man's eyes drifted to the long welted scar that ran like a pink raindrop down the side of Pete's face. "You start drinking when you came home?"

Pete studied the deepening color in the sky, the hills that seemed humped against a fire burning just beyond the earth's rim. "It runs in my family. I don't think the war had much to do with it," he said.

"That's a stand-up way to look at it."

"How much sobriety you have?"

"A couple of years, more or less."

"You have a two-year chip?" Pete said.

"I'm not big on chips. I do the program my own way."

Pete folded his hands and didn't reply.

"You got wheels?" the man said.

"I hitched a ride with a guy who smelled like a beer truck. I asked him to come in with me, but he said Jesus's first miracle was turning water into wine, and his followers weren't hypocrites about it. I couldn't quite fit all that together."

"Want to get some coffee and a piece of pie after the meet? I'm springing," the man in overalls said.

During the meeting, Pete forgot about his conversation with the man he'd met on the back steps. A woman was talking about going on a dry drunk and experiencing flashbacks that returned her to the inside of a blackout. Her voice, like that of a benighted soul forced to witness light, became threaded with tension as she told the group she might have killed someone with her automobile. The room was quiet when she finished speaking, the people in the pews and folding chairs staring at their feet or into space, their faces wan, each knowing the speaker's story could have been his or her own.

After the meeting, the man in overalls helped stack chairs and wash out cups and the coffeemaker. He glanced in the direction of the woman who thought she might have committed vehicular homicide. He lowered his voice. "That one is about to talk herself into Huntsville pen," he said to Pete.

"What you hear and who you see here stays here. That's the way it's supposed to work," Pete said.

"Anybody who believes that has a lot more trust in people than I do. Let's get something to eat, and I'll take you home."

"You don't know how far I live."

"Believe me, I got nothing better to do. My girlfriend boosted my truck and took off with a one-legged Bible salesman," the man in overalls said. He stared across the row of pews at the woman who had spoken of a dry drunk earlier; his forehead creased with furrows. The woman stood at a window, her attention fixed on the darkness outside, her hands resting on the sill as though they weren't attached to her arms. "Goes to show you, doesn't it?" he said.

"Show you what?" Pete said.

"That woman over there, the one confessed to killing somebody who might not exist. She looks like she just figured out she's created a bigger mess than the one she was already in."

Pete didn't answer. Ten minutes later he drove to a restaurant with the man in overalls, who said his name was Bill, and ordered a piece of cake and a glass of iced tea.

"You got a girl?" Bill said.

"I like to think I do," Pete replied.

"She's in the program, too?"

"No, she's normal. I never could figure why she got involved with the likes of me."

"Where y'all living?"

"A low-rent joint up the road."

Bill seemed to wait for the next words Pete would speak.

"I've been thinking about something," Pete said. "That woman back yonder at the meet?"

"The wet-brain?"

"I wouldn't call her that."

Bill picked up the check and studied it, then looked irritably in the direction of the waitress.

"She was willing to confess to something maybe she didn't do," Pete continued. "Or if she did do it, she was willing to confess to it and maybe go to prison. For her, it didn't make any difference. She just wants to be forgiven for whatever she's done wrong in her life. That takes guts and humility I don't reckon I have."

"That broad can't add," Bill said, getting up with the check in hand. "I'll meet you outside. We need to haul freight. I got to get some shut-eye."

Pete waited in the parking lot, chewing on a plastic soda straw, looking at the stars, Venus winking above a black mountain in the west. What had Bill said earlier about a two-year sobriety chip? He hadn't bothered to accept it? That one didn't quite slide down the pipe. That would be like turning down the Medal of Honor because the ceremony conflicted with an evening of color-matching your socks.

"Ready to roll?" Bill said, exiting the café.

Pete removed the soda straw from his mouth and looked at Bill in the glow of a neon beer sign.

"Problem?" Bill said.

"No, let's boogie," Pete said.

"You still haven't told me where you live."

"At the red light, turn east and keep going till you run out of pavement."

"I thought you said you lived up the road, not east," Bill said, trying to smile.

"I guess I'm not that sharp when it comes to the cardinal points of the compass. Actually, our place is so far back in the sticks, we got to bring the sunshine in on a truck," Pete replied. "That's a fact."

Bill was quiet as they drove eastward through hardpan

countryside dotted with mesquite and old tires and scrap metal that sparkled like mica under the moon. He put a mint on his tongue and sucked on it and looked sideways at Pete as the SUV hit chuckholes that jarred the frame. "How much farther?"

"Another five or six miles."

"What the hell do you do out here?"

"I'm shaving and treating fence posts for a fellow."

"That's interesting. I didn't know there was that much wood around here."

"It's what I do."

"How about your girl?"

"She's got a little Internet business."

"Selling what? Lizard turds?"

"She does right well with it."

Bill drove past another mile marker. Set back between two hills was a lighted house with a gasoline truck parked in the yard and a windmill in back. Horses stood motionlessly in a railed pen where the grass was nubbed down to the dirt.

"Excuse me," Bill said, reaching across Pete.

"What are you doing?"

"It's my Beretta. You see that jackrabbit go across the road? Hang on."

Bill pulled onto the shoulder and got out, staring at a dry wash running from a culvert into a tangle of brush that had leaves like thick green buttons. Out in the moonlight, away from the shadows, were cactuses blooming with yellow and red flowers. A nine-millimeter semiauto hung from Bill's right hand. "Want to take a shot?" he said.

"What for?"

"Sometimes in hot weather, they get worms. But if you gut and skin them right and hang them from wire overnight, so all the heat drains out, they're safe to eat. Come on, hop out."

Pete opened the SUV's door and stepped down on the gravel,

the wind warm on his face, a smell like dried animal dung in his nostrils. The highway was empty in both directions. On the other side of the border, he thought he could see electric lights spread across the bottom of a hill.

"Follow me down here," Bill said. "You can have the first shot. He's gonna spook out of the brush in just a minute. Jackrabbits always do. They don't have the smarts to stay put, like a cottontail does. You never hunted rabbits when you were a kid?"

Pete took his soda straw out of his pocket and put it in his mouth. "Not often. Our farm was so poor the rabbits had to carry their own feed when they hopped across it."

Bill grinned. "Come on, we'll flush him out. Afraid of rattlers?"

"Never given them much thought."

"Think I'm gonna rape you?"

"What?"

"Just a bad joke. But your behavior strikes me as a little bit queer."

"How are you using the word 'queer'?"

"That's what I mean. You're wrapped too tight, trooper. If you ask me, you need to get your pole polished."

Bill seemed to lose interest in the conversation. He reached down and picked up a rock. He studied the clump of brush with buttonlike leaves at the bottom of the wash and flung the rock into it hard enough to break a branch and make a clattering sound far down the wash. "See him scoot? Told you he was in there," he said.

"Yeah, you called it."

Bill turned and faced Pete. His nine-millimeter was pointed downward, along his thigh, the butterfly safety pushed to the fire position. He formed a pocket of air in one cheek, then the other, like a man rinsing his mouth. "Yes, sir, you're a mite spooky, Pete. A hard man to read, I'd say. I bet you blew up some hajji ass over there, didn't you?"

Pete tried to remember giving his name to Bill. Maybe he had, if not at the meet, perhaps at the café. *Think, think, think,* he told himself. He could feel his scalp tightening. "I'd better be getting on home. I'd like to introduce you to my girlfriend."

"She's waiting on you, huh?"

"Yeah, she's a good one about that."

"Wish I was you. You bet I do," Bill said. He looked southward into the darkness, his thoughts hidden. Then he released the magazine on his gun and stuck it in his pocket. He cleared the chamber and inserted the ejected round into the top of the magazine and shoved the magazine back into the frame with the heel of his hand. "Think fast," he said, throwing the gun to Pete.

"Why'd you do that?"

"See if you were paying attention. Scared you, didn't I?"

"Pert' near," Pete replied. "You're quite a card, Bill."

"Not when you come to know me," Bill said. "No, sir, I wouldn't say I was a card at all. Just stick my piece back in the glove box, will you?"

Five miles farther down the road, the hills flattened and the moon sat on the horizon like a huge, bruised white balloon. Up ahead, Pete could see a passing lane, then a brightly lit convenience store and gas-pump island. "We're just about two miles or so from the dirt track that goes to our house," he said. "I can get off up yonder if you want."

"In for a penny, in for a pound. I'll take you all the way."

"I got to be honest about something, Bill."

"You kill somebody with your car while you were in a blackout?"

"The reason I don't have a lot of sobriety is I want to drink."

"You mean now?"

"Now, yesterday, last week, tomorrow, next month. When I catch the bus, the undertaker will probably have to set a case of Bud on my chest to keep me in the coffin."

"What are you trying to tell me?"

"Like they say, unless you've reached your bottom, you're just jerking on your dork. Pull into the store yonder."

"Sure that's what you want to do?"

"Hell, yes, it is. What about you?"

"One or two cold brews wouldn't hurt. I'm no fanatic. What about your girlfriend?"

"She doesn't complain. You'll like her."

"I bet I will," Bill said.

He pulled the SUV into the gas island and got out to fill the tank while Pete went inside the convenience store. The air was thick and warm and smelled of burned diesel. Hundreds of moths had clustered on the overhead lights. Pete took two packs of pepperoni sausage from a shelf and two cartons of king-size beers from the cooler. The cans were silver and blue and beaded with moisture and cold inside the cardboard. He set them on the counter and waited while another customer paid for a purchase, clicking his nails on top of one carton, looking around the store as though he had forgotten something. Then he adjusted his belt and made a face and asked the cashier where the men's room was. The cashier lifted his eyes only long enough to point toward the rear of the store. Pete nodded his thanks and walked between the shelves toward the back exit, out of view from the front window.

Seconds later, he was outside in the dark, running between several eighteen-wheelers parked on a grease-compacted strip of bare earth behind the diesel island. He dropped down into an arroyo and ran deeper into the night, his heart beating, clouds of insects rising into his face, clotting in his mouth and nostrils. The heat lightning flaring in the clouds made him think of the flicker of artillery rounds exploding beyond the horizon, before the reverberations could be felt through the earth.

He crawled through a concrete culvert onto the north side

of the two-lane state highway, then got to his feet and began running across a stretch of hill-flanged hardpan traced with serpentine lines of silt and gravel that felt like crustaceans breaking apart under his shoes.

He had created a geographic forty-five-degree angle between his present location and the Fiesta motel, where Vikki waited for him. The distance, by the way the crow flies, was probably around forty-five miles. With luck, if he ran and walked all night, he would be at the motel by sunrise. As he raced across the ground, the lightning threw his shadow ahead of him, like that of a desperate soldier trying to outrun incoming mail.

Chapter
12

W HEN HACKBERRY HOLLAND was captured by the Chinese south of the Yalu and placed in a boxcar full of marines whose clothes smoked with cold, he tried to convince himself during the long transportation to the POW camp in No Name Valley that he had become part of a great historical epic he would remember one day as one remembers scenes from *War and Peace*. He would be a chronicler who had witnessed two empires collide on a snowy waste whose name would have the significance of Gallipoli or Austerlitz or Gettysburg. A man could have a worse fate.

But he quickly learned that inside the vortex, you did not see the broad currents of history at work. No grand armies stood in position behind rows of cannons that were given the order to fire in sequence, almost in tribute to their own technological perfection rather than as a means of killing the enemy. Nor did you see the unfolded flags flapping in the wind, the caissons and ambulance wagons being wheeled into position, the brilliant colors of the uniforms and the plumes on the helmets of the officers and the sun shining on the drawn sabers. You saw and remembered only the small piece of ground you had occupied, one that would forever be filled with sounds and images that you could not rinse from your dreams.

You remembered shell casings scattered along the bottom of a trench, field dressings stiff with blood, frozen dirt clods raining down on your steel pot, the chugging sound of a 105 round arching out of its trajectory, coming in short. You remembered the rocking of the boxcar, the unshaved jaws of the men staring back at you out of their hooded parkas; you remembered the face of hunger in a shack where fish heads and a dollop of rice were considered a banquet.

When Hackberry returned from San Antonio after the shooting death of Isaac Clawson, he pulled off his boots on the back steps and walked inside the house in his socks, undressed in the bath, and stayed in the shower until there was no more hot water in the tank. Then he dried himself and put on fresh clothes and took his shoeshine kit out on the steps and used the garden hose and a can of Kiwi polish and a brush and a rag to clean Isaac Clawson's blood from the sole and welt of his right boot.

He had burst into the motel room where Isaac Clawson died, not knowing what was on the other side of the door, and stepped into a pool of Clawson's blood, printing the carpet with it, printing the walkway outside, smearing it into the grit and worn fabric that marked the passage of a thousand low-rent trysts.

And that was the way he would always remember that moment—as one of ineptitude and unseemliness and violation. Later, after the arrival of a journalist and a photographer, someone had placed a hand towel over Clawson's head and face. The towel didn't cover his features adequately and provided him neither anonymity nor dignity. Instead, it seemed to add to the degradation done to him by the world.

The shooter, who was probably Preacher Jack Collins, had gotten away. In his wake, he had left the ultimate societal violation for others to clean up. For Hackberry, those details and none other would always define the death of Isaac Clawson. Also, he would never lose the sense that somehow, by stepping in Clawson's blood, he had contributed to the degradation of Clawson's person.

Hackberry used a second rag to wipe the moisture from the hose off his boots. When his boots were dry and clean and smooth to the touch, he slipped them on his feet and put his rags, his shoe brush, and the can of Kiwi polish in a paper bag, soaked the bag with charcoal starter, and burned it in the metal trash barrel by his toolshed. Then he sat down on the steps and looked at the sun rising above the poplars at the back of his property.

Inside the shadows, he saw a doe with twin fawns looking back at him. Two minutes later, Pam Tibbs pulled her cruiser into the driveway and rang the bell.

"Back here," Hackberry yelled.

When she came around the side of the house, she was holding a thermos in one hand and a bag of doughnuts in the other. "You get some sleep?" she said.

"Enough."

"You coming to the office?"

"Why wouldn't I?"

"You eat yet?"

"Yeah, I think I did. Yeah, I'm sure I did."

She sat on the step below him and unscrewed the top of the thermos and popped open the bag of doughnuts. She poured coffee into the thermos top and wrapped a doughnut in a napkin and handed both to him. "You worry me sometimes," she said.

"Pam, I'm your administrative superior. That means we don't personalize certain kinds of considerations."

She glanced at her watch. "Until eight A.M. I'll do what I damn please. How do you like that? Can I get a cup out of your kitchen?"

He started to answer, but she opened the screen door and went inside before he could speak. When she came back out, she filled her cup and sat down beside him. "Clawson went in without backup. His death is not on either one of us," she said.

"I didn't say it was."

"But you thought it."

"Jack Collins got away. We were probably within a hundred feet of him. But he got out of the motel and out of the parking lot and probably out of San Antonio while I was tracking an ICE agent's blood all over the crime scene."

"That's not what's bothering you, is it?"

When he blinked, like a camera lens *clatch*ing open and closing just as quickly, he saw the faces of the Asian women staring up at him from the killing ground behind the stucco church, grains of dirt on their lips and in their nostrils and hair.

"Ballistics shows that all the women were killed by the same weapon," he said. "There was probably only one shooter. From what the FBI knows about Collins, he seems to be the one most capable of that kind of mass murder. We could have put Collins out of business."

"We will. Or if we don't get to him first, the feds will."

Hackberry looked at the doe with her fawns in the poplar trees and could feel Pam's eyes on the side of his face. He thought of his twin sons and his dead wife and the sound the wind made at night when it channeled through the grass in the pasture. Pam moved her foot slightly and touched the side of her shoe against his boot. "Are you listening to me, Hack?"

He could feel a great fatigue seep through his body. He cupped his hands on his knees and turned his head toward her. There was no mistaking the look in her eyes. "I'm too old," he said.

"Too old for what?"

"The things young people do."

"Like what?"

"You got me. How about we change the subject?"

"You're a stubborn and unteachable man. That's why somebody needs to look after you."

He got to his feet, shifting a growing pocket of pain out of his spine. "I must have committed some terrible sins in my past life," he said.

She drank from her coffee, her gaze lifting to his. He let out his breath and went inside to get his hat and gun before going to the office.

THREE DAYS LATER, at five P.M., Ethan Riser called Hackberry at the department and asked him to have a drink.

"Where are you?" Hackberry asked.

"At the hotel."

"What are you doing down here?"

"Soliciting some help."

"The FBI can't handle its problems on its own?"

"I heard you like Jack Daniel's."

"The word is 'liked,' past tense."

"I'll meet you at that joint down the street," Ethan Riser said.

One block from the jail, behind the Eat Café, was a saloon with a sign over the bar that warned the customer YOU ARE STANDING ON THE HARDEST FLOOR IN TEXAS, SO YOU BEST NOT LAND FACEDOWN ON IT. The floor was made from old railroad ties that were grimed black with diesel and creosote and cinders and smoke from prairie fires and anchored to their crossbeams with rusted steel spikes. The bar itself was fitted with a brass footrail that had three cuspidors pushed neatly under it. On top of the bar were a bowl of hard-boiled eggs and a jar of pickled hogs' feet and another jar that contained a urine-yellow liquid and a rattlesnake whose thick coils and open mouth were pressed against the glass. The lights behind the bar were hooded with green plastic shades, and a wood-bladed fan turned slowly on the ceiling.

Ethan Riser was standing at the far end of the bar, a cone-shaped glass of draft beer in one hand, a leather cup in the other.

"What's up?" Hackberry said.

Ethan Riser rattled five poker dice in the leather cup and rolled them on the bar. "Your grandfather really put John Wesley Hardin in the can?"

"He locked him in chains and nailed the links to the bed of a wagon and drove him there personally, after first raking him off the top of his horse."

"Know how Hardin died?"

"He was rolling dice in the Acme saloon in El Paso. He said, 'You got four sixes to beat' to the man drinking next to him. Then he heard a pistol cock behind his head. Then next thing he heard was a pistol ball entering his skull just above the eye."

"I wish I could roll four sixes, but I can't," Riser said. "I've got a psychopath on the loose that some other people want to cut a deal with, even if this lunatic has murdered a federal agent."

"Jack Collins?"

"These people I work with, or under, think Collins can help us nail somebody we've wanted to take off at the neck for a long time. A Russian by the name of Josef Sholokoff. Ever hear of him?"

"No."

"I think my colleagues are wrong on two counts. I believe Collins is a button man others hire and discard like used Kleenex. I don't think he's wired in to people of any importance. Second, I don't believe in making deals with the killers of federal agents." Riser saw the expression in Hackberry's eyes, a brief flicker of disappointment that seemed to make Riser reexamine what he had just said. "Okay, I don't believe in making deals with guys who mow down defenseless women, either."

"Why tell me all this?"

"Because you're smart and not political. Because you've been around awhile and you don't care a lot about what people think of you or what happens to you."

"You know how to say it, Mr. Riser." Hackberry signaled to the bartender. He leaned on his elbows and waited for Riser to continue. Out of the corner of his eye, he could see the beer in Riser's glass going flat.

"We think we got a break down by the Big Bend," Riser said. "A guy caused a commotion in a convenience store, and the clerk called it in. The guy had been putting gas in his SUV, and his buddy had gone inside to buy beer. Except the buddy left the beer on the counter and went out the back door and hauled ass."

The bartender set a glass of ice and carbonated water and lime slices in front of Hackberry.

"You drink that?" Riser asked.

"Go on about the guy."

"He came into the convenience store and wanted to know where Pete went. The clerk said he didn't know. The guy called him a liar and pulled a semiauto out of his overalls. The clerk called nine-one-one, and the sheriff decided to lift some prints off the fuel-pump handle. They got a hit. The guy with the semiauto is Robert Lee Motree, also known as Bobby Lee Motree. He did six months in the Broward County stockade for illegal possession of a firearm. He's also worked for a New Orleans private investigative service owned by a guy named Arthur Rooney. You recognize that name?"

"Yeah, but I thought Rooney ran some escort fronts in Houston or Dallas," Hackberry said.

"That's the same guy. Rooney got blown out of New Orleans by Katrina and is in Galveston now." Riser seemed to hesitate, as though his words were leading him into an area he hadn't fully given himself consent to enter.

"Go on," Hackberry said.

"Rooney is a careful man, but we put a tap on his current

punch of the day. He made a call from her apartment to a contract hitter by the name of Hugo Cistranos. On the tape, it sounds like Rooney and Cistranos are going to clip Jack Collins."

"Why?"

"Get this. Collins cut off Rooney's finger with a barber's razor on Rooney's own desktop." Riser started laughing.

"What's the Russian's role in all this?"

"We're not sure. He's a big player in Arizona and Nevada and California. He owns whole networks of whores and porn studios and has a lot of outlaw bikers muling his tar and crystal meth up from the border. How much China white do you see here?"

"Not much. It's upscale stuff. Addicts with money can smoke it and not worry about needles and AIDS."

"DEA says a two-million-dollar shipment was off-loaded from a two-engine plane that landed on a highway in your county last week."

"Tell them thanks for letting us in on that."

"If you were looking for Vikki Gaddis and Pete Flores down in the Big Bend, where would you start?"

"I'd have to give that some thought."

"You don't like us much, do you?" Riser drank from his beer and wiped his mouth.

"I like y'all just fine. I just don't trust you," Hackberry said.

THAT NIGHT HACKBERRY ate dinner by himself in a back booth at a restaurant out on the highway, his Stetson crown-down on the seat beside him. Working-class families were lined up at the salad bar, and country music filtered through the swinging doors of the lounge annex on the far side of the cashier's counter. He saw Pam Tibbs enter the front door with an athletic-looking man dressed in sport clothes and shined loafers, his dark hair wet-combed and sun-bleached at the tips, his face confident and tanned and unwrinkled by either worry or age. Pam wore a purple skirt and black pumps and a black top with a gold cross and chain; she had just had her hair cut and looked not only lovely but ten years younger than her age in the way that women look when they love someone. When she saw Hackberry, she jiggled her fingers at him and went inside the lounge with her friend.

Ten minutes later, she came back out of the swinging doors and sat down across from Hackberry. He could smell her perfume and the hint of bourbon and ice and crushed cherries on her breath. "Join us," she said.

"Who is 'us'?" he asked, and wondered if she caught the tinge of resentment in his voice.

"My cousin and me. His wife will be here in a few minutes," she said, her fingers spreading on the table, her expression not quite able to contain her surprise at his reaction.

"Thanks, I have to get home."

"Hack?"

"What?"

"Come on."

"Come on, what?"

He felt her foot touch his under the table. "Ease up," she said.

"Pam—"

"I mean it. Give yourself a break. People can't be alone all the time."

"You're my chief deputy. Act like it," he said. He looked sideways to see if anyone had heard him.

"What if I am?" she said, leaning forward now.

"I'd like to finish my dinner."

"You make me mad. I want to hit you sometimes."

"I'm going to get some salad."

"Your chicken-fried steak will get cold."

Hackberry thought he might have discovered the source of many unexplained brain aneurysms.

* * *

THAT NIGHT HE returned home and sat on a folding chair in the yard under a sky that roiled with thunderclouds. It was not a rational act. The hour was late, the wind bending the poplar trees at the foot of his property, the air filled with bits of desiccated matter that stung his face like insects. Overhead, yellow pools of dry lightning flared and pulsed in the clouds but made no sound. Even though he had soaked the lawn that morning, the ground under his feet felt as hard as brick. Five or six deer had clustered down in the trees as though preparing for an impending storm. Then he realized the deer were there for other reasons. On a rise just above his property, he saw the silhouettes of four coyotes slink across the crest. When lightning lit the sky behind them, he saw the yellow-gray of their coats, the peculiar way they hung their heads, the neck bones and jaws loose and not completely connected, a suggestion of slather on the teeth and lips.

Was this what it was all about? he wondered. One creature killing and eating another? Or even worse, the fanged predator with eyes in the front hunting down and tearing apart the gentle grass-eating animal born with eyes on the sides of its head, forever condemned to be food for coyotes and wolves and cougars and, finally, man with his sharpened stick?

What was it that had bothered him about Ethan Riser? The fact that he could drink normally and walk away from it? That he represented an organization with power that had almost global reach? Or Hackberry's refusal to accept the notion that the Ethan Risers of the world were functional and made the system work and, in spite of all their inadequacies and failures, did an enormous amount of good?

No, that wasn't it, either. Some people dwelled apart and didn't fit. It was that simple. Preacher Jack Collins was one of them. In all probability, he was a psychopath who, upon his death, would continue to look upon himself as normal, stepping through a hole in the dimension still convinced it was the world that was wrong and not he. But there were both male and female counterparts to men like Jack Collins. They wore badges or Roman collars or climbed fire ladders into flaming buildings or did triage in battalion aid stations and, like Collins, never discussed their difference or the events in their lives that had sawed them loose from the seminal glue holding the rest of humankind together.

Saint Paul had written that perhaps there were angels living among us. If so, perhaps this was the bunch he was talking about. But before any one of them congratulated himself, he needed to be aware of the dues that went with membership. If an individual, through either his own volition or events over which he had no control, found himself taking up residence in a country undefined by flags or physical borders, he could be assured of one immediate and abiding consequence: He was on his own, and solitude and loneliness would probably be his companions unto the grave.

The greatest irony was that celibacy often went with the residency, less out of spiritual choice than circumstance. And those who called celibacy a gift were usually, in Hackberry's opinion, those who lived twenty-four hours a day inside the iron maiden, their flesh tormented by the spikes of their unacknowledged desire.

He leaned forward in his folding chair and stretched his lower back, his sciatica like a fire creeping along his spinal cord.

He saw the cruiser turn off the road and come up his driveway. He heard the doorbell ring but did not bother to get up to answer it. When Pam Tibbs came around the side of the house, he saw that she had changed out of her evening clothes into jeans and a departmental khaki shirt. She was wearing her gun belt and cuffs and slapjack and Mace.

"What are you doing here?" he said.

"This month I go on at oh-one-hundred Saturdays," she replied.

"That doesn't address the question."

"You always sit in the yard by yourself at one in the morning?"

"Sometimes my back lights up and I have to wait for it to pass."

She was standing in front of him, looking down at him, the curly ends of her hair hanging against her cheeks, her eyes bright in the shadows. He could hear her breathing and see her breasts rising and falling under her shirt. "You want me to resign?" she said.

"No, I just want you to accept certain realities."

"Like what?"

"You're still a young woman. The world is yours. Don't mistake sympathy or admiration or friendship for love."

"Who the hell are you to tell me what to think?"

"Your goddamn boss is what I am."

"You never swear, Hack. You're going to start now?"

"I told you, I'm old. You need to let me alone, Pam."

"Then run me off," she said. "Until then I'm not going anywhere."

She was standing closer to his chair, closer than she should have been. He stood up, towering over her. He could smell the heat in her clothes and the warm odor in her hair. She put her hands on both of his hips and pressed the crown of her head into the center of his chest. He could feel his mouth go dry and a thickness growing in his loins.

"The best women always fall in love with the wrong men," he said. "You're one of those, kid."

"Don't call me that."

"You're late for your shift," he said.

He left her there and went inside the house and locked the door behind him.

Chapter
13

L<small>IAM</small> E<small>RIKSSON HAD</small> parked his pickup truck, one with a camper shell inserted in the bed, down in a sandy bottom thinly shaded by mesquite trees. A shiny green liquid, one with the viscosity of an industrial lubricant, wound through the pebbled creek bed, and gnats and horseflies hung in the brush along the banks. In the distance was a long stretch of baked flatland that glimmered like salt and, beyond it, a range of blue hills. Bobby Lee Motree sat on a rock and took a longneck from a bucket of ice and cracked off the cap.

"I don't see how you can cut up a sweet piece like that," he said.

"Business is business. Why be sentimental about it? Besides, I found it, so it ain't no skin off my ass," Liam replied.

Liam stood at the rear door of his camper shell, touching the blade of a hacksaw with his thumb. He was bare-chested and wore a straw hat with a wilted brim, like one a female gardener would wear, and hiking shorts with big snap pockets and alpine shoes with lugs on the soles. He had shaved off his orange beard after he had screwed up at the check-cashing store in San Antonio; now the lower half of his face looked like emery paper. Or maybe the skin of a freshly exhumed corpse, Bobby Lee thought.

"You should have left your beard, or maybe just trimmed or dyed it," Bobby Lee said.

"Something eating on you?"

Yeah, there was. But exactly how much information could he trust Liam with? Bobby Lee bit on his lip and thought about it.

Liam grinned, showing the gaps in his teeth, and locked down a pump shotgun in a machinist vise that was bolted to the bed of his truck. He had already wood-rasped the stock into a pistol grip and machine-sanded the wood smooth. He set the hacksaw blade flush with the pump and began sawing.

"I think I've figured out where the soldier boy is living," Bobby Lee said.

"How'd you do that?" Liam asked, still grinning.

"He led me south, then way to hell and gone out east. I think he's probably about the same distance in the exact opposite direction."

"You were always good at ciphering things out, Bobby Lee. Matter of bloodline, maybe," Liam said. "I'm referring to the fact that Robert E. Lee is in your pedigree."

Was Liam coming on wise? Bobby Lee narrowed his eyes. All right, let's take a run at it, he thought. "We've worked lots of gigs, me and you."

"We've splattered the walls, bud. They're never gonna know who did any of it, either," Liam said.

"But this current deal has gotten complicated." Bobby Lee let his words hang in the air.

Liam stopped sawing, not raising his eyes. He wiped the cut in the shotgun's barrel with an oily rag. "Does this have something to do with that call you got from Hugo?"

"Hugo says we get rid of the girl and the soldier. Then we do

Nick Dolan and his wife, with special instructions for the wife. Then we do Preacher."

Liam began sawing again, his back turned to Bobby Lee. "I suspect I misheard you on that last part."

"Jack cut off Artie Rooney's finger, and now he's shaking him down for a half mil. Hugo says it's time for Jack to join the Hallelujah Chorus."

Liam turned around. "Do Preacher? You're actually serious? You haven't started fooling with acid again?"

"I'm taking you into my confidence, Liam. I don't like the way things have turned out. But Preacher is slipping. I think it's because of the deal behind the church."

"Yeah, well, nobody planned that one. If that's on anybody, it's on Hugo."

"You in or not, Liam?"

"Cap Preacher? That's like trying to kill death."

"He's got a weakness. It's got something to do with sugar. Or candy or pastry. I don't get it. But he's got something wrong with him. A hooker I knew said Jack almost died once because of something he ate."

"You're that scared of him?" Without waiting for an answer, Liam casually resumed cutting off the shotgun's barrel, the muscles in his back rippling like warm tallow as he worked.

Bobby Lee felt a blood vessel pulse in his temple. He took a sip of his beer before he spoke. "Want to add anything to that last remark?"

"Why would I want to do that?"

"Because I'm having a little trouble handling it."

"I was talking about myself. Preacher scares the hell out of me. He's a mean motor scooter and crazy besides."

Bobby Lee started to speak again but this time held his tongue. He cracked open another beer and drank from it, realizing irrefutably that he had made his problems worse by taking Liam into his confidence. He had stood up for Liam with Preacher, and this was what he got for it. Liam was no different from any other gutter rat in the business. He had no mercy, either. He had proved that when he went to work on the owner of the diner, what-was-his-name, Junior Kraut Face or something. Now Bobby Lee had both Preacher and Liam to worry about, plus the fact that he hadn't gotten paid, plus the fact that Preacher had popped a federal agent, which was sure to bring down a ton of heat on all of them.

Liam finished sawing through the shotgun's barrel and sailed it across the creek bed into a cluster of sandstone boulders. He listened as the barrel tinkled and rolled down the side of a ravine. He begin fitting a series of twelve-gauge shells into the magazine, pushing them in with his thumb until the spring in the loading tube came tight. "I already took out the sportsman's plug," he said. "Five double-aught bucks. You want to see the paint fly? These babies can do it."

He aimed at a jackrabbit running across the hardpan, leading it with the sawed tip of the barrel, one eye closed. Then he breathed out a popping sound and lowered the gun. He grinned and smacked Bobby Lee on the shoulder, causing him to spill beer down the front of his shirt. "Relax, enjoy the time you got," Liam said. "That's my philosophy. Life's a party, right?"

Bobby Lee took a drink from his bottle, eyeing Liam with the caution he would show a snake coiled in the shade of scrub brush.

"You spoke up for me when Preacher wanted to rip my ass," Liam said. "I'm not forgetting that. We're buds. Crack me a beer."

DANNY BOY LORCA was squatted behind the jail at sunup Monday morning when Hackberry parked his truck and started inside. Danny Boy's skin had the dark, smudged coloration of someone who cooked as a matter of course over open charcoal pits or who cleared and burned brush for a living or who worked land that had been blackened by wildfires. His thick hair, cut like an Apache's, did not look unwashed as much as dull and ash-powdered, the scars from jailhouse-knife beefs of years ago like dead worms on his hands and forearms. He was drawing a picture in the dirt with a sharpened stick.

"What you got there, Danny Boy?" Hackberry asked.

"Face I saw in a dream."

"You here to see me about something?"

Danny Boy stood up. He wore jeans that were so tight that they looked painted on his body, and a long-sleeve calico shirt notched around the upper arms with purple garters. Stuffed in his clothes, he had the shape of a giant banana. "Pete Flores called me. He needs me to get him a car. Him and Vikki Gaddis want to go to Montana."

"Come inside."

"I been dry three days. I'm staying clear of jail for a while," Danny Boy said, not moving. The sky in the west was a metallic blue still caught between darkness and first light, the horizon layered with a long band of steel-colored clouds that could have been either dust or rain mist. Danny Boy sniffed at the air and stared at the sky as though he had just heard a brief rumble of thunder that had no source.

"I thought we were friends," Hackberry said. "I thought you trusted me. You think I'll do you harm?"

Danny Boy's eyes seemed full of sleep when he looked back at Hackberry. Hackberry could not remember seeing Danny Boy smile, not ever. "Pete said he got away from a guy who was trying to kill him. Somewhere down by Big Bend. He said the guy was at an A.A. meeting in a church. If Pete can get holt of a car, he's gonna drive straight through to Montana."

"Where's Pete staying?"

Danny Boy shook his head, indicating that he didn't know or he wasn't prepared to say.

"How about Vikki?"

"Waitressing and playing in a restaurant or a club. I told Pete I didn't have no money, but he better not be thinking about stealing a car. He says he ain't going down for the murder of them Asian women."

"He won't. I promise."

"Last night I dreamed about rain. I woke up and thought it was hitting on my roof. But it was grasshoppers flying into the windmill and the screens. You say Pete ain't going down for them murders. But Pete was there when they got killed. Guys like Pete have a hard time in jail. They try to go their own way and get in trouble. He'll be in Huntsville for a long time."

"Not if I can help it."

But Danny Boy had lost interest in the conversation in the same way he had lost interest years ago in the promises of most white people. He was staring at the face he had drawn in the dirt. The Apache haircut, the wide brow, the square jaw, and the small eyes all looked like his own. He rubbed the sole of his shoe back and forth across the drawing, smearing it back into the earth.

"Why'd you do that?"

"He's one of them ancient rain gods. There was a bunch of them living here when this was a giant valley full of corn. But the rain gods went away. They ain't coming back, either."

"How do you know that?"

"They got no reason to. We don't believe in them no more."

AT EIGHT A.M. Hackberry called Pam Tibbs into his office.

"Yes, sir?" she said.

"I have a general idea where Vikki Gaddis and Pete Flores

might be. My back is flaring up, and I need you to drive me," he said.

"You ought to see a doctor," she said. Her eyes left his. "Sorry."

"I depend on you because you're smart, Pam. I'm not patronizing you when I say that."

"You don't have to explain yourself."

He let it pass. "We'll be back late tonight or maybe tomorrow. Get whatever you need out of your locker." But he couldn't let it pass after all. Why did she bother him like this? "I *know* I don't have to explain myself. I was trying to . . . Never mind."

"What?"

"Nothing. Would you get me an aspirin, please? Bring the box."

At eight-thirty A.M., Hackberry and Pam Tibbs were doing eighty miles an hour down the four-lane, the emergency flasher rippling silently. Hackberry lay back in the passenger seat, half asleep, his Stetson tilted over his eyes, his long legs extended.

Where do you look for a guitar-picking woman in the state of Texas?

Anywhere.

Where do you look for a guitar-picking woman who sings "Will the Circle Be Unbroken" to a beer-joint audience?

In a place that will probably remember the experience for a long time.

Hackberry knew his errand was probably a foolish one. He was out of his jurisdiction and trying to save young people who trusted neither him, his department, nor the system he represented. Cassandra had been given knowledge of the future and simultaneously condemned to a lifetime of being disbelieved and rejected. The wearisome preoccupation of the elderly—namely, the conviction that they had already seen the show but could never pass on the lessons they had learned from it—was not unlike Cassandra's burden, except the anger and bitterness of old people was not the stuff of Homeric epics.

Hackberry shifted in the seat, pulling his hat lower on his face, and tried to get out of his funk. The cruiser hit a bump and forced his eyes open. He hadn't realized how far he and Pam had driven. He saw the shapes of mountains in the south and the buildings and planted trees and the planned neighborhoods of a small town spread along the side of a long geological slope that looked as though the land had suddenly tilted into the sky.

"You fell asleep," Pam said.

"Where are we?"

"Not far from the convenience store where Bobby Lee Motree pulled a semiauto on the night clerk. Did the FBI get you a mug shot of him yet?"

"They will eventually. They have their own problems to deal with."

"Why do you make excuses for them?"

"Because a lot of them are decent people."

"I bet they love their grandmothers and they're kind to animals, too." She glanced sideways at him, her expression hidden behind her aviator shades, her mouth a flat line.

"My grandfather was a Texas Ranger," Hackberry said. "He and some of his friends went on a raid into Mexico after Pancho Villa crossed the river and killed a bunch of civilians. My grandfather and his friends attacked a train loaded with Villa's soldiers. The Texans had captured a Lewis gun. They caught a bunch of those poor devils in an uncoupled cattle car that was rolling downhill. My grandfather said their blood was blowing out of the boards and fanning in the wind like the discharge from a chute in a slaughterhouse."

"I don't get your point."

"My grandfather was an honest lawman. He did some things that bothered his conscience, but you don't judge a person by one episode or event in his life, and you don't judge people categorically, either. Ethan Riser is a good man."

"You really were an ACLU lawyer."

Hackberry removed his hat and ran a comb through his hair. He could feel his gun belt biting into his hips. "Put it on pause, will you, Pam?"

"Say again?"

"That must be the convenience store yonder," he said.

They parked and introduced themselves to the assistant manager. He had the manic look and behavioral manner of someone who might have spent his life inside a windstorm. His description of Bobby Lee Motree was not helpful. "You tend to forget what people look like when they're waving a pistol in your face," he said.

"You don't happen to have the surveillance tape, do you?" Hackberry said.

"Them FBI people took it."

"Have you ever seen Pete Flores?"

"Who?"

"The kid who left the beer on your counter and took off. The one with the long scar on his face."

"No, sir. I can tell you one thing about him, though. That boy can flat haul ass."

"How's that?"

"After the weirdo with the gun drove off, I went out back looking for the kid with the scar. I saw him there on the other side of the road in the moonlight, his shirttail flying, heading due north. He went over the top of a rail fence like he had wings on."

"Did you get the weirdo's tag number?" Hackberry asked.

"There was mud smeared on it." The assistant manager lifted up a baseball bat and dropped it on top of the counter. "The next time I see that guy, I'm gonna park his head over Yellow House Peak. Them FBI people are gonna be hauling off a man with no head."

Hackberry and Pam got back in the cruiser, the air conditioner running, the sun white and straight overhead. "Where to?" Pam asked.

"Danny Boy Lorca said Pete told him he'd met a guy at an A.A. meeting who tried to kill him," Hackberry said. "How many A.A. meetings are held on a given night in a rural area like this?"

"Not many. Maybe one or two," she said.

"You ever attend one?"

"My mother did."

"Let's go back to that last town."

She pulled out on the road, blowing gravel off the back tires. "I've never seen you drink," she said.

"What about it?"

"I thought maybe you went to A.A. meetings at one time or another."

"No, I just don't drink anymore. When people ask about it, that's what I tell them. 'I used to drink, but I don't anymore.' "

She looked across the seat at him, her eyes unreadable behind her shades. "Why'd you quit?"

There was a taste like pennies in his saliva. He rolled down the window and spat. He wiped his mouth and stared at the countryside sweeping by, the grass on the hillsides brown and bending in the wind, a cattle truck parked by a turnout where a historical marker stood, the cattle bawling in the heat. "I quit because I didn't want to be like other members of my family."

"Alcoholism runs in your family?"

"No, killing people does," he said. "They killed Indians, Mexicans, gunmen, Kaiser Bill's heinies—anyone they could get in their sights, they blew the hell out of them."

She concentrated on the road and was silent a long time.

At the intersection of the county and state highways, Hackberry used a pay phone to call the regional hotline of Alcoholics Anonymous. The woman who answered said that only one meeting was available in the area on the night Hackberry asked about. It was held in a white frame church house just north of the intersection where Hackberry was calling from.

"There're some early-bird meetings. I also have a schedule for Terlingua and Marathon, if you don't mind driving a piece," she said.

"No, I think the one at the church is the one I'm interested in. That's the only one here'bouts on Tuesday nights, right?"

"That's right."

"Who can I talk to there?"

"Anybody at the meeting."

"No, I mean right now."

"You think you're going to drink?"

"I'm an officer of the law, and I'm investigating a multiple homicide . . . Hello?"

"I have to think about what you just told me." There was a short pause. "I finished thinking about it. Thanks for calling the A.A. hotline. Goodbye." The line went dead.

Hackberry and Pam drove through town and found the church on the east side of the state highway. A rail of a man was hammering shingles on the roof, his denim shirt buttoned at the throat and neck against the heat, his armpits dark with sweat, his knees spread like a clamp on the roof's spine. Pam and Hackberry got out of the cruiser and looked up at him, trying to shield their eyes from the glare.

"You the pastor?" Hackberry called up.

"I was when I got up this morning."

"I'm looking for a young man named Pete Flores. Maybe he attended an A.A. meeting here."

"I wouldn't know," the man said.

"Why not?" Hackberry said.

"They don't use last names."

"I've got a picture of him. Mind if I come up?"

"Doubt if it'll do any good."

"Why not?"

"I let them use the building, but I don't go to their meetings, so I'm not real sure who attends them."

"Give me the picture, Hack. I'll take it up," Pam said.

"I'm fine," Hackberry said. He mounted the ladder and climbed steadily up the rungs, his neutral expression held carefully in place as a bright red fire blossomed in the small of his back. He worked the photo Ethan Riser had given him out of his pocket and handed it to the pastor. The pastor studied it, his uncut hair stuck like wet black points on the back of his neck.

"No, sir, I never saw this fellow at my church. What'd he do?" said the pastor.

"He's a witness to a crime and may be in danger."

The pastor looked at the photo again, then handed it back to Hackberry without comment.

"You said you never saw him at your church."

"No, sir, I haven't."

"But maybe you saw him somewhere else."

The pastor took the photo back, his face starting to show the strain of squatting on the roof's slant. "Maybe I saw a kid in a filling station or up at the café. He wasn't in uniform, though. He had a scar on his face. It looked like a long drop of pink wax running down his skin. That's why I remember him. But the soldier in this picture don't have a scar."

"Think hard, Reverend. Where'd you see him?"

"I just don't recall. I'm sorry."

"You ever hear of a woman here'bouts who likes to sing country spirituals in nightclubs or beer joints?"

"No, sir. But you must do mighty interesting work. Let me know if you ever want to trade jobs."

* * *

BOBBY LEE'S FRUSTRATION with events and with Liam's weather-vane personality was starting to reach critical mass. It was Liam's truck that had broken down on the state highway, forcing them to call for a tow to a shithole with one restaurant and one mechanic's shop. It was Liam who had left vinyl garbage bags spread all over the bottom of his camper shell, causing the mechanic to ask if they were trying to get a jump on deer season. It was Liam who had droned on and on about how Bobby Lee had screwed up at the convenience store, his eyes as self-righteous and mindless as a moron's, his tombstone teeth too large for his mouth.

They were in a booth at the back of the restaurant, Liam's gym bag by his foot, a change of clothes and a shaving kit and the cut-down shotgun zipped inside. They were waiting for the mechanic's brother-in-law to drive them forty-five miles to the motel where Bobby Lee's SUV was parked under the porte cochere.

"If you hadn't pulled your piece on a nerd in a convenience store, we wouldn't be having this problem," Liam said. "We could be using your vehicle instead of mine. I told you I had transmission trouble last week. You can't get information out of a nerd without sticking a gun up his nose?"

"I didn't pull my piece. You got that? It fell out of my belt. But I didn't pull it deliberately, Liam. How about giving it a rest?"

The waitress brought their food and poured more water in their glasses. They stopped speaking while she tended to the table. She set a basket with packaged crackers between them, then retrieved salt and pepper shakers from another table and set them by the basket. Bobby Lee and Liam waited. She loomed over them, her big shoulders and wide hips and industrial-strength perfume somehow shrinking the space around them.

"You guys want anything else?" she asked.

"No, we're good here," Bobby Lee said.

"I need some steak sauce," Liam said.

Bobby Lee smoldered in silence until the waitress brought a bottle of A.1. to the table and went away.

"What are you so heated up about?" Liam asked.

"Take off that hat."

"What for?"

"It's stupid. It looks like a woman's."

Liam stuffed a complete slice of white bread in his mouth and chewed it with his mouth open.

"We got to have an understanding, Liam. I trusted you when I told you maybe Preacher has got to go off the board. I got to know we're on the same wavelength here. I can't have you bitching me out all the time."

"You don't like to hear the truth, that's your problem."

Outside, the sun was red on the horizon, dust rising off the hills in a brown nimbus. Bobby Lee felt as though someone had stuck a metal key into the base of his neck and wound up his nerve endings as tightly as piano wire. He started to eat, then set down his fork and stared emptily at his plate.

He had played the whole deal wrong. Liam was not to be trusted or confided in; he was a whiner who scapegoated his friends. But if Liam wasn't a bud, who was? Who was the purist in their midst? Who was the guy who did the work less for the money than for the strange visions that seemed to crawl across the backs of his eyelids?

"Looks like you're doing some heavy thinking," Liam said.

"You think I blew it for us at the convenience store, that I should have handled it different, that I should have let the soldier take off on me and not even go inside."

"I thought you said to drop it."

"I just want you to put yourself in my place and tell me what you would have done, Liam."

"When this is over, we'll both get laid. I got a couple of discount coupons from *Screw* magazine." Liam waited, grinning idiotically.

Bobby Lee looked into Liam's eyes. They were a translucent blue, their moral vacuity creating its own kind of brilliance, the pupils like dead insects trapped under glass. They were the eyes of a man to whom there was no significant reality beyond the tips of his fingers.

"When this is over, I'm going back to college. My sister has a house in Lauderdale. I'm gonna take her kids to Orlando," Bobby Lee said.

"Everybody says that, but it doesn't work that way. Can you see yourself selling shoes to old guys in Miami Beach with smelly socks?"

"I'm studying to be an interior decorator."

But Liam wasn't listening. His attention had shifted to a man and woman who were sitting at a booth by the entrance to the restaurant.

"Don't turn around yet, but check out John Wayne over there," he said. "I'm not kidding. From the side, he looks just like Wayne. He's even got Calamity Jane with him. She must be his traveling punch. Who said western movies are dead?"

Chapter 14

THE AIR-CONDITIONING WAS turned up full-blast in the restaurant, fogging the bottoms of the windows. Hackberry and Pam had taken a booth close to the front counter. Family people were eating dinner in the back section, which was separated from the front by a latticework partition decorated along the top with plastic flowers. A church bus pulled up in front, and a throng of preteens came in and piled into the empty booths. Workingmen were drinking beer at the counter and watching a baseball game on a flat-screen television high on the wall. As the sun set on the hills, the interior of the restaurant was lit with a warm red glow that did not subtract from its refrigerated coolness but only added to its atmosphere of goodwill and end-of-the-day familiality.

Hackberry put his hand over his mouth and yawned and stared at the menu, the words on it swimming into a blur.

"How's your back?" Pam asked.

"Who said anything about my back?"

"Back pain saps a person's energy. It shows in a person's face."

"What shows in my face are too many birthdays."

"Do you know we covered a hundred square miles of Texas today?"

"We might do twice that tonight."

"I think they're in Mexico."

"Why?"

"Because that's what I would do."

"Vikki Gaddis might. Pete won't."

The waitress returned to the table and took their order and went away. Pam sat stiffly in the booth, her shoulders pushed against the backrest. "Vikki will blow Dodge, but Pete will hang tough? Because that's what swinging dicks do? Girls aren't swinging dicks, you're saying?"

"Pete is one of those unfortunate guys who will never accept the possibility that their country will use them up and then spit them out like yesterday's bubble gum. Can you stop using that language?"

She scratched at a place between her eyes and looked out the window, her badge glinting on her khaki shirt.

As they waited for their food, Hackberry felt the day catch up to him like a hungry animal released from its leash. He ate three aspirin for the pain in his back and gazed idly at the people in the restaurant. Except for the television set on the wall and the refrigerated air, the scene could have been lifted out of the year 1945. The people were the same, their fundamentalist religious views and abiding sense of patriotism unchanged, their blue-collar egalitarian instincts undefined and vague and sometimes bordering on nativism but immediately recognizable to an outsider as inveterately Jacksonian. It was the America of Whitman and Jack Kerouac, of Willa Cather and Sinclair Lewis, an improbable confluence of contradictions that had become Homeric without its participants realizing their importance to the world.

If someone were to ask Hackberry Holland what his childhood had been like, he would answer the question with an image rather than an explanation. He would describe a Saturday-afternoon trip to town to watch a minor-league baseball game with his father the history professor. The courthouse square was bordered by elevated sidewalks inset with tethering rings that bled rust like a ship's scuppers. A khaki-painted World War I howitzer stood in the shadows of a giant oak on the courthouse lawn. The dime store, a two-story brick building fronted with a wood colonnade, featured a popcorn machine that overflowed onto the concrete like puffed white grain swelling out of a silo. The adjacent residential neighborhood was lined with shade trees and bungalows and nineteenth-century white frame houses whose galleries were sunken in the middle and hung with porch swings, and each afternoon at five P.M. the paperboy whizzed down the sidewalk on a bicycle and smacked the newspaper against each set of steps with the eye of a marksman.

But more important in the memory of that long-ago American moment was the texture of light after a sun shower. It was gold and soft and stained with the contagious deep green of the trees and lawns. The rainbow that seemed to dip out of the sky into the ball diamond somehow confirmed one's foolish faith that both the season and one's youth were eternal.

Now Hackberry dipped a taco chip in a bowl of red sauce and put it in his mouth. He picked up his glass of iced tea and drank from it. A bunch of the kids from the church bus brushed by the table on their way to the restroom. Then they were gone, and he found himself looking through the latticework partition at the face of a man who seemed familiar but not to the degree that Hackberry could place him. The man wore a gardener's hat, the wide brim shadowing his features. The waitress working the back of the restaurant kept moving back and forth behind the latticework, further obstructing Hackberry's view.

Hackberry pinched the fatigue out of his eyes and straightened his spine.

"You developed back trouble from your time as a POW?" Pam said.

"I guess you could say I didn't have it when I went to Korea, but I did when I returned."

"You draw disability?"

"I didn't apply for it."

"Why is it I knew you were going to say that?"

"Because you're omniscient."

He was grinning. She propped her knuckles under her chin and tried not to laugh, then gave it up, her eyes crinkling, holding on his, a smile spreading across her face.

The waitress brought their Mexican dinners to the table, gripping each plate with a damp dish towel, the heat and steam rising into her eyes. "Be careful. It's real hot," she said.

LIAM WAS ORDERING dessert, his eyes doing a breast inventory as the waitress leaned over and picked up his dirty dishes.

"Want a little R and R across the border tonight?" he said after the waitress was gone.

"What I can't understand is why we haven't been able to find the motel. It's the Siesta motel, right?" Bobby Lee said, ignoring Liam's suggestion.

"I looked on the Internet. There's no such motel down here. You want to get laid tonight or not?"

"I want to find the soldier and his squeeze and do our job and go home."

"That's when we take care of Preacher?"

"I didn't say that."

"Maybe it's the smart move."

"In what way?"

"He and Hugo always get the high end on payday. Why should a guy get extra pay because he's crazy?"

"Preacher is smart in a different way. That doesn't mean he's crazy," Bobby Lee said.

"Having second thoughts?"

"We're soldiers. We do what we're told," Bobby Lee said, picking up the salt shaker and looking at it.

"You're lots of things, Bobby Lee, but soldier isn't one of them."

"Want to explain that?"

"What did you say you're studying? Interior design? I bet you'll be good at it."

Bobby Lee put a matchstick in his mouth. "I got to take a drain," he said. He went into the restroom and soaped his hands and forearms and rinsed his skin clean and cupped cold water into his face with both hands. He had to swallow when he looked into the mirror. His bald spot seemed to be spreading outward. His eyebrows formed a single black line across his brow, giving his face a crunched look, as though a great weight were pressing down on his head. His throat was starting to sag under his chin; his unshaved jaw had specks of gray. He was twenty-eight years old.

This whole gig stank. Worse, he'd allied himself with Liam Eriksson, who had just mocked him to his face. Bobby Lee sat on the stool inside the toilet stall and checked the bars on his cell phone, then punched in Preacher's number.

"Yeah?" Jack's voice said.

"Jack, glad you're there, man."

"What's going on, Bobby Lee?"

"Where are you?"

"Like the Beach Boys say, 'I get—'"

"Yeah, I know, you get around."

"Got some news for me?" Jack said, undisturbed by Bobby Lee's impatience.

"Not exactly."

"What did you call me for?"

"Just checking in."

"Having trouble with Liam?"

"How'd you know?"

"You got a lot of talent, Bobby Lee. Of the seven deadly sins, envy is the only one that doesn't have a trade-off."

"You lost me."

"Lust, hate, covetousness, pride, sloth, greed, and gluttony bring with them an appreciable degree of pleasure. But an envious man gets no relief. It's like a guy drinking liquid Drano because another guy has wine on his table. One thing you can be sure about, though. The man who envies you will eventually blindside you proper."

"Liam envies me?"

"What does a fellow like me know?"

"A lot. You know a lot, Jack."

"Something going on, boy?"

"Nothing I can't take care of."

"That's the way to talk."

"See you, Jack."

Bobby Lee closed his cell phone and stared at the back of the stall door. It was patinaed with drawings of genitalia that had been scratched into the paint. For just a moment he wondered if the drawings were not an accurate representation of the thoughts that went on inside Liam's head. How could he have been willing to throw in his lot with a bozo like Liam and betray a pro like Jack? Jack might be a religious head case, but he was no Judas, and Hugo and Liam were. Taking off Artie Rooney's finger seemed like an extreme measure, but at least with Jack, you always knew where you stood.

So where did that leave Bobby Lee?

Answer: playing it cool, gliding on that old-time R&B. A little time would pass and all this would be over and he'd be bone-fishing in the Keys, eating fried conch, drinking St. Pauli Girl beer, and watching a molten-red sun slip into the waters off Mallory Square.

As he started back toward the booth, he glanced through the latticework partition that separated him from the front of the restaurant. Suddenly, he realized he was looking at the couple Liam had told him to turn around and check out. The woman wore jeans and a khaki shirt and a badge on her breast. The tall man Liam had said looked like John Wayne was sitting across from her in the booth, his Stetson crown-down on the seat. He was cutting up his food, his profile silhouetted against the sunset. Bobby Lee could also see the holstered white-handled blue-black thumb-buster revolver that hung from his gun belt.

Bobby Lee also had no doubt who the tall man was. He had seen both him and the female deputy next to the diner where Vikki Gaddis had worked, with a guy who was probably a fed, maybe even the one Preacher capped later, all three of them talking to the owner of the diner, Junior Whatever in handcuffs. The tall guy's name was Holland, that was it, Holland, the county sheriff, a big wheel in Dipshit, Texas, and the woman was his deputy, and now the two of them were right here, maybe forty feet from Bobby Lee and Liam's booth.

Bobby Lee went straight back into the restroom, into the stall, and punched in Liam's number.

"You fall in the commode?" Liam said.

"The guy in the booth, the one you said looked like John Wayne, that's the sheriff."

"Sheriff?"

"You couldn't see his gun belt below the table. His name's Holland. I saw him questioning Vikki Gaddis's boss, the guy from the diner. The deputy was there, too. With a guy who looked like a fed. I think the fed was the guy Preacher smoked in that motel in San Antonio. I saw his picture in the paper." Bobby Lee could hear Liam breathing into the cell phone.

"They haven't made us," Liam said. "We walk out together, calm and cool and collected."

"The cash register is right by their fucking booth."

"Create a distraction."

"Hang my dick out the men's room door?"

"You have matches?"

Bobby Lee pulled the wet kitchen match out of his mouth. "What about it?"

"Start a fire in the wastebasket."

"Look, Liam—"

"Do it," Liam said, and broke the connection.

Not good, Bobby Lee thought, his heart starting to seize up in his chest.

Another man came into the restroom and began relieving himself in the urinal, making a lot of noise. Bobby Lee combed his hair in the mirror until the man had finished and gone back outside. Bobby Lee looked at the wads of discarded paper towels overflowing from the wastebasket. The paper was damp and would smolder like leaves burning on a fall day.

But for what? To bring emergency vehicles and firemen and more cops to the restaurant while Liam and Bobby Lee tried to walk discreetly away, with no vehicle, no way to get out of town, carrying a gym bag, with half the people in the restaurant remembering they had seen Bobby Lee in the can before smoke started gushing through the door?

Right.

Bobby Lee went out the back exit into the warmth of the evening, into the smell of the cooling land, into the touch of a raindrop on his brow.

Liam was on his own, he told himself. Better that Liam pay the check and walk out quietly rather than the two of them try it together, doubling their chances of recognition. What was wrong with that? Only Liam would recommend starting a fire in a confined situation in order not to draw attention.

Bobby Lee walked around the side of the building, angling toward the mechanic's shed across the street, glancing sideways through the window at the booth where the sheriff and his deputy were still eating. He saw the sheriff stand up, pick up his hat, then replace it on the seat. The sheriff said something to the deputy, his expression pleasant, unhurried. Then he walked behind a bunch of kids who were headed toward the restroom.

Bobby Lee didn't think twice about the opportunity that had just been presented to him. He flipped open his cell phone and punched redial, the adrenaline pounding in his ears, his heart swelling against his ribs.

"What now?" Liam said.

"The sheriff just made you. He's headed for your booth. Get the fuck out of there," he said. Bobby Lee clicked off his cell phone, the chimes ringing in his closed palm. He crossed the road hurriedly in the shadow of a striated mesa, an acrid stench like the smell of a tar pot rising into his face.

AT LEAST EIGHT or nine boys had gotten up at once and headed toward the men's room, walking ahead of Hackberry, causing him to pause between a booth and a table while a youth minister tried to form the boys into a line. Hackberry glanced back at his booth. Pam had gotten up from the seat and picked up the check and was computing the tip, counting out four dollar bills and some change on the tabletop. She looked pretty, framed against the window, the tips of her hair touched by the late sun, her shoulders muscular inside her khaki shirt, her bottom a little too wide for her jeans, her chrome-plated .357 high up on the right hip. When she realized he was staring at her, her cheeks colored and her expression took on an uncharacteristic vulnerability.

He winked and gave her the thumbs-up sign, but if asked, he couldn't have explained why.

The events and the images of the next few moments were kaleidoscopic in nature and seemed to lack causality, coherence, or rational sequence. The young boys crowding into the men's room were still unruly, but in the innocent way that all boys on a cross-country trip were unruly. An apple-cheeked bovine man in a western suit the color of tin was ladling meatballs off a platter onto the plates of his grandchildren. A workingman at the counter wiped beer foam off his chin and asked the waitress to change the television channel. A woman held up her water glass against the light and examined a dead fly floating in it. A minister in a lavender Roman collar was eating a steak, dipping each bite into a pool of ketchup that he had sprinkled with black pepper; his wife was telling him he was eating his food too fast. At the dessert bar, a teenage girl was upset because she had dropped and sunk the dipper in a container of hot fudge.

And Hackberry Holland, walking toward the restroom, squeezing between the diners, saw in the corner of his eye the man in the straw gardener's hat wrestling open a gym bag by his foot, ripping a thirty-inch-long object loose from a tangle of underwear and shirts and socks. As Hackberry stared in disbelief, as though watching a slow-motion film that had nothing to do with reality, he saw that the object was a cut-down pump shotgun, the hacksawed steel still bright from the cut, loose shotgun shells spilling out of the gym bag onto the floor.

His next thoughts flashed across his mind in under a second, in the way that a BB arches into space and disappears:

Where had he seen the man's face?

In a photo, maybe.

Except the face in the photo had an orange beard of the kind a Nordic seafarer might have.

Was this how it ended, with a flash from a shotgun muzzle and a burst of light inside the skull before the report ever reached his ears?

Hackberry tilted a table upward, spilling food and plates onto the floor, and flung it at the man in the gardener's hat, who was raising the shotgun toward Hackberry's chest. The first discharge blew a shower of splinters and shreds of red-and-white-checkered cloth all over Hackberry's shoulder and left arm and down the side of his pants.

No one in the room moved. Instead, they looked stunned, shrunken, frozen inside clear plastic, as though a sonic boom had temporarily deafened them. Hackberry got his revolver free of its holster just as he heard the shooter jack another round into the chamber of his weapon. The second blast went high, over the top of the table. Glass caved out of the front window into the parking lot. Only then did people begin screaming, some trying to hide under tables or behind the booths. Someone kicked open a fire exit, setting off an alarm. The boys from the church bus had piled over one another into the men's room, their faces stretched tight with fear.

Hackberry was crouched behind the table and a wood post, a bent fork or spoon biting through the cloth of his trousers into his knee. He pointed his revolver through a space between the table and the wood post and let off two rounds in the direction of the shooter, the .45's frame kicking upward in his hand. He fired again and saw stuffing from a booth floating like chicken feathers in the gloom. He heard the shooter work the pump on his twelve-gauge and a spent shell casing clink and roll on a hard surface.

Hackberry hung on to the post and pulled himself erect, a tree of pain blooming in his back. He ran for the cover provided by the last booth in the shooter's row, letting off one round blindly at the shooter, his boots as loud as stones striking a wood surface.

The room became absolutely quiet, as though the air had been sucked out of it. Hackberry rose in a half-crouch and pointed his revolver at the place where the shooter had been. The gym bag was still on the floor. The shooter and the shotgun shells he had spilled from the bag were gone.

Hackberry straightened his back, his weapon still pointed in front of him, the hammer on full cock, the sight on the tip of the barrel trembling slightly with the tension of his grip on the frame. He glanced over his shoulder. Where was Pam? The window behind her booth was blown out, one vinyl seat of the booth and the wedges of glass protruding from the window frame painted with red splatter. Hackberry wiped his mouth with his free hand and widened his eyes and tried to think clearly. What was the formal name for the situation? Barricaded suspect? The clinical language didn't come close to describing the reality.

"Give it up, partner. Nobody has to die here," he said.

Except for a cough, the muted crying of a woman, and a sound like somebody prizing open a stuck window, the room remained silent.

"He went in the girls' bathroom," a burr-headed boy in short pants said from under a table.

A latticework alcove had been built around the entrance to the women's restroom, obscuring the doorway. Hackberry walked at an angle toward the door, silverware and broken glass crunching under his boots, his eyes locked on the door through the spaces in the latticework.

Had Pam been hit? The second shotgun blast had traveled right across the booth where she had been counting out the tip on the tabletop.

"He's got a little girl in there. Don't go in there," a voice said from behind an overturned chair.

It was the minister in the lavender Roman collar. He was bleeding from his cheek and neck; the heel of one hand sparkled with ground glass. His wife was on her knees beside him, gripping his arm, her body rounded into a ball.

"You saw him?" Hackberry asked.

"He grabbed the girl by the neck and pulled her with him," the minister said.

"Can you get to the front door?" Hackberry asked.

"Yes, sir," the minister replied. "I can."

"When I start into the women's room, you stand up and take as many people with you as you can. Can you do that for me, sir?"

"You're going in there?"

"We'll bring the girl out of there safely. When you get out front, find my deputy. Her name is Pam Tibbs. Tell her exactly what you told me."

"Who's the man with the shotgun?"

"His name is Eriksson. My deputy will recognize the name. Better get going, Reverend."

"You said 'we.' "

"Sir?"

"You said 'we'll' get the girl out. Who's 'we'?"

A moment later, Hackberry closed the distance between himself and the doorway while the minister and his wife began herding a group of twelve to fifteen people toward the front of the restaurant. Hackberry pressed his back against the wall, his revolver pointed upward. He could see the red sunset flowing through the destroyed front window and hear sirens in the distance. "Hear that sound, Eriksson?" he said.

There was a beat. "How'd you make me?"

"I didn't. If you hadn't shot at me, I would have walked past you."

"You're lying."

"Why would I lie?"

Eriksson had no answer. Hackberry remembered that originally, a second man had been sitting in Eriksson's booth, someone who had probably blown Dodge and left Eriksson to take the fall for both of them.

"Your partner screwed you, bub," Hackberry said. "Why take his weight? Send the little girl out, and it'll be taken into consideration. You did security work in Iraq. That'll be a factor, too. Get a good defense lawyer, and with the right kind of post-traumatic-stress-disorder mambo, you might even skate. It beats eating a two-hundred-and-thirty-grain round from a forty-five."

"You're gonna drive me out of this county. You're gonna get me into Mexico. Or I waste the girl."

"Maybe I can arrange that."

"No, you don't arrange anything. You do it."

"How do you want to work that? Want me to bring a vehicle around back and load you and the girl up?"

"No, you put your piece on the floor, slide it to me with your foot, then you walk in with your fingers laced on the back of your neck."

"That doesn't sound workable, Eriksson."

"Maybe you'd like to see her brains floating in the toilet bowl."

Hackberry heard the voice of a little girl crying. Or rather, the voice of a child whose fear had gone beyond crying into a series of hiccups and constrictions of air in the nostrils and throat, like someone having a seizure. "Be stand-up. Let her go, partner," Hackberry said.

"You want her? No problem. Kick the piece inside and come in after it. Otherwise, all bets are off. Think I'm jerking your johnson? Stick your head in here."

Hackberry could hear a dronelike whirring sound in his ears, one he associated with wind blowing out of a blue-black sky across miles of snowy hills and ice splintering under the weight of thousands of advancing Chinese infantry.

"I'll make it easy for you," Eriksson said. He opened the bathroom door slightly, allowing Hackberry a brief view of the restroom's interior. Eriksson was holding the little girl by the neck of her T-shirt while he screwed the cut-down pump into her shoulder bone. "I got nothing to lose," he said.

"I believe you," Hackberry said. He stepped backward, opened the cylinder to his revolver, and dumped his four spent rounds and two unfired ones into his palm and threw them clattering across the floor. He squatted, placed his revolver on the floor, and shoved it with one foot into the restroom.

"Walk in behind it," Eriksson said.

Then Hackberry was in the enclosure with him, staring into the muzzle of the shotgun.

"Go on, little girl," Eriksson said. "I wasn't gonna hurt you. I just had to say that."

"Yes, you were. You hurt me bad," she said, cupping her hand to one shoulder.

"Get out of here, you little skank," Eriksson said. He bolted the door behind her, his attention never leaving Hackberry. "Slickered you, motherfucker."

Hackberry let his eyes become dead and unseeing, let them drift off Eriksson's face to a spot on the wall. Or perhaps to a patch of red sky that should not have been visible inside a women's restroom.

"Did you hear me?" Eriksson asked.

"You're a smart one," Hackberry said.

"You got that right."

Then Eriksson seemed to realize something was wrong in his environment, that he had not seen or taken note of something, that in spite of his years of vanquishing his enemies and shaving the odds and orchestrating events so that he always walked away a winner, something had gone terribly wrong. "Get on your cell," he said.

"What for?"

"What do you mean, what for? Tell your people to stay away from the building. Tell them to bring a car to the back."

"You're not getting a car."

"I'll get a car or you'll catch the bus, whichever you prefer."

"You're leaving here in cuffs."

Eriksson took his own cell phone from his pocket and tossed it to Hackberry. It bounced off Hackberry's chest and fell to the floor. "Pick it up and make the call, Sheriff," Eriksson said.

"I said you're a smart one. A smart man is a listener. Listen to what I say and don't turn around. No, no, keep your eyes on me. You do not want to turn around."

"Are you senile? I'm holding a shotgun in your face."

"If you turn around, you'll lose your head," Hackberry said. "Look straight ahead. Kneel down and place your weapon on the floor."

Eriksson's lips parted. They were dry, caked slightly with mucus. His hands tightened on the twelve-gauge. He crimped his lips, wetting them before he spoke. "This has got a hair trigger. No matter what happens, you're gonna have a throat full of bucks."

"Believe what I tell you, Eriksson. Don't move, don't back away from me, don't turn around. If you do any of those things, you will die. I give you my word on that. No one wants to see that happen to you. But it's your choice. You lower your weapon by the barrel with your left hand and place it on the floor and step away from it."

"I think you're a mighty good actor, Sheriff, but I also think you're full of shit."

Eriksson stepped backward, out of Hackberry's reach, turning his line of vision toward a frosted back window that had been wedged open with a tire tool. For just a moment, the aim of his shotgun angled away from Hackberry's chest. Outside, a huge cloud of orange dust gusted across the sun.

Eriksson's translucent blue eyes were charged with light. His face seemed to twitch just before he saw Pam Tibbs standing slightly beyond the window ledge, her khaki shirt speckled with taco sauce, her chrome-plated revolver aimed in front of her with both hands. That was when she squeezed the trigger, driving a soft-nosed .357 round through one side of his head and out the other.

Chapter
15

PREACHER JACK COLLINS lived at several residences, none of which carried his name on a deed or a rental agreement. One of them was located south of old Highway 90, within sight of the Del Norte Mountains, twenty miles deep into broken desert terrain that looked composed of crushed stone knitted together by the roots of scrub brush and mesquite and cactus that bloomed with bloodred flowers.

On the mountain behind his one-bedroom stucco house was a series of ancient telegraph poles whose wires hung on the ground like strands of black spaghetti. Behind the poles was the gaping opening of a rock-walled root cellar that had been shored up with wood posts and crossbeams that either had collapsed or that insects had reduced to the weightless density of cork.

One starlit night, Preacher had sat in the entrance and watched the desert take on the gray and blue and silver illumination that it seemed to draw down into itself from the sky, as though the sky and the earth worked together to both cool the desert and turn it into a pewter artwork. Then he had realized that a breeze was blowing into his face and flowing over his arms and shoulders and into the excavation at his back. The root cellar was not a root cellar after all. Nor was it a mine. It was a cave, deep and spiraling, one that had probably been formed by water millions of years ago, one that led to the other side of the mountain or a cavern far beneath it. Perhaps early settlers had framed up the walls and ceilings with timbered support, but Preacher was convinced no human hand had contributed to its creation.

He spent many evenings sitting on a metal chair in front of the cave, wondering if the wind echoing inside it spoke to him and if indeed the desert was not an ancient vineyard made sterile by man's infidelity to Yahweh. Paradoxically, that thought comforted him. The sinfulness of the world somehow gave him a greater connection to it, made him more acceptable in his own eyes and simultaneously reduced the level of his own iniquity. Except Preacher had one problem he could not rid himself of: He had filled the ground with the bodies of Asian women and watched while Hugo's bulldozer had scalloped up the earth and pushed the backfill over them. He told himself he had been acting as an agent of God, purging the world of an abomination, perhaps even preempting the moral decay and diseases that had awaited them as prostitutes on the streets of a corrupt nation.

But Preacher was having little success with his rationalization for the mass execution of the helpless and terrified women who waited for him nightly in his sleep. When Bobby Lee Motree arrived at Preacher's house in the desert, Jack was delighted by the distraction.

He set up two metal chairs in front of the cave and opened cold bottles of Coca-Cola for the two of them and watched while Bobby Lee drank his empty, his throat pumping, one eye fastened curiously on Preacher. Bobby Lee was wearing a muscle shirt and his top hat and his brown jeans that had yellow canvas squares stitched on the knees. He was full of confidence and cheer at being back in Preacher's good graces; he unloaded his burden, telling Preacher how Liam got popped by the female deputy sheriff in the restaurant and how that rat bastard Artie Rooney had told Hugo to smoke everybody—the soldier and his girl, the Jewish guy and his wife and maybe even the Jewish guy's kids, and finally, Preacher himself.

"If you cain't trust Artie Rooney, who can you trust? The standards of our profession have seriously declined," Preacher said.

"I was thinking the same thing," Bobby Lee replied.

"That was a joke."

"Yeah, I knew that. I can always tell when you're joking."

Preacher let the subject slide. "Tell me again how this Holland fellow spotted Liam. I didn't quite get all that."

"I guess he recognized him, that's all."

"Even though Liam had shaved off his beard and was sitting in a crowded restaurant and the sheriff had never seen him and had no reason to be looking for Liam there?"

"Search me. Weird stuff happens."

"But the sheriff didn't make you?"

"I was in the can, taking a dump."

"How'd you get out during all that shooting if you were in the can?"

"It was a Chinese fire drill. I ran outside with the crowd."

"And just strolled on off, a fellow with no car, a fellow everybody saw sitting with Liam just a few minutes earlier?"

"Most of them were pouring the wee-wee out of their shoes. Why should they worry about me?"

"Maybe you were just lucky."

"I told you the way it was."

"Young people believe they're never going to die. So they've got confidence that old men like me don't have. That's where your luck comes from, Bobby Lee. Your luck is an illusion produced by an illusion."

Bobby Lee's obvious sense of discomfort was growing. He shifted in his chair and glanced at the stars and the sparkle of the desert and the greenish cast at the bottom of the sky. "Is that hole behind us one of those pioneer storage places where they kept preserves and shit?"

"Maybe it goes down to the center of the earth. I'm going to find out one day."

"Sometimes I just can't track what you're saying, Jack."

"My uncle was in the South Pacific. He said he dynamited a whole mountain on top of the Japs who wouldn't surrender and were hiding in caves. He said you could hear them at night, like hundreds of bees buzzing under the ground. I bet if you put your ear to the ground, you might still hear them."

"Why do you talk about stuff like that?"

"Because I'm doubting your truthfulness, and you're starting to piss me off."

"I wouldn't try to put the glide on you. Give me some credit," Bobby Lee said, his eyes round, unblinking, the pupils dilated like drops of ink in the dark.

"Bobby Lee, you either gave up Liam or this fellow Holland is a special kind of lawman, the kind who doesn't quit till he staples your hide on the barn door. Which is it?"

"I didn't give up Liam. He was my friend," Bobby Lee replied, propping his hands on his knees, tilting his face up at the sky. His unshaved jaw looked as though grains of black pepper and salt had been rubbed into the pores. Preacher looked at him for a long time, until Bobby Lee's face began to twitch and his eyes glistened. "You want to keep hurting and insulting me, go ahead and do it. I came out here to see you because you're my friend. But all you do is run me down," Bobby Lee said.

"I believe you, boy," Preacher said.

Bobby Lee cleared his throat and spat. "Why do you do it?" he asked.

"Do what?"

"Our kind of work. We're button men. We push people's off button and shut down their motors. A pro does it for money. It's not supposed to be personal. You're a pro, Preacher, but with you, it's not the money. It's something nobody ever asks you about. Why do you do it?"

"Why are you asking me?"

" 'Cause you're the only man I could ever relate to."

"You see the glow in the land? It's the bone in the soil that does that. Inside all that alluvial soil and lava flow and sedimentary rock, there's millions of dead things letting off energy, lighting the way for the rest of us."

"Go on."

Preacher picked a mosquito off his neck and squeezed it between his thumb and finger. He wiped the blood on a piece of Kleenex. "That's all. You asked a question and I answered it."

"I don't get it. Lighting the way, what?"

"Don't fret yourself, boy. I need to know everything about this fellow Holland. I want to know why he was down by Big Bend. I want to know how he recognized Liam."

"I'm one guy. You got us into all this, Jack. How am I supposed to fix everything?"

Preacher didn't respond. In the wind, his face looked as serene and transfixed as though it had been bathed in warm water, his lips parted slightly, his teeth showing. In his eyes was a black reflection that made even Bobby Lee swallow, as though Preacher saw a presence on the horizon that no one else did. "You're not mad at me, are you?" Bobby Lee said, trying to smile.

"You? You're like a son to me, Bobby Lee," Preacher answered.

BOBBY LEE DROVE away from the stucco house before first light, and Preacher prepared breakfast for himself on a propane stove and ate from a tin plate on his back steps. As a red glow fingered its way across the plain from the east, Preacher mounted his crutches and worked his way down the incline toward a mesa that was still locked in shadow. He crossed the opening to an arroyo and stumped through a depression of soft baked clay that cracked and sank beneath his weight with each step he took. He thought he could see petroglyphs cut in the layered rock above his head, and he was convinced he was traversing an alluvial flume that probably had irrigated verdant fields when an agrarian society had lived in harmony with the animals and a knife blade hammered out of primitive iron drew no blood from them or the people who had been sent to dwell east of Eden.

But Preacher Jack's thoughts about a riparian paradise brought him no peace. When he looked behind him, the funnel-shaped indentations of his crutches in the dried-out riverbed reminded him of coyote tracks. Even the drag of his footprints was serpentine and indistinct, as though his very essence were that of a transient and weightless creature not worthy of full creation.

He wished to think of himself as a figure emblazoned retroactively on biblical legend, but the truth was otherwise. He had been a burden to his mother the day he was born, as well as a voyeur to her trysts. Now he lusted for the woman who had bested him both physically and intellectually and, in addition, had managed to pump one .38 round into his calf and one through the top of his foot. The memory of her scent, the heat in her skin and hair, the smear of her saliva and lipstick on his skin caused a swelling in his loins that made him ashamed.

She had not only eluded him but indirectly had gotten Liam Eriksson killed and involved a sheriff named Holland in the case, probably the kind of rural hardhead a pro didn't mess with or, if necessary, you paid somebody else to pop.

Preacher turned in a circle and began thudding his way back toward his house. The hills and mesas were pink in the sunrise, the air sweet, the leaves of the mesquite brushing wetly against his trousers and wrists and hands. He wanted to breathe the morning into his chest and cast out the funk and depression that seemed to screw him into the earth, but it was no use; he had never felt so alone in his life. When he closed his eyes, he thought he saw a boxcar on a rail siding, his mother sitting on a stool inside the open door, cutting carrots and onions into a pot in which she would make a soup that she would heat on an open fire that evening. In the dream, his mother lifted her face into the sunlight and smiled at him.

Maybe it was time to put aside doubt and self-recrimination. A man could always become captain of his soul if he tried. A man didn't have to accept the hand fate had dealt him. Moses didn't. Neither did David. Wasn't it time to continue his journey into a biblical past and to become a son of whom his mother could be proud, regardless of deeds he had performed on behalf of Artie Rooney, regardless of the nightmares in which a line of Asian women tried to hold up their palms against the weapon that jerked sideways in his grasp, almost as though it possessed a will stronger than his own?

The answer lay in the Book of Esther. The story had been written twenty-three hundred years before he was born, and it had waited all these centuries for him to step inside it and take on the role that should have been his, that was now being offered to him by an invisible hand. He drew the freshness of the morning into his lungs and felt a pang in his chest as sharp as a piece of broken glass.

AT FIVE A.M. Nick Dolan woke to the sound of raindrops striking the banana fronds below his bedroom window. Briefly, he thought he was at his grandfather's house off Napoleon Avenue in New Orleans. His grandfather had lived in a shotgun house

with a peaked tin roof and ceiling-high windows flanged by ven-
tilated shutters that could be latched during the hurricane season. There was a pecan tree in the backyard with a rope swing,
and the ground under its branches was soft and moldy and green
with flattened pecan husks. Even in the hottest part of the day,
the yard was breezy and stayed in deep shade and the neighborhood children gathered there each summer afternoon at three
o'clock to await the arrival of the Sno-Ball truck.

The grandfather's house was a safe place, far different from
Nick's neighborhood in the Ninth Ward, where Artie Rooney
and his brothers and their friends had made life a daily torment
for Nick.

Nick sat on the side of the bed and cupped his hand lightly
on Esther's hip. She was turned toward the wall, her dark hair
and paleness touched with the shadows the moonlight created
through the window. He slipped her nightgown up her thigh and
hooked his finger over the elastic of her panties and pulled them
down far enough so he could kiss her lightly on the rump, something he always did before congress with her. He could feel the
nocturnal intensity of her body heat through her gown and hear
the steady, undisturbed sound of her breathing against the wall.
The touch of his hand or his lips seemed to neither awaken nor
arouse her, and he wondered if her deep slumber was feigned or
if indeed she had dreamed herself back into a time when Nick
had not exchanged their happiness for success in the skin trade.

He put on his slippers and robe and ate a bowl of Grape-Nuts
and drank a glass of cold milk in the kitchen and, at six A.M.,
disarmed the burglar alarm and retrieved the newspaper from
the front yard. The morning was cool and damp and smelled of
water sprinklers and Nick's closely cropped St. Augustine grass
that his Mexican gardeners had mowed late yesterday and the
night-blooming flowers Esther constantly fertilized with coffee
grounds and bat guano and fish blood and black dirt bagged

from a swamp outside Lake Charles, all of which created a fecund odor Nick associated with a Louisiana graveyard that lay so deep in shadow it was never penetrated by sunlight.

Enough with thoughts about graveyards, he told himself, and went back in the house, the rolled newspaper fat in his hand. Nor did he wish to dwell on thoughts about schoolyard bullies and personal failure and the slippage of his fortune onto the shoals of financial ruin. He wanted to be with Esther, inside her warm embrace, inside the glow of her thighs with the smell of her hair in his face and the rhythm of her breath on his cheek. It didn't seem a lot to ask. Why had the Fates ganged up against him? He pulled the plastic rain sheath off the newspaper and unrolled the paper on the breakfast table. The lead story dealt with the murder of a young mother and her two children. The primary suspect was an estranged boyfriend. The woman's face looked familiar. Had she worked in his club? Yeah, it was possible. But what if she had? What was worse, the daily drudgery and humiliation and penury of a welfare recipient or knocking down some quasi-serious bucks by cavorting a few hours on a pole for the titty-baby brigade?

Nick knew the secret source of his discontent. His money had been his validation and his protection from the world, his payback for every time he had been shoved down on line at school or at the movie theater or chased crying into his yard by the army of street rats who claimed they were avenging the death of Jesus. Now a large part of Nick's income was gone, and some bad ventures in commodities and mortgage companies were about to wipe out the rest of it.

Nick had nail wounds in his wrists and hands for other reasons. Although Esther pretended differently, she would probably never forgive him for his involvement in the deaths of the Asian women, regardless of the fact that he was almost as much a victim as they were. At least that was the way he saw it.

A shadow moved across the breakfast table. Nick turned in his chair, startled, knocking over his glass of milk.

"You want oatmeal?" Esther said.

"I already ate," he replied.

"Why are you up so early?"

"Restless, I guess."

"Go on back to bed."

"Do you want to?"

"Want to what?"

"Sleep some more?"

"I'm going to fix some tea."

"Maybe neither one of us got enough sleep," Nick said, stifling a yawn. "It's only six-twenty. We could take a little nap. Later, we can go out for breakfast. Want to do that?"

"My aerobics class is at seven-thirty."

"Better not miss the aerobics. That's important. They let men in there? I could use that. Jumping up and down and sweatin' to the golden oldies or whatever." He stiffened his fingers and jabbed them against the softness of his stomach. Then he did it again, harder.

She gave him a curious look and filled a pan with water and placed it on the gas burner. "Sure you don't want some oatmeal?"

"I'm starting a diet. I need to reform myself physically, maybe get plastic surgery while I'm at it."

Nick went upstairs and shaved and brushed his teeth and got fully dressed, putting on a tie and a white shirt, more as a statement of independence from his sexual and emotional need than as preparation to go to work at his restaurant, which didn't open until eleven. He went back downstairs, deliberately walking through the kitchen, pulling a carton of orange juice out of the refrigerator, sucking his teeth, whistling a tune, ignoring Esther's presence.

"Where are you going?" she said.

"Downstairs and pay some bills. While there's still money in the bank for me to pay the bills. Tell the kids I'll drive them to the pool later."

"What's with the attitude?" she asked.

"The flower beds smell like litter boxes with fish buried in them. We need to load the weed sprayer with Lysol and douche all the beds."

"Listen to you. You see the paper? A whole family is killed, and you're talking about how the garden smells. Count your blessings. Why the dirty mouth in your own kitchen? Show a little respect."

Nick squeezed the heels of his hands against his temples and went down the half-flight of stairs into the glacial coldness of his office. He sat behind his desk in the darkness and planted his forehead on the desk blotter, the gold tie hanging from his throat like an ear of boiled corn, his flaccid arms like rolls of bread dough at his sides. He banged his head up and down on the blotter.

"I couldn't help but hear y'all talking. Maybe you could take a page from the papists. Celibacy probably has its moments," a voice said from the darkness.

"Jesus Christ!" Nick said, his head jerking up.

"Thought we should go over a few things."

"I had the alarm on. How'd you get in?" Nick said, focusing on the man who sat in the stuffed leather chair, a pair of walking canes propped across his shoe tops.

"Through the side door yonder. I came in before y'all went to bed. Fact is, I browsed two or three of your books and took a little nap here in the chair and used your bathroom. You need to tidy up in there. I had to dig clean hand towels out of the closet."

Nick picked up the phone receiver, the dial tone filling the room.

"I came here to save your life and the lives of your wife and children," Preacher said. "If I were here for another reason . . .

Well, we don't even need to talk about that. Put the phone down and stop making an ass of yourself."

Nick replaced the receiver in the cradle. The back of his hand looked strangely white and soft, cupped around the blackness of the receiver. "Is it money?"

"I say something once, and I don't repeat it. You're not deaf, and you're not lacking in intelligence. If you pretend to be either one, I'm going to leave. Then your family's fate is on you, not me."

Nick's fingers were trembling on top of the desk blotter. "It's about Artie Rooney and the Asian girls, isn't it? Were you the shooter? Hugo said the shooter was a religious nutcase. That's you, right?"

Preacher's face remained impassive, his greased hair combed back neatly, his forehead shiny in the gloom. "Rooney is going to have you and Mrs. Dolan killed, and maybe your children, too. If the shooter can get in close, he wants your wife shot in the mouth. He also plans to have me killed. That gives us a lot of commonalities. But you say the word, and I'll be gone."

Nick felt his mouth drying up, his eyes watering, his rectum constricting with fear and angst.

"Are you going to get emotional on me?" Preacher asked.

"Why should you care about us?"

"I've been sent. I am the one who has been sent." Preacher tilted his face up. He seemed to smile in a self-deprecating manner, in a way that was almost likable.

"What the hell are you talking about?" Nick wiped at his nose with the back of his wrist, not expecting an answer, not wanting to listen any more to a lunatic.

"You watch television shows about witness protection and that kind of thing?"

"Everybody does. That's all that's on TV."

"Want to live in a box in Phoenix in summertime with sand and rocks for a yard and bikers with swastika tats for neighbors? Because outside of cooperating with me, that's the only shot you've got. Artie Rooney has an on-again, off-again business relationship with a Russian by the name of Josef Sholokoff. His people come out of the worst prisons in Russia. Want me to tell you what they did to a Mexican family in Juárez, to the children in particular?"

"No, I don't want to hear this."

"Cain't blame you. You know a man name of Hackberry Holland?"

"No . . . Who? Holland? No, I don't know anybody by that name."

"You recognize the name, though. You've seen it in the newspaper. He's a sheriff. You read about the death of the ICE agent in San Antonio. Holland was there."

"I told you, I don't know this Holland guy. I'm a restaurateur. I got into the escort business, but I don't do that anymore. I'm going broke. I'm not a criminal. Criminals don't go broke. Criminals don't file bankruptcy. They don't see their families put on the street."

"Were you interviewed by the ICE agent? Has Holland been to see you?"

"Me? No. I mean, maybe the man from Immigration and Customs came to my home. I don't know anybody named Holland. You say something only once to other people, but other people got to say it ten times to you?"

"I think Sheriff Holland wants to do me injury. If he takes me off the board, you go off the board, too, because I'm the only person standing between you and Artie Rooney and his Russian business partners."

"I made mistakes, but I'm not a thief. You stop dragging me into your life."

"You're telling me I'm a thief?"

"No, sir."

"You have a pistol in your drawer, a Beretta nine-millimeter. Why don't you take it out of the drawer and hold it in your hand and point it at me and call me dishonorable again?"

"If you found my gun, you took the bullets out."

"Could be. Or maybe not. Open the drawer and pick it up. The weight should tell you something."

"I apologize if I said something I shouldn't."

Preacher leaned forward in the chair. He was wearing a brown suit with light stripes in it, and the cast was gone from his leg. "You take Mrs. Dolan and your children out of town for a while. You pay cash everywhere you go. A credit card is an electronic footprint. You don't call your restaurant or your lawyer or your friends. Artie Rooney may tap your phone lines. I'll give you a cell phone number where you can contact me. But I'll be the only person you'll be talking to."

"Are you crazy? Nobody is this arrogant." Nick opened the side drawer to his desk and looked at the gun lying inside it.

"A crazy person is psychotic and has a distorted vision of the world. Which of us is the realist? The one who has survived among the predators or the one who pretends to be a family man while he lives off the earnings of whores and puts his family at mortal risk?"

Nick tried to hold his gaze on Preacher's.

"You want to say something?" Preacher asked. "Pick up the gun."

"Don't tempt me."

"Did you ever fire it?"

"No."

"Pick it up and point it at me. Hold it with both hands. That way your fingers will stop trembling."

"You don't think I'll pick it up?"

"Show me."

Nick rested his hand in the drawer. The steel frame and checkered grips of the nine-millimeter felt solid and hard and reassuring as he curved his fingers around them. He lifted the gun out of the drawer. "It's light. You took the clip out."

"It's called a magazine. It feels light because you're scared and your adrenaline gives you strength you normally don't have. The firing mechanism has a butterfly safety. The red dot means you're on rock and roll. Pull back the hammer."

"I don't want to."

"Do it, little fat man. Do it, little Jewish fat man."

"What did you call me?"

"It's not what I call you. It's what Hugo calls you. He also calls you the Pillsbury Doughboy. Fit your thumb over the hammer and pull it back, then aim the front sight at my face."

Nick set down the gun on the desk blotter and removed his hand from the grips. He was breathing audibly through his nostrils, his palms clammy, a taste like soured milk climbing into his mouth.

"Why cain't you do it?" Preacher asked.

"Because it's empty. Because I'm not here to entertain you."

"That's not why at all. Push the button by the trigger guard."

Nick picked up the gun and squeezed the release on the magazine. The magazine fell from the frame and clunked on the desktop, the loading spring stacked tight with brass-jacketed shells.

"Pull back the slide. You'll see a round in the chamber. The reason you didn't point the gun at me is because you're not a killer. But other men are, and they don't think two seconds about the deeds they do. Those are the men I'm trying to protect your family from. Some of us are made different in the womb and are not to be underestimated. I'm one of them, but I think I'm different from the others. Is everything I say lost on you? Are you ignorant as well as corrupt?"

"No, you make me want to blow your fucking head off."

The door to the upstairs opened, and light flooded down the

staircase. "Who's down there?" Esther said. Before anyone could answer her question, she descended the stairs, gripping an empty pot by the handle. She stared down at Preacher. "Who are you?"

"A friend."

"How'd you get in my house?"

"The side door was open. I've explained this. Why don't you sit down?"

"You're one of them, aren't you?"

"One of who?"

"The gangsters who have been plaguing our lives."

"You're wrong."

"He's about to leave, Esther," Nick said.

"You're one of those who abducted my husband," she said.

"I wouldn't call it that."

"Don't lie."

"You shouldn't use that term to me, madam."

She stepped closer to him. "The Asian women, the prostitutes, the illegals or whatever they were, you're here about them. You're the one who did it."

"Did what?"

"Killed them. It was you, wasn't it?"

"Why do you say that?" Preacher's mouth twitched slightly, his words catching in his throat.

"Your eyes are dead. Only one kind of man has eyes like that. Someone who murders the light behind his own eyes. Someone who has tried to scrub God's fingerprint off his soul."

"Don't you talk to me like that, woman."

"You call me 'woman'? A dog turd off the sidewalk calls me 'woman' in my own house?"

"I came here to—"

"Shut up, you worthless gangster," she said.

"By God, you won't talk to me like—" he began.

She swung the stainless-steel pot, still caked with oatmeal, across his face. The sound reverberated like a brass cymbal inside the room. Before he could recover from the shock, she hit him again, this time on the head. When he tried to raise his arms, she rained down one blow after another on his neck, shoulders, and elbows, gripping the handle with both hands, chopping downward as though attacking a tree stump.

"Esther!" Nick said, coming from behind his desk.

When Preacher lowered his arms, she swung the pot again, catching him right above the ear. He got to his feet and stumbled to the side door, blood leaking out of his hair. He jerked open the door and climbed the short flight of concrete steps into the yard, grabbing the higher steps for support, his palms smearing with bird shit.

Esther picked up his walking canes and followed him into the yard, through the citrus and crepe myrtle trees and windmill palms and hibiscus. He headed for the street, trying to outdistance her, looking back over his shoulder, his hatchet face quivering, his broken movements like a land crab's. She flung his walking canes at his head. "Just so you don't have any reason to come back," she said.

Preacher crashed through the hedge onto the sidewalk and saw Bobby Lee fire up his vehicle down the street, just as a water truck passed and splattered Preacher from head to foot. The eastern sky was the blue of a robin's egg and ribbed at the bottom with strips of crimson and purple cloud. The colors were majestic, the royal colors of David and Solomon, as though the sky itself had conspired to mock his grandiosity and foolish pride and vain hope that salvation would ever be his.

Chapter
16

Early Saturday morning, Hackberry walked down to his barn and skimmed the bugs from the secondary tank he kept for his registered Missouri foxtrotters, a chestnut named Missy's Playboy and a palomino named Love That Santa Fe. Then he turned on the spigot full blast and let the water run until it overflowed the aluminum sides and was clean of insects and dust and cold to the touch and tinted a light green from the pieces of hay floating in it. Both foxtrotters were still colts and gave themselves the liberty of nuzzling him and poking at his pockets for treats, their breath heavy and warm and grassy on the side of his face. Sometimes they pulled a glove from his pocket or grabbed the hat from his head and ran away with it. But this morning they were not playful and instead kept staring down the pasture, motionless, ears back, nostrils dilating in the wind that blew out of the north.

"What's wrong, boys? A cougar been around?" Hackberry said. "You guys are too big to be bothered by such critters as that."

He heard his cell phone chime in his khakis. He opened it,

looking toward the railed fence at the north end of the pasture, seeing nothing but a solitary oak framed against the sunrise and an abandoned clapboard shack his neighbor kept hay in. He placed the phone against his ear. "You up, Hack?" a voice said.

"What's going on, Maydeen?"

"I just got a weird call. Some guy says he has to talk with you but won't give his name."

"What's he want?"

"He said you're in danger. I asked him in danger of what. He said I didn't want to know. He said he's using a cell phone he bought off a street person, so I could forget about tracing the call."

"What'd you tell him?"

"That I'd deliver the message. If he calls again, you want me to give him your number?"

"Yeah, go ahead."

"There's something else. I asked him if he'd been drinking. He said, 'I wish I was just having the DTs. I wish this was all a dream. But those Asian women didn't shoot themselves.' "

A half hour later, while Hackberry was watering his flower beds, his cell phone chimed in his pocket again. "Hello?" he said. There was no reply. "Is this the same man who called my office earlier?"

"Yes."

Hackberry leaned over and turned off the water faucet. "You wanted to warn me about something?"

"Yes."

"Want to tell me what it is?"

"Jack Collins, that's his name. People call him Preacher."

"What about him?"

"He thinks you're after him. He thinks you and me have met."

"What's your name?"

"Collins killed the Thai women. He's hooked up with Hugo

Cistranos and Arthur Rooney. He thinks he's a character out of the Bible."

"Are you telling me you're in danger, sir?"

"I don't care about me."

"Collins is trying to hurt your family?"

"You've got it all wrong. He thinks he's protecting us. Collins says Arthur Rooney plans to kill us."

"Let us help you. Meet me someplace."

"No. I made this call because—"

"Because what?"

"I don't want your blood on me. I don't want the Asian women's blood on me. I don't want that soldier and his girlfriend hurt, either. I didn't plan any of this."

Nobody does, bud, Hackberry thought.

"Did you make a nine-one-one call about this some time ago and try to warn the FBI about Vikki Gaddis and her boyfriend?"

"No."

"I think you did. I heard your voice on the tape. I think you're probably a good man. You shouldn't be afraid of us."

"Artie Rooney says he wants my wife shot in the mouth. I'm not a good man. I let all this happen. I said what I had to say. You're never gonna hear from me again."

The signal went dead.

Hackberry called Maydeen. "Get ahold of Ethan Riser. Tell him I think we've got a solid lead on Jack Collins."

"Ethan who?"

"The FBI agent. Tell him to call me at the house."

"Is there somebody out to get you, Hack?"

"Why should I be a threat to anybody?"

"Because you're stubborn as a cinder block and you don't give up and all the shitbags know it."

"Maydeen, would you please—" He shook his head and closed his phone.

Throughout the day, Hackberry waited for Ethan Riser to call back. At the office, he cleaned out the paperwork in his in-basket, drove a sick female inmate from the jail to the hospital, ate lunch, shot a game of pool in the saloon, placed an ad for a road-gang guard in the newspaper (eight dollars an hour, no benefits, must not be an ex-felon), and returned home for supper.

Still no call from Ethan Riser.

He washed his dishes and dried them and put them away, then sat on the porch as the evening cooled and plumes of dust rose off the land and a purple haze formed in the sky. Occasionally, he sensed a hint of rain in the air, a touch of ozone, a shift in the breeze that was ten degrees cooler, a ripping sound in a bank of black clouds on the horizon. When he strained his eyes, he thought he saw lightning on a distant hill, like gold wires sparking against the darkness.

From where he sat, he could see both the southern and northern borders of his property, the railed pastures he watered with wheel lines, the machine shed where he parked his tractor and his four-stall barn and his tack room filled with bridles and snaffle bits and saddles and hackamores and head stalls and three-inch-diameter braided rope leads and horsefly spray and worming syringes and hoof clippers and wood rasps, the poplar trees he had planted as windbreaks, his pale, closely clipped lawn that looked like a putting green in a desert, his flower beds that he constantly weeded and mulched and fertilized and watered by hand every morning. He could see every inch of the world he had created to compensate for his solitude and to convince himself the world was a grand place and well worth fighting for and, in so doing, had found himself without someone to enjoy it beside in equal measure.

But maybe it was presumptuous of him to conclude that his ownership of the ranch was more than transitory. Tolstoy had said the only piece of earth a person owned was the six feet he claimed with his death. The gospel of Matthew said He makes His sun rise on the evil and the good, and sends rain on the just and the unjust. Just across the border was a moral insane asylum where drug dealers did drive-bys in SUVs on entire families, where coyotes stole the life savings of peasants who simply wanted to work in the United States, and where any freshly created hump in the countryside could contain a multiple burial.

Wasn't the potential for devolvement back into a simian society always extant within? Hackberry had seen American soldiers sell out their own in a prison camp south of the Yalu. The purchase price had been a warm shack to sleep in, an extra ball of rice, and a quilted coat with lice eggs in the seams. A trip into any border town gave one little doubt that hunger was the greatest aphrodisiac. It wouldn't take much to create the same kind of society here, Hackberry thought. The collapse of the economy, the systemic spread of fear, the threat of imagined foreign adversaries would probably be enough to pull it off. But one way or another, his home and his ranch and the animals on it and he himself would become dust blowing in the wind.

He stood up from his wicker chair and leaned his shoulder against one of the lathe-turned wood posts on the porch. The sun had burned into a red spark between two hills, and again he thought he smelled impending rain in the south. He wondered if all old men secretly searched for nature's rejuvenation in every tree of lightning pulsing silently inside a storm cloud, in every raindrop that struck a warm surface and reminded one of how good summer could be, of how valuable each day was.

The chime of his cell phone interrupted his reverie.

"Hello?" he said.

"It's Ethan. I hear you're having problems with anonymous callers."

"Remember the guy who called in the nine-one-one warning about Vikki Gaddis? My bet is he's from around New Orleans."

"You a dialectical linguist?"

"On the tape, the caller sounded like he had a pencil between his teeth. The guy who called me had an accent like the Bronx or Brooklyn, except not quite. You only hear that accent in New Orleans or close by. I think this is the same guy who called while he was drunk."

"Your dispatcher said this guy gave you a lead on Jack Collins."

"The caller said Collins has taken an undue interest in me. I don't give a lot of credence to that, but I do think the caller is obsessed with guilt and is hooked up with Arthur Rooney."

"I think you're underestimating Collins's potential, Sheriff. From everything we know about him, he believes he's the victim, not the perpetrator. You know the story of Lester Gillis?"

"Who?"

"Baby Face Nelson, a member of the Dillinger gang. He carried the photos and addresses and tag numbers of cops and FBI agents everywhere he went. He passed two agents in their car and made a U-turn and ran them off the road and killed both of them with seventeen bullet holes in him. I think Collins is the same kind of guy, except probably crazier. Get this: Baby Face Nelson had the last rites of the Catholic Church and had his wife wrap his body in a blanket and leave him in front of a cathedral because he didn't want to be cold." Riser started laughing.

"Arthur Rooney is originally from New Orleans, isn't he?" Hackberry said.

"The Ninth Ward, the area that got hit hardest by Katrina."

"Can you get me the names of his old business associates?"

"Yeah, I guess I could do that."

"Guess?"

"I've got certain parameters I have to abide by."

"Your colleagues still want to use Jack Collins to get to the Russian, what's-his-name?"

"Josef Sholokoff."

"So I have limited access to your information, even though I may be the target of the guy your colleagues want to cut a deal with?"

"I wouldn't put it that way."

"I would. Tell your colleagues that if Jack Collins comes around here, they're going to be interviewing his corpse. See you, Mr. Riser." Hackberry clicked off his cell phone and had to restrain himself from sailing it over the top of his windmill.

One hour later, he looked out the window and saw Pam Tibbs turn off the state road and drive under his arch and park her pickup in front of the house. She got out and seemed to hesitate before coming up the flagstones that led through his yard. She wore earrings and designer jeans and boots and a magenta silk shirt that was full of lights.

He stepped out on the porch. "Come in," he said.

"I didn't want to bother you," she said.

"You didn't necessarily catch me in the middle of inventing the wheel."

"Maydeen gave me two tickets to the rodeo. We can probably still catch the last hour or so, or just go to the fair."

"Is everything okay?"

"Sure. No problems."

He walked into the yard, the spray from his sprinklers iridescent in the glow of the porch light. She looked up into his face, an expectation there that he couldn't quite define. He scratched at the top of his forehead. "I had dreams about Korea for a long time," he said. "Once in a while I still go back there. It's the way we're made. If certain things we do or witness don't leave a stone bruise on the soul, there's something wrong with our humanity."

"I'm all right, Hack."

"It doesn't work that way, kiddo."

"Don't assign me patronizing names." When he didn't reply,

she put her hands on her hips and stared into the darkness, her eyes fighting with an emotion she didn't plan to discuss or perhaps even recognize. "Eriksson looked into my face just before I shot him. He knew what was about to happen. I've always heard the term 'mortal fear' used to describe moments like that. But that wasn't it. He saw the other side."

"Of what?"

"The grave, judgment, eternity, whatever people want to call it. It was like he was thinking the words 'It's forever too late.'"

"Eriksson dealt the play and got what he deserved. You saved my life, Pam. Don't let a sonofabitch like that rob you of *your* life."

"You can be pretty hard-edged, Hack."

"No, I'm not. Eriksson was a killer for hire." He cupped his palm around the back of her neck. "He preyed on the defenseless and used what was best in people to turn them into his victims. We're the children of light. That's not a hyperbole."

Her eyes wandered over his face as though she feared mockery or insincerity in his words. "I'm not a child of light, not at all."

"You are to me," he said. He saw her swallow and her lips part. His palm felt warm and moist on the back of her neck. He removed it and hooked his thumbs in his pockets. "I'd really like to go to that rodeo. I'd like to buy some candied apples and caramel corn at the fair, too. Anybody who doesn't like rodeos and county fairs has something wrong with him."

"Get mad at me if you want," she said. She put her arms around him and hugged herself against him and pressed her face against his chest and her body against his loins. He could smell the perfume behind her ears and the strawberry shampoo in her hair and the fragrance of her skin. He saw the windmill's blades ginning in the starlight, the disengaged rotary shaft turning impotently, the cast-iron pipe dry and hard-looking above the aluminum tank. He rested his cheek on top of Pam's head, his eyes tightly shut.

She stepped away from him. "Is it because you feel certain people shouldn't be together? Because they're the wrong age or color or gender or their bloodline is too close? Is that how you think, Hack?"

"No," he replied.

"Then what is it? Is it because you're my boss? Or is it just me?"

It's because it's dishonorable for an old man to sleep with a young woman who is looking for her father, he thought.

"What did you say?"

"I said nothing. I said let me buy you a late supper. I said I'm happy you came by. I said let's go to the fair."

"All right, Hack. If you say so. I won't—"

"Won't what?"

She smiled and shrugged.

"You won't what?" he repeated.

She continued to smile, her feigned cheerfulness concealing her resignation. "I'll drive," she said.

THAT NIGHT AFTER she dropped him off, he sat for a long time in his bedroom with the lights turned off. Then he lay down on top of the bedcovers in his clothes and stared at the ceiling, the heat lightning flickering on his body. Outside, he heard his horses running in the pasture, their hooves heavy-sounding, swallowed by the wind, as though they were wrapped in flannel. He heard his garbage-can lid rattle on the driveway, blown by the wind or pulled loose from the bungee cord by an animal. He heard the trees thrashing and wild animals walking through the yard and the twang of his smooth wire when a deer went through his back fence. Then he heard a noise that shouldn't have been there, a car engine in closer proximity to his house than the state road would allow.

He sat up and slipped his boots on and went out on the porch.

A car had pulled off the asphalt and driven onto the dirt track beyond the northern border of his property. The car's lights were off, but the engine was still running. Hackberry went back into the bedroom and removed his holstered revolver from under his bed and unsnapped the strap from the hammer and let the holster slide off the barrel onto the bedspread. He walked back outside and crossed the yard to the horse lot. Missy's Playboy and Love That Santa Fe were standing by their water tank, frozen, looking to the north, the wind drifting a cloud of dust across them.

"It's okay, fellows. We're just going to check this guy out," Hackberry said, walking between them, the white-handled .45 hanging from his left hand.

As Hackberry approached the north fence on the pasture, the driver of the car shifted into gear without apparent urgency, the lights still off, and turned in a circle, dead tree branches and uncropped Johnson grass raking under the car's frame. Then he drove in a leisurely fashion onto the asphalt and continued down the road, clicking on his headlights when he passed a clump of oaks on the bend.

Hackberry went back to the house, set his revolver on the nightstand, and gradually fell asleep. He dreamed of a rodeo bull exploding out of a bucking chute. The rider's bones seemed to be breaking apart inside his skin as the bull reared and corkscrewed between his thighs. Suddenly, the rider was in the air, his wrist still tied down with a suicide wrap, his body over the side, whipped and dirt-dragged and flung into the boards and finally horned.

Without ever quite waking from the dream, Hackberry reached for his revolver and clenched its white handles in his palm.

* * *

PREACHER CONSIDERED HIMSELF a tolerant man. But Bobby Lee Motree could be a challenge.

"Holland is an old man," Bobby Lee said over the cell phone. "When he was running for Congress, he was known as a drunk and a gash hound. He got religion after he started representing a Mexican farmworkers' union, probably because he'd already screwed up everything else he touched. His first wife dumped him and cleaned out his bank account. His second wife was a Communist organizer of some kind. She died of cancer. The guy's a loser, Jack."

Preacher was sitting at a card table in the shade behind his stucco house, watching a lizard crawl across the top of a big gray rock while he talked. The table was spread with a clean cloth. On top of the cloth, Preacher had disassembled his Thompson machine gun. Next to the disassembled parts were a can of lubricant and a bore brush and a white rag stained yellow with a fresh application of oil. While he talked, Preacher touched the oiled surface of the Thompson's barrel and studied the wispy tracings his fingerprints left on the steel.

"Listen, Jack, if it's not broken, you don't fix it," Bobby Lee said. "The guy couldn't even save his own grits. Liam would have capped him if that cunt of a deputy hadn't shown up."

"Don't use that term around me."

"We're talking about popping a Texas sheriff, and you're worried about language?"

Preacher wiped his fingertips on the gun cloth and studied a hawk flying above the mountainside, its shadow racing across the slope.

"You there?" Bobby Lee said.

"Where else would I be?"

"I'm just saying Holland is a retread and a rural schmuck who surrounds himself with other losers. Why borrow trouble?" Bobby Lee said.

"The man has the Navy Cross."

"So, rah-rah, he's a swinging dick. Maybe he ran in the wrong direction."

"You have a serious problem, Bobby Lee."

"What's that?"

"You come to conclusions without looking at the evidence. Then you find reasons to justify your shoddy conclusions. It's like inventing a square wheel and trying to convince yourself you like your wagon to ride a little rough."

"Jack, you smoked a federal agent. You want to add another cop to your tally? They not only execute in this state, they have beer parties at the prison gates when they do it. I'm risking my life throwing in with you. We've got Hugo and Artie Rooney to deal with. Then there's Vikki Gaddis and the soldier boy. What's next, dropping a hydrogen bomb on Iran?"

"I'll handle Artie Rooney."

"You ought to get laid. You know what Hugo said? I'm quoting Hugo, I didn't say it, it's Hugo talking, not me. He said, 'Preacher's last sexual encounter was a visit to his proctologist.' How long has it been since you got your ashes hauled?"

Preacher watched the lizard's throat puff out in a red balloon on the rock. The lizard's tongue uncoiled and wrapped around a tiny black ant and pulled the ant into the lizard's mouth. "I'm glad you're on my side, Bobby Lee. You have loyalty in your lineage. That's why General Lee stuck with the state of Virginia, isn't it? Loyalty has no surrogate. Blood will out, won't it?"

There was a long silence. "Why are you always ridiculing me? I'm the only guy who stood with you. You really hurt my feelings, man."

"You got a point. You're a good boy, Bobby Lee."

"That means a lot to me, Jack. But you got to quit renting space in your head to bozos who couldn't shine your shoes."

"Artie Rooney is going to pay me a half million dollars. Ten percent of that will go to you."

"That's generous of you, man. You got a kind heart."

"In the meantime, Artie is going to leave the Jews alone. That one isn't up for grabs."

"You still worried about the Jews after what Ms. Dolan did to you? What about the Gaddis broad and the soldier boy? Are they out?"

"They're in."

"They're in?"

"You heard me."

"What about Holland?"

"I'll give it some thought."

"I think he saw me. I pulled off the road to case his place. I thought he was asleep. He came outside and saw my car. But it was too dark for him to get my tag or see my face. If we leave him alone, he'll forget about it."

"You didn't tell me that."

"So I just did. Use your head, Jack. Artie Rooney hijacked Josef Sholokoff's whores. Who do you think Rooney is gonna put that on? You got the rep from L.A. to Miami. Mexican cops think you walk through walls. Artie gets on the phone, tells Sholokoff you're a psycho, tells him you're working for Nick Dolan, and gets you permanently out of his hair. You taught me to be a fly on the wall, Jack."

"Want to spell that out?"

"That agent you capped wasn't just a fed, he was from ICE. They're fanatics, worse than Treasury agents. You got any idea of how hot you are?"

"You just said 'you.'"

"Okay, 'we.'"

"Call me when you find Vikki Gaddis."

"Is this girl worth clipping? Think about it. A waitress from a truck stop?"

"Did I say anything about clipping her? Did you hear me say that?"

"No."

"You find her, but you don't touch her."

"Why should I want to touch her? It's not me who's got—"

"Got what?"

"An obsession. Like a tumor on the brain. The size of a carrot."

Again Preacher let his silence speak for him; it was a weapon Bobby Lee never knew how to deal with.

"You still there?"

"Still here," Preacher said.

"You're the best there is, Jack. Nobody else could have done what you did behind the church. It took guts to do that."

"Say again?"

"To step across the line like that, to grease every one of them, to burn the whole magazine and bulldoze them under and mark it off. It takes maximum cojones to do a mass whack like that, Jack. That's why you're you."

This time Preacher's silence was not of his own volition. He took the cell phone from his ear and opened his mouth to clear a blockage in his ear canal. The side of his face felt both numb and hot to the touch, as though he had been stung by a bee. He stared at the gray rock. The lizard was gone, and at the base of the rock, he saw a spray of tiny purple flowers that looked like tiny violets. He wondered how any flower that lovely and delicate could grow in the desert.

"You still there? Talk to me, man," he heard Bobby Lee's voice say. Preacher closed his cell phone without replying. He picked up the Thompson and ran a bore brush through the barrel and swabbed it with a clean oil patch. He folded a piece of white paper and inserted it in the open chamber, reflecting the sunlight up through the rifling. The inside of the barrel was immaculate, the whorls of light an affirmation of the gun's mechanical integrity and reliability. He lifted up the drum and snapped it cleanly into place under the barrel and laid the gun across his lap, his palms resting on the wood stock and steel frame. He could hear whirring sounds in his head, like wind blowing in a cave or perhaps the voices of women whispering to him through the ground, whispering inside the wildflowers.

AT THAT SAME moment, one hundred miles away, three bikers were headed down a two-lane highway, full-bore, their arms wrapped with jailhouse tats, the points of their shoulders bright with sunburn. Sometimes, out of boredom, they lazed across the solid yellow stripe or stopped at a roadside rathole for a beer and a grease burger or caught a live hillbilly band at a shitkicker nightclub or steak house. But otherwise, they burned their way across the American Southwest with the dedication of Visigoths. The crystal that coursed in their veins, the dirty thunder of their exhaust flattening against the asphalt, the blowtorch velocity of the wind on their skin, the surge of the engines' power into their genitalia, blended together in a paean to their lives.

They topped a rise and turned onto a dirt road and followed it for two miles until they came out on the cusp of a sloping plain of alluvial grit and alkali and green mesquite. They stopped between two dun-colored bluffs, and their leader consulted a topographical map without dismounting, then used binoculars to study a small stucco house set against a mountain that contained a shadow-darkened opening in its face. "Bingo," he said.

The three men dismounted and touched fists and parked their hogs down in a gulley and built a fire and cooked their food on sticks. When they had finished eating, they pissed on the flames in the sunset and rolled out their sleeping bags and smoked weed and, like spectators at an exotic zoo, silently watched a coyote with a stiffened back leg try to keep up with a pack climbing a hill. Then they fell asleep.

On the fair side of the plain, the stucco house was quiet. A solitary figure sat on a metal chair in front of the opening to a shored-up cave, staring at the mantle of gold light on the hills, his expression as removed from earthly concerns as that of a man whose severed head had just been placed on a platter.

Chapter 17

Bᴜᴛ ɪɴ ᴛʜᴇ morning, the man who lived upon occasion in the stucco house was not to be found. The bikers had approached the house on foot from three directions, the sun still buried beneath the earth's rim, the light so weak their bodies cast no shadows on the ground. A compact car was parked twenty yards away from the house, the doors unlocked, the keys hanging in the ignition. The bikers kicked open the front and back doors of the house, turned over the bed, raked the clothes out of the closets, and tore the plywood out of the ceiling to see if Preacher was hiding in an attic or crawl space.

"The mine shaft," one of them said.

"Where?" another said.

"Up on the mountain. There's no other place he could be. Josef said he's on crutches."

"How'd he know we were coming?"

"The Mexicans say he walks through walls."

"That's why their country would make a great golf course, as long as it was run by white people."

The bikers spread out and approached the opening on the

283

mountainside, their weapons hanging loosely at their sides. They wore needle-nosed cowboy boots that were metal-plated around the heels and toes, jeans that were stiff with grit and road grime, and shirts whose sleeves were razored off at the armpits. Their hair was sunburned at the tips and grew in locks on the backs of their necks. Their bodies had the tendons and lean hardness of men who lifted weights daily and for whom narcissism was a virtue and not a character defect.

Their leader was named Tim. He stood two inches taller than his companions and wore a gold earring in one earlobe and a beard that ran along his jawline like a cluster of black ants. A Glock semiautomatic hung from his right hand. He paused in front of the cave and slipped the gun into the back of his belt, as though enacting a private ritual unrelated to what anyone thought of him. He took a breath and entered the cave. He produced a penlight from his jeans, clicked it on, and shone it into the darkness.

"It's a mine?" one of his companions said.

"I can feel a breeze blowing through it. It's got to have a second opening."

"You see the guy?"

"No, that's why I said it's got a second opening. Maybe he went through it and out the other side."

"Where's it go?"

Tim continued to walk deeper into the cave, the beam of his penlight watery and diffuse on the walls. "Come have a look at this."

"At what?"

"Did you see *Snakes on a Plane*?"

The two bikers who had remained outside the cave stepped into the darkness. Tim aimed the penlight in front of him, pointing it down a passageway that twisted into the mountain.

"Jesus!" one of them said.

"They go where there's food or water. Maybe a cougar dragged its kill in here," Tim said. "You ever see that many in one place?"

"Maybe Collins is a ghoul. Maybe he dumps his victims in here."

"Go down and check it out. They rattle before they strike. They're not rattling. You'll be okay."

"How about that one on the ledge behind you?"

The other two bikers waited, smiles on their faces, expecting Tim to jump. Instead, he turned around and shone the light into a diamondback's eyes. He picked up a piece of splintered timber that had fallen from the roof. He poked at the snake's head with it, then bedeviled it in the stomach, and finally, lifted it up in a coil and flipped it into the darkness.

"You're not afraid of snakes?"

"I'm afraid of bad information. I think this Texas bunch is jerking Josef around. This guy Collins is a hitter, not a pimp. Hitters don't boost somebody else's whores."

"Where do you think he went?"

"One thing is for sure. He didn't go out the other side."

"Then where is he?"

"Probably watching us."

"No way. From where?"

"I don't know. The guy has been killing people for twenty years and never went inside."

"This blows, Tim."

They were outside the cave now, the stucco house still in shadow, the morning cool, the wind ruffling the mesquite. The three men stared at the surrounding hills, looking for the glint of binoculars or the lens on a telescopic rifle sight.

"Who are we supposed to check in with?"

"The guy who ratted out Collins. His name is Hugo Cistranos."

"What are we gonna do?"

Tim slipped the Glock from behind his belt and strolled down the gravel path from the cave to Preacher's compact car. He circled the car, taking careful aim, and shot out each tire. He went inside the house and closed all the windows, like a man securing his home from an impending storm. He found a candle in a kitchen drawer, lit it, and melted the wax in a pool so he could affix it to the drainboard. Then he shut the front door and turned on the propane stove and shut the kitchen door behind him as he exited the house.

"Let's fang down some frijoles," he said.

Sheriff Hackberry Holland had just picked up Danny Boy Lorca for public intoxication and locked him in a cell upstairs when Maydeen told him Ethan Riser was on the phone.

"How you doing, Mr. Riser?" Hackberry said, picking up the receiver on his desk.

"Can't you call me Ethan?"

"It's a southern inhibition."

"You were right about the origins of your mystery caller. We think his name is Nick Dolan. He was a floating casino operator in New Orleans before Katrina."

"How'd you ID him?"

"His name was in Isaac Clawson's notes. Clawson figured the Thai murder victims for prostitutes somebody was smuggling into the country, so he started running down anybody with major ties to escort services. It appears Clawson was giving Arthur Rooney a hard look and decided to check out Nick Dolan at the same time. Evidently, he interviewed Dolan at his vacation home in New Braunfels."

"Why are y'all just finding this out?"

"Like I told you, Clawson liked to work alone. He didn't put everything he did in the official file."

"But so far you're not absolutely sure Dolan is the same guy who called me?"

"Dolan knows Rooney. Dolan has been mixed up with prostitution for the last two years. Clawson had him in his bombsights. Also, Dolan just dissolved his partnership in his escort services and fired all the strippers at his nightclub. Either Clawson scared the shit out of him, or Dolan has developed problems of conscience."

"You haven't interviewed him yet?"

"No."

"You're putting a tap on him instead?"

"Did I say that?"

"I think you're calling me because you don't want me to find Dolan on my own."

"Some people have a way of putting themselves in the middle of electric storms, Sheriff."

"I don't think the problem is mine. Your colleagues want Collins as a conduit to this Russian out on the West Coast. I think they might want to use Dolan as bait. In the meantime, I'm a hangnail."

This time Ethan Riser was silent.

"You're telling me I'm bait, too?" Hackberry said.

"I can't speak for the actions of others. But I sleep nights. I do so because I treat people as honestly as I can. Watch your ass, Sheriff. Guys like us are old school. But there's not many of us left."

A FEW MINUTES LATER, Hackberry filled a Styrofoam cup with black coffee, dropped three sugar cubes in it, and removed a folded-up checkerboard and a box of wood checkers from his bottom desk drawer. He walked up the old steel stairs to the second floor and pulled up a chair to Danny Boy Lorca's cell. He sat down and placed the coffee and the checkerboard inside the bars and unfolded the checkerboard on the concrete floor. "Set 'em up," he said.

"I fell off the wagon again," Danny Boy said, sitting up on the edge of his bunk, rubbing his face. His skin was as dark as smoked leather, his eyes dead, like coals that have been consumed by their own fire.

"One day you'll quit. Between now and then, don't fret yourself about it," Hackberry said.

"I dreamed it rained. I saw a dried-out field of corn stand up straight in the rain. I had the same dream for three nights."

Hackberry's eyes crinkled at the corners.

"You don't pay no attention to dreams, huh?" Danny Boy said.

"You bet I do. Your move," Hackberry said.

THE THREE BIKERS checked in to a motel next to a truck stop and nightclub, partially because the portable sign in front of the nightclub said LADIES FREE TONIGHT—TWO-FERS 5 TO 8. They showered and changed into fresh clothes and drank Mexican beer at the bar and picked up a woman who said she worked at the dollar store in town. They also picked up her friend, who was sullen and suspicious and claimed she had a ten-year-old boy waiting alone at home.

But when Tim showed the friend his tin Altoids box packed to the brim with a lovely white granular cake of nose candy, she changed her mind and joined him and her girlfriend and the other two bikers for a couple of lines, some high-octane weed, and an order-in pizza back at the motel.

Tim had rented a room at the end of the building, and while his companions and their new friends went at it full-throttle on two beds, he drank a soda outside and crushed the can in one hand and threw it in the trash. He sat on a bench under a tree throbbing with cicadas and opened his cell phone. He could hear the bedstead banging against the motel wall and the cacophonous laughter of the two dimwits his friends had picked up, as if their laughter were outside them and not part of anything that was funny. He put an unlit cigarette in his mouth and tried to clear his head. What would the smart money do in a situation like this? You didn't blow a hit for Josef Sholokoff. You also didn't mess up when you took on a guy like Jack Collins, at least if he was as good as people said he was.

The eaves of the motel were lit with pink neon tubing. The light was fading from the sky, and the air was purple and dense and moist, with a smell of dust in it that suggested a drop in the barometer, perhaps even a taste of rain. The fronds on a palm tree by the entrance to the motel straightened and rattled in the wind. He thought about going back inside and trying out one of the dimwits. No, first things first. He dialed a number on his cell phone. While he listened to the ring, he wondered what was keeping the pizza man with their order.

"Hugo?"

"Yeah, who's this?"

"It's Tim."

"Tim who?"

"Tim who works for Josef. Lose the charade. You want an update or not?"

"You got Preacher?"

"We're working on it."

"Explain that."

"We had him boxed, but he disappeared. I don't know how he did it."

"Preacher is onto you but he got away? Do you have any idea what you're telling me?"

"It sounds like you overloaded on your Ex-Lax."

"You listen, asshole—"

"No, you listen. The guy has got no wheels and no house to go back to. We'll find him. In the meantime—"

"What do you mean, he has no house to—"

"There was a propane accident in his kitchen. Some vandals blew the tires off his car at about the same time. Everything is under control. Here's the good news. You said you were looking for a broad."

"No, I said Preacher was looking for a broad. He's got an obsession about her. You said you shot out his tires? What the fuck do you think this is? Halloween?"

"Man, you just don't listen, do you?"

"About what?"

"The broad and the soldier you're looking for. She has chestnut hair and green eyes, looks like a fine piece of ass, sings Gomer Pyle spirituals to beer-drinking retards who don't have a clue? If that sounds right, I know where you can find her."

"You found Vikki Gaddis?"

"No, Michelle Obama. You got a pencil?"

"There's one here somewhere. Hang on."

"One day you guys have to explain to me how you got into the life."

Inside the motel room, the women got up and dressed in the bathroom. The woman from the dollar store came out first, blotting her face with a towel, smoothing her hair out of her face. She was overweight and round-shouldered, her arms big like a farm girl's; without makeup, her face was as stark as a pie plate. "Where's the pizza?" she asked.

"The guy must have got lost," one biker said.

The other biker wanted to use the bathroom, but the second woman had locked the door. "What are you doing in there?" he said, shaking the knob.

"Calling my son. Hold your water," she said through the door.

"I love family values," he said.

The second woman came out of the bathroom. Unlike her friend, her bone structure looked like it had been created from an Erector Set. Her face was triangular in shape, her skin bad, her eyes filled with a glint that seemed to teeter without cause on malevolence.

"Your kid okay?" one of the bikers said.

"You think I'd be here if he wasn't?" she replied.

"Not everybody is such a good mother."

The two women went out the door. A beaded sky-blue sequined purse hung on a string from the overweight woman's shoulder. She looked back once, smiling as though to say good night.

Tim came back into the room and sat down in a chair by the window. He pulled off his metal-sheathed boots and cupped his hands on his thighs, staring at the floor. "We've got to clean this up."

"You talk to Josef?"

"To this lamebrain Hugo. He says we spit in the tiger's mouth."

"A guy on crutches with no car or house? I think this guy is some kind of urban legend."

"Maybe."

"I'm hungry. You want me to call the pizza place again or go out?"

"What I want you to do is let me think a minute."

"You should have got laid, Tim."

Tim stared at the nicked furniture, the yellowed curtains on the windows, the bedclothes piled on the floor. On the chair by the television set was a gray vinyl handbag, the brass zipper pulled tight. "There's something wrong," he said.

"Yeah, we're wandering around in a giant skillet. Is this whole state like this?"

"Who ordered the pizza?"

"The skinny broad."

"What'd she say?"

"'I want two sausage-and-mushroom pizzas.'"

"Pick up the receiver and hit redial."

"I think you're losing it, man."

"Just do it."

"This phone doesn't have a redial."

"Then get the number off the pizza menu on the desk and call it."

"Okay, Tim. How about a little serenity here?"

Someone knocked on the door. The biker who had picked up the phone replaced the receiver in the cradle. He started toward the door.

"No!" Tim said, holding up his hand. He got up from his chair in his sock feet and clicked off the light. He pulled back the window curtain just far enough to see the walkway.

"Who is it?" the other biker asked him.

"I can't tell," Tim said. He removed the Glock from his overnight bag. "What do you want?" he said through the door.

"Pizza delivery," a voice said.

"What took you so long?"

"There was an accident on the highway."

"Set it on the walkway."

"It's in the warmer."

"If you set it down, it won't be in the warmer any longer, will it?"

"It's thirty-two dollars."

Tim put on the night chain and took out his wallet. He eased the door open, the chain links tightening against the brass slot. The delivery man was older than he expected, blade-faced, his nose sunburned, an orange-and-black cloth cap pulled low on his brow.

"How much did you say?"

"Thirty-two dollars even."

"I've only got a hundred."

"I have to go back to the car for change."

Tim held on to the hundred and closed the door and waited. A moment later, the delivery man returned and knocked again. Tim cracked the door and handed the hundred-dollar bill to him. "Count the change out on the top of the box. Keep five for yourself."

"Thank you, sir."

"What's your name?"

"Doug."

"Who's with you in your car, Doug?"

"My wife. When I get off, we're going to visit her mother at the hospital."

"You take your wife on deliveries so you can go to the hospital together?"

The delivery man began blinking uncertainly.

"I was just asking," Tim said. He shut the door and waited. Then he went to the curtain and peeled it from the corner of the window and watched the pizza man turn his car around and drive back onto the highway. He opened the door and squatted down and lifted the two heavily laden cartons of pizza from the concrete. They were warm in his hand and smelled deliciously of sausage and onions and mushrooms and melted cheese. He watched the taillights of the delivery car disappear down the road, then closed the door and replaced the chain. "What are you guys looking at?" he said to his companions.

"Hey, you're just being careful. Come on, let's scarf."

They ordered beer brought over from the nightclub, and for the next hour, they ate and drank and watched television and rolled joints out of Tim's stash. Tim even became silently amused at his concern over the pizza man. He yawned and lay back on the bed, a pillow behind his head. Then he noticed again the vinyl handbag one of the women had left behind. It had fallen from the chair and was lodged behind the television stand. "Which one of the broads was carrying a gray purse?" he said.

"The bony one."

"Check it out."

But before the other biker could pick up the handbag, there was another knock on the door. "We need a turnstile here," Tim said.

He got up from the bed and went to the window. This time he pulled the curtain all the way back so he could have a clear view of the walkway and door area. He went to the door and opened it on the chain. "You forgot your purse?" he said.

"I left it here or in the club. It's not at the club, so it must be here," the woman said. "Everything is in it."

"Hang on." He shut the door, his hand floating up to release the chain.

"Don't let her in, man. If women can have a hard-on, this one has got a hard-on. I'll get her purse," one of the other bikers said.

Tim slipped the night chain from its slot.

"Tim, wait."

"What?" Tim said, twisting the doorknob.

"There ain't a wallet in the purse. Just lipstick and tampons and used Kleenex and hairpins."

Tim turned around and looked back at his friend, the door seeming to swing open of its own accord. The woman who had knocked was hurrying across the parking lot toward a waiting automobile. In her place stood a man Tim had never seen. The man was wearing a suit and a white shirt without a tie, and his hair was greased and combed straight back, his body trim, his shoes shined. He looked like a man who was trying to hold on to the ways of an earlier generation. His weight was propped up by a walking cane that he held stiffly with his left hand. In his right hand, snugged against his side, was a Thompson machine gun.

"How'd you—" Tim began.

"I get around," Preacher said.

The spent casings shuddering from the bolt of his weapon clattered off the doorjamb, rained on the concrete, and bounced and rolled into the grass. The staccato explosions from the muzzle were like the zigzags of an electric arc.

Preacher limped toward the waiting car, the downturned silhouette of his weapon leaking smoke. Not one room door opened, nor did one face appear at a window. The motel and the neon-pink tubing wrapped around its eaves and the palm tree etched against the sky by the entrance had taken on the emptiness of a movie set. As Preacher drove away, he stared through the big glass window of the front office. The clerk was gone, and so were any guests who might have been waiting to register. From the highway, he glanced back at the motel again. Its insularity, its seeming abandonment by all its inhabitants, the total absence of any detectable humanity within its confines, made him think of a snowy wind blowing outside a boxcar on a desolate siding, a pot of vegetables starting to burn on an untended fire, although he had no way to account for the association.

Chapter 18

Vikki Gaddis got off work at the steak house at ten P.M. and walked to the Fiesta motel with a San Antonio newspaper folded under her arm. When she entered the room, Pete was watching television in his skivvies. His T-shirt looked like cheesecloth against the red scar tissue on his back. She popped open the newspaper and dropped it in his lap. "Those guys were at the restaurant three nights ago," she said. "They were bikers. They looked road-fried."

Pete stared down at the booking-room photographs of three men. They were in their twenties and possessed the rugged good looks of men in their prime. Unlike the subjects of most booking-room photography, none of the men appeared fatigued or under the influence or nonplussed or artificially amused. Two of them had served time in San Quentin, one in Folsom. All three had been arrested for possession with intent to distribute. All three had been suspects in unsolved homicides.

"You talked to them?" Pete asked.

"No, they talked to me. I thought they were just hitting on me. I sang four numbers with the band, and they tried to get me to sit down with them. I told them I had to work, I was a waitress and just sang occasionally with the band. They thought it was funny that I sang 'Will the Circle Be Unbroken.' "

"Why didn't you tell me?"

"Because I thought they were jerks and not worth talking about."

Pete began reading the newspaper story again. "They were machine-gunned," he said. He bit a hangnail. "What'd they say to you?"

"They wanted to know my name. They wanted to know where I was from."

"What'd you tell them?"

"That I had to get back to work. Later, they were asking the bartender about me."

"What in particular?"

"Like how long I'd been working there. Like had I ever been a professional folksinger. Like didn't I used to live around Langtry or Pumpville? Except these guys had California tags, and why should they know anything about little towns on the border?"

Pete turned off the television but continued to stare at the screen.

"They're contract killers, aren't they?" she said.

"They didn't follow you after you got off work. They didn't come around the motel, either. Maybe you were right—they were just jerks trying to pick you up."

"There's something else."

He looked at her and waited.

"I talked with the bartender before I got off tonight. I showed him the newspaper. He said, 'One of those bikers was talking about calling up some guy named Hugo.' "

"You're just telling me all this now?" Pete said.

"No, you're not listening. The bartender—" She gave up and sat down on the bed beside him, not touching him. "I can't think straight." She pushed at her forehead with the heel of her hand. "Maybe they did follow me home and I didn't see them. What if they found out where we're living and they called up this guy Hugo and told him?"

"I don't get it, though. Who killed them?" Pete said. "The story doesn't say what kind of machine gun the shooter used. There's a lot of illegal stuff available now—AKs, Uzis, semiautos with hell-triggers."

"What difference does that make?"

"The story says there were shell casings all over the crime scene. If the guy had a Thompson with a drum on it—"

"Pete, will you just spit it out? What are you saying? You talk in hieroglyphics."

"The guy who killed all the women behind the church used a Thompson. They're hard to come by. They shoot forty-five-caliber ammunition. The ammo drum will hold fifty rounds. Maybe the guy who killed the women behind the church is the same guy who machine-gunned the bikers."

"That doesn't make sense. Why would they be killing each other?"

"Maybe they're not working together." Pete read more, running his thumb down to the last paragraph. He set the paper aside and rubbed his palms on his knees.

"Say it," she said.

"The shooter had a limp. Maybe he uses a walking cane. A trucker saw him from the highway."

Vikki got up from the bed. Her face was pale, the skin tight against the bone, as though she were staring into a cold wind. "He's the man I shot, isn't he?"

Pete began putting on his trousers.

"Where you going?"

"Out."

"To do what?"

"Not to drink, if that's what you're asking."

Her eyes remained accusatory, locked on his.

"I brought all this on us, Vikki. You don't have to say it."

"Don't leave."

"More of the same isn't gonna cut it."

"I'm not mad at you. I'm just tired."

"I'll be back."

"When?"

"When you see me."

"What are you going to do?"

"Boost a car. I wasn't just a crewman in a tank. I was a mechanic. See, there's an upside to getting french-fried in Baghdad."

"Damn you, Pete."

HUGO CISTRANOS WAS sitting on a canvas chair on the beach in his Speedos, the waves capping and sliding in a yellow froth up on the sand. The air smelled like brass and iodine. It smelled of the crusted seaweed around his feet and the ruptured air sacs of the jellyfish that lay in a jagged line at the water's edge. It smelled of the fear that fouled his heart and pooled in his glands that no amount of suntan lotion could hide.

He tried Preacher's cell phone again. He had already left six messages, then had listened to a recording tell him Preacher's mailbox was full. But this time the cell phone not only rang, Preacher picked up. "What do you want?" he said.

"Hey, Jack, where you been?" Hugo said. "I was worried sick, man."

"About what?"

"About whatever has been going on over there. Where are you?"

"Looking for a new house."

"Looking for—"

"I had a fire, a propane explosion."

"You're kidding?"

"During the fire, somebody shot out my car tires, too. Maybe one of the firemen."

"I read about that motel gig in the *Houston Chronicle*. That's what brought it on? Those punks torched your place?"

"What motel?"

"Jack, I'm your friend. Those guys worked for the Russian out on the coast. I don't know why they were after you, but I'm glad they got clipped. I suspect they were sent out here to do a payback on Artie and everybody who works for him, including me."

"I think you got it figured, Hugo."

"Look, I called about a couple of other issues, even though I was worrying about you, not hearing from you and all." A red Frisbee sailed out of nowhere and hit Hugo on the side of the head. He picked it up and flung it savagely in a little boy's direction. "Artie wants to settle with you. He wants me to take care of the money transfer."

"Settle? This isn't a suit."

"He's offering you two hundred thou. That's all the cash he's got. Why not call it slick and put it behind you?"

"You said 'issues,' in the plural."

"We think we know where the broad is."

"Try to use proper nouns. That's the specific name of a person, place, or thing."

"Vikki Gaddis. I don't know if the soldier is still with her or not. You want to handle it, or you want Bobby Lee and a couple of new guys to tune her up and maybe deliver her anywhere you want?"

"You don't put a hand on her."

"Whatever you say."

"How'd you find her?"

"Long story. What do you want me to tell Artie?"

"I'll get back to you with wire instructions for an offshore account."

"That creates an electronic trail, Jack. We need to meet."

"I'll drop by."

"No, we need to get everybody together at one time and talk things out."

"Where's the Gaddis girl?"

Hugo's mind was racing. Why had he believed he could out-think a sociopath? His plated chest was heaving as though he had run up a hill. His skin felt encrusted with sand; sweat and sand seeped from his armpits. His mouth was dry, and the sun was burning through the top of his head. "Jack, we've been in the game a long time together."

"I'm waiting."

"You got it. I'm on your team. You got to believe me on that."

He gave Preacher the name of the town and the name of the steak house where Vikki Gaddis had been seen, not revealing his source. Then he wiped his mouth. "You got to tell me something. How'd you get to those bikers? How'd you set that up, man?"

"Whores sell information. They also sell out their johns if the price is right. Some of them take a high degree of pleasure in it," Preacher said.

As Hugo's heart slowed, he realized an opportunity had just presented itself, one he had not thought about earlier. "I'm your friend, Jack. I've always looked up to you. Be careful when you're down there on the border. That sheriff and his deputy, the ones who nailed Liam? They were here."

"This fellow Holland?"

"Yeah, he was talking to Artie. About you, man. Artie told him he never heard of you, but this guy has you made for the deal behind the church. I think he's got political ambitions or something. He was asking ugly questions about your family, about your mother in particular. What the fuck does that guy care about your mother?"

Hugo could hear the wind between his ear and the cell phone, then the connection went dead.

Got you, you crazy sonofabitch, he said to himself.

He slipped on his shades and watched the little boy's red Frisbee sail gently aloft, out over the waves, seagulls cawing emptily around it.

PETE WALKED DOWN the road in the dark, under the pink stucco arch painted with roses, past the closed-down drive-in theater and the circular building with service windows constructed to resemble a bulging cheeseburger and the three Cadillacs that appeared to be buried nose-first in the hardpan. The wind was up, and the combination of dust and humidity it created felt like the filings from damp sandpaper in his hair and on his skin. At the edge of town, he followed a train spur northeast, walking along the edge of the embankment onto a wide flat plain where the main track pointed miles into the distance, the night sky gleaming on the rails.

A half hour later, as he walked into a basin, he heard a double-header coming at low speed down the track, the flat-wheelers and empty grain cars rocking on the grade. He moved out into the scrub brush until the first locomotive passed, then began to run beside the open door of an empty flat-wheeler. Just before the car wobbled past a signal light mounted on a stanchion, he leaped inside the car, pushing his weight up on his hands, rolling onto a wood floor that smelled of chaff and the warm, musky odor of animal hides.

He lay on his back and watched the hills and stars slip by the open door. He did not remember when he had slept an entire night without dreaming or waking suddenly, the room filling with flashes that had nothing to do with car lights on a high-way or electricity in the clouds. The dreams were inhabited by disparate elements and people and events, most of them seemingly disconnected but held together in one fashion or another by color and the nauseating images the color suggested—the wet rainbow inside a bandage that had been peeled off an infected wound, a viscous red spray erupting from the hajjis who had been crawling on a disabled tank, trying to pry open the hatches, when Pete let off on them with Ma Deuce, a .50-caliber that could shred human beings into dog food. The victims in the dreams were many but not necessarily people he had known or seen—soldiers, children, sunken-faced old women and men whose teeth were an atrocity to look at. Paradoxically, for Pete, sleeplessness was not the problem; it was the solution.

Except he couldn't hold a job. He daydreamed and dropped wrenches in machinery, couldn't concentrate on what others were saying, and sometimes could not count the change in the palm of his hand. In the meantime, Vikki Gaddis was not only financially supporting him but had become the target of a collection of killers because of his irresponsibility and bad judgment.

He found a piece of burlap on the boxcar floor and stuffed it under his head and fell asleep. For some reason he didn't understand, he felt himself rocking off to sleep, almost like an embryonic creature being carried safely inside its mother's womb.

When he woke, he could see the lights on the outskirts of Marathon. He rubbed the sleep out of his face and dropped from the flat-wheeler onto the ground. He waited for the train to pass him, then crossed the tracks and found the two-lane road that led into town and eventually to his cousin's used-car lot.

It was located appropriately in a tattered neighborhood that seemed leached of its color. A high fence surrounded the lot and the sales office, topped by rolls of razor wire. Pete walked down a side street, away from the streetlights on the two-lane county road, glancing over his shoulder at an eighteen-wheeler shifting down at the intersection. The lot was filled with oversize pickup trucks and SUVs whose commercial value had plummeted during the price rise of gasoline to four dollars a gallon. Pete looked up and down the line of unsold and marked-down vehicles, wondering which would be easiest to hotwire. Between an Expedition and a Ford Excursion, he saw the gas-guzzling junker his cousin had sold him and whose crankshaft had fallen out on the highway. The cousin had wrecker-hauled it back onto the lot and placed a for-sale sign inside the windshield. What did that say about the quality of the other vehicles his cousin was offering for sale?

Pete found a break in the spirals of razor wire at the back of the property and laced his fingers in the fence, preparing to climb over. Down the aisle between two rows of vehicles, he saw the chain-locked gates he would have to exit with whatever truck or SUV or compact shitbox he managed to boost. He had a collapsible Schrade utility tool in his pocket, one that contained pliers and wire cutters and screwdrivers and small wrenches of every kind, but nothing approaching the strength and size needed to cut a chain or padlock.

Through the front fence, he saw a sheriff's cruiser pass on the county road and turn in to a diner at the intersection. How many blunders could one guy make in one night?

He sat down on a greasy hump of dirt out of which a cluster of pines grew and put his face in his hands. He watched the sheriff's cruiser drive away from the diner, then his attention focused on a lighted phone booth between the diner and the corner of the intersection.

It was time to call for the cavalry, although he was afraid of what the cavalry was about to tell him. He walked to the telephone booth and made a collect call to the residence of William Robert Holland in Lolo, Montana.

But Pete's intuitions had been correct. Billy Bob told him his only recourse was to surrender himself to his cousin Hackberry Holland; he even gave Pete Hackberry's number. He also told Pete the FBI probably had a tap on his phone and that the clock was likely ticking on Pete.

Pete could hear the sorrow and pity in his friend's voice, and it made his heart sink. In his mind's eye, he saw the two of them years ago, cane-fishing under a tree on a green river, their cold drinks and bread-and-butter sandwiches lying on a blanket in the shade.

After Pete hung up, sweat was creaking in his ears, and the bodies of insects were thudding against the Plexiglas sides of the booth. He folded back the accordion door hard against the jamb and began walking down the two-lane toward the railroad tracks. Up ahead, he saw a lone compact car stopped at the traffic light, the driver waiting listlessly behind the steering wheel, his features lit by the glow from an AutoZone sign. The traffic light seemed to be stuck on red, but the driver waited patiently for it to change, although there were no other vehicles on the street.

The driver had a long nose and high cheekbones, the hair combed straight back, streaked with gel or grease. His facial structure could have been called skeletal except for the fact that the flesh was lumpy, as though it were covered with bee stings, suggesting carnality and decadence rather than deprivation. His gaze was focused on the traffic signal, like a modern parody of a Byzantine saint experiencing the dark night of the soul.

Pete started across the intersection, in front of the compact's high beams, just as the traffic signal changed. The driver of the compact had to slam on his brakes. But Pete did not move. He continued to stare into the brilliance of the headlights, red and yellowish-green circles burning into his eye sockets. He spread his arms against the air. "Sorry for being on the planet," he said.

The driver pulled slowly around him, his window down. "You have a problem of some kind?"

"Yes, sir, I do. See, the light was red when I started across the street. Because it turns from red to green doesn't mean the driver of a car can run over whatever is in front of him."

"That's interesting to know. Now, how about taking your hand off the roof of my car? I don't particularly enjoy looking into somebody's armpit."

"I like your 'Support the Troops' ribbons. You must have bought a shitpile of them. What d'you think about bringing back the draft so the rest of y'all can kick some rag-head ass over in the Sandbox?"

"Move away, kid."

"Yes, sir, I'm very glad to," Pete said. He began picking up rocks from the asphalt. "Let me he'p you on your way. Is there a late-night pinochle game down at the AMVETS tonight?"

The driver's eyes roamed over Pete's face. His expression was one of curiosity rather than fear or apprehension. "Get yourself some help. In the meantime, don't ever fuck with me again."

"I thank you for straightening me out, sir. Happy motoring. God bless and Godspeed."

As the driver pulled away, Pete flung one rock after another at the compact, whanging them off the doors and roof and trunk. Then he picked up a half-brick and chased after the compact and threw the brick as hard as he could, pocking a hole in the rear window. But the driver never accelerated or touched the brake pedal. He simply drove steadily down the road toward the main highway that led out of town, leaving Pete in the middle of the street, wrapped in self-loathing and a level of impotent rage that sat on his brow like a crown of thorns.

AFTER PREACHER GOT back on the four-lane and resumed his journey, he looked in the rearview mirror at his broken window. Lunatic or drunken or drug-induced behavior had never been a source of worry or concern to him. Unhinged people like that kid back there flinging rocks at a stranger's car were just a reminder that Preacher didn't have to validate himself, that moral imbeciles had taken over the institution a long time ago. Check out the French General Assembly under Robespierre, he thought. Check out the crowd at a televangelical rally. If they had their way, there would be an electric chair on every street corner in Texas, and half the population would be bars of soap.

He pushed his speed up to sixty-five, staying under the seventy-mile-an-hour limit. The backseat was stacked with the boxed possessions he had salvaged from his destroyed house. His Thompson, for which he had paid eighteen thousand dollars, was concealed between the backseat and the trunk. He would miss his stucco house at the base of the mountain, but eventually, he knew he would return to it. He was sure the cave in the mountainside and the sounds the wind made blowing inside its walls held portent not only for him but for the unwinding scroll of which his story was a part. Was it too big a leap of faith to conclude the whistling of the wind was nothing less than the breathing of Yahweh inside the earth?

Weren't all our destinies already written on scrolls that we unwound and discovered in incremental fashion? Perhaps the past and the present and the future were already written on the wind, not in transient fashion but whispered to us with unerring accuracy if we would only bother to listen. The three bikers had thought they would kill him in his own house, little knowing of the power that inhabited the environment they had invaded. He wondered what they'd thought when he'd let off on them in the motel room. There had been regret in their eyes, certainly, and desperation and fear, but most of all just regret. If they could have spoken, he was sure they would have renounced everything in their lives in order to live five more seconds so they could make their case and convince either Preacher or whoever governed the universe that they would devote the remainder of their lives to piety and acts of charity if they could just have one more season to run.

Preacher steered around an eighteen-wheeler, the tractor rig's high beams turning his pocked rear window into a fractured light prism. Had the rock thrower been drunk? The man hadn't smelled of booze. Obviously, he had been in Iraq or Afghanistan. Maybe the VA was dumping its nutcases on the street. But there was a detail about the kid Preacher couldn't forget. In his obsession to find Vikki Gaddis, he had thought little about her boyfriend, the kid Hugo and Bobby Lee always referred to as "the soldier boy." What had Bobby Lee said about him? That the kid had a scar on his face that was as long as an earthworm?

No, it was just coincidence. Yahweh didn't play jokes.

Or did He?

Chapter
19

AT TWO A.M. the air-conditioning compressor outside Hackberry's window gasped once, made a series of clunking sounds like a Coke bottle rolling down a set of stairs, and died. Hackberry opened the windows and the doors, turned on the ceiling fan in his bedroom, and went back to sleep.

A huge bank of thunderclouds had moved out of the south and sealed the sky. The clouds were lit by igneous flashes that rippled across the entirety of the heavens in seconds and died far out over the hills. It was cool in the room under the revolving blades of the fan, and Hackberry dreamed he was in a naval hospital in the Philippines, sedated with morphine, a hospital corpsman no older than he pulling the syringe from his arm. A sun shower was blowing in from the bay, and outside his window, an orchid tree bloomed on the lawn, its lavender petals scattered on the clipped grass. In the distance, where the bay merged with water that was the dark blue of spilled ink, he could see the gray hulking outline of an aircraft carrier, its hard steel edges smudged by the rain.

The hospital was a safe place to be, and the memories of a

POW camp south of the Yalu seemed to have little application in his life.

He heard thunder and wind in his sleep and the twang of wire on his back fence and tumbleweed bouncing against the side of his house and matting in his flower beds. Then he smelled rain blowing through his screens, sweeping in a rush across the housetop, filling the room with a freshness that was like spring or memories of hot summers when raindrops lit upon a heated sidewalk and created a smell that convinced you the season was eternal and one's youth never faded.

The mist drifted through the window, touching his skin, dampening his pillow. He got up and closed the window and, in the distance, saw lightning strike a hillside, flaring inside a grove of blighted oaks that looked like gnarled fingers inside the illumination. He lay back down, his pillow over his face, and fell asleep again.

OUT ON THE road, a compact car passed in the darkness, its headlights off. There was a solitary hole in the back window, its edges shaped into a crystalline eye superimposed on the car's dark interior. The driver steered with both hands around a rock that had rolled onto the road, avoiding a fence post and a tangle of barbed wire that had tilted out of a hillside. He passed a barn and a pasture with horses and a water tank in it, then turned out into a field and drove across a long stretch of Johnson grass and parked his car in a streambed next to a hill, the dry rocks crackling under his tires. He removed the submachine gun from behind his backseat, and the paper bag that contained two ammunition drums, then sat down on a flat rock, his hat tilted on his face, his unpressed secondhand pin-striped suit dotted with rain, a walking cane propped against his knee.

The wind blew open his coat and ruffled the brim of his hat, but his eyes did not blink, nor did his face show any expression. He stared listlessly at the grass bending around him and at a stump fire smoldering in the rain. The smoke from the fire smelled like burning garbage and made him clear his throat and spit. He fitted the ammunition drum onto his Thompson and pulled and released the bolt, feeding a round into the chamber. He remained seated for a long time, staring at nothing, the Thompson resting on his lap, his hands as relaxed as a child's on its barrel and stock.

He did not know the hour and never wore jewelry or a watch when he worked. He did not measure the passage of time in terms of minutes or hours but in terms of events. There were no vehicles on the county road. There was no sign of activity inside the house he was about to invade. There were no insomniacs or early risers turning on lights in the neighborhood. There was a fire burning in the grass, and horses were nickering in the darkness, the smoke providing a plausible explanation for their sense of alarm. The sky was booming with thunderous explosions; not those of dry lightning but the kind that promised serious rain, perhaps even the kind of monsoon that gave back life to a desert. In spite of the acrid tinge of smoke inside the mist, the night was as lovely and normal as one could expect during the late summer in Southwest Texas.

Preacher stuffed his trousers inside the tops of his boots and upended his Thompson in one hand, the other gripping his cane, then began walking through a thicket toward the ranch house in the distance, his face as impervious as molded plastic to both the brambles and the rain.

WHEN SERGEANT KWONG visited Hackberry in his dreams, a burp gun was always hanging on a strap from his shoulder, and an ice hook dripped from the fingers of his right hand. Hackberry could even see the half-moons of dirt inside Kwong's nails and the shine of his quilted coat that was slathered with dried mud, the sleeves marked with mucus where he had wiped his nose.

In the dream, Kwong fitted the hook through one of the iron squares in the sewer grate above Hackberry's head and hoisted the grate onto a cusp of yellowed snow where Kwong had urinated. Hackberry was sitting with his back against the dirt wall of the hole, his knees drawn up before him, the inverted steel pot he defecated in resting by his foot. Kwong's massive body was silhouetted against a salmon-colored sky, his face dark with shadow under a short-billed cloth cap tied with earflaps under his chin. His unshaved jaw was as big as a gorilla's, the hair in his nose white with ice crystals, his breath fogging. Hackberry could hear other POWs being pulled out of their holes, shoved into a line, the guards talking louder, more clipped, angrier than usual, kicking anyone who didn't move fast enough.

Kwong dropped the iron grate heavily onto the snow, shaking the hook free. "Climb up, cocksuck. Today your day," he said.

Inside his dream, Hackberry tried to force himself back to the hospital in the Philippines, back to the moment when the navy corpsman had injected him with morphine and he could arbitrarily turn his head on the pillow and see the orchid tree blooming on the lawn and in the distance the misty gray outline of the aircraft carrier in the rain.

On the north side of the pasture, Preacher walked steadily through the Johnson grass, its wetness glistening on his boots, the butt of the Thompson riding on his hip, his walking cane spearing into the soft dirt. The palomino and chestnut geldings in the horse lot were spooking in the curds of smoke from the stump fire, whinnying, their ears back. High overhead, a plane with lighted windows was making an approach to a private airport, gliding through the rain and flickers of lightning to a safe harbor. The sheriff's neighbors were sound asleep, confident of the sunrise and the goodness of the day that awaited them. As Preacher thought of these things, his energies grew in magnitude and intensity, like bees stirring to life inside a hive after a boy has disturbed it with a rock. He cast aside his walking cane and climbed through the rails of the horse lot and continued toward the house, the discomfort gone from his leg and foot, a marching band blaring in his head.

The two horses ran in different directions from him, their back hooves kicking blindly at the air. Up ahead, the house was dark, the windmill on the far side chained up, the blades and rudder trembling stiffly in the wind.

WHEN HACKBERRY JERKED awake, he tried to sit up in bed, then heard metal clink and felt his left wrist come tight against a chain. He pushed himself up against the bedstead, his vision unfocused, his left hand suspended foolishly in the air as though his motor controls had been cut.

"Whoa, hoss," Preacher said. He was sitting in a chair in the corner, the Thompson across his lap. He had removed his hat and placed it crown-down on the dresser. His clothes were damp and smudged with ash and mud, his face and boots shiny with rainwater. "It's already a done deal. Don't hurt yourself unnecessarily."

Hackberry could hear himself breathing. "You're the one they call Preacher?"

"You knew I was coming, didn't you?"

"No. For me, it's not personal."

"I was told you were asking Arthur Rooney about me, about my private life and such."

"Whoever told you that is a damn liar."

"Yeah, he probably is. But nonetheless, you've been looking for me, Sheriff Holland. So I found you instead."

"I should have locked my door."

"Think your broken air conditioner was coincidental?"

"You did it?"

"No, a man who works for me did."

"What's your business here, Mr. Collins?"

"You have to ask that?"

"Jack Collins is your real name? The one given you at birth?"

"What difference does it make?"

"In case you haven't figured it out, nicknames are forms of disguise. I hear you're supposed to be the left hand of God."

"I never claimed it."

"You let others do that for you. You don't discourage them."

"I don't study on what other people say or think. Why do you keep favoring the other side of your bed, Sheriff?"

"I have problems with sciatica. I can't lie in one position."

"Is this what you're looking for?" Preacher said, holding up Hackberry's revolver.

"Maybe."

"If you're going to keep a weapon close by your bed, it should be a small one, a derringer or an Airweight you can tuck under your mattress or pillow so an intruder cain't find it without waking you up. You favor a thumb-buster forty-five? That's a lot like carrying around a junkyard on your hip, isn't it?"

Hackberry looked through the screen door at the rain blowing in the pasture, his horses playing in it, rearing in mock combat, a stump fire glowing orange and hot under a log each time the wind fed fresh oxygen into the flames. "Do what you came to do and be done," he said.

"I wouldn't rush my fate if I were you."

"You lecture others, a man who killed nine unarmed women, some of them hardly more than children? You think you're the scourge of God? You're a pimple on creation. I've known your kind all my life. You're always looking for a cause or a flag to hide under. There's no mystery to your psychological makeup,

Collins. Your mother probably wanted you aborted and cursed the day you were born. I think you were despised in the womb."

Preacher's mouth was a stitched seam, as though he were taking the measure of each word Hackberry used. He huffed air out his nostrils indifferently. "Could be. I never got to know her real well. You're a recipient of the Navy Cross."

"So what?"

"I checked out your background. You don't fit easily into one shoe box. You were a womanizer and a drunkard. While you were married and running for Congress, you were hiring Mexican girls down on the border. You ever carry diseases home to your wife?"

The ammunition drum on the Thompson rested between Preacher's knees; the index finger of his right hand was poised outside the trigger guard. "The question isn't a complicated one," he said.

"You name it and I did it. Until I met the woman who became my second wife."

"The Marxist?"

"She was an organizer for the United Farm Workers and a friend of Cesar Chavez."

"That's how you took up with the papists?"

"There're worse groups."

"The situation with those Asian women wasn't of my selection."

"I dug them up. I saw your handiwork up close and personal. Run your bullshit on somebody else."

"You found them?"

"At least one girl had dirt clenched in her palm. You know what that indicates?"

Preacher raised his index finger in the air. "I didn't have control of what happened out there."

"You're using the passive voice."

"What?"

"It involves manipulation of language to avoid admission of guilt."

"You a grammarian besides a war hero?"

"There's nothing heroic about my history. I informed on two fellow POWs."

Preacher seemed to have lost interest in the subject. He scratched idly at his cheek with four fingers. "You afraid?"

"Of what?"

"The other side."

"I've already been there."

"Say again?"

"I looked into the eyes of a man just like you. He carried a burp gun that was made in China or Russia. He was a cruel man. I suspect his cruelty masked his innate cowardice. I never met a cruel man or a bully who wasn't a coward."

Preacher waved his hand at the air. "Be quiet."

At first Hackberry thought his words had reached inside Preacher's defense system, then realized the vanity of his perception. Preacher had risen from his chair, his attention fixed on the road, the Thompson slanted downward. He moved to the window. "She's not the brightest bulb in the box, is she?"

"Who?"

"Your deputy, the one who killed Liam. She just turned on her interior light to write in her log."

"She patrols this road when she has the night shift. She's not part of this, Collins."

"Oh, yes, she is, my friend."

"You sonofabitch, you motherfucker."

"What did you call me?"

"I'm the guy who came after you, Collins. Not my deputy. She takes orders. She's not a player."

"You insult my mother, but you ask immunity for your female

friend? Her fate is on your conscience. Think back: the unlocked doors, pursuing me outside your jurisdiction, the killing of Liam Eriksson. You engineered this, Sheriff. Look into my face. Look inside me. You see yourself."

Preacher had leaned down to speak, his breath sour, a tiny web of saliva at the corner of his mouth. Hackberry grabbed Preacher's shirt with one hand and knotted the cloth in his fist and pulled Preacher toward him. He spat full in his face, then gathered his spittle a second time and spat on him again and again, until his mouth was empty of moisture.

Preacher jerked away from him and drove the butt of the Thompson into the bridge of Hackberry's nose, using both hands. He hit him again, this time in the head, splitting the scalp, raking the steel butt plate down Hackberry's ear.

Preacher picked up his hat from the dresser and walked toward the side door. "I'll be back to deal with you later. I'll be the last thing you ever see. And you'll beg to take back every word you said about my mother."

Blood leaked out of Hackberry's hair into his eyes. He watched impotently as Preacher went out the door into the yard, the Thompson tilted downward in his silhouette like a black exclamation point against the glow of the cruiser's headlights.

Hackberry strained against the manacle on his left wrist, forming his fingers into a cone, trying to pull the back of his hand through the steel's circumference, blood running in strings down his thumb, braiding off his nails. He got to his feet and, with both arms outstretched, jerked against the chain, which was locked by the other manacle around a thick dowel on the bedstead. Through the window, he could see Preacher far down the driveway, approaching Pam Tibbs's cruiser, the rain swirling like spun glass around him, thunder rippling across the sky.

Hackberry saw Pam reach up and turn off the dome light. Then, for a reason he didn't understand, the light went back on.

Hackberry yelled at the top of his voice just as the bedstead splintered apart. Preacher fitted the Thompson to his shoulder, his right elbow pointed outward like a chicken's wing, and aimed through the iron sights.

The eruption of fire from the barrel was like the jagged and erratic contortions of an electrical arc. The .45-caliber rounds blew the glass out of the back and side windows and stitched across the doors, ripping stuffing out of the seats, exploding a side mirror, tattering the hood, flattening a tire in under a second.

Hackberry tore the handcuffs loose from the destroyed bedstead and found his holstered revolver on the floor where Preacher had placed it. He ran barefoot into the side yard just as Preacher let off another burst, this time holding the Thompson against his hip, spraying the cruiser from one end to the other. A flame glowed under the hood, then seemed to drip from the engine onto the asphalt and race backward toward the gasoline tank. There was no transition between the moment of ignition and the explosion that followed. A fireball exploded from the car's frame, filling the windows, roasting the interior, rising into the darkness in a dirty red-black scorch that gave off a smell like an incinerator behind a rendering plant. Hackberry felt the whoosh of heat float across the lawn and touch his face.

"Collins!" he shouted. He saw Preacher turn, framed against the burning car. Hackberry raised his revolver and aimed with both hands and fired once, the report deafening, the recoil like the kick of a jackhammer. He steadied the front sight and fired two more shots, but he was too far away from his target, and he heard the rounds strike stone or the top of a rise and whine into the darkness with a sound like the tremolo of a broken banjo string.

He saw Preacher move out of the light and head for the north pasture, unhurried, holding the Thompson by the pistol grip, the barrel pointed at the sky, glancing back at Hackberry only once.

The rain steamed on the smoldering remains of the cruiser, the flames in the grass burning outward in a ring, the mesquite starting to catch and flare like fireflies. There was no movement anywhere near the cruiser. The airbags in the front seat had inflated and exploded in the heat and were now draped on the steering wheel and blackened seats and dashboard like curtains of ash. Hackberry could feel his eyes brimming with water. He followed Preacher into the pasture, the rain blowing in his face, his two geldings terrified. Inside the flash of lightning in the clouds, he thought he saw Preacher climbing through the rails of the north fence. He fired once, or was it twice, with no effect.

He stepped on a fence clip and felt the aluminum tip slice through the ball of his foot. Then Preacher was out in the pasture, out of the shadows, past the stump fire. Hackberry paused at the fence and fired again. This time he saw Preacher's coat jump, as though a gust of wind had caught it and flapped it loose from his side. Hackberry climbed through the fence and went deeper into the Johnson grass, toward a thicket behind which a compact car was parked.

Preacher opened the compact's door. Almost as an afterthought, he turned and faced Hackberry, his Thompson lowered. He smiled at the corner of his mouth. "You're a persistent man, Holland."

Hackberry raised his revolver with both hands, cocked back the hammer, and sighted on Preacher's face. "Send me a postcard and tell me how you like hell," he said. He squeezed the trigger. But the hammer snapped on a spent cartridge.

"You lose, bub," Preacher said.

"Be done with it."

"I don't have to. I'm stronger than you are. I'll live inside your thoughts the rest of your life. The woman I just killed will become my friend and haunt your sleep. Welcome to the great shade."

Preacher got in his car, started the engine, and drove slowly out of the field. After he had passed the burned shell of the cruiser, he turned on his headlights and proceeded down the county road toward town, the pocked hole in his rear window glinting like a crystal eye.

Hackberry walked out of the field onto the asphalt, the blood in his hair mixing with the rain, running through his eyebrows and down his face. In the way that dreams turn out to be only dreams, he saw an image in the mist that made no sense, that was out of place and time, that was like the reversal of a film whose frames contained material that was unacceptable and had to be corrected.

Pam Tibbs was climbing from the rain ditch that paralleled the far side of the road, her clothes powdered with soot, her face smudged and streaked with rain.

"Oh, Pam," he said.

She stepped out on the road, her eyes watering in the black smoke blowing off the cruiser's tires. She seemed disoriented, as though the earth were shifting under her feet. She looked at him woodenly. "I'd gotten out of the cruiser. I thought I hit a deer. A doe with two fawns ran in front of me. One of the fawns was making a sound like it was hurt or frightened. But they're not here. I think the explosion knocked me unconscious."

"I was sure you were dead."

"You're hurt," she said.

"I'm fine."

"Is Collins still here?"

"He's gone. You have your cell?"

He saw that it was already in her hand. He took it from her, but his fingers were shaking so badly that she had to make the 911 call for him.

Chapter 20

PETE CAUGHT A ride back to the motel on a poultry truck and slept through the morning, trying to block out the memories of the previous night, which included his fight with Vikki, his failed attempt to boost a car, his admission of fear and inadequacy to his friend Billy Bob in Montana, and his rage and attack upon the driver of the compact car at the traffic light.

How could one guy screw up so often, so bad, and in so short a time? When he woke at noon, a poisonous lethargy seemed to grip both his body and spirit, as though he had been drinking for two days and all his tomorrows had been mortgaged. He was sure that if a high wind blew away the motel and left him behind, he would discover that creation was a vast empty shell as well as a sham, a stage set that hid no mysteries, and he was an insignificant cipher in the middle of it.

Vikki was nowhere in sight. His only companion was a roach the size of a cigar butt climbing up the curtain by the television set. He put on his shirt, not bothering to button it, and sat on the side of the bed and wondered what he should do next.

Billy Bob had said to trust his cousin the sheriff. But what about the feds? Sometimes they hung witnesses out to dry. Pete had heard stories about the Justice Department prosecuting cases that couldn't be won, turning over the names of confidential informants to defense lawyers who passed the names on to their clients and exposed the informants to violent and perhaps fatal retribution.

His and Vikki's names would be in the newspapers. Vikki had pumped two rounds into this guy Preacher when he had tried to force her into his car. Pete had never seen the man's face and knew nothing of his history or background but had little doubt what he would do to Vikki if he got his hands on her.

But what if Pete continued to do nothing? So far he and Vikki had been lucky. If they just had money or passports or a car. Or a weapon. But they had none of these things, and now, to compound his problems, he had fought with Vikki.

The rains had passed when he went outside, but the sky was sealed from horizon to horizon with clouds that were as heavy and gray as lead, like a giant lid pressing the humidity and heat back into the earth. In the convenience store that doubled as a Greyhound bus stop, he bought a box of saltine crackers and a can of Vienna sausages. He also bought a coned-up straw hat from a Mexican who was selling hats and serapes and garish velvet paintings of either the Crucifixion or the Sacred Heart of Jesus off the back of a pickup truck. He bought a bottle of Coca-Cola from the outside machine, and just as the sun was breaking through the overcast, spearing columns of light onto the desert, he squatted down in the shade of the store and began eating the sausages sandwiched between crackers, drinking from the soda, moistening the dried-out saltines to the point where they were almost chewable.

He could not explain adequately to himself why he had bought the hat, which had cost six dollars, except for the fact that squatting down on his haunches, the leather of his colorless cowboy boots spiderwebbing with cracks, eating his lunch in the hot shade of a convenience store on the outer edges of the Great American Desert, his hat slanted down on his brow, was like a conduit back into a time when he had thought of the world in terms of chimerical holograms rather than events— bobber-fishing in a green river, Angus grazing in red clover, sunlit showers breaking on bluebonnets in the spring, harvest moons that were as big and brown and dust-veiled as a planet that had strayed from its orbit.

Pickup trucks and country music and dancing to the "Bandera Waltz" under Japanese lanterns at a beer garden on the banks of the Frio. Barbecues and fish frys and high school kids on hayrides and other kids hanging out on horseback in front of the IGA. Dinner on the ground and devil in the bush and baptism by immersion and outdoor preachers ranting in ecstasy with their eyes rolled back in their heads. If he could just reach back a couple of years and put his hand on all of it and hold on to it and never let anyone talk him into giving it up.

That was the secret: to hold on to the things you loved and never give them up for any reason, no matter how strong the entreaty.

He walked down the street to the town's one block of business buildings, stepping up on an elevated sidewalk that still had tethering rings inset in the concrete. He passed a shut-down bank that had been constructed in 1891, a barbershop with a revolving striped pole in a plastic tube, a used-appliance store, a café that advertised bison burgers in water-based white paint on the window, a barroom that was as long and narrow and dark as a boxcar. The town's library was tucked compactly inside a one-story limestone building that once sold recapped automobile tires.

In the reference section, he found a stack of phone books for all the counties in Southwest Texas. It took him only five minutes to find the number he needed. He borrowed a pencil from the reference librarian and wrote the number on a piece of scrap paper. The librarian's hair was almost blue, her eyes very tiny and bright behind her glasses; her facial skin was wrinkled with deep folds that had the coloration of a pink rose. "You're not from here, are you?" she said.

"No, ma'am. I'm a visitor."

"Well, you come back here any time you want."

"I surely will."

"You're a nice young man."

"Thank you. But how do you know what I am?"

"You removed your hat when you entered the building. You removed it even though you thought no one was watching you. Your manners are those of a naturally considerate and respectful person. That makes you a very nice young man."

Pete walked back to the motel, left a note for Vikki on her pillow, and hitchhiked thirty miles west of town to a desolate crossroads that reminded him of the place where the Asian women had died and his life had changed forever. He entered a phone booth, took a deep breath, and dialed a number on the phone's console. In the distance, he could see a mile-long train inching its way along a stretch of alkali hardpan, like a black centipede, heat waves warping the horizon.

"Sheriff's Department," a woman said. It was a voice he had heard before.

"Is this the business line?" he asked.

"That's the number you dialed. Did you want to report an emergency?"

"I need to talk to Sheriff Holland."

"He's not in right now. Who's calling, please?"

"When will he be in?"

"That's hard to say. Can I he'p you with something?"

"Patch me through. You can do that, cain't you?"

"You need to give me your name. Is there a reason you don't want to give me your name?"

He could feel sweat pooling inside his armpits, his own stale odor rising into his face. He folded back the door of the booth and stepped outside, the receiver pressed against his ear.

"Are you there, sir?" the woman said. "We've spoken before, haven't we? You remember me? Your name is Pete, isn't it?"

"Yes, ma'am, that's what I go by."

"We want you to come see us, Pete. You need to bring Ms. Gaddis with you."

"That's why I want to talk to the sheriff."

"The sheriff is at the hospital. A man tried to kill him and Deputy Tibbs last night. I think you know the man we're talking about."

"This guy Preacher? No, I don't know him. I know his name. I know he tried to kidnap and maybe kill Vikki. But I don't *know* him."

"We've been trying to he'p you, soldier. Sheriff Holland in particular."

"I didn't ask him to." He could hear sweat creaking between his ear and the phone receiver. He held the receiver away from his head and wiped his ear with his shoulder. "Hello?"

"I'm still here."

"How bad are the sheriff and the deputy hurt?"

"The sheriff is having some X-rays done. You're not a criminal, Pete. But you're not acting real bright, either."

"What's your name, ma'am?"

"Maydeen Stoltz."

Pete looked at his watch. How long did it take to trace a call? "Well, Miss Maydeen, why don't you pull your head out of your hole and give me the sheriff's cell phone number? That way I won't have to trouble you anymore."

He thought he could hear her ticking a ballpoint on a desk blotter.

"I'll give you his number and tell him to expect your call in the next few minutes. But you listen to me on this one, smartass. Last night we almost lost two of the best people either one of us will ever know. You give that some thought. And if you talk to me like that again and I catch up with you, I'm gonna slap the daylights out of you."

She gave him the sheriff's cell number, but he had nothing to write with and had to draw the numerals on the dusty shelf under the phone console with his finger.

He went inside the small grocery store at the intersection, the smell of cheese and lunch meat and insect spray and stale cigarette smoke and overripe fruit enough to make him choke. At the back of the store, he stared through the smoky glass doors of the coolers, his arms folded across his chest as though he were protecting himself from an enemy. Inside one door, the Dr Peppers and root beers and Coca-Colas stood end to end in neat racks. Behind the next door were six-pack upon six-pack of every brand of beer sold in Texas, the amber bottles beaded with coldness, the cardboard containers damp and soft, waiting to be picked up gingerly by caring hands.

One six-pack of sixteen-ouncers, he thought. He could space them out through the afternoon, just enough to flatten the kinks in his nervous system. Sometimes you needed a parachute. Wasn't it better to ease into sobriety rather than to be jolted into it?

"Find what you want?" the woman behind the counter said. She weighed at least 250 pounds and swelled out like an inverted washtub below the waistline. She was smoking a cigarette and flicking the ash into a bottle cap, her lipstick rimmed crisply on the filter, a V-shaped yellow stain between her fingers.

"Where's the men's room?" he asked.

She drew in on her cigarette and exhaled the smoke slowly,

taking his measure. "About four feet behind you, the door with the sign over it that says 'Men's Room.' "

He went in the restroom and came back out wiping the water off his face with a paper towel. He slid open the door to the cold box and lifted out a six-pack of Budweiser, balancing it on his palm, the cans coated with moisture and hard and clinking against one another inside the plastic yoke. The cashier was smoking a fresh one, blowing the smoke through her fingers while she held the cigarette to her mouth. He set the six-pack on the counter and reached for his wallet. But she didn't ring up the purchase.

"Ma'am?"

"What?"

"You have a reason for acting so damn weird?"

"Weird in like what way?"

"For openers, staring at me like I just climbed out of a spaceship."

She dropped her cigarette into a bucket of water under the counter. "*I* don't have a reason for staring at you."

"So—"

"*He* might."

Her gaze drifted out the front window of the store, past the two gas pumps under the porte cochere. A town constable's patrol car was parked beside the telephone booth. A man wearing a khaki uniform and shades was sitting behind the wheel, the engine off, the doors open to let in the breeze while he wrote on a clipboard.

"That's Howard. He asked who was just using the phone," the woman said.

"I reckon that could have been me."

"I saw you at the A.A. meeting at the church."

"That could have been me, too."

"You still want the beer?"

"What I want is a whole lot of gone between me and your store."

"I cain't he'p you do that."

"Ma'am, I'm in a mess of trouble. But I haven't harmed anybody, not intentionally, anyway."

"I expect you haven't."

Her eyes were full of pity, the same kind of pity and sorrow he had heard in the voice of his friend Billy Bob. Pete folded his arms across his chest again and watched the town constable get out of his patrol car and walk under the porte cochere and pull open the front door of the store. In those few seconds, a line of stitches seemed to form and burst apart across Pete's heart.

"Were you using that booth out there?" the constable asked. His skin was sun-browned, his shirt peppered with sweat, his eyes hidden by his shades.

"Yes, sir, just a few minutes ago."

"You owe the operator ninety-five cents. Would you take care of it? She's ringing it off the hook."

"Yes, sir, right away. I didn't know I went overtime."

"You want the beer?" the clerk said.

"I surely do."

Pete hefted the six-pack under his arm, got his change and an extra three dollars in coins, and walked back out to the booth. The sun was hammering down on the hardpan and the two-lane asphalt state highway, glazing the hills, alkali flats, and the distant railroad track where the freight train had stopped and was baking in the heat.

He ripped open the tab on a sixteen-ouncer and set it on the shelf below the phone and punched in Sheriff Holland's cell phone number. As the phone rang, he gripped the sweaty coldness of the can in his left palm.

"Sheriff Holland," a voice said.

"Your cousin Billy Bob—"

"He's already called me. You going to come see us, Pete?"

"Yes, sir, that's what I want to do."

"What's holding you up?"

"I don't want to go to Huntsville. I don't want to see this guy Preacher and his friends come after Vikki."

"What do you think they're doing now, son?"

I ain't your son, a voice inside him said. "You know what I mean."

"How have people been treating you?"

"Sir?"

"Since you came back from Iraq, how do people treat you? Just general run-of-the-mill people? They been treating you all right?"

"I haven't complained."

"Answer the question."

"They've treated me good."

"But you don't trust them, do you? You think they might be fixing to slicker you."

"Maybe unlike others, I don't have the luxury of making mistakes."

"I have an idea where you might be, Pete. But I'm not going to call the sheriff there. I want you and Ms. Gaddis to come in on your own. I want y'all to help me put away the guys who killed those poor Asian women. You fought for your country, partner. And now you have to fight for it again."

"I don't like folks using the flag to get me to do what they want."

"You drinking?"

"Sir?"

"You were drinking when you called in the original nine-one-one by the church house. If I were you, I'd lay off the hooch till I got this stuff behind me."

"You would, would you?"

"I had my share of trouble with it. Billy Bob says you're a good man. I believe him."

"What do we do, just walk into your office?" Pete said. He looked at the cloud of vapor on top of the aluminum beer can. He looked at the brassy bead of the beer through the tab. His windpipe turned to rust when he tried to swallow.

"If you want, I'll send a cruiser."

Pete picked up the beer can and pressed its coldness against his cheek. He could see the train starting to move on the track, the black gondolas clanging against their couplings as though they were fighting against their own momentum.

He sat down on the floor of the booth, pulling the phone and its metal-encased cord with him, the six-pack splaying open on the concrete pad. He felt as though he had descended to the bottom of a well, beyond the sunlight, beyond hope, beyond ever feeling wind on his face again or smelling flowers in the morning or being a part of the great human drama most of the world took for granted, a man with red alligator hide for skin and a bagful of sins that would never be forgiven. He pulled his knees up to his face, his head bent forward, and began to weep silently.

"You still with me, bud?"

"Tell Miss Maydeen I'm sorry for sassing her. I also apologize to you and your deputy for getting y'all hurt. I also owe an apology to some guy I attacked at a traffic light last night. I think I'm plumb losing my mind."

"You assaulted somebody?"

"I threw rocks at his car. I busted a hole in his rear window with a brick."

"Where was this?"

Pete told him.

"What kind of car?"

"A tan Honda."

"You busted a big hole in the window?"

"Just under the size of a softball. It was elongated. It looked like the eye of a Chinaman staring out the window."

"You don't remember the license number, do you?"

Pete was still holding the sixteen-ouncer. He set it on the ground outside the booth. He pushed it over with the sole of his boot. "One letter and maybe two numbers. Y'all already got a report on it?"

"You could say we may have had contact with the driver."

A few moments later, Pete picked up the cans he had dropped and took them back inside the store and set them on the counter. "Can I get a refund?" he said.

"If you hold your mouth right," the cashier said.

"What?"

"That's a joke." She opened the register drawer and counted out his cash. "There's some showers in back. Hang around if you feel like it, cowboy."

"I got someone waiting on me."

She nodded.

"You're a nice lady," he said.

"I hear that lots of times," she said. She stuck another filter-tip in her mouth and lit it with a BIC, blowing the smoke at an upward angle, gazing through the window at the way the two-lane warped in the heat and dissolved into a black lake on the horizon.

"I didn't mean anything, ma'am."

"I look like a 'ma'am'? It's 'miss,' " she said.

TWO DAYS AFTER the invasion of his home by Jack Collins, Hackberry Holland and Pam Tibbs flew in the department's single engine plane to San Antonio, borrowed an unmarked car from the Bexar County Sheriff's Office, and drove into Nick Dolan's neighborhood. The enclave atmosphere and the size of the homes, the Spanish daggers and hibiscus and palm and umbrella trees and crepe myrtle and bougainvillea in the yards, and the number of grounds workers made Hackberry think of a foreign country, in the tropics, perhaps, or out on the Pacific Rim.

Except he was not visiting a neighborhood as much as a paradox. The dark-skinned employees—maids retrieving the trash cans from the curb, yardmen with ear protectors clamped on their heads operating mowers and leaf blowers, hod carriers and framers constructing an extension on a house—were all foreigners, not the repressed and indigenous people Somerset Maugham and George Orwell and Graham Greene had described in their accounts of life inside dying European and British empires. Those who owned and lived in the big houses in Nick Dolan's neighborhood were probably all native-born but had managed to become colonials in their own country.

When Hackberry had called Nick Dolan's restaurant and asked to interview him, Dolan had sounded wired to the eyes, clearing his throat, claiming to be tied up with business affairs and trips out of state. "I got no idea what this is about. I'm dumbfounded here," he said.

"Arthur Rooney."

"Artie Rooney is an Irish putz. I wouldn't piss in his mouth if he was dying of thirst. Let me rephrase that: I wouldn't cross the street to see a pit bull rip out his throat."

"Has the FBI talked with you, Mr. Dolan?"

"No, what's the FBI got to do with anything?"

"But you talked to Isaac Clawson the ICE agent, didn't you?"

"Maybe that name is familiar."

"I appreciate your help. We'll be out to see you this evening."

"Hold on there."

It was late when Hackberry and Pam arrived at Nick's house, and shadows were spreading across the lawn, fireflies lighting in smoky patterns inside the trees. Nick Dolan ushered them right through the house into his backyard and sat them down on rattan chairs by a glass-topped table already set with a pitcher of limeade and crushed ice and a plate of peeled crawfish and a second plate stacked with pastry. But there was no question in Hackberry's mind that Nick Dolan was a nervous wreck.

Nick began talking about the grapevine that laced the trellises and the latticework over their heads. "Those vines came from my grandfather's place in New Orleans," he said. "My grandfather lived uptown, off St. Charles. He was a friend of Tennessee Williams. He was a great man. Know what a great man is? A guy who takes things that are hard and makes them look easy and doesn't complain. Where's your gun?"

"In the vehicle," Hackberry said.

"I always thought you guys had to have your gun on you. You want some limeade? Try those crawfish. I had them brought live from Louisiana. I boiled and veined them myself. I made the sauce, too. I mash up my own peppers. Go ahead, stick a toothpick in one and slop it in the sauce and tell me what you think. Here, you like chocolate-and-peanut-butter brownies? Those are my wife's specialty."

Pam and Hackberry looked at Nick silently, their eyes fastened on his. "You're making me uncomfortable here. I got high blood pressure. I don't need this," Nick said.

"I think you're the anonymous caller who warned me about Jack Collins, Mr. Dolan. I wish I'd taken your warning more to heart. He put a couple of dents in my head and almost killed Deputy Tibbs."

"I'm lost."

"I also think you're the person who called the FBI and told them Vikki Gaddis and Pete Flores were in danger."

Before Hackberry had finished his last sentence, Nick Dolan began shaking his head. "No, no, no, you got the wrong guy. We're talking about mistaken identity here or something."

"You told me Arthur Rooney wants to murder both you and your family."

Nick Dolan's small round hands were closing and opening on the glass tabletop. His stomach was rising and sinking, his cheeks blading with color. "I got in some trouble," he said. "I wanted to get even with Artie for some things he did to me. I got mixed up with bad people, the kind who got no parameters."

"Is one of them named Hugo Cistranos?"

"Hugo worked for Artie when Artie ran a security service in New Orleans. We all got flooded out by Katrina and ended up in Texas at the same time. I don't got anything else to say about this."

"I'm going to find Jack Collins, Mr. Dolan. I'd like to do it with your help. It'll mean a lot for you down the line."

"You mean I'll be a friend of the court, something like that?"

"It's a possibility."

"Stick your 'friend of the court' stuff up your nose. This crazy fuck Collins, excuse my language, is the only guy keeping us alive."

"I'm not sympathetic with your situation."

"You don't have a family?"

"I looked into Collins's face. I watched him machine-gun my deputy's cruiser."

"My wife beat the shit out of him with a cooking pot. He could have killed both of us, but he didn't."

"Your wife beat up Jack Collins?"

"There's something wrong with the words I use that you can't understand? I got an echo in my yard?"

"I'd like to speak with her, please."

"I'm not sure she's home."

"You know what obstruction of justice is?" Pam Tibbs said.

"Yeah, stuff they talk about on TV detective shows."

"Explain this," Pam said. She picked up a brownie from the

plate and set it back down. "It's still hot. Tell your wife to come out here."

Nick Dolan stared into space, squeezing his jaw with one hand, his eyes out of sync. "I caused all this."

"Caused what?" Pam said.

"Everything."

"Where's your wife, Mr. Dolan?" Pam asked.

"Drove away. Fed up. With the kids in the car."

"They're not coming back?" she asked.

"I don't know. Vikki Gaddis came to my restaurant and applied for a job as a singer. I wish I'd hired her. I could have made a difference in those young people's lives. I told all this to Esther. Now she thinks maybe I'm unfaithful."

"Maybe you can still make a difference," Hackberry said.

"I'm through talking with y'all. I wish I'd never left New Orleans. I wish I had helped the people rebuild in the Ninth Ward. I wish I'd done something good with my life."

Pam looked at Hackberry, blowing her breath up into her face.

THAT NIGHT A storm that was more wind and dust and dry lightning than rain moved across Southwest Texas, and Hackberry decided not to fly back home until morning. He and Pam ate in a Mexican restaurant on the Riverwalk, a short distance from the Alamo. Their outdoor table was situated on flagstones and lit by gas lamps. A gondola loaded with mariachi musicians floated past them on the water, all of the musicians stooping as they went under one of the arched pedestrian bridges. The river was lined with banks of flowers and white stucco buildings that had Spanish grillwork on the balconies, and trees that had been planted in terraced fashion, creating the look of a wooded hillside in the middle of a city.

Pam had spoken little during the plane ride to San Antonio and even less since they had left Nick Dolan's yard.

"You a little tired?" Hackberry said.

"No."

"So what are you?"

"Hungry. Wanting to get drunk, maybe. Or catch up with Jack Collins and do things to him that'll make him afraid to sleep."

"Guys like Collins don't have nightmares."

"I think you've got him figured wrong."

"He's a psychopath, Pam. What's to figure?"

"Why didn't Collins shoot you when your revolver snapped empty?"

"Who knows?"

"Because he's setting you up."

"For what?"

"To be his executioner."

Hackberry had just raised his fork to his mouth. He paused under a second, his eyes going flat. He put the forkful in his mouth. He watched a gondola emerge from under a stone bridge, the musicians grinning woodenly, a tree trailing its flowers across their sombreros and brocaded suits. "I wouldn't invest a lot of time thinking about this guy's complexities," he said.

"They all want the same thing. They want to die, and they want their executioner to be worthy of them. They also want to leave behind as much guilt and fear and depression in others as they can. He aims to mess you up, Hack. That's why he tried to take me out first. He wanted you to watch it. Then he wanted you to pop him."

"I'll try to honor his wishes. You don't want a glass of wine or a beer?"

"No."

"It doesn't bother me."

"I didn't say it did. I just don't want any." She wiped her

mouth with her napkin and looked away irritably, then back at him again, her gaze wandering over the stitches in his scalp and the bandage across the bridge of his nose and the half-moons of blue and yellow bruising under his eyes.

"Would you stop that?" he said.

"I'm going to fix that bastard."

"Don't give his kind power, Pam."

"Is there anything else I'm doing wrong?"

"I'll think about it."

She set down her knife and fork and kept staring at him until she forced him to look directly at her. "Lose the cavalier attitude, boss. Collins is going to be with us for the long haul."

"I hope he is."

"You still don't get it. The feds are using Nick Dolan as bait. That means they're probably using us, too. In the meantime, they're treating us like beggars at the table."

"That's the way it is. Sometimes the feds are—"

"Assholes?"

"Nobody is perfect."

"You ought to get yourself some Optimist Club literature and start passing it out."

"Could be."

She pulled at an earlobe. "I think I'll have a beer."

He fought against a yawn.

"In fact, a beer and a shot of tequila with a salted lime on the side."

"Good," he said, filling his mouth with a tortilla, his attention fixed on the mariachi band blaring out Pancho Villa's marching song, "La Cuca-racha."

"You think I should go back to school, maybe get a graduate degree and go to work for the U.S. Marshals' office?"

"I'd hate to lose you."

"Go on."

"You have to do what's right for yourself."

She balled her hands on her knees and stared at her plate. Then she exhaled and started eating again, her eyes veiled with a special kind of sadness.

"Pam?" he said.

"I'd better eat up and hit the hay. Tomorrow is another day and another dollar, right?"

HACKBERRY WOKE AT ONE A.M. in his third-story motel room and sat in the dark, his mind cobwebbed with dreams whose details he couldn't remember, his skin frigid and dead to the touch. Through a crack in the curtains, he could see headlights streaming across an overpass and a two-engine plane approaching the airport, its windows brightly lit. Somehow the plane and cars were a reassuring sight, testifying to the world's normality, the superimposition of light upon darkness, and humanity's ability to overcome even the gravitational pull of the earth.

But how long could any man be his own light bearer or successfully resist the hands that gripped one's ankles more tightly and pulled downward with greater strength each passing day?

Hackberry was not sure what an alcoholic was. He knew he didn't drink anymore and he was no longer a whoremonger. He didn't get into legal trouble or associate himself for personal gain with corrupt politicians; nor did he drape his cynicism and bitterness over his shoulder like a tattered flag. But there was one character defect or psychological impairment that for a lifetime he had not been able to rid himself of: He remembered every detail of everything he had ever done, said, heard, read, or seen, particularly events that involved moral bankruptcy on his part.

Most of the latter occurred during his marriage to his first wife, Verisa. She had been profligate with money, imperious toward those less fortunate than herself, and narcissistic in both her manner and her sex life, to the degree that if he ever thought of her at all, it was in terms of loathing and disgust. His visceral feelings, however, were directed at himself rather than his former wife.

His drunkenness and constant remorse had made him dependent on her, and in order not to hate himself worse for his dependence, he had convinced himself that Verisa was someone other than the person he knew her to be. He gave himself over to self-deception and, in doing so, lost any remnant of self-respect he still possessed. Southerners had a term for the syndrome, but it was one he did not use or even like to think about.

He paid Verisa back by driving across the border and renting the bodies of poor peasant girls who twisted their faces away from the fog of testosterone and beer sweat he pressed down upon them.

Why was he, the vilest and most undeserving of men, spared from the fate he had designed for himself?

He had no answer.

He turned on the night-light and tried to read a magazine. Then he slipped on his trousers and walked down to the soda machine and bought an orange drink and drank it in the room. He opened the curtain so he could see the night sky and the car lights on the elevated highway and the palm trees on the lawn swelling in the wind.

Not far away, 188 men and boys had died inside the walls of the Spanish mission known as the Alamo. At sunrise on the thirteenth day of the siege, thousands of Mexican soldiers had charged the mission and gotten over the walls by stepping on their own dead. The bodies of the Americans were stacked and burned, and no part of them, not an inch of charred bone, was ever located. The sole white survivors, Susanna Dickinson and her eighteen-month-old child, were refused a five-hundred-dollar payment by the government and forced to live in a San Antonio brothel.

Pam Tibbs had taken the room next to his. He saw the light go on under the door that connected their rooms. She tapped lightly on the door. He got up from his chair and stood by the door, not speaking.

"Hack?" she said.

"I'm fine."

"Look out your window in the parking lot."

"At what?"

"Look."

He went to the window and gazed down at the rows of parked cars and the palm trees on the lawn and the tunnels of smoky light under the surface of the swimming pool. He could see nothing of note in the parking lot. But for just a second he thought he saw a shadow cross the clipped grass between two palms that were scrolled with strings of tiny white lights, then disappear through a piked gate on the far side of the pool.

He went back to the door that connected his and Pam's rooms and slid the bolt. "Open your side," he said.

"Just a minute," she said.

A few seconds later, she pulled open the door, wearing jeans, her shirt hanging outside her belt. Her hairbrush lay on top of her bedspread.

"What did you see?" he asked.

"A guy in a tall hat like the Mad Hatter's. He was standing by our car. He was looking up at the motel."

"He do anything to the car?"

"Not that I saw."

"We'll check it out tomorrow."

"You couldn't sleep?" she said.

"About every third night, a committee holds a meeting in my head."

She sat down on the stuffed chair in front of him. She was

wearing moccasins without socks and no makeup, and the side of her face was printed with the pillow. "I need to tell you something, and I need to do so because it involves something you won't acknowledge yourself. Collins cuffed you to your bed, but you tore it apart trying to stop him from killing me. You went after him when you had only a pistol and he had a Thompson machine gun. He could have cut you in half, but you went after him anyway."

"You would have done the same."

"It doesn't matter. You did it. A woman never forgets something like that."

He smiled at her in the darkness and didn't reply.

"Don't you like me physically? Do you think I'm not pretty? Is it something like that?"

"The problem isn't you, Pam. It's me. I misused women when I was young. They were poor and illiterate and lived in hovels across the river. My father was a university professor. I was an attorney and a war hero and a candidate for Congress. But I used these women to hide my own failure."

"What does that have to do with me?"

"I don't want to use someone."

"That's what it would be, then? 'Use'?"

"How about we kill this conversation?"

She got up and walked past his chair, beyond his line of vision. He felt her fingers touch his collar and the hair on his neck. "Everybody is made different. Gay people. Young women who want father figures. Men who need their mothers. Fat girls who need a thin man to tell them they're beautiful. But I like you for what you are and not out of a compulsion. I never put strings on a relationship, either." She rested her palm on his shoulder blade. "I admire you more than any human being I've ever met. Make of that what you want."

"Good night, Pam," he said.

"Yeah, good night," she said. She leaned over him, folding her arms on his chest, her chin on his head, pressing her breasts against him. "Fire me for this if you like. You were willing to give your life to save mine. God love you, Hack. But you sure know how to hurt someone."

Chapter
21

BOBBY LEE HAD driven through the darkness and into the morning with the sunrise at his back, the flood of warm air and light spreading before him across the plains, lifting mesas and piles of rock out of the shadows that had pooled on the hardpan, none of it offering any balm to his soul.

He had put his money on Preacher because Preacher was smart and Artie Rooney wasn't. He was double-crossing Hugo because Hugo was a viper who'd park one behind your ear the first time the wind vane swung in the opposite direction. Where did that leave him? He had teamed up with a guy who was smart and had large amounts of money in offshore accounts and had probably read more books than most college professors. But Preacher was not necessarily smart in the way a survivor was smart. In fact, Bobby Lee was not sure Preacher planned to be a survivor. Bobby Lee wasn't sure he liked the prospect of becoming the copilot of a guy who had kamikaze ambitions.

He drove across a cattle guard onto Preacher's property and stared disbelievingly at the stucco house that the bikers had destroyed and Preacher had paid a dozer operator to blade into a two-story pile of scorched debris. Preacher was now living in a polyethylene tent at the foot of the mountain behind the concrete slab the dozer had scraped clean. His woodstove sat outside it, and next to it was a vintage icebox with an oak door and brass hinges and handle and a drawer underneath that could be filled with either crushed or chopped-up block ice. Behind the tent, against the mountain, was a portable blue chemical toilet.

Clouds had moved across the sun, and the wind was blowing hard when Bobby Lee entered the tent, the flap tearing loose from his hands before he could retie it. He sat down on Preacher's cot and listened to the brief silence when the wind slackened. "Why do you stay out here, Jack?"

"Why shouldn't I?"

"The cops aren't interested in your house getting blown up?"

"It was caused by an electrical short. I make no trouble for anyone. I'm a sojourner who checks books out of the library. These are religious people. Disrespect their totems and feel their wrath. But they don't take issue with a polite and quiet man."

Preacher was sitting in a canvas chair in front of a writing table, wearing a soiled long-sleeve white shirt and small non-prescription reading glasses and unpressed dark slacks with pin stripes and a narrow brown belt that was notched tightly into his rib cage. On the table was a GI mess kit with a solitary fried egg and blackened wiener in it. A Bible was open next to it, the pages stiff and rippled and tea-colored, as though they had been dipped in creek water and left to dry in the sun.

"You're losing weight," Bobby Lee said.

"What are you not telling me?"

Bobby Lee's brow furrowed, the implicit criticism like the touch of a cigarette to his skin. "Holland was at the Dolan house. Then he went to a motel with the woman who capped Liam. That's all I know. Jack, let go of the Dolan family. If we got to take care of the Gaddis girl, let's get on with it. Hugo told you where she's working. We grab her and the soldier boy, and you finish whatever it is you got to do."

"Why do you think Hugo told us where she was working?"

"If we see Hugo or any of his talent around, we splatter their grits. That number you did on those bikers was beautiful, man. A hooker dimed them for you after she screwed them? You know some interesting broads. Remind me not to get in the sack with any of them."

"My mother is buried here."

Bobby Lee wasn't making the connection. But he seldom did when Preacher started riffing. The wind was blowing harder against the tent, vibrating the aluminum poles, straining the ropes tied to the steel pins outside. A ball of tumbleweed smacked against the side, freezing momentarily against it, then rolling away.

"You asked why I live here. My mother married a railroad man who owned this land. He died of ptomaine," Preacher said.

"You inherited the place?"

"I bought it at a tax sale."

"Your mom didn't leave a will?"

"What business is it of yours?"

"It isn't, Jack," Bobby Lee said. "Those guys you had to deal with in the motel room? They were Josef Sholokoff's people?"

"They didn't have time to introduce themselves."

"I have to line out something to you. About Liam. It's eating my lunch. I set him up in that café. I called him on my cell and said that Holland had made him. I split and let him take the fall."

Preacher gazed at Bobby Lee, his legs crossed, his wrists hanging off the arms of the chair. "Why you telling me this, boy?"

"You said I was like a son to you. You meant that?"

Preacher crossed his heart, not speaking.

"I got a bad feeling. I think you and me might go down together. But I don't see that I've got a lot of choices right now. If we get cooled out, I don't want a lie between us."

"You're a mixed bag of cats, Bobby Lee."

"I'm trying to be straight up with you. You're a purist. There's not many of your kind around anymore. That doesn't mean I like eating a bullet."

"Why do you think we're going to get cooled out?"

"You tried to machine-gun a deputy sheriff. Then you had a chance to clip the sheriff and didn't. I think maybe you've got a death wish."

"That's what Sheriff Holland probably thinks. But you're both wrong. In this business, you recognize the great darkness in yourself, and you go inside it and die there, and then you don't have to die again. Why do you think the Earp brothers took Doc Holliday with them to the OK Corral? A man coughing blood on his handkerchief with one hand and covering your back with a double-barrel ten-gauge won't ever let you down. So you fed ole Liam to the wolves, did you?"

Bobby Lee looked away from Preacher. Then he corrected his expression and stared straight into Preacher's face. "Liam made fun of me after I stood up for him. He said I was lots of things, but I would never be a soldier. What was that about a great darkness inside us?"

If Bobby Lee's question registered on Preacher, he chose to ignore it. "I'm going to rebuild my house, Bobby Lee. I'd like for you to be part of that. I'd like for you to feel you belong here."

"That makes me proud, Jack."

"You look like you want to ask me something."

"Maybe we could put some flowers on your mother's grave. Where's she buried?"

The wind was thumping the tent so hard, Bobby Lee could not be sure what Preacher said. He asked him to repeat the statement.

"I never quite get through to you," Preacher shouted.

"The wind's howling."

"She's underneath your feet! Where I planted her!"

ON THE FAR end of the same burning, windswept day, one on which the monsoonal downpour had been baked out of the topsoil and dust devils formed themselves out of nothing and spun across the plains and, in the blink of an eye, broke apart against monument rocks, Vikki Gaddis walked from the Fiesta motel to the steak house where she waited tables and sometimes sang with the band. The sky had turned yellow as the heat went out of the day, the sun settling into a melted orange pool among the rain clouds in the west. In spite of the humidity and dust, she felt a change was taking place in the world around her. Maybe her optimistic mood was based on the recognition that no matter what a person's situation was, eventually it would have to change, for good or bad. Perhaps for her and Pete, change was at hand. There was a greenish tint to the land, as though a patina of new life had been sprinkled on the countryside. She could smell the mist from the grass sprinklers on the center ground and the flowers blooming in the window boxes of the motel at the intersection, a watered date-palm oasis in the midst of a desert, a reminder that a person always had choices.

Pete had told her of his conversation with the sheriff whose name was Hackberry Holland and the offer of protection the sheriff had made. The offer was a possibility, a viable alternative. But to step across a line into a world of legal entanglement and processes that were irreversible was easier said than done, she thought. They would be risking the entirety of their future, even their lives, on the word of a man they didn't know. Pete kept reassuring her that Billy Bob would not have given him Hackberry's name if he were not a good person, but Pete had an incurable trust in his fellow man, no matter how much the world hurt him, to the point where his faith was perhaps more a vice than a virtue.

She remembered an incident that had occurred when she was a little girl and her father had been awakened at two in the morning by the chief of police in Medicine Lodge and told to pick up an eighteen-year-old black kid who had escaped from a county prison in Oklahoma. The boy, who had been arrested for petty theft, had crawled through a heating duct in January and had almost been fried before he kicked a grille from an air vent that, by sheer chance, gave onto an unsecured part of the building. He had ridden a freight train into Kansas with two twisted ankles and had hidden out in his aunt's house, where in all probability he would have been forgotten, since his criminal status was marginal and not worth the expense of finding and bringing him back.

Except the escapee had the IQ of a seven-year-old and phoned the county prison collect and asked the jailer to mail his possessions to Medicine Lodge. He made sure the jailer wrote down his aunt's correct address. A ninety-day county bit had now been augmented by a mandatory minimum of one year in McAlester Pen.

Three days later, Vikki watched her father and an Oklahoma sheriff's deputy lead the escapee in an orange jumpsuit and waist and leg chains to the back of an Oklahoma state vehicle and lock him to a D-ring inset in the floor. The escapee was limping badly and could not have weighed over a hundred pounds. His arms were like sticks. His skin seemed to be possessed of a disease that leached it of color. His hair had been cut so that it resembled a rusty Brillo pad glued to his scalp.

"What's gonna happen to him, Daddy?" Vikki had asked.

"He'll be cannibalized."

"What's that mean?"

"Honey, it means on a day like this, your old man would like to be a full-time musician."

What would her father say about her and Pete's situation now? She had always identified her father more with his music than with his career as a lawman. He was always happy, his tanned skin crinkling at the corners of his eyes, and seldom let the world injure him. He lent money to people who could not pay it back and befriended drunkards and minorities and didn't allow either politics or organized religion to carry him away. He had collected all the Carter Family's early music and was immensely proud to have known the patriarch of the family, Alvin Pleasant Carter, who, in a postcard to Vikki's father, had called him "a fellow musicianer." His favorite Carter family song was "Keep on the Sunny Side of Life."

Where are you now, Daddy? In heaven? Out there among the mesas or inside the blowing clouds of dust and rain? But you're somewhere, aren't you? she said to herself. *You always said music never dies; it lives on the trade winds and wraps all the way around the world.*

She had to wipe a tear from her eye before she went inside the steak house.

"A couple of famous fellows were asking about you," the bartender said.

"How do you define 'famous'?"

The bartender was an ex–rodeo rider nicknamed Stub, for the finger he had pinched off when he caught it in a calf-rope at the Calgary Stampede. He was tall and had a stomach shaped like a water-filled enema bottle and hair that was as slick and black as patent leather. He wore black trousers and a long-sleeve white shirt and a black string tie and was drying champagne glasses and setting them upside down on a white towel while he talked. "They were in last night and wanted to meet you, but you were busy."

"Stub, would you just answer the question?"

"They said they were from the Nitty Gritty Dirt Band."

"They're hanging out here rather than Malibu because they like the weather in late August?"

"They didn't say."

"Did you give them my name?"

"I said your name was Vikki."

"Did you give them my last name or tell them where I live?"

"I didn't tell them where you live."

"What are their names?"

"They left a card here. Or I think they did." He looked behind him at two or three dozen business cards in a cardboard box under the cash register. "They liked your singing. One of them said you sounded like Mother something."

"Maybelle?"

"What?"

"I sound like Mother Maybelle?"

"I don't remember."

"Stub—"

"Maybe they'll come in tonight."

"Don't talk about me to anyone. No one, not for any reason. Do you understand?"

Stub shook his head and dried a glass, his back to her.

"Did you hear me?"

He sighed loudly, as though a great weight had been unfairly set on his shoulders. She wanted to hit him in the head with a plate.

Until nine-thirty P.M. she served dinners from the kitchen and drinks from the bar to tourists on their way to Big Bend and family people and lonely utility workers far from home who came in for a beer and the music. Then she took her guitar from a locked storage compartment in back and removed it from the case and tuned the strings she had put on only last week.

The Gibson had probably been manufactured over sixty years

ago and was the biggest flattop the company made. It had a double-braced red spruce top and rosewood back and sides. It was known as the instrument of choice of Elvis and Emmylou or any rockabilly who loved the deep-throated warm sound of early acoustic guitars. Its sunburst finish and pearl and flower-motif inlay and dark neck and silver frets seemed to capture light and pools of shadow at the same time and, out of the contrasts, create a separate work of art.

When she made an E chord and ticked the plectrum across the strings, the reverberation through the wood was magical. She sang "You Are My Flower" and "Jimmie Brown the Newsboy" and "The Western Hobo." But she could hardly concentrate on the words. Her gaze kept sweeping the crowd, the tables, the utility workers at the bar, a group of European bicyclists who came in sweaty and unshaved with backpacks hanging from their shoulders. Where was Pete? He was supposed to meet her at ten P.M., when the kitchen closed and she usually started cleaning tables and preparing to leave.

A man who was alone at a front table kept spinning his hat on his finger while he watched her sing; one side of his face was cut with a grin. He wore exaggerated hillbilly sideburns, cowboy boots, a print shirt that looked ironed on his tanned skin, jeans that were stretched to bursting on his thighs, and a big polished brass belt buckle with the Stars and Bars embossed on it. When she glanced at him, he gave her a wink.

Over the heads of the crowd, she saw Stub answer the phone. Then he replaced it in the cradle and said something to a drink waitress, who walked up to the bandstand and told Vikki, "Pete said to tell you not to eat dinner, he's going to the grocery to fix y'all something."

"He's going to the grocery at ten o'clock?"

"They stay open till eleven. Count your blessings. My old man is watching rented porn at his mother's house."

Vikki laid her guitar in its case, fastened the clasps, and locked the case in the storage room. At closing time, Pete still had not shown up. She went to the bar and sat down, her feet hurting, her face stiff from smiling when she didn't feel like it.

"Pretty fagged out?" a voice beside her said.

It was the cowboy with the Confederate belt buckle. He had not sat down but was standing close enough that she could smell the spearmint and chewing tobacco on his breath. He was holding his hat with both hands, straightening the brim, pushing a dent out of the crown, brushing a spot out of the felt. He put it on his head and took it back off, his attention focusing on Vikki. "You off?" he said.

"Am I what?"

"You need a ride? Every foot of wind out there has got three feet of sand in it."

Stub compressed a small white towel in his palm and dropped it on the bar in front of the cowboy. "Last call for alcohol," he said.

"Include me out."

"Good, because this is a family-type joint that closes early. Then Vikki helps me clean up. Then I walk her home."

"Glad to hear it," the cowboy said. He put a breath mint in his mouth and cracked it between his molars, grinning while he did it.

Stub watched him leave, then set a cup of coffee in front of Vikki. "Those guys come back?" he asked.

"The ones who claim they're with the Nitty Gritty Dirt Band?"

"You don't believe they're the genuine article?"

She was too tired to talk about it. She lifted her coffee cup, then replaced it in the saucer without drinking from it. "I won't be able to sleep," she said.

"You want me to walk you home?"

"I'm fine. Thanks for your help, Stub."

He picked up a business card tucked under the register. "I dug this one out of the box," he said. He set it in front of her.

She picked it up and looked at the printing across the face. "It says 'Nitty Gritty Dirt Band.'"

"The guy wrote something on the back. I didn't read it."

She turned the card over in her palm. "It says he loved my singing."

"Who?"

"Jeff Hanna. His name is right there."

"Who's Jeff Hanna?"

"The guy who founded the Nitty Gritty Dirt Band."

She walked back to the motel. The stars had come out, and in the west, the bottom of the sky was still lit with a glow that was like a flare burning inside a green vapor. But she could take no comfort in the beauty of the stars and late-summer light on a desert plain. Each time a car or truck passed her, she unconsciously moved away from the asphalt, averting her face, her eyes searching for a sidewalk that led to a building, a driveway to a house, a swale that fronted a filling station.

Would they live this way the rest of their lives?

She unlocked her door and went inside her motel room. The air conditioner was cranked up all the way, moisture running down its side onto the rug. Pete had not returned from the grocery store, and she was exhausted and hungry and scared and incapable of thinking about the next twenty-four hours. Only Pete would choose to prepare a late and complicated dinner on the night they had to make a decision that would either confirm their status as permanent fugitives or place them in the hands of a legal system they didn't trust.

She undressed and went into the shower and turned on the hot water. The steam rolled out of the stall in a huge cloud and fogged the mirror and glistened on the plaster walls and puffed through the partially open door into the bedroom.

When she had been a teenager, her father had always teased her about her love for stray animals. "If you're not careful, you'll find a fellow just like one of those cats or dogs and run off with him," he had said.

Who had she found?

Pete, bumbling his way into the maw of mass murderers.

As she stared at her reflection through a small hole in the fogged mirror, she was stricken with shame and guilt by her own thoughts. Today was her birthday. She had forgotten it, but Pete had not.

She was filled with unrelieved anger at herself and the intractability of their situation. For the first time in her life, she understood how people could deliberately injure and even kill themselves. Their desperation didn't have its origins in depression. The warm tub of water was cosmetic; the quick downward movement across the forearms was born out of rage at the self.

She got into the shower and washed her hair and lathered her breasts and underarms and thighs and abdomen and buttocks and calves, holding her face so close to the hot spray that her skin turned as red as a blister. How would they take back their lives? How would they free themselves from the fear that waited for them every morning like a hungry animal? The only sanctuary they had was a motel room with a clanking air conditioner dripping rust on the rug, a bed stained with the fornications of others, and curtains they could close on a highway that led back to a rural crossroads and a mass burial ground she couldn't bear to think about.

She propped her forehead against the stall, the jet of shower water exploding on her scalp, the steam seeping into the bedroom where the night chain on the door hung down on the jamb. She had started out the evening thinking about choices. The rain had changed the land, and the sunset had reshaped the mountains and cooled the desert. He who was the alpha and the omega made all things new, didn't He? That was the promise, wasn't it?

But when you were in a room that seemed to have no exit except false doors painted on the walls, how were you supposed to choose? What kind of cruel joke was that to play on anyone, much less on those who had tried to do right with their lives?

She squeezed her eyes tightly shut and kept her head pressed so hard against the shower wall that she thought her skin would split.

PETE STEERED HIS basket to the deli counter and dropped a rotisserie chicken, a carton of potato salad, and a carton of coleslaw inside. Then he lifted a six-pack of ice-cold Dr Pepper out of the cooler and a half-gallon of frozen yogurt from the freezer and headed for the bakery. He picked up an angel food cake and found a loaf of French bread that was still soft. The baker was working late and was cleaning up behind the pastry counter. Pete asked her to scroll "Happy Birthday, Vikki" on his cake.

"Special girl, huh?" she said.

"Yes, ma'am, ain't none better," he replied.

He paid up front and, with a grocery bag in each arm, began the one-mile walk toward the motel. The sun's afterglow had finally died on the horizon, and he could see the evening star bright and twinkling above a rock ridge that looked carved from decaying bone. The wind had stopped completely, and under an overhang of trees, he thought he could smell an autumnal odor like gas and chrysanthemums in the air. An eighteen-wheeler passed him, its brakes hissing, a backwash of heat and diesel fumes enveloping him. He veered away from the road's edge, walking now on an uneven surface, gravel breaking under his feet, his coned-up Mexican straw hat bobbing on his head. Up ahead, under a chinaberry tree, was a shut-down Sno-Ball stand, a cluster of bright red cherries painted on a wood sign above its shuttered serving counter. In the distance, when a vehicle approached from the west, he could dimly see the abandoned drive-in theater and the weed-grown miniature-golf course and the silhouettes of the Cadillac car bodies buried nose-down in the hardpan. Vikki must be at the motel by now, he thought. Waiting for him, worrying, maybe secretly regretting she had ever hooked up with him.

He thought the word "Vikki," so it became a sound in his head rather than a word. He thought it in a way that turned the word into a heart with blood pumping in it and curly hair and strangely colored recessed eyes and breath that was sweet and skin that smelled as fresh as flowers opening in the morning. She was smart and pretty and brave and talented and took no credit for any of it. If he had money, they could go to Canada. He had heard about Lake Louise and the blue Canadian Rockies and places where you could still cowboy for a living and drive a hundred miles without seeing a man-built structure. Vikki talked all the time about Woody Guthrie and Cisco Houston and the music of the Great American West and the promise the land had held for the generation that came out of the 1940s. Montana, British Columbia, Wyoming, the Cascades in Washington, what did it matter? Those were the places for a new beginning. He had to turn things around and make it up to Vikki for what he had done. He had to separate himself from the nine murdered Asian women and girls who lived in his dreams. Didn't all dead people grow weary and eventually go toward a white light and leave the world to its illusions?

If it cost him his life, he had to make these things happen.

He shifted the sack that was cupped in his right forearm so he wouldn't bruise the cake inside. Behind him, he heard the tires of a diesel-powered vehicle pulling off the asphalt onto the gravel.

"Pete, want a ride?" the driver of the pickup said. He was grinning. A felt hat with a wilted brim hung on the gun rack behind him. He wore a print shirt that was as taut on his torso as his sun-browned skin.

"I don't have far to go," Pete replied, not recognizing the driver.

"I work with Vikki. She said y'all are cooking up a meal tonight. Special occasion?"

"Something like that," Pete said, still walking, looking straight ahead.

"That sack looks like it's fixing to split." The driver was steering with one hand, keeping his pickup on the road's shoulder, tapping the brake to keep the idle from accelerating his vehicle past Pete.

"Don't remember me? That's 'cause I'm in the kitchen. Bending over the sink most of the time."

"Don't need a lift. Got it covered. Thanks."

"Suit yourself. I hope Vikki feels better," the driver said. He started to pull back on the asphalt, craning out the window to see if the lane was clear, his shoulders hunched up over the wheel.

"Hang on. What's wrong with Vikki?" Pete said.

But the driver was ignoring him, waiting for a church bus to pass.

"Hey, pull over," Pete said, walking faster, the bottom of one bag starting to break under the weight of the damp six-pack of Dr Pepper. Then the bottom caved, cascading the six-pack and a box of cereal and a quart of milk and a container of blueberries onto the gravel.

The driver of the pickup pulled his vehicle back onto the safety of the shoulder, leaning forward, waiting for Pete to speak again.

"Vikki's sick?" Pete said.

"She was holding her stomach and looking kind of queasy. There's a nasty kind of flu going around. It gives you the red scours for about a day or so."

"Park up yonder," Pete said. "It'll take me a minute."

The driver didn't try to conceal his vexation. He looked at the face of his watch and pulled into darkness under the chinaberry tree and cut his lights, waiting for Pete to pick up his groceries from the roadside and carry them to the bed of the truck. The driver did not get out of his vehicle or offer to help. Pete made one trip, then returned to pick up the bag that had not broken. The back window of the truck was black under the tree's overhang, the hood ticking with heat. The driver sat with his arm propped casually on his window, rolling a matchstick on his teeth.

Pete walked to the passenger side and got in. A pair of handcuffs hung from the rearview mirror.

"Them are just plastic," the driver said. He grinned again, his pleasant mood back in place. He wore a brass buckle on his belt that was embossed with the Stars and Bars and was burnished the color of browned butter. "You got a knife?"

"What for?"

"This floor rug keeps tangling in my accelerator. It like to got me killed up the road."

Pete worked his Swiss Army knife out of his jeans and opened the long blade and handed it to the driver. The driver started sawing at a piece of loose carpet with it. "Strap yourself in. The latch is right there on your left. You got to dig for it."

"How about we get on it?"

"State law says you got to be buckled up. I tend to be conscious of the law. I did a postgraduate study in cotton-picking 'cause I wasn't, know what I mean?" The driver saw the expression in Pete's face. "Ninety days on the P farm for nonsupport. Not necessarily anything I'd brag to John Dillinger about."

Pete stretched the safety belt across his chest and pushed the metal tongue into the latch and heard it snap firmly into place. But the belt felt too tight. He pushed against it, trying to adjust its length.

The driver tossed the piece of sawed fabric out the window and folded the knife blade back into the handle with his palm. "My niece was wearing it. Hang on. We ain't got far to go," he said. He took the gearshift out of park and dropped it into drive.

"Give me my knife."

"Just a second, man."

Pete pressed the release button on the latch, but nothing happened. "What's the deal?" he said.

"Deal?"

"The belt is stuck."

"I got my hands full, buddy," the driver replied.

"Who are you?"

"Give it a break, will you? I got a situation here. Do you believe this asshole?"

An SUV had pulled off the road beyond the Sno-Ball stand and was now backing up.

"What the fuck?" the driver of the pickup said.

The SUV was accelerating, its bumper headed toward the pickup, the tires swerving through the gravel. The driver of the pickup dropped his gearshift into reverse and mashed on the accelerator, but it was too late. The trailer hitch on the SUV plowed into the truck's grille, the steel ball on the hitch and the triangular steel mount plunging deep into the radiator's mesh, ripping the fan blades from their shaft, jolting the pickup's body sideways.

Pete jerked at the safety belt, but it was locked solid, and he realized he'd been had. But the events taking place around him were even more incongruous. The driver of the SUV had cut his lights and leaped onto the gravel, holding an object close to his thigh so it could not be seen from the road. The man moved hurriedly to the driver's door of the pickup, jerked it open, and, in one motion, thrust himself inside and grabbed the driver by the throat with one hand and, with the other, jammed a blue-black .38 snub-nose revolver into the driver's mouth. He fitted his thumb over the knurled surface of the hammer and cocked it back. "I'll blow your brains all over the dashboard, T-Bone. You've seen me do it," he said.

T-Bone, the driver of the pickup, could not speak. His eyes bulged from his head, and saliva ran from both sides of his mouth.

"Blink your eyes if you got the message, moron," the man from the SUV said.

T-Bone lowered his eyelids and opened them again. The driver of the SUV slid the revolver from T-Bone's mouth and lowered the hammer with his thumb and wiped the saliva off the steel onto T-Bone's shirt. Then, for no apparent reason other than unbridled rage, he hit him in the face with it.

T-Bone pressed the flat of his hand to the cut below his eye. "Hugo sent me. The broad is at the Fiesta motel," he said. "We couldn't find the Fiesta 'cause we were looking for the Siesta. We had the wrong name of the motel, Bobby Lee."

"You follow me to the next corner and turn right. Keep your shit-machine running for three blocks, then we'll be in the country. Don't let this go south on you." Bobby Lee Motree's eyes met Pete's. "It's called a Venus flytrap. Rapists use it. It means you're screwed. But 'screwed' and 'bullet in the head' aren't necessarily the same thing. You roger that, boy? You've caused me a mess of trouble. You can't guess how much trouble, which means your name is on the top of the shit list right now. Start your engine, T-Bone."

T-Bone turned the ignition. The engine coughed and blew a noxious cloud of black smoke from the exhaust pipe. Something tinkled against metal, and antifreeze streamed into the gravel as the engine caught, then steam and a scorched smell like a hose or rubber belt cooking on a hot surface rose from the hood. Pete sat silent and stiff against the seat, pushing himself deeper into it so he could get a thumb under the safety strap and try to work it off his chest. His Swiss Army knife was on the floor, the red handle half under the driver's foot. A car went by, then a truck, the illumination of their headlights falling outside the pool of shadow under the chinaberry tree.

"My piece is under the seat," T-Bone said.

"Go ahead."

"I need to talk to Hugo."

"Hugo doesn't have conversations with dead people. That's what you're gonna be unless you do what I say."

T-Bone bent over, his gaze straight ahead, and lifted a .25 auto from under the seat. He kept it in his left hand and laid it across his lap so it was pointed at Pete's rib cage. A thin whistling sound like a teakettle's was building inside the hood. "I didn't mean to get in your space, Bobby Lee. I was doing what Hugo told me."

"Say another word, and I'm going to seriously hurt you."

Pete remained silent as T-Bone followed Bobby Lee's SUV out of town and up a dirt road bordered by pastureland where black Angus were clumped up in an arroyo and under a solitary tree by a windmill. Pete's left hand drifted down to the latch on the safety belt. He worked his fingers over the square outline of the metal, pushing the plastic release button with his thumb, trying to free himself by creating enough slack in the belt to go deeper into the latch rather than pull against it.

"You're wasting your time. It has to be popped loose with a screwdriver from the inside," T-Bone said. "By the way, I ain't no rapist."

"Were you at the church?" Pete asked.

"No, but you were. Way I see it, you got no kick coming. So don't beg. I've heard it before. Same words from the same people. It ain't their fault. The world's been picking on them. They'll do anything to make it right."

"My girlfriend is innocent. She wasn't part of anything that happened at that church."

"A child is created from its parents' fornication. Ain't none of us innocent."

"What were you told to do to us?"

"None of your business."

"You're not on the same page as the guy in the SUV, though, are you?"

"That's something you ain't got to worry about."

"That's right. I don't. But you do," Pete said.

Pete saw T-Bone wet his bottom lip. A drop of blood from the cut under his eye slipped down his cheek, as though a red line were being drawn there with an invisible pencil. "Say that over."

"Why would Hugo send you after us and not tell Bobby Lee? Bobby Lee is working on his own, isn't he? How's the guy named Preacher fit into all this?"

T-Bone glanced sideways, the shine of fear in his eyes. "How much you know about Preacher?"

"If Bobby Lee is working with him, where's that leave you?"

T-Bone sucked in his cheeks as though they were full of moisture. But Pete guessed that in reality, his mouth was as dry as cotton. The dust from the SUV was corkscrewing in the pickup's headlights. "You're a smart one, all right. But for a guy who's so dadburned smart, it must be strange to find yourself in your current situation. Another thing I cain't figure out: I talked with your girlfriend at the steak house. How'd a guy who looks like a fried chitling end up with a hot piece of ass like that?"

Up ahead, the brake lights on the SUV lit up as brightly as embers inside the dust. To the south, the ridges and mesas that flanged the Rio Grande were purple and gray and blue and cold-looking against the night sky.

Bobby Lee got out of his vehicle and walked back to the truck, his nine-millimeter dangling from his right hand. "Cut your lights and turn off your engine," he said.

"What are we doing?"

"There's no 'we.'" Bobby Lee's cell phone hung from a cord looped over his neck.

"I thought we were working together. Call Hugo. Call Artie. Straighten this out."

Bobby Lee screwed the muzzle of a nine-millimeter against T-Bone's temple. The hammer was already cocked, the butterfly safety off.

"You use your nine on your—"

"That's right, I do," Bobby Lee said. "A fourteen-rounder, manufactured before the bunny huggers got them banned. Hand me your piece, butt-first."

T-Bone lifted his hand to eye level, his fingers clamped across the frame of his .25. Bobby Lee took it from him and dropped it in his pocket. "Who's down here with you?"

"A couple of new people. Maybe Hugo's around. I don't know. Maybe—"

"Maybe what?"

"There's a lot of interest in Preacher."

Bobby Lee removed the nine-millimeter's muzzle from T-Bone's temple, leaving a red circle that seemed to glow against the bone. "Get out."

T-Bone stepped carefully from the door. "I was supposed to grab the girl and call Hugo and not do anything to her. I didn't pull it off, so I saw the kid carrying his groceries on the road, and I took a chance."

Bobby Lee was silent, busy with thoughts inside of which people lived or died or were left somewhere in between; his thoughts shaped and reshaped themselves, sorting out different scenarios that, in seconds, could result in a situation no human being wanted to experience.

"If you see Preacher—" T-Bone said.

"I'll see him."

"I just carry out orders."

"Do I need to jot that down so I got the wording right?"

"I ain't worth it, Bobby Lee."

"Worth what?"

"Whatever."

"Tell me what 'whatever' is."

"Why you doing this to me?"

"Because you piss me off."

"What'd I do?"

"You remind me of a zero. No, a zero is a thing, a circle with air inside it. You make me think of something that's less than a zero."

T-Bone's gaze wandered out into the pasture. More Angus were moving into the arroyo. There were trees along the arroyo, and the shadows of the cattle seemed to dissolve into the trees' shadows and enlarge and darken them at the same time. "It's fixing to rain again. They always clump up before it rains."

Bobby Lee was breathing through his nose, his eyes unfocused, strained, as though someone were shining a light into them.

T-Bone closed his eyes, and his voice made a clicking sound, but no words came from his throat. Then he hawked loudly and spat a bloody clot on the ground. "I got ulcers."

Bobby Lee didn't speak.

"Don't shoot me in the face," T-Bone said.

"Turn around."

"Bobby Lee."

"If you look back, if you call Hugo, if you contact anybody about this, I'm gonna do to you what you did to that Mexican you tied up in that house in Zaragoza. Your truck stays here. Don't ever come in this county again."

"How do I know you're not—"

"If you're still sucking air after about forty yards, you'll know."

Bobby Lee rested his forearm on the truck window and watched T-Bone walk away. He slowly turned his gaze on Pete. "What are you looking at?"

"Not a whole lot."

"You think this is funny? You think you're cute?"

"What I think is you're standing up to your bottom lip in your own shit."

"I'm the best friend you got, boy."

"Then you're right. I'm in real trouble. Tell you what. Pop me out of this safety belt, and I'll accept your surrender."

Bobby Lee walked around to the other side of the vehicle and opened the door. He pulled a switchblade from his jeans and flicked it open. He sliced the safety strap in half, the nine-millimeter in his right hand, then stepped back. "Get on your face."

Pete stepped out on the ground, got to his knees, and lay on his chest, the smell of the grass and the earth warm in his face. He twisted his head around.

"Eyes front," Bobby Lee said, pressing his foot between Pete's shoulder blades. "Put your hands behind you."

"Where's Vikki?"

Bobby Lee didn't reply. He stooped over and hooked a hand-cuff on each of Pete's wrists, squeezing the teeth of the ratchets as deep as he could into the locking mechanism. "Get up."

"At the A.A. meeting, you said you were in Iraq."

"What about it?"

"You don't have to do this stuff."

"Here's a news flash for you. Every flag is the same color. The color is black. No quarter, no mercy, it's 'burn, motherfucker, burn.' Tell me I'm full of shit."

"You were kicked out of the army, weren't you?"

"Close your mouth, boy."

"That guy, T-Bone, you saw yourself in him. That's why you wanted to tear him apart."

"Maybe I can work you in as a substitute."

Bobby Lee opened the back door of the SUV and shoved Pete inside. He slammed the door and lifted the cell phone from the cord that hung around his neck, punching the speed dial with his thumb. "I got the package," he said.

Chapter 22

VIKKI DRIED HERSELF and wrapped the towel around her body and began brushing her teeth. The mirror was heavily fogged, the heat and moisture from her shower escaping through the partially opened door into the bedroom. She thought she heard a movement, perhaps a door closing, a half-spoken sentence trailing into nothingness. She squeezed the handle on the faucet, shutting off the water, her toothbrush stationary in her mouth. She set the toothbrush in a water glass. "Pete?" she said.

There was no response. She tucked the towel more securely around her. "Is that you?" she said.

She heard electronic laughter through the wall and realized the people in the next room, a Hispanic couple with two teenage children, had once again turned up the volume on their television to full jet-engine mode.

She opened the door wide and tied a hand towel around her head as she walked into the bedroom. She had left only one light burning, a lamp by the table in the far corner. It created more shadows than it did illumination and softened the neediness of the room—the bedspread that she avoided touching, the sun-faded curtains, the brown water spots on the ceiling, the molding that had cracked away from the window jambs.

She felt his presence before she actually saw him, in the same way one encounters a faceless presence in a dream, a protean figure without origins, from an unknown place, who can walk through walls and locked doors, and in this instance place himself in the cloth-covered chair by the closet, on the far side of the bed, the only telephone in the room two feet from his hand.

He had made himself comfortable, one leg crossed on his knee, his pin-striped suit in need of pressing, his white shirt starched, his shoes buffed, his knit necktie not quite knotted, his shave done without a mirror. Like the dream figure, he was a study in contradiction, his shabby elegance not quite real, his rectangularity that of a grandiose poseur sitting in a soup kitchen.

He kept his eyes on hers and did not lower them to her body, but she could see the flicker of hunger around his mouth, the hollows in his cheeks, his suppressed need to lick his tongue across his bottom lip.

"You," she said.

"Yes."

"I hoped I would never see you again."

"Worse men than I are looking for you, missy."

"Don't you talk down to me."

"You don't wonder how I got in?"

"I don't care how you got in. You're here. Now you need to leave."

"But that's not likely, is it?"

"By your foot."

"What?"

"What's that by your foot?"

He looked down at the carpet. "This?"

"Yes."

"A twenty-two derringer. But it's not for you. If I were a different sort of fellow, it might be. But it's not." He cupped his hand to lift his leg gingerly off his knee and set it down. "You did me up proper on the highway."

"I stopped to help you because I thought you had a flat. You repaid the kindness by trying to abduct me."

"I don't 'abduct' people, miss. Or Ms."

"Excuse me. You kill them."

"I have. When they came after me. When they tried to kill me first. When they were part of a higher plan that I didn't have control over. Sit down. Do you want your bathrobe?"

"I don't have one."

"Sit down anyway."

She felt as if a hot coal had been placed on her scalp. Moisture was leaking out of the towel she had wrapped on her head. Her face stung, and her eyes burned. She could feel drops of sweat networking down her thighs like lines of ants. His eyes dropped to her loins, then he looked away quickly and pretended to be distracted by the noise the air conditioner made. She sat down at the small table against the wall, her knees close together, her arms folded across her chest. "Where's Pete?" she asked.

"He was rescued by a friend of mine."

"Rescued?" She paused and said the word a second time. "*Rescued?*" She could taste the acidity in her saliva when she spoke.

"Do you want me to leave without resolving our problem? Do you want to leave Pete's situation undecided? He's out there somewhere on a dark road in the hands of a man who believes he's a descendant of Robert E. Lee."

"Who are you a descendant of? Who the fuck are you?"

The fingers of Preacher's right hand twitched slightly. "People don't speak to me that way."

"You think a mass killer deserves respect?"

"You don't know me. Maybe I have qualities you're not aware of."

"Did you ever fight for your country?"

"You might say in my own way I have. But I don't make claims for myself."

"Pete was burned in his tank. But the real damage to him happened when he came back home and met you and the other criminals you work with."

"Your friend is a fool or he wouldn't be in this trouble. I don't appreciate the coarseness of your remarks to me."

Again she could feel a pool of heat building inside her head, as though the sun were burning through her skull, cooking her blood, pushing her out on the edges of a place she had never been. Her towel was starting to slip loose, and she gathered it more tightly around her, pressing its dampness against her skin with her arms.

"I'd like for you to go away with me. I'd like to make up for any harm I did to you. Don't speak, just listen," he said. "I have money. I'm fairly well educated for a man without much formal schooling. I have manners, and I know how to care for a fine woman. I have a rented house on a mountaintop outside Guadalajara. You could have anything you want there. There would be no demands on you, sexual or otherwise."

She thought she heard a train in the distance, the massive weight and power of the locomotive grinding dully on the track, the vibrations spreading through the hardpan like the steady tremors given off by an abscessed wisdom tooth.

"Give Pete back to me. Don't hurt him," she said.

"What will you give me in turn?"

"Take my life."

"Why would I want to do that?"

"I put two bullets in you."

"You don't know me very well."

"You know why you're here. Go ahead and do it. I won't resist you. Just leave Pete alone." Her eyes seemed to go in and out of focus, the room shimmering, a dark liquid swelling up from her stomach into her throat.

"You offend me."

"Your thoughts are an offense, and you don't hide them well."

"What thoughts? What are you talking about?" The skin under his left eye wrinkled, like putty drying up.

"The thoughts you don't want to admit are yours. The secret desires you mask with your cruelty. You make me think of diseased tissue with insects crawling on it. Your glands are filled with rut, but you pretend to be a gentleman wishing to care for and protect a woman. It's embarrassing to look at the starvation in your face."

"Starvation? For a woman who insults me? Who thinks she can tongue-lash me after I saved her from a man like Hugo Cistranos? That's right, Hugo plans to kill you and your boyfriend. You want me to hit the speed dial on my cell phone? I can introduce your friend to an experience neither of you can imagine."

"I need to get dressed. I don't want you to watch me."

"Dressed to go where?"

"Out. Away from you."

"You think you're controlling the events that are about to happen around you? Are you that naive?"

"My clothes are in the dresser. I'm going to take them into the bathroom and dress. Don't come in there. Don't look at me while I'm removing my clothes from the drawer, either. After I'm dressed, I'll be going somewhere. I'm not sure where. But it won't be with you. Maybe I'll end here, in this room, in this dirty room, in this godforsaken place on the edge of hell. But you won't be a part of it, you piece of shit."

His facial expression seemed divided in half, as though his motor controls were shutting down and the muscles on one side of his face were collapsing. His right hand trembled. "You have no right to say these things."

"Kill me or get out. I can't stand being around you."

He stooped over and picked up the blue-black white-handled derringer from the carpet. He was breathing raggedly through his nose, his eyes small and hot under his brow. He approached her slowly, his white shirt catching the pink glow of the neon outside the window, giving his face a rosy hue it didn't possess on its own. He stood in front of her, his stomach flat behind his shirt and his tightly notched belt, an odor of dried perspiration wafting from his suit. "Say that last part again."

"I hate being in the presence of a man like you. You're what every woman dreads. Your physical touch causes nausea."

He lifted the barrel of the derringer to her mouth. Through the wall, she could hear the electronic laughter from the neighbor's television set. She could hear the locomotive pulling a mile-long string of gondolas and boxcars between the hills, the reverberations shaking the foundation of the motel. She could hear Preacher's dry exhalations just above her forehead. He put his left hand under her chin and lifted her line of vision to his. When she tried to turn away, he pinched her jaws and jerked her head straight. "Look into my eyes."

"No."

"You're afraid?"

"No. Yes."

"Of what?"

"Of what I'll see there. You're evil. I think you carry the abyss inside you."

"That's a lie."

"In your sleep, you hear a howling wind, don't you? It's like the sound the wind makes at night on the ocean. Except the wind is inside you. I read a poem once by William Blake. It was about the worm that flies at night in the howling storm. I think he was writing about you."

He released her, almost flinging her face from his hand. "I

couldn't care less about your literary experience. It's you who's the agent of the devil. It's inherent in your gender. From Eden to the present."

Her head was lowered, her arms still folded across her bosom, her back starting to tremble. He reached in his pocket with his left hand. She felt something touch her cheek. "Take it," he said.

She showed no response other than to wrap herself more tightly in her own skin, and curl her shoulders and spine into a tighter ball, and keep her eyes fixed on the tops of her folded arms.

He pushed an object that was both sharp and yielding against her cheek, jabbing the jawbone, trying to force her head up. "I said take it."

"No."

"There's six hundred dollars in the clip. Cross into Chihuahua. But don't stop till you get to Durango. Hugo Cistranos's people are everywhere. South of Durango, you'll be safe." He held the money clip with two fingers in front of her. "Go ahead. No strings."

She spat on the money clip and on the bills and on his fingers. Then she began to weep. In the silence that followed, the pink glow of his shirt and the odor of his perspiration and the proximity of his loins to her face seemed to crush the air out of her lungs, as though the only reality in the world were the figure of Preacher Jack Collins hovering inches from her skin. She had never realized that silence could be so loud. She believed its intensity was like the creaking sounds a drowning person hears as he sinks to the bottom of a deep lake.

He traced the double muzzles of the derringer across her temple and hairline and along her cheek. She closed her eyes, and for a moment she thought she heard the electronic laughter from the television set subsumed by a train engine blowing through a tunnel, its whistle screaming off the walls, a lighted dining car filled with revelers disappearing into the darkness.

When she opened her eyes, she saw a cell phone in his hand, saw his thumb touch a single button, saw the phone go out of her line of vision toward his ear. "Cut him loose," he said.

Then the room was quiet again, and she felt the hot wind of the desert puffing through the door and saw an eighteen-wheeler driving by on the state highway, its trailer outlined with strings of festive lights, the stars winking above the hills.

EVEN BEFORE THE sun had broken the edge of the horizon, Hackberry Holland knew the temperature would reach a hundred degrees by noon. The influence of the rainstorm and the promise it had offered had proved illusory. The heat had lain in abeyance through the night, collecting in stone and warm concrete and sandy river bottoms that boiled with grasshoppers; at dawn it had come alive again, rising with the sun inside a warm blanket of humidity that shimmered on the fields and hills and made the eyes water when you stared too long at the horizon.

At seven-thirty A.M. Hackberry raised the flag on the pole in front of his office, then went inside and tried again to reach Ethan Riser. He did not know what had happened to Pete Flores since Pete had called from a phone booth and told Hackberry he remembered one letter and two numbers from Jack Collins's car tag, or at least the tag of the tan Honda that Flores had showered rocks on. Hackberry had given the Texas DMV the single letter and two digits and asked that they run every combination possible through the computer until they found a match with a Honda. He had also called Riser and told him of the call from Flores.

The DMV had come back with 173 possibles. Riser not only did not get back to him; he had stopped returning Hackberry's calls altogether. Which raised another question: Was Riser like too many of his colleagues, cooperative and helpful as long as the locals were useful, then down the road and gone after he got what he needed?

Or maybe Riser had been told by his superiors to stay away from Hackberry and worry less about local problems and concentrate on putting Josef Sholokoff out of business.

On occasion, federal agencies practiced a form of triage that went beyond the pragmatic into a marginal area that was one step short of ruthless. Psychopaths were sprung from custody without their victims or the prosecution's witnesses being notified. People who had trusted the system with their lives discovered they had been used and discarded as casually as someone flicking away a cigarette butt. Most of these people usually had the power and social importance of fish chum.

By ten A.M. Hackberry had left two messages with Riser. He opened his desk drawer and removed a thick brown envelope that contained the eight-by-ten crime-scene photos taken behind the church at Chapala Crossing. Besides their morbid subject matter, the photos contained a second kind of peculiarity: None of the uniformed deputies, the paramedics, the federal personnel, or the forensic team from Austin wore any expression. In photo after photo, their faces were empty of emotion, their mouths down-hooked at the corners, as though they were playing roles in a film that was not supposed to make use of sound or any display of feeling. The only photography he could compare it with was the black-and-white news footage taken during the mass burials at the death camps liberated by American forces in early 1945.

He returned the photos to the drawer.

What had happened to Pete Flores and Vikki Gaddis? What was the next move Preacher Jack Collins would make? What kind of cage could contain the evil that had perpetrated the slaughter at Chapala Crossing?

* * *

AT TWO-THIRTY THAT afternoon Danny Boy Lorca was driving his converted army-surplus flatbed truck up the two-lane from the Mexican border, the wind as hot as a blowtorch through the window, the unmuffled roar of the engine shaking the cab, his fuel gauge ticking on empty. He saw the hitchhikers in the distance, standing on the roadside between two low hills whose sides had been scorched by a wildfire. There was no other traffic on the road. The outlines of the two hitchhikers were warping in the heat, the glaze on the road like a pool of tar. As he drew closer, he realized one of the hitchhikers was a woman. A guitar case rested by her foot. Her denim shirt was pasted to her skin with perspiration. The man next to her wore a coned-up straw hat and a shirt he had sawed off at the armpits. The top of one arm was wrinkled with scar tissue that looked like the material in an overheated lampshade.

Danny Boy pulled to the side of the road, glancing warily in the rearview mirror. "Y'all came back," he said through the passenger window.

"Will you give us a ride?" the woman asked.

Danny Boy never answered questions whose answer seemed obvious, in the same way he did not say hello or goodbye to people when their actions or presence were obvious.

Pete Flores swung a duffel bag onto the truck bed and placed Vikki's guitar case between it and the cab. He opened the passenger door, blowing on his hand after he did, waiting for Vikki to get inside. "Wow," he said, looking at his hand. "How long has your truck been in the sun?"

"It's a hunnerd and seven," Danny Boy said.

"Thank you for stopping," Vikki said.

Pete climbed inside and shut the door. He started to offer his hand, but Danny Boy was concentrating on the wide-angle mirror.

"You know the cops are looking for you? Federal agents and state people and Sheriff Holland, too. A federal agent got killed."

"I reckon they found us," Pete said.

Danny Boy pulled back onto the road, his shirt open on his leathery chest, his neck beaded with dirt rings. "Maybe this ain't the best place for y'all."

"We don't have any other place to go," Pete said.

"If it was me, I'd get on a freight and go to Canada and follow the harvest, maybe. A cook on them crews can make good money. I'd find a place that ain't been ruined and settle down."

Pete stuck his arm out the window, turning his palm into the airflow so it would vane up his arm and inside his shirt. "We're working on it," he said.

"Them people you got mixed up with? They're out there."

"Which people? Out where?" Vikki asked.

"They're out there at night. They come up the arroyos. They ain't wets, either. They go past my place. I see them in the field."

"Those are harmless farmworkers," Pete said.

"No, they ain't. See the sky. We had one night of hard rain, the way it used to be. But we didn't get no more. Them rain gods were giving us a chance. But they ain't coming back while all these drug dealers and killers are here. There's a hole in the earth, and down inside it is the place where all the corn came from. That's where all power comes from. Don't nobody know where the hole is anymore."

Vikki looked sideways at Pete.

"Tell her," Danny Boy said.

"Tell her what?"

"That I ain't drunk."

"She knows that. Danny Boy is okay, Vikki." Pete gazed out the window, the wind climbing up his bare arm, puffing inside his shirt. "That's Ouzel Flagler's place. I wish I hadn't been there when some bad hombres came in."

"That's where you met them guys?"

"Probably. I'm not sure. I was in a blackout most of the day.

I know I bought mescal from Ouzel that day. Ouzel's mescal always leaves its mark, like an earth grader has rolled over your head."

Ouzel Flagler's brick bungalow, cracked down the middle, with a plank bar built on one side of the house, was veiled briefly by a cloud of dust blowing off the hardpan, balls of tumbleweed skipping across its roof. Under a white sun, amid the tangled wire and all the rusted construction equipment Ouzel had hauled onto his property, a cluster of rheumy-eyed longhorns was standing by a recessed pool of rainwater, the sides of the depression strung with green feces.

"Don't look at it," Vikki said.

"At what?"

"That place. It's not part of your life anymore."

"What I did that night is on me, not on Ouzel."

"Will you stop talking about it, Pete? Will you just stop talking about it?"

"I got to get gas up yonder," Danny Boy said.

"No, not here," Vikki said.

Danny Boy looked at her, his eyes sleepy, the muscles in his face flaccid. "The needle is below the E. It's three miles to the next station."

"Why didn't you tell us you were out of gas when we got in?" she said.

Danny Boy shifted down and angled the truck off the road into the filling station, steering with his hands in the ten-two position, bent slightly forward like a student driver beginning his first solo, his face impassive. "You can walk across the highway and maybe catch a ride while I'm inside," he said. "I got to use the restroom. I forgot to tell you about that when you got in, even though it's my truck. If you don't have a ride by the time I leave, I'll pick y'all up again."

"We'll wait in the truck. I'm sorry," Vikki said.

Danny Boy went inside the station and paid for ten dollars' gas in advance.

"Why were you getting on his case?" Pete said.

"Ouzel Flagler's brother owns this station."

"Who cares?"

"Pete, you never learn. You just never learn."

"Learn what? About Ouzel? He has Buerger's disease. He's a sad person. He sells a little mescal. What's the big deal? You stood up to that killer. I'm really proud of you. We don't have to be afraid anymore."

"Please shut up. For God's sake, for once just shut up." She blotted the humidity out of her eyes with a Kleenex and stared at the highway winding into the sun's white brilliance. The terrain, untouched by shade or shadows, glaring and coarse and rock-strewn, made her think of a dry seabed and huge anthills or a planet that had already gone dead.

Danny Boy pulled the gas spigot out of the tank and clanked it back into place on the pump, then used the outside washroom and climbed back into the cab, his face still wet from a rinse in the lavatory. "On a day like this, ain't nothing like cold water," he said.

None of them took note of the man on the other side of the black glare on the filling station window. He had just come out of the back of the store and was drinking a soda, upending it, his neck swollen by a chain of tumors. His head seemed recessed into his shoulders, reminiscent of a perched carrion bird's. He finished his soda, dropped the can into the wastebasket, and seemed to think for a long time. Then he picked up the telephone.

Chapter 23

PETE AND VIKKI had climbed down from Danny Boy Lorca's truck cab, retrieved a duffel bag and guitar case from the truck bed, and entered the building dehydrated, sunburned, and windblown with road grit. Their clothes stiff with salt, they sat down in front of Hackberry's desk as though his air-conditioned office were the end of a long journey out of the Sahara. They told him of their encounter with Preacher Jack Collins and Bobby Lee and the man named T-Bone and the fact that Collins had let them go.

"We got on the bus early this morning, but it broke down after twenty miles. So we hitchhiked," Pete said.

"Collins just cut you loose? He didn't harm you in any way?" Hackberry let his gaze linger on Vikki Gaddis.

"It happened just like we told you," Vikki said.

"Where do you think Collins went?" Hackberry asked.

"Collins is y'all's business now. Tell us what you want us to do," Pete said.

"I haven't quite thought it through," Hackberry said.

"Repeat that, please?" Vikki said.

"I've got two empty cells. Go up the iron stairs in back and check them out."

"You're offering us jail cells?" she said.

"The doors would stay unlocked. You can come and go as you like."

"I don't believe this," she said.

"You can use the restroom and the shower down here," Hackberry said.

"Pete, would you say something?" Vikki said.

"Maybe it's not a bad idea," he replied.

Pam Tibbs came into the office and leaned against the doorjamb. "I'll go with you, honey."

"With luck, we can probably find an iron staircase by ourselves," Vikki said. "Excuse me, I forgot to call you 'honey.' "

"Suit yourself, ma'am," Pam said. She waited until they were out of earshot before she spoke again. "How do you read all that stuff about Collins and Bobby Lee Motree and this character T-Bone?"

"Who knows? Collins probably has psychotic episodes."

"Vikki Gaddis has a mouth on her, doesn't she?"

"They're just kids," Hackberry said.

"That doesn't mean you should put your ass in a sling for them."

"Wouldn't dream of it."

Maydeen Stoltz walked into the room. "Ethan Riser is on the phone. Want me to take a message?"

"Where's he calling from?" Hackberry asked.

"He didn't say."

"Ask him if he's in town."

"Like that? 'Are you in town?' "

"Yeah, tell him I want to ask him to dinner. Would you please do it, Maydeen?"

She went back into the dispatcher's office, then returned. "He's in San Antonio."

"Put him through."

"I'm going to get a job on a spaceship," she said.

A moment later, the light on Hackberry's desk phone went on, and he picked up the receiver. "Hey, Ethan. How are you?"

"You called me by my first name."

"I'm trying to get a perspective on a couple of things. Is there any development with Nick Dolan's situation?"

"Not a lot."

"Have y'all interviewed him yet?"

"No comment."

"So he's still bait?"

"I wouldn't use that particular term."

"Hang on." Hackberry covered the receiver with his palm. "Keep those kids out of here."

"I'm kind of busy," Riser said. "What can I help you with?"

"How valuable is Pete Flores to you?"

"He's the weak sister in the mass killing. He can give us names. It takes just one thread to pull a sweater loose."

"I don't think 'weak sister' is a good term for a kid like that."

"Maybe not. But Flores made his choice when he signed on with the bunch who murdered those women and girls. We can use him to testify against the others. That means he goes into custody as a material witness."

"Custody? In the can?"

"That's a certainty. Flores has made an art form out of flight."

"How about witness protection?"

"Maybe down the line. But he cooperates or he takes the weight for the others. Let's be honest. These guys running skag and meth and girls into the country are Mobbed up all the way to Mexico City. Our jails are full of MS-13 and Mexican Mafia hitters. Flores may have his throat cut before he ever sees a grand jury. It's too bad. The kid might be a war hero, but those women and girls who ate the forty-five rounds aren't here to mourn for him."

Hackberry took the phone from his ear and opened and closed his mouth to clear a sound like cellophane crinkling inside his head. Outside, the flag was popping and straightening in a flume of yellow dust.

"You still with me, Sheriff?" Riser said.

"Yeah, copy that. Listen, isn't Hugo Cistranos the key? Don't tell me y'all don't have dials on this guy. Why aren't you squeezing him instead of chasing Flores and Vikki Gaddis around?"

"I don't get to call all the shots, Sheriff."

Hackberry could sense the change in Riser's mood. Through his office door, he could see Pam Tibbs escorting Flores and Gaddis to a small room that was used for interviews. "I can appreciate your situation," he said.

"Sorry I haven't gotten back to you. I had to go back to Washington, and I'll probably have to take off again tomorrow. What's all this about? If I were you, I'd ease up. You're a combat veteran. Sometimes you have to lose a few for the greater good. That might sound Darwinian, but those who believe different belong in monasteries."

"This is all about nailing Josef Sholokoff, isn't it?"

"Neither of us makes the rules."

"Have a good trip to Washington."

"Let me be up-front again. I'll try to keep you in the loop. But the word is 'try.' "

"You couldn't be more clear, Mr. Riser." Hackberry replaced the receiver in the cradle. Pam Tibbs stood in the doorway. He looked woodenly at her.

"I hope Bonnie and Clyde appreciate this," she said.

"Bring a cruiser around to the back door. Bonnie and Clyde were never here. Indicate that to Maydeen on your way out."

"You got it, boss man."

"Don't call me that."

* * *

THE THERMOMETER HAD just peaked at 119 degrees when Nick Dolan carried his bag out of the Phoenix airport and hailed a cab, one with more dents than it should have had. The driver was from the Mideast and had festooned the inside of the cab with beadwork and pictures of mosques and words from the Koran and was burning incense on the dashboard and playing Arabian music on a tape deck. "Where to, sir?" he said.

"I'm not sure. Where can you get a blow job in Mecca?"

"Excuse me, sir?"

"The Embassy Suites."

"In Phoenix?"

"What's your name?"

"Mohammed."

"I'm shocked. No, I want to go to the Embassy Suites in Istanbul. Do you hand out earplugs with that music?"

"Earplugs? What earplugs, sir?"

"The Embassy Suites off Camelback."

"Yes, sir. Thank you, sir. Hang on, sir." The driver floored the cab, swinging out into traffic, throwing Nick across the seat with his luggage.

"Hey, we're not on a hijack mission here," Nick said. He knew his histrionic display at the driver's expense was a mask for the fear that once again had taken up residence in his breast and was feeding at his heart. He had gotten the phone number of Josef Sholokoff from his old partner in the escort business and had made an appointment to meet Sholokoff at his house at nine P.M. that evening. The fact that Sholokoff had given Nick easy access to his home only increased Nick's sense of insecurity.

"Hey, Mohammed, you ever hear of a guy named Josef Sholokoff?" Nick said. He gazed out the window, waiting for the driver's reply. He watched the palm trees and stucco homes on the boulevard zoom by, the gardens bursting with flowers.

"Hey, you up there in the clouds of incense, you know a guy by the name of—"

The driver's eyes locked on Nick's inside the rearview mirror. "Yes, sir, Embassy Suites," he said. He turned up the volume, filling the cab with the sounds of flutes and sitars.

Nick checked in to the hotel and undressed down to his boxer shorts and strap undershirt. His suite was on the fifth floor and overlooked the outdoor swimming pool; he could hear children shouting and splashing in the water. He started to go into the bathroom and take a shower but felt so weak he thought he was going to collapse. He fixed a glass of ice and bourbon from the hospitality bar and sat down in a chair and picked up the telephone. He could see his reflection in the mirror on the bathroom door. It was that of a small, puffy, round man in striped underwear, his childlike hand clenching a thick water glass, his pale legs knotted with clumps of varicose veins, his face a white balloon with eyes and a mouth painted on it. He punched his wife's cell phone number into the phone.

"Hello?" she said.

"It's me, Esther."

"Where the hell are you?"

"In Phoenix."

"Arizona?"

"Yeah, what are you doing?"

"What am *I* doing? I'm pulling weeds in the flower bed. Which is what you should be doing. You're actually in Arizona? Not just down the street having a nervous breakdown?"

"I didn't tell you because I thought you'd be upset. I got a return flight booked at six-forty-five in the morning. So it's not like I'm really gone."

"You're over a thousand miles away, but that's not gone?"

"I'm gonna see this guy Josef Sholokoff. I called him up at his house."

"This guy is worse than Jack Collins."

"Nothing is gonna happen. I'll be at his house. He's not gonna hurt me in his own house."

"I think I'm going to faint. Hold on, I got to get in the shade."

"Did you know Esther was the name of Bugsy Siegel's wife?"

"Who cares? Is my husband totally nuts?"

"I'm saying I'm no Benny Siegel, Esther."

There was a long silence on the other end of the line.

"You there?" he said. "Esther? What's wrong?"

Then he realized she was crying. "Don't be sad," he said. "You're brave. I married the bravest, prettiest woman in New Orleans. We're gonna start over again. We got the restaurant. We got each other and the kids. The rest of it doesn't matter. Hello?"

"Come home, Nick," she said.

Nick showered and, for the next half hour, lay nude on top of his king-size bed, the points of his feet and hands spread in a giant X, like Ixion fastened to his burning wheel. Then he put cold water on his face and neck, and dressed in slacks and loafers and a fresh shirt, and called for a cab. He walked out of the hotel and stood under the porte cochere, his head as light as helium. The city was beautiful in the summer twilight, the palm trees tall and rustling, the mountaintops sharply etched against a magenta sky, the outdoor cafés filled with families and young people for whom death was an abstraction that happened only to others.

The dented cab that pulled up for him looked altogether too familiar. Nick opened the back door, and a sweet-sick cloud of incense that made him think of perfumed camel flop covered his skin and clothes. "Mohammed," Nick said.

"Tell me where you want to go, sir," the driver said.

"To the home of Josef Sholokoff," Nick replied, getting in the back. He wondered if he was actually trying to get Mohammed to talk him out of his mission. "I got the address on this piece of paper. It's up there in the hills somewhere."

"Not good, sir."

"When we get there, I want you to wait for me."

"Not good at all, sir. No, not good. Very bad, sir."

"You're my man. You gotta have my back."

The driver was turned all the way around in the seat, looking aghast at his fare. "I think you have been given very poor advice about your visit, sir. This is not a nice man. Would you like to go to the baseball game? Or I can drive you by the zoo. A very nice zoo here."

"You people blow yourselves up with bombs. You afraid of some Russian schmuck who probably can't get it up without watching one of his own porn films?"

Mohammed pushed down the flag on his meter. "Hang on, sir," he said.

The cab snaked its way up a mountain that was just north of a golf resort. From the window Nick could see the great golden bowl of the city, the flow of headlights through its streets, the linear patterns of palm trees along the boulevards, the concrete canals brimming with water, the chains of sun-bladed swimming pools that extended for miles through the neighborhoods of the rich. The west side of town, where the hardscrabble whites and poor Hispanics lived, was another story.

"You watch trash TV, Mohammed?" Nick asked. "*Jerry Springer*, that kind of crap?"

"No, sir." Mohammed looked in the rearview mirror. "Maybe sometimes."

"Those people, the guests, they don't get paid for that."

"They don't?"

"No."

"Then why do they do it to themselves?"

"They think they'll be immortal. They get inside a movie or a television show, and they think they got the same magic as celebrities. Look down there. That's what it's about. The big score."

"You are a very smart man. That's why I do not understand you."

"What don't you understand?"

"Why you are going to the home of a man like Josef Sholokoff."

Mohammed pulled the cab up to the locked gates of a compound that was sculpted back into the mountain. Inside the walls, the lawn was a deep, cool green in the shadows, the sod soggy from soak hoses, the citrus trees heavy with fruit, the balconies on the upper stories of the house scrolled with Spanish-style ironwork. The gates swung inward electronically, but no security personnel or even gardeners were in sight. Mohammed drove to the carriage house and stopped.

"You're gonna wait, right?" Nick said.

"I think so, sir."

"Think?"

"I have a wife and children to consider, sir."

"The guy sells dirty movies. He's not Saddam Hussein."

"They say he kills people."

Yeah, that, too, Nick said to himself.

By the side of the house were a flagstone patio and a swimming pool that glittered like diamonds from the underwater lighting. A half-dozen women lay on beach chairs or on float cushions in the pool. Four men were playing cards on a glass-topped table. They wore print shirts with flower or parrot designs and golf slacks and sandals or loafers. Their demeanor was that of men who felt neither threatened nor ill at ease with their role in the world nor aggrieved by tales of carnage or privation or suffering on the evening news. Nick knew many like them when he ran the cardroom for Didoni Giacano in New Orleans. They turned their lethality on and off as easily as one did a light switch, and they did not consider themselves either violent or aberrant. Ultimately, it was their personal detachment from their deeds that made them so frightening.

The overseer of their game sat in a high chair, the kind used by an umpire on a tennis court. He was a small, fine-boned man with a long jaw and narrow cranium. His grin exposed his teeth, which were long and crooked and looked tea-stained and brittle, as though they would break if their possessor bit into a hard surface. His nose was scarred by acne, his nostrils were full of gray hair, the shape of his eyes more Asian than Occidental. "There he is, right on time," he said.

"I'm Nick, if you're talking about me. You're Mr. Sholokoff?"

"This is him, boys," the man in the chair said to the men playing cards.

"I thought maybe we could talk in private."

"Call me Josef. You want a drink? You like my ladies? Your eyes keep going to my ladies."

"I feel like I'm at the public pool here."

"Tell me what you want. You had a long trip out. Maybe you want to relax in one of my cottages back there. See the Negro girl down at the shallow end? She's starting her movie career. Want to meet her?"

"I didn't have anything to do with killing those women you were running into the country."

Sholokoff seemed barely able to contain his mirth. "So you think I'm a human smuggler? And you've come out here to tell me you never did me any injury? Maybe you got a wire on you. You got a wire? You working for the FBI?"

"Hugo Cistranos had the women killed. He used to do hits in New Orleans for Artie Rooney. I wanted to get even with Artie for some things he did to me a long time ago. I thought it was him bringing the Asian women in. I thought I was gonna put them to work for me. I came to these kinds of conclusions because I was a dumb fuck who should have stayed in the restaurant and nightclub business. I don't want my family hurt. I don't care what y'all do to me. I'm getting a crick in my neck looking up at you here."

"Get him a chair," Sholokoff said. "Bring me the artwork, too."

One of the cardplayers brought a white-painted iron chair from the lawn for Nick to sit in; another went inside the house and returned with a manila folder in his hand.

Sholokoff opened the folder on his lap and sorted through several eight-by-ten photos, glancing at each of them appraisingly, the grin never leaving his face.

"These guys aren't Russians?" Nick asked, nodding at the cardplayers.

"If they were Russian, my little Jewish friend, they would eat you alive, toenails and all."

"How do you know I'm Jewish?"

"We know everything about you. Your family name was Dolinski. Here, look," Sholokoff said. He tossed the folder into Nick's lap.

The photos spilled out in Nick's hands: his son, Jesse, entering the San Antonio public library, the twin girls crossing a busy street, Esther unloading groceries in the driveway.

"Your wife's family came from the southern Siberian plain?" Sholokoff said.

"Who took these pictures?"

"They say Siberian women rule their men. Is that true?"

"You leave my family out of this."

Sholokoff propped his elbows on the arms of the chair, elevating his shoulders up around his neck, his face still split with a grin. "I got a deal for you. And if you don't like it, I got maybe one other deal. But there's not many deals on the table for you. Think real hard about your choices, Mr. Dolinski."

"I came here to tell you the truth. Everyone says you're a good businessman, the best at marketing the product you're in. A good businessman wants facts. He doesn't want bullshit. That's what Artie Rooney and Hugo Cistranos sell, one hundred percent bullshit. You don't want the facts about those women, I'm out of here."

"You said you wanted to get even with Arthur Rooney. What did Arthur Rooney do to you?"

Nick glanced sideways at the cardplayers and at the women floating on cushions in the pool or lying on beach chairs. "When we were kids, him and his friends did a swirlie on me at the movie theater."

"Explain this 'swirlie' to me."

"They used my face to scrub out the toilet bowl. It was full of piss when they did it."

Sholokoff's laughter caused a convulsion in his cheek muscles that was like rictus in a corpse. He held a stiffened hand to his mouth to make it stop. Then his men started laughing, too. "You were paying back a guy because he washed your hair in piss? Now you're in Phoenix bringing Josef a great truth about the operation of his business. I am in awe of you. You are what they call a great captain of industry. Now here are the deals for you, Mr. Dolinski. You ready?

"You can give Josef your restaurant and your vacation house on the river. Then Arthur Rooney and Hugo won't be doing swirlies on your head anymore. Or you can take the second deal. This one is more interesting, one I like a lot more. Your wife has all the marks of a Siberian woman, a strong face and big tits and a broad ass. But I got to try her out first. Can you fly her out here?"

The men at the card table did not look up from their game but laughed under their breath. The hot wind blowing across the face of the mountain rustled the palm and bottlebrush trees and scattered bits of leaves on the surface of the pool. The women's bodies looked as hard and sleek as those of seals.

Nick stood up from the chair. His feet were sweaty and felt like mush inside his socks. "I met some of your whores when I was running an escort service in Houston. They talked about you a lot. They kept using words like 'rodent' or 'ferret.' But they weren't just talking about your face. They said your dick looked like a thumbtack. They said that was how come you got into porn. You got secret desires to be a human tampon."

Sholokoff began laughing again, but much more quietly and not nearly as convincingly. One of his eyes seemed frozen in place, as though a separate and ugly thought were hidden in it.

"And here's my deal to you, you Cossack cocksucker," Nick continued. "You come around me or my family, I'm gonna mortgage or sell my restaurant, whichever is quicker, and use every dollar of the money to have your bony worthless ass greased off the planet. In the meantime, you might run a VD test on your skanks and Lysol your pool. I think I saw a couple of them lined up at the free herpes clinic in West Phoenix."

Nick walked back across the lawn toward the carriage house. He could hear chairs scraping behind him and the voice of Josef Sholokoff starting to rise, like that of a man tangled inside his own irritability and his unwillingness to concede its origins.

Be there for me, Mohammed, Nick thought.

Mohammed was having his own troubles. He had moved the cab from near the carriage house to a spot by the corner of the building—probably, Nick suspected, to avoid seeing women dressed only in bikini bathing suits. But two of Sholokoff's men had come out the front door and were blocking the driveway. Nick headed straight down the drive toward the electronic gates. Behind him, he heard Mohammed stepping on the gas, then the sound of tires whining across a slick surface.

Nick looked over his shoulder and saw Sholokoff's cardplayers coming around the side of the house. Nick broke into a jog, then a run.

The cab was fishtailing across the lawn, blowing fountains of black soil and water and divots of grass from under the fenders, exploding a birdbath across the grille, destroying a flower bed in order to get on the driveway again. Mohammed swerved past Nick and hit the brakes. "Better get in, sir. I think we're in deep excrement," he said.

Nick piled into the backseat, and Mohammed floored the accelerator. The front end of the cab crashed into the gates just before they could lock shut, flinging them backward on their hinges, breaking both of the cab's headlights. The cab careened into the street, one hubcap bouncing over the opposite curb, rolling like a silver wheel down the mountainside.

Nick sat back in the seat, his lungs screaming for air, his heart swollen the size of a bass drum, sweat leaking out of his eyebrows. "Hey, Mohammed, we did it!" he shouted.

"Did what, sir?"

"I'm not sure!"

"Why are you shouting, sir?"

"I'm not sure about that, either! Can I buy you a drink?"

"I don't drink alcohol, sir."

"Can I buy you a late dinner?"

"My ears are hurting, sir."

"Sorry!" Nick shouted.

"My family is waiting supper for me, sir. I have a wife and four children at home. I have a very nice family."

"Can I take all of you to a late dinner?"

"That's very good of you, sir. My family and I would love that," Mohammed said, pressing his palm to one ear, starting to shout himself. "I could hear you talking to those men. These are very dangerous men. But you spoke up to them like a hero. You are a very nice and brave man. Hang on, sir."

Chapter
24

THE PREVIOUS DAY Hackberry Holland had given over the back bedroom and the half-bath of his house to Vikki Gaddis and Pete Flores. In the first silvery glow on the horizon the next morning, he could not account to himself for his actions. He owed Flores and Gaddis nothing on a personal basis. He was incurring legal and political risk, and at the least, he was ensuring the permanent enmity of Immigration and Customs Enforcement and the FBI. Age was supposed to bring detachment from all the self-evaluative processes that kept people locked inside their heads. As with most of the other aphorisms associated with getting old, he thought this one a lie.

He showered and shaved and dressed and went out to the horse lot to clean off the top of the tank for his foxtrotters and to fill it with fresh water. On the lip of the tank, he had constructed a safety "ladder" out of chicken wire for field mice and squirrels who, during drought or severe heat spells, would otherwise climb up the water pipe onto the tank's edge in order to drink and fall in and drown. The chicken wire was molded over the aluminum rim, extending into the water, so small animals could climb back out. While Hackberry skimmed bird feathers and bits of hay off the tank's surface, his two foxtrotters kept nuzzling him, breathing warmly on his neck, nipping at his shirt when he paid them no mind.

"You guys want a slap?" he said.

No reaction.

"Why'd we bring these kids to our house, fellows?"

Still no response.

He went inside the barn and used a push broom to begin cleaning the concrete pad that ran the length of the stalls. The dust from the dried hay and manure floated in the light. Through the barn doors, he could see the wide sweep of the land and hills that were rounded like a woman's breasts, and the mountains to the south, across the Rio Grande, where John Pershing's buffalo soldiers had pursued Pancho Villa's troops fruitlessly in 1916. Then he realized there was a difference in the morning. Dew was shining on the windmill and the fences; there was a softness in the sunrise that had not been there yesterday. The air was actually cool, blessed with a breeze out of the north, as though the summer were letting go, finally surrendering to its own seasonal end and the advent of fall. Why couldn't he resign himself to the nature of things and stop contending with mortality? What was the passage from Ecclesiastes? "One generation passeth away, and another generation cometh, but the earth abideth forever"?

Eleven thousand years ago people who may or may not have been Indians lived in these hills and wended their way along the same riverbeds and canyons and left behind arrowheads that looked like Folsom points. Nomadic hunters followed the buffalo here, and primitive farmers grew corn and beans in the alluvial fan of the Rio Grande, and conquistadores carrying the cross and the sword and the cannon that could fire iron balls into Indian villages had left their wagon wheels and armor and bones under cactuses whose bloodred flowers were not coincidental.

Right here he had found the backdrop for the whole human comedy. And what was the lesson in any of it? Hackberry's father the history professor had always maintained the key to understanding our culture lay in the names of Shiloh and Antietam. It was only in their aftermath that we discovered how many of our own countrymen—who spoke the same language and practiced the same religion and lived on the same carpetlike, green, undulating, limestone-ridged farmland—we would willingly kill in support of causes that were not only indefensible but had little to do with our lives.

At six A.M. Hackberry saw Pam Tibbs's cruiser turn off the asphalt road and come under the arch and up his driveway. She parked the cruiser and unchained the pedestrian gate on the horse lot and walked toward him with a big brown paper bag hanging from her right hand.

"Are Gaddis and Flores up yet?" she said.

"I didn't notice."

"Did you eat?"

"Nope."

"I brought you some melted-cheese-and-egg-and-ham sandwiches and some coffee and a couple of fried pies."

"I have a feeling you're going to tell me something."

"Talk to the state attorney's office. Get somebody on your side."

"Wars of enormous importance are always fought in places nobody cares about, Pam. This is our home. We take care of it."

"That's what this is about, isn't it? The outside world came across the moat."

Hackberry propped the push broom against a stall and took two folding chairs out of the tack room and set them up on the concrete pad. He took the paper bag from Pam's hand and waited for her to sit down. Then he sat down and opened the bag but did not remove anything from it.

"Some of the Asian women had eight-ball hemorrhages. I see their eyes staring at me in my sleep. I want Collins dead. I want this guy Arthur Rooney dead and this guy Hugo Cistranos dead. The feds are after a Russian out in Phoenix. Their workload is greater than ours, and their priorities are different from ours. It's that simple."

"I doubt they'll be that tolerant."

"That's their problem."

"Flores seems like a nice kid, but he's a five-star fuckup."

"Y'all talking about me?" Pete said from the doorway.

Pam Tibbs's face turned as red as a sunburn. Pete was smiling, silhouetted against the sunrise, wearing a T-shirt and a pair of fresh jeans he had tucked into his boots.

"We were wondering if you and Vikki would like to have breakfast with us," Hackberry said.

"There's something I didn't pass on yesterday," Pete said. "I don't think it's a big deal, but Vikki did. When Danny Boy picked us up, he had to stop for gas at that filling station run by Ouzel Flagler's brother. I just thought I'd mention it."

Pam Tibbs looked at Hackberry, her lips pursed, her eyes lidless.

"Some people say Ouzel is mixed up with Mexican dope mules and such, but I don't set a lot of store in that. He seems pretty much a harmless guy to me. What do y'all think?" Pete said.

The first morning that he woke in Preacher's tent, Bobby Lee could feel the difference in the temperature. He pushed open the flap and felt a great cushion of cool air rising off the earth, glazing the mesas and monument rocks and creosote brush and spavined trees with dew, even staining the soil with dark areas of moisture, as though an erratic rain shower had blown across the land during the night.

Preacher was still asleep on his cot, his head deep in a striped pillow that had no pillowcase and had been stained by the grease from his hair. Bobby Lee went outside and used the chemical toilet and started a fire in the woodstove. He filled a spouted metal pot with water from the hundred-gallon drum Preacher had paid four Mexicans to mount on eight-foot stanchions; he poured coffee grounds into the pot and set it on the stove. When the sun broke above the horizon, the wood framing of Preacher's new house, constructed by the same Mexicans—all illegals who spoke no English—stood out in skeletal relief against the vastness of the landscape, as though it did not belong there or, if it did, it marked the beginning of a great societal and environmental change about to take place. The wind came up, and Bobby Lee watched the burned books from Preacher's house that had been bulldozed into a pile of debris blow away in gray and blackened scraps of paper. Was a change of some kind taking place before Bobby Lee's eyes? Was he witness to events that, as Preacher constantly suggested, were prophesied thousands of years ago?

Preacher had told Bobby Lee he would be part of the new place. If his name was not on the deed, he would nonetheless be bonded to the property and the house by Preacher's word. Was it possible for Preacher and Bobby Lee to get the mow-down behind them and resolve their problems with Hugo Cistranos and Artie Rooney and this Russian Sholokoff? It happened. He knew retired button men in Miami and Hallandale who had done thirty or forty hits in New York and Boston and Jersey and never gone down on a serious beef and today had no one looking at them. The guys who had killed Jimmy Hoffa and Johnny Roselli had never been in custody, guys who might have even been involved with the murder of John Kennedy. If those guys could skate, anybody could.

When the coffee boiled, he used a dish towel to pour a tin cup full from the pot, then lifted the cup to his mouth. The coffee, grounds and all, scalding hot, landed on his stomach lining like a cupful of acid.

He went back inside the tent. Preacher was up, pulling on his pants. "You look like you're having some kind of discomfort there, Bobby Lee," he said.

"I think I got an ulcer."

"You got coffee out there?"

"I'll get you some." *Thanks for the concern,* Bobby Lee said to himself. He went back outside and filled a second tin cup. He opened the wooden icebox and took out a perforated can of condensed milk and a box of sugar cubes. "You take sugar or you don't?" he called out.

"You don't remember?" Preacher said through the flap.

"I get it mixed up."

"Two cubes and a half teaspoon of canned milk."

Bobby Lee brought the cup back inside the tent and placed it in Preacher's hand. "You're not diabetic?"

"No, I told you that."

"So you avoid alcohol out of principle rather than for health reasons?"

"Why should you care, Bobby Lee?"

"Just one of those things. Liam and me were talking once about how you got medical issues of some kind."

Preacher was standing up over his writing table, unshaved, wearing an unironed white shirt. He drank from his cup, touching his lips gingerly against the rim. "Why would you and Liam be talking about my health?"

"I don't remember the circumstances."

"You think I have a health problem that people need to know about?"

"No, Jack, I know you're good about taking care of yourself, is all. Liam and me were just making conversation."

"But a man like Liam Eriksson was intensely concerned about my well-being?"

"Wish I hadn't brought it up."

"Did Liam bring it up?"

"Maybe. I don't remember."

Preacher sat down on his unmade cot and set his coffee on the writing table. Before going to bed, he had been playing blackjack against himself. The deck was splayed facedown on the table. Two cards had been dealt faceup to the imaginary player. The dealer's hole card was facedown. The second dealer's card had not been dealt. "What do you reckon has given you that ulcer?"

"Everything went south because of the Asian women. It was a mistake that just happened. You and me shouldn't have to pay the price. It's not fair."

"You're still a fish."

"About *what*?"

"We weren't hijacking the women. We were hijacking the heroin in their stomachs. They started going nuts on us, and Hugo decided to waste the whole bunch and use the lot behind the church as a storage area. He was going to dig them up later."

"That's sick."

"But this Holland fellow came along and changed all that. What I'm saying to you is there are no accidents."

Bobby Lee wasn't about to enter into Preacher's psychotic frame of reference. "What if we get out of the country for a while? Let everything cool off?"

"You disappoint me."

"Come on, don't talk to me like that, man."

"We've got Arthur Rooney and Hugo to deal with. Sholokoff is going to send another hit team after us. I've got all that federal heat coming down on me because of that fellow from ICE. I don't think I'm quite finished with Sheriff Holland, either. He spat on me. The girl did, too."

"Jesus, Jack."

"Also, I've still got my commitments with the Jewish family."

"That last bit just won't go down the pipe. I can't fathom that, man. It's absolutely beyond me."

"That I'm not bothered because Mrs. Dolan got upset and attacked me?"

"In a word, yeah."

"Mrs. Dolan is Jewish royalty. For some, a woman is a pair of thighs and breasts, something you can put your seed in so she can wash it out. But I don't think you're that kind, Bobby Lee."

Bobby Lee let the image slide off his face. "I got to ask you something."

"Is my mother really buried under this tent?"

"That's part of it."

"What's the rest?"

"Like what happened to her?"

"How did she end her days?"

"Yeah, I mean like she got sick or she was old or she got hurt in an accident?"

"That's a complex question. See, I'm not sure if she's under this tent, or if only part of her is. I buried her after a hard freeze. I had to build a fire on the ground and use a pickax to chop the grave. So I didn't go very deep with it. Not knowing a lot back then about predators and such, I didn't cover the mound with stones. When I came back a year later, critters had dug her up and strung her around about forty or fifty yards. I put what I could back in the hole and packed the dirt down tight, but to tell the truth, I'm not sure how much of her is down there. There were a lot of other bones around."

"Jack, did you—"

"What?"

"Shit happens. Like did you have to do something to your mother?"

"Yeah, it does. Get me a refill, will you? My leg is hurting."

Bobby Lee went outside with Preacher's cup just as the Mexican carpenters arrived to resume the framing on Preacher's house. Bobby Lee went back inside the tent, forgetting to add either sugar or condensed milk to the cup. Preacher was staring into space, his expression like a blunted ax blade. He took the cup from Bobby Lee's hand. The coffee was even hotter now than when Bobby Lee had first made it.

"Answer the question, Jack."

"Did I kill my own mother? Good God, son, what kind of person do you think I am? Let me show you something." Preacher picked up the splayed deck from the writing table and squared the cards between his palms. He turned up the dealer's hole card and looked at it blankly. It was the ace of spades. The imaginary player's two cards were a ten and an ace of hearts. Preacher squeezed the top card off the deck with his thumb and flopped it faceup on top of the dealer's ace. "Queen of spades," he said. "Blackjack. See, the story is already written, Bobby Lee. A fellow just has to be patient, and his queen comes along."

"You actually let the Gaddis girl spit on you?"

Preacher placed his tin cup to his mouth and drank it to the bottom without ever flinching, his lips discoloring from the intense heat. He thought for a long time and pulled at the corner of his eye. "She did it because she was scared. I don't fault her for it. Besides, she's not the woman I want or I'm supposed to have."

"I never can figure you out."

"Life is a flat-out puzzle, isn't it?" Preacher said.

"CAN YOU CLIP a horse's feet?" Hackberry said.

Pete was mucking out a stall in the back of the barn with a broad-billed coal shovel. He straightened from his work, his skin and hair damp in the gloom. "Sir?"

Hackberry repeated the question.

"I've done it once or twice," Pete said.

"Good, you can help me now. You ever give a horse his penile procedure?"

"I don't remember."

"You'd remember."

They put headstalls on both colts and tethered one to the hitching post in front of the barn and walked the palomino named Love That Santa Fe around the side into the shade.

"Santa Fe doesn't like people messing with his back feet, so he tends to spook," Hackberry said.

"Yes, sir."

"Hold the lead."

"Yes, sir, got it."

"You say you've done this before?"

"Sure."

"When you hold the lead and the farrier is working in back, don't stand catty-corner to him. If the horse spooks, he'll pull away from you and fall backward on the farrier."

"I can see that might be a problem."

"Thank you." Hackberry bent over and cradled the hind left foot of the horse against his thighs and began trimming the edges of the hoof, the half-moon strips of horn dropping into the dust. He felt Santa Fe surge and try to straighten his leg and pull against the lead. "Hold him," Hackberry said.

"I'm not exactly playing with myself up here," Pete said.

Hackberry smoothed the edges and bottom of the hoof with his rasp, still fighting the resistance of a three-year-old horse weighing eleven hundred pounds. "Dammit, boy, hold him," he said.

"I'd sure like to get a job in your department. I bet it's fun," Pete said.

Hackberry dropped Santa Fe's foot to the ground and straightened up, closing his eyes, waiting for the pain in his lower back to go to the place that pain eventually went to.

"You got sciatica?"

"Get the chairs back out of the tack room, will you?"

"Yes, sir."

Hackberry pressed his hands against the barn wall and stretched one leg at a time behind him, like a man trying to push down a building. He heard Pete unfold the chairs and set them on the ground. Hackberry sat down and removed his hat and wiped his forehead with the back of his wrist. It was comfortable in the shade, the heat of the day trapped inside the sunshine, the wind puffing the mulberry tree in the backyard.

"Who was the shooter at the church?" Hackberry said.

"The one actually did it?"

"Who was he?"

"This guy Preacher, I guess."

"You guess?"

"I didn't see it. I got out of the truck to take a leak and took off when the shooting started."

"Who had the Thompson?"

"The guy named Hugo. It was in a canvas bag with the ammo pan. He said it belonged to the most dangerous man in Texas."

"Did you ever see Preacher?"

"No, sir, I never saw him. The only guy I saw up close was Hugo. It was in the dash light of the truck. There were other guys out there in the dark, but I don't know who they were. One guy had a beard, I think. I just saw him in the headlights for a second. Maybe the beard was red or orange."

"Was his name Liam or Eriksson?"

"I don't know, sir."

"Who hired you for the job?"

"An ole boy I was drinking with. But he didn't show up at the convoy."

"Convoy?"

"There was one truck and an SUV and a couple of cars."

"Where were you drinking when you met the guy who hired you?"

"At Ouzel's place. Or at least I think I was."

"What was this ole boy's name?"

"I don't know. I was drunk."

"So as far as you know, the shooter could have been Hugo, not Preacher?"

"It could have been anybody. I told you, sir, I took off."

"Did you see the women?"

"Yes, sir."

Pete was sitting in one of the two folding chairs he had set up, his eyes averted, his shoulders rounded like the top of a question mark. He folded his arms across his chest and lowered his chin.

"Did you talk to the women?"

"A girl fell down getting into the truck, and I he'ped her up."

Hackberry could hear the wind gusting through the grass and the screens on the far side of the barn. "By that time you knew you weren't bringing in wets?"

"Yes, sir."

"Who did you think these women were?"

"I didn't want to know."

"Housemaids?"

"No, sir."

"Fieldworkers?"

"No, sir."

"Did you think they were going to start up a laundry?"

"I figured they were prostitutes. And I figured if they weren't prostitutes already, somebody was fixing to turn them into prostitutes." Pete's eyes were shiny when he glanced sideways at Hackberry.

"You think I'm being too hard on you?"

"No, sir."

"That's good, because the feds are going to be a lot harder."

"I don't care. I got to live with what I did. Fuck them."

"They're just doing their job, Pete. But that doesn't mean we won't do ours."

"I cain't translate that."

"What that means is I don't think your legal value is worth horse piss on a hot rock."

"Is that good or bad?"

"I suspect both of us will find out directly."

Pete stared in confusion at the sky and at the wind in the trees and at the shimmer of sunlight on the water brimming over the edge of the horse tank. "I wish I'd ate an AK round in Baghdad."

HACKBERRY HAD TOLD Pete and Vikki to stay close to the house, then had gone to town in his truck to buy groceries. Pete and Vikki sat on the gallery in the late-Saturday-afternoon haze and drank limeade from a pitcher that was beaded with moisture from the icebox. In the west, great orange and mauve-tinted clouds rose out of the hills, as though a brush fire were racing up the arroyos on their opposite slopes. Vikki tuned her sunburst Gibson and formed an E chord and ticked the plectrum across the strings, the notes rolling out of the sound hole.

Pete wore his straw hat, even though they were sitting in shade. "You know those big herds the drovers used to move from Mexico up the Chisholm and the Goodnight-Loving? Some of them came right through here. Lot of those cows went plumb to Montana."

"What are you thinking about?" she asked.

"Montana."

"Maybe Montana is not all you think it is."

"I suspect it's that and more. People say British Columbia is even better. They say Lake Louise is green like the Caribbean and has a big white glacier at the head of it and yellow poppies all around the banks. Can you imagine having a ranch in a place like that?"

"You're the dreamer, Pete."

"A song-catcher is calling me a dreamer?"

"I said 'the' dreamer. Of the two of us, it's you who has the real vision."

"You sing spirituals in beer joints."

"They're not really beer joints. So there's nothing special about what I've done. You're the poet. You have faith in things there's no reason to believe in."

"Want to take a walk?"

"Sheriff Holland wants us to stay close by."

"It's Saturday evening, and we're sitting on the front porch like old people," he said. "What's the harm?"

She put away her Gibson, snapped the latches on the case, and set the case inside the door. In the south pasture, the quarter horses had moved into the shadows created by the poplar trees. The sky was golden, the tannic smell of dead leaves on the wind. Up on a hillside, Vikki thought she saw a reflection, an ephemeral glitter, like sunlight striking on a piece of foil that had gotten caught in the branch of a cedar tree. Then it was gone. "I'll leave a note," she said.

They walked up the road into shade that was lengthening from a hill, the breeze at their backs, the two foxtrotters walking along the railed fence with them. They rounded a curve and saw a deer trail that switchbacked up a hillside. Vikki shaded her eyes with one hand and stared at the place where the trail disappeared into an arroyo strewn with rocks that looked like yellow chert. She stared at the hillside until her eyes watered.

"What are you looking at?" Pete asked.

"I thought I saw a reflection behind that boulder up there."

"What kind of reflection?"

"Like sunlight hitting glass."

"I don't see anything."

"I don't, either. At least not now," she said.

"In Afghanistan, I'd pray for wind."

"Why?"

"If there were a lot of trees and the wind started to blow and one thing in the trees didn't move with the wind, that's where the next RPG was coming from."

"Pete?"

The change in her voice made him turn his head and forget about the reflection on the hillside or his story about Afghanistan.

"I'm afraid," she said.

"You've never been afraid of anything. You're braver than I am."

"I think you're right about Montana or British Columbia. I think we're about to turn over our lives to people we don't know and shouldn't trust."

"Sheriff Holland seems to be on the square."

"He's a county sheriff in a place nobody cares about. He's an elderly man whose back is coming off his bones."

"Don't let him hear you say that."

"It's the goodness in you that hurts you most, Pete."

"Nothing hurts me when you're around."

He put his arm over her shoulders, and the two of them walked past the last fence on Hackberry Holland's property and followed a trail between two hills that led to a creek and the back lot of an African-American church where the congregation had assembled in the shade of three giant cottonwoods. The creek was of a sandy-red color and had been dammed up with bricks and chunks of concrete, forming a pool that swelled out into the roots of the trees.

The men were dressed in worn suits and white shirts and ties that didn't match the color of their coats, the women in either white dresses or dark colors that absorbed heat as quickly as wool might.

"Will you look at that," Vikki said.

"You didn't get dunked when you were baptized?"

"There're no white people there at all. I think we're intruding."

"They're not paying us any mind. It's worse if we walk away and make noise. There's a willow tree yonder. Let's sit under it a minute or two."

The minister escorted a huge woman into the pool, the immersion gown she wore ballooning up like white gauze around her knees. The minister cupped one hand behind her neck and lowered her backward into the pool. Her breasts were as taut and dark and heavy as watermelons under her gown. The surface of the pool closed over her hair and eyes and nose and mouth, and she grasped the minister's arm with a rigidity that indicated the level of her fear. On the bank, the leaves of the cottonwoods seemed to flicker in the wind with a green-gold kinetic light.

The minister raised his eyes to his congregants. "Jesus told the apostles to go not unto the Gentiles. He sent them first unto the oppressed and the forlorn. And that's how our shackles have been broken, my brothers and sisters. I now baptize Sister Dorothea in the name of the Father, the Son, and the Holy Spirit. And we welcome our white brethren who are watching us now from the other side of our little Jordan."

Vikki and Pete were sitting in the shade on a pad of grass under the willow tree. Pete plucked a long, thin blade of grass and put it in his mouth. "So much for anonymity," he said.

She brushed at a fly on the side of his face, then looked in a peculiar way at the back of her hand. "What's that?" she said.

"What's what?" Pete said. His arms were locked around his knees, his attention fixed on the baptism.

"There was a red dot on my hand."

"Just then?"

"Yes, it moved across my hand. I saw it when I touched your face."

He got to his feet and pulled her erect, looking up through the leaves at the side of the hill. He pushed her behind him, deeper into the shade, under the cover of the tree.

"Give me your hand," he said.

"What are you doing?"

"Looking for an insect bite."

"I wasn't bitten by an insect."

He looked out again from under the tree's canopy at the hillside, his eyes sweeping over the scattered rocks, the piñon and juniper spiked into soil that was little more than gravel, the shadows inside an arroyo and the scrub brush that grew along its rim, the shale that had avalanched down from a collapsed fire road. Then he saw a glassy reflection at the top of a ridge and, for under a second, an electric red pinpoint racing past his feet.

"It's a laser sight," he said, stepping backward. "Get behind the tree trunk. They don't have the angle yet."

"Who? What angle?"

"That bastard Hugo or whoever works for him. That's what Collins said, right? Hugo wanted to do both of us? They cain't get a clear shot yet."

"There's a sniper up there?"

"Somebody with a laser sight, that's for sure."

She took a deep breath and blew it out. She opened her cell phone and stared at it. Her blue-green eyes were bright in the shade, locked on his. "No bars," she said.

"We don't have a lot of time. A nine-one-one call wouldn't he'p us."

"What do you want to do?"

The fact that her question indicated options seemed testimony to the quality he admired most in her, namely her refusal to let others control her life, regardless of the risk she had to incur. He wanted to hold her against his chest. "Wait them out," he said.

"What if they work their way down the hill?"

His head was hammering. If he yelled out to the congregants, they would scatter and run, and the rifleman on the hill would have no reason not to fire round after round through the branches of the willow.

"Pete, I'd rather die than live like this."

"Live like how?"

"Hiding, being afraid all the time. Nothing is worth that."

"Sometimes you have to live to fight another day."

"But we don't fight another day. We hide. We're hiding now."

"You told Jack Collins to go to hell. You spit on him."

"I told him to rape me if he wanted. I told him I wouldn't resist."

Pete rubbed his palm across his mouth. His hand was dry and callused and made a grating sound on his skin. "You didn't tell me that."

"Because I didn't want to hurt you."

"I think I'm going to kill that fellow if I catch up with him. You don't think I'll do it, but there's a part of me you don't know about."

"Don't talk like that."

"You stay here. Don't move for any reason. I need your word on that."

"Where are you going?"

"I'm gonna take it to them."

"That's insane."

"It's the last thing that guy up there expects."

"No, you're not going out there by yourself."

"Let go of me, Vikki."

"We do it together, Pete."

He tried to pry her hands from his arm. "I can make that boulder over yonder, then head up the arroyo."

"I'll follow you if you do."

There was nothing for it. "We cross the creek and get into the cottonwoods. Then we go through the back door of the church and out the front."

"What about the black people?" she said.

"We're out of choices," he replied.

THE TWO MEN had followed the couple down below by first climbing the hill and then walking the ridgeline, peeking over the summit when necessary, threading their way through rocks and twisted juniper trunks that had been bleached gray by the sun. One of the men carried a bolt-action rifle on a leather sling. A large telescopic sight was mounted above the chamber, the front lens capped with a dustcover. Both men were breathing hard and sweating heavily and trying to avoid looking directly into the western sun.

They couldn't believe their bad luck when they crawled up to the edge of the summit and saw the couple walking under a willow tree.

"We stumbled into a colored baptism," the man with the rifle said.

"Keep the larger picture in mind, T-Bone. Let the coloreds take care of themselves," the other man said.

T-Bone peered through his telescopic sight and saw a flash of skin through the branches. He activated his laser and moved it across the leaves until it lit upon the side of someone's face. Then the wind gusted and the target disappeared. He paused and tried again, but all he could see was the pale green uniformity of the tree's canopy. "I'd scrub this one, Hugo," he said.

"You're not me," Hugo said. His browned skin was powdered

with dust so that the whites of his eyes looked stark and theatrical in his face. He folded a handkerchief in a square and positioned it on a rock so he could kneel without causing himself more discomfort than necessary. He drummed his fingers on a piece of slag and took the measure of the man he was with, his impatience and irritability barely restrained. "Keep your head down, T-Bone."

"That's what we've been doing. My back feels like the spring on a jack-in-the-box."

"Don't silhouette on a hill, and don't let the sunlight reflect on your face. It's like looking up at an airplane. You might as well be a signal mirror. Another basic infantry lesson—you shouldn't have all that civilian jewelry on you."

"Thanks for passing that on, Hugo. But I say we wait till dark and start over at the house."

Hugo didn't reply. He was wondering if they could work their way down the arroyo for at least two clear shots, then get back over the ridge and down to their vehicle before the black people realized what had happened in their midst.

"Did you hear what I said?" T-Bone asked.

"Yes, I did. We take them now."

"I just don't get what's going on. Why'd Preacher and Bobby Lee turn on us? Why didn't they pop the kid and his girl when they had the chance?"

"Because Preacher is a maniac, and Bobby Lee is a treacherous little shit."

"So we're doing this for Arthur Rooney?"

"Don't fret yourself about it."

"Those bikers Preacher hosed down?"

"What about them?"

"They worked for Josef Sholokoff?"

"Could be, but they're not our concern," Hugo said, cupping his hand on T-Bone's shoulder. T-Bone had sweated through his clothes, and his shirt felt as soggy as a wet washcloth. Hugo wiped his palm on his trousers. He looked down at the top of the willow tree and at the sandy-red stream and at the black minister and his congregants, who seemed distracted by something the white couple were doing.

"Get ready," Hugo said.

"For what?"

"Our friends are about to make their move. Put a little more of your heart in it. That boy down there made a fool out of you, didn't he?"

"I never said that. I said Bobby Lee double-crossed us. I never said anybody made a fool out of me. People don't make a fool out of me."

"Sorry, I just misspoke."

"I don't like this. This whole gig is wrong."

"We take them now. Concentrate on your shot. The priority is the boy. Take the girl if you can. Do it, T-Bone. This is one thing you're really good at. I'm proud of you."

T-Bone wrapped the rifle sling around his left forearm and clicked off the safety. He moved into a more comfortable position, his left elbow anchored in a sandy spot free of sharp rocks, the steel toes of his hobnailed work shoes dug into the hillside, his scrotum tingling against the ground.

"There they go. Take the shot," Hugo said.

"The minister is walking a little girl into the creek."

"Take the shot."

"Flores and the girl are holding hands. I cain't see for a clear shot."

"What are you talking about?"

"The minister and a little girl are right behind them."

"Take the shot."

"Stop yelling."

"You want me to do it? Take the shot."

"There's colored people everywhere. You whack them and it's a hate crime."

"They can afford to lose a few. Take the shot."

"I'm trying."

"Give me the rifle."

"I'll do it. Let them get clear." T-Bone raised the barrel slightly, leading his target, his unshaved jaw pressed into the stock, his left eye squinted shut. "Ah, beautiful. Yes, yes, yes. So long, alligator boy."

But he didn't pull the trigger.

"What happened?" Hugo said.

T-Bone pulled back from the crest, his face glistening and empty, like that of a starving man who had just been denied access to the table. "They went up the steps into the back of the church. I lost them in the gloom. I didn't have anything but a slop shot."

Hugo hit the flat of his fist on the ground, his teeth gritted.

"It's not my fault," T-Bone said.

"Whose is it?"

T-Bone worked the bolt on his rifle and opened the breech, ejecting the unfired round. It was a soft-nosed .30-06, its brass case a dull gold in the twilight. He fitted it back into the magazine with his thumb and eased the bolt back into place and locked it down so the chamber was empty. He rolled on his back and squinted up at Hugo, his eyelashes damp with perspiration. "You bother me."

"I bother *you*?"

"Yeah."

"You care to tell me why?"

"'Cause I never saw you scared before. Has ole Jack Collins got you in his sights? 'Cause if you ask me, somebody has got you plumb scared to death."

Chapter 25

WHEN HACKBERRY GOT back home from the grocery store in town, the sun had melted into a brassy pool somewhere behind the hills far to the west of his property. The blades on his windmill were unchained and ginning rapidly in the evening breeze, and inside the shadows on his south pasture, he could see well water gushing from a pipe into the horse tank. Once again he thought he smelled an odor of chrysanthemums or leakage from a gas well on the wind, or perhaps it was lichen or toadstools, the kind that grew carpetlike inside perennial shade, often on graves.

For many years Saturday nights had not boded well for him. After sunset he became acutely aware of his wife's absence, the lack of sound and light she had always created in the kitchen while she prepared a meal they would eat on the backyard picnic table. Their pleasures had always been simple ones: time with their children; the movies they saw every Saturday night in town, no matter what was playing, at a theater where Lash La Rue had once performed onstage with his coach whip; attending Mass at a rural church where the homily was always in Spanish; weeding their flower beds together and, in the spring, planting vegetables from seed packets, staking the empty packets, crisp and stiff, at the end of each seeded row.

When he thought too long on any of these things, he was filled with such an unrelieved sense of loss that he would call out in the silence, sharply and without shame, lest he commit an act that was more than foolish. Or he would telephone his son the boat skipper in Key West or the other twin, the oncologist, in Phoenix, and pretend he was checking up on them. Did they need help buying a new home? What about starting up a college fund for the grandchildren? Were the kingfish running? Would the grandkids like to go look for the Lost Dutchman's mine in the Superstitions?

They were good sons and invited him to their homes and visited him whenever they could, but Saturday night alone was still Saturday night alone, and the silence in the house could be louder than echoes in a tomb.

Hackberry hefted the grocery sacks and two boxed hot pizzas from his truck and carried them through the back door of the house into the kitchen.

Pete Flores and Vikki Gaddis were waiting for him at the breakfast table, both of them obviously tense, their mouths and cheeks soft, as though they were rehearsing unspoken words on their tongues. In fact, inside the ambience of scrubbed Formica and plastic-topped and porcelain perfection that was Hackberry's kitchen, they had the manner of people who had wandered in off the highway and had to explain their presence. If they had been smokers, an ashtray full of cigarette butts would have been smoldering close by; their hands would have been busy lighting fresh cigarettes, snapping lighters shut; they would have blown streams of smoke out the sides of their mouths and feigned indifference to the trouble they had gotten themselves into. Instead, their forearms were pressed flat on the yellow table, and there was a glitter in their eyes that made him think of children who were about to be ordered by a cruel parent to cut their own switch.

Whatever was bothering them, Hackberry did not appreciate being treated as a presumption or an authority figure with whom they had to reconcile their behavior. He set the groceries and the pizza boxes on the table. "What did I miss out on?"

"Somebody was trying to take a shot at us," Pete said.

"Where?"

"Up yonder from your north pasture. On the other side of a hill. There's a church house by a stream."

"You said 'trying.' You saw the shooter?"

"We saw the laser sight," Pete said.

"What were y'all doing at the church?"

"Taking a walk," Vikki said.

"Y'all just strolled on up the road?"

"That about says it," Pete replied.

"Even though I said stick close by the house?"

"We were watching some people get baptized. We were sitting under a willow tree. Vikki saw the red dot on my face and on her hand, then I saw it on the ground," Pete said.

"You're sure?"

"How do you mistake something like that?" Pete said.

"Why wouldn't the shooter fire?"

"Maybe he was afraid of hitting one of the black people," Pete said.

"The bunch we're dealing with doesn't have those kinds of reservations," Hackberry said.

"You think we made this up?" Vikki said. "You think we want to be here?"

Hackberry went to the sink and washed his hands, lathering his skin well up on his arms, rinsing them a long time, drying the water with two squares of thick paper towel, his back turned to his guests so they could not see his expression. When he turned around again, his neutral demeanor was back in place. His gaze dropped to Pete's pants legs. "You ran across the creek?" he said.

"Yes, sir. Then on inside the church house. You could say we were bagging ass."

"You think it was Jack Collins?"

"No," Vikki said. "He's done with us."

"How do you know what's in the head of a lunatic?" Hackberry said.

"Collins let us live, so now he feels he's stronger than we are. He won't test himself again," she said. "He tried to give me money. I spit on his money and I spit on him. He's not a lunatic. Everything he does is about pride. He won't risk losing it again."

"So who was the guy with the laser sight?" Hackberry said.

"It's got to be Hugo Cistranos," Pete said.

"I think you're right," Hackberry said. He opened the top on one of the boxed pizzas. "You spat on Jack Collins?"

"You think that's funny?" she said.

"No, I did the same. Maybe he's getting used to it," he said.

"Where you going, Sheriff?" Pete said.

"To make a phone call." Hackberry walked through the hallway toward the small room in back that he used as a home office. He heard footsteps behind him.

"I apologize for my rudeness," Vikki said. "You've been very kind to us. My father was a police officer. I'm aware of the professional risk you're taking on our behalf."

Better hang on to this one, Pete, Hackberry thought. He sat behind his desk and called Maydeen at the department and told her to put a cruiser on his house. Then he left messages at both of the phone numbers he had for Ethan Riser. Through the side window, he had a fine view of his south pasture. His quarter horses and the windmill and poplar trees were silhouetted against the purple coloring in the west like dimly backlit components in an ink wash. But the fading of the light, the gray aura that seemed to rise from the grass, gave him a sense of terminus that was like a knife blade in his chest. If the two young people had not been staying with him, he would have driven to town and visited his wife's grave, regardless of the hour.

In some ways, Vikki Gaddis and Pam Tibbs reminded him of Rie. Rie's detractors had called her a Communist and jailed her and her friends and turned a blind eye to the acts of violence done to them inside and outside of jail, but never once did she allow herself to be afraid.

Hackberry turned off his desk lamp and looked through the window into the darkness that seemed to be spreading across the land. Was it a suggestion of the Great Shade that we all feared? he wondered. Or a visual harbinger of what some called end-times, that morbid apocalyptical obsession of fanatics who seemed to delight in the possibility of the world's destruction?

But the greater question, the one that sank his heart, was whether or not he would ever see his wife again, on the other side, reaching through the light to take his hand and ease him across.

The phone made his face jerk. It was Ethan Riser.

"I'm returning your call. What's up?" Riser said.

"Hugo Cistranos may be in my neighborhood," Hackberry said. "What kind of leash did you have on this guy?"

"You're asking me if he's under surveillance?"

"I know you have him tapped. Where is he?"

"I don't know. Somebody saw him?"

"We may have a guy with a laser sight in the neighborhood, but I can't confirm that. Have you gotten any more feedback on those license numbers that may belong to Jack Collins?"

"I'm at my granddaughter's wedding reception right now. I returned your call as a professional courtesy. Either tell me specifically what is on your mind or call me back during business hours on Monday."

"I need your assurances about Pete Flores."

"In regard to what?"

"If I bring him in, you don't stuff him into the wood chipper."

"We don't stuff people in wood chippers."

"Sell that stuff to somebody else." The line was silent. Hackberry felt a rush of blood in his head that made him dizzy. He swallowed until his mouth was dry again and waited for the tautness to go out of his throat before he spoke. "Flores didn't see the mass killing. All he can do is put Cistranos at the scene. You already know Cistranos is dirty on the mass homicide. You must have wiretap evidence by this time. You must have information from CIs. Maybe you've already flipped Arthur Rooney. I think the only reason you haven't picked up Cistranos is he's bait. You don't need the kid, do you?"

"If you're in contact with Pete Flores, you tell him he'd better get his ass into an FBI office."

"That kid got fried in a tank because he believed in his country. You think he belongs in a federal prison or a place like Huntsville?"

"I'd like to say it's been good talking to you. But instead, I think I'll just say goodbye."

"Don't blow me off, Agent Riser. You guys are determined to hang Josef Sholokoff from a meat hook, and you don't care how you get him there."

But Hackberry was already talking to a dead connection.

EARLY SUNDAY MORNING, the sun was barely above the hills when Pam Tibbs turned the cruiser, with Hackberry in the passenger seat, in to Ouzel Flagler's place. They rumbled across the cattle guard, the cloud of dust from the cruiser drifting back amid the junked farm tractors and construction machinery and rusted-out tankers and tangles of fence wire strewn over the property. The Sunday-morning quiet was starkly palpable, almost unnatural, in its contrast to the visual reminders of Ouzel's customers'

Saturday-night fun at the blind-pig bar he operated: beer cans and red plastic cups and fast-food containers scattered across a half acre, a discarded condom flattened into a tire track, ashtrays and at least one dirty plastic diaper dumped on the ground.

"We're not any too soon," Hackberry said, peering through the windshield.

Ouzel and his wife and two grandchildren were exiting the side door of their house. All of them were dressed for church, Ouzel in brown shoes and a blue tie dotted with dozens of tiny white stars and a dark polyester suit that shone as brightly as grease.

"You want to take him in?" Pam asked.

But Hackberry's attention was fixed on the abandoned machinery.

"Did you hear me?"

"I think I underestimated Ouzel's potential," he replied. "Cut off his vehicle. Keep his wife away from a phone while I talk to him."

"You look like somebody put thumbtacks in your breakfast cereal."

"This place is really an eyesore, isn't it? Why in the hell do we allow something like this to exist?"

She looked at him curiously. When they got out of the cruiser, she picked up her baton from between the seats and slipped it through the ring on her belt. Hackberry stepped in front of Ouzel, raising his hand. "Hold up, partner, you'll have to be late for the sermon this morning," he said.

"What's wrong?" Ouzel said.

"Ask your family to go back inside. My deputy will stay with them."

"We get too loud here last night?"

"Deputy Tibbs, leave me your baton," Hackberry said.

She looked at him strangely again, then slipped the baton from its ring and handed it to him, her eyes lingering warily on his.

"I don't know what's going on here," Ouzel said.

Pam placed her hands on the two small children's shoulders and began walking them toward the side door. But the wife—a broad-faced, hulking peasant of a woman who was known for her bad disposition and her clean brown beautiful hair—did not move and stared straight into Hackberry's face, her dark eyes like lumps of coal that were no longer capable of giving off heat. "These are our grandkids," she said.

"Yes?"

"We take them to church because their mother won't," she said. "They're good kids. They don't need this."

"Mrs. Flagler, you and your husband are not victims," Hackberry said. "If you cared about those children, you wouldn't be involved with criminals who transport heroin and crystal meth through your property. Now go back in your house and don't come out until you're told to."

"You heard him, ma'am," Pam said. Before she entered the Flagler house, she looked back over her shoulder at Hackberry, this time with genuine concern.

Ouzel's Lexus was parked incongruously under a cottonwood tree, its tinted windows and waxed surfaces darkly splendid in the shade.

"You aren't afraid birds will corrode your paint?" Hackberry said.

"I parked it there a few minutes ago so it'd be cool when we got in," Ouzel said.

"There's a man in the neighborhood with a laser-sighted rifle. I think you brought him here," Hackberry said.

"I don't know anything about that. No, sir, I don't know anything about rifles. Never did. Never had much interest." Ouzel's gaze swept the great panorama of plains and mountains to the south, as though he were simply passing the time of day in idle conversation with a friend.

Hackberry placed the flat of his hand on the hood of the Lexus. Then he picked a leaf off a ventilator slit and let it blow away in the wind. "What'd it cost you, sixty grand, something like that?"

"It wasn't that much. I got a deal." Ouzel looked back at his house from the shadows the tree made. When he rotated his neck, the bulbous purple swellings in his throat raking against the stiffness of his collar, his small eyes sunk into black dots, Hackberry thought he could detect an odor that was reminiscent of a violated grave or the stench given off by an incinerator in which dead animals were burned. He wondered if he was starting to step across an invisible line.

"Why you staring at me like that?" Ouzel said.

"We let you skate on the sale of illegal booze because it was easier to keep an eye on you than it was to monitor a half-dozen vendors we couldn't keep track of. But that was a big mistake on our part. You got mixed up with the dope traffickers across the river, and they've been using the back of your property as a corridor ever since. How much of your construction equipment is operational?"

"None of it. It's junk. I sell parts off it."

"When is the last time you saw Hugo Cistranos, Ouzel?"

"I cain't say that name rings bells."

Hackberry laid Pam Tibbs's metal baton on the hood of the car. It rolled off, bouncing on the bumper before it struck the dirt with a pinging sound. He picked it up and reset it on the hood, then grabbed it when it rolled again, resetting it until it balanced, the tiny scratches showing like cats' whiskers in the paint. He watched the baton contemplatively and moved it once more, pushing it audibly across the hood's surface. "A couple of young people were almost killed yesterday. You sicced the shooter on them. Now you're on your way to your church with your grandchildren. You're a special kind of fellow, Ouzel." Hackberry spun the baton on the car hood the way one might spin a bottle. "What do you think we ought to do about that?"

Ouzel's eyes flicked back and forth from the baton to Hackberry's face. "About what?" he said.

"I'm going to bring a forensic team out here. They're going to examine every grader and dozer and front-end loader on the place. They'll take soil samples from the blades and buckets and treads and see if they match the soil behind the church at Chapala Crossing. If your equipment was used in a mass burial, the DNA from the dead will still be on the metal. That will make you an accessory to a mass murder. If you don't ride the needle, you'll go down for the rest of your life. I'm talking about Huntsville, Ouzel. Do you understand what kind of place Huntsville is?"

"I didn't know anything about those Asian women till I saw it on TV."

"Who used your equipment?"

"I don't control what happens here. Sometimes I see lights in the dark at the south end of my property. Maybe somebody put one of the dozers on a flatbed and took it away. I kept the blinds shut. In the morning it was back. Other people have keys to everything I own here."

"Which people?"

"They're in Mexico. Maybe a couple come from Arizona. They don't tell me anything. After the dozer was back, some guys came to see me." Ouzel touched his wrist and the back of his left hand, a sorrowful light swimming into his eyes. "They—"

"They what?"

"Walked me out to my shed and put my hand in my own vise."

"Was Hugo Cistranos one of them?"

"I don't know his last name. But the first name was Hugo."

"Who did you call about my young friends?"

"All I got is a phone number. I don't have the name that goes with the number. When something happens, when I see something that's important, I'm supposed to call that number. Sometimes Hugo answers. Sometimes a woman. Sometimes other guys."

"Give me the number."

Ouzel took a ballpoint pen from his pocket and a piece of paper from his wallet, his hands shaking. He started to write on top of his car hood but instead propped one foot on the bumper and smoothed the paper on his leg and wrote out the number there so he would not risk damaging the finish on his car.

"When did you last call this number?"

"Friday."

"When you saw Vikki Gaddis and Pete Flores?"

"I was at my brother's filling station. They were riding in Danny Boy Lorca's truck. They came in for gas." Ouzel's eyes wandered to the baton. "Can you take that off my car?"

"Do you have any idea at all of the suffering you're party to?"

"I never made anybody suffer. I just tried to support my family. You think I want these animals running my life? I'm sorry for those women who died. But tell me this: They didn't know what happens when you become a prostitute and have yourself smuggled into somebody else's country? How about what they did to my hand? How about the trouble I'm in? I just wanted to take my grandkids to church this morning."

Hackberry had to wait a long time before he replied. "Is there anything else you want to tell me, Ouzel?"

"I get immunity of some kind, right?"

"I'm not sure you've really given me anything. Your memory comes and goes, and a lot of what you say is incomprehensible. I also think for every true statement you make, you surround it with five lies."

"How about this? The one they call Preacher. You know that name?"

"What about him?"

"He was here."

"When?"

"Yesterday. He was looking for the guy named Hugo. I gave him that phone number just like I did you. It belongs to a resort or something. In the background I've heard people talking about shooting cougars and African animals, the kind that got those twisted horns on their heads. I gave it to Preacher, and he looked at it and said, 'So that's where the little fellow is.' If you're gonna bust me, don't cuff me in front of the kids. I'll get in the cruiser on my own."

Hackberry picked up the baton from the car hood and let it hang from his right hand. It felt heavy and light at the same time. He could feel the comfortable solid warmth of the metal in his palm and the blood throbbing in his wrist. In his mind's eye, he could see images of things breaking—glass and chrome molding and light filaments.

"Sheriff?" Ouzel said. "You won't let the kids see me in cuffs, huh?"

"Get out of my sight," Hackberry said.

ON THE WAY back to the department, with Pam Tibbs behind the wheel, the weather started to blow. Directly to the north, giant yellow clouds were rising toward the top of the sky, dimming the mesas and hills and farmhouses in the same way a fine yellow mist would. Hackberry rolled down his window and stuck his hand into the wind stream. The temperature had dropped at least ten degrees and was threaded with flecks of rain that struck his palm like sand crystals.

"When I was about twelve years old and we were living in Victoria, we had a downpour on a sunny day that actually rained fish in the streets," he said to Pam.

"Fish?" she said.

"That's a fact. I didn't make it up. There were baitfish in the gutters. My father thought a funnel cloud probably picked up a bunch of water from a lake or the Gulf and dropped it on our heads."

"Why are you thinking about that now?"

"No reason. It was just a good time to be around, even though those were the war years."

She removed her sunglasses and studied the side of his face. "You're acting a little strange this morning."

"Better keep your eyes on the road," he said.

"What do you want to do with that phone number Ouzel gave you?"

"Find out who it belongs to, then find out everything you can about the location."

"What are you planning to do, Hack?"

"I'm not big on seeing around corners," he replied. He heard her drum her fingers on the steering wheel.

At the office, Maydeen Stoltz told him that Danny Boy Lorca had been picked up for public drunkenness and was sleeping it off in a holding cell upstairs. "Why didn't somebody just drive him home?" Hackberry asked.

"He was flailing his arms around in the middle of the street," she replied. "The Greyhound almost ran over him."

Hackberry climbed the spiral steel stairs at the back of the building and walked to the cell at the far end of the corridor where overnight drunks were kept until they could be kicked out in the morning, usually without charges. Danny Boy was asleep on the concrete floor, his mouth and nostrils a flytrap, his hair stained with ash, his whole body auraed with the stink of booze and tobacco.

Hackberry squatted down on one haunch, gripping a steel bar for balance, a bright tentacle of light arching along his spinal cord, wrapping around his buttocks and thighs. "How you doing, partner?" he said.

Danny Boy's answer was a long exhalation of breath, tiny bubbles of saliva coming to life at the corner of his mouth.

"Both of us have got the same problem, bub. We don't belong in the era we live in," Hackberry said. Then he felt shame at his grandiosity and self-anointment. What greater fool was there than one who believed himself the overlooked Gilgamesh of his times? He had not slept well during the night, and his dreams had taken him back once again to Camp Five in No Name Valley, where he had peered up through a sewer grate at the gargoyle-like presence of Sergeant Kwong and his shoulder-slung burp gun and quilted coat and earflapped cap, all of it backlit by a salmon-pink sunrise.

Hackberry retrieved a tick mattress from a supply closet and laid it out in front of Danny Boy's cell and lay down on top of it, his knees drawn up before him to relieve the pressure on his spine, one arm across his eyes. He was amazed at how fast sleep took him.

It wasn't a deep sleep, just one of total rest and detachment, perhaps due to his indifference toward the eccentric nature of his behavior. But his iconoclasm, if it could be called that, was based on a lesson he had learned in high school when he spent the summer at his uncle Sidney's ranch southeast of San Antonio. The year was 1947, and a California-based union was trying to organize the local farmworkers. Out of spite, because he had been threatened by his neighbors, Uncle Sidney had hired a half-dozen union hands to hoe out his vegetable acreage. Somebody had burned a cross on his front lawn, even nailing strips of rubber car tires on the beams to give the flames extra heat and duration. But rather than disengage from his feud with homegrown terrorists, Uncle Sidney had told Hackberry and an alcoholic field picker named Billy Haskel, who had pitched for Waco before the war, to mount the top of the charred cross on the roof of the pickup and chain-boom the shaft to the truck bed. Then Uncle

Sidney and Billy Haskel and Hackberry had driven all around the county, confronting every man Uncle Sidney thought might have had a hand in burning a cross on his lawn.

At the end of the day, Uncle Sidney had told Hackberry to dump the cross in a creek bed. But Hackberry had his own problems. He had been ostracized by his peers for dating a Mexican girl he picked tomatoes with in the fields. He asked his uncle if he could keep the cross on the truck for a few more days. That Saturday night he took his Mexican girlfriend to the same drive-in theater where he had already lost a bloody fistfight after the one occasion when he had tried to pretend the color line for Mexicans was any different than it was for black people.

As the twilight had gone out of the sky and the theater patrons had filtered to the concession stand in advance of the previews, Hackberry's high school friends had assembled around the pickup, leaning against its surfaces, drinking canned beer, touching the boomer chain on the cross, touching the blackened shell-like wood of the cross itself, talking louder and louder, their numbers swelling as an excoriated symbol of rejection became a source of ennoblement to all those allowed to stand in its presence. That moment and its implications would stay with Hackberry the rest of his life.

Perhaps only fifteen minutes had passed before he opened his eyes and found himself looking squarely into Danny Boy Lorca's face.

"Why were you waving your arms in the middle of the street?" Hackberry said.

"'Cause all my visions don't mean anything. 'Cause everything around us is kindling waiting to burn. A drunk man can flip a match into the weeds on the roadside and set the world on fire. Them kind of thoughts always make me go out there flapping my arms in the wind."

Danny Boy didn't say where "there" was, and Hackberry didn't ask. Instead, he said, "But you did your job. It's on us if we don't listen to guys like you."

"Then how come I got this gift? Just to be a wino in a white man's jail?"

"Think of it this way. Would you rather be sleeping overnight in my jailhouse or be one of those people who have no ears to hear?"

Danny Boy sat up, his thick hair like a helmet on his head, the bleariness in his eyes unrelieved. He looked at the ceiling and out into the corridor and at the clouds of yellow dust moving across the skylight. Then his head turned as he focused on Hackberry's face. His eyes seemed to possess the frosted blue sightlessness of a man with severe cataracts. "You're gonna find the man you been looking for."

"A guy named Preacher?"

"No, it's a Chinaman, or something like a Chinaman. The guy you always wanted to kill and wouldn't admit it."

"WE'VE GOT THE location of the phone number," Pam said from the top of the steel stairs. "It's a game farm up by the Glass Mountains." Her gaze wandered over Hackberry's face. "Have you been asleep?"

"I dozed off a little bit," he said.

"You want to contact the sheriff in Pecos or Brewster?"

"See who'll give us a cruiser at the airport."

"We're not sure Cistranos is at the game farm."

"Somebody is there. Let's find out who they are."

"There's something else. Maydeen got a call from a guy who wouldn't identify himself. He wouldn't talk to anyone but you. His number was blocked. She told him to hold on while she got a pad and wrote down his remarks. He hung up on her."

"Who do you think it was?"

"He said you and he had unfinished business. He said you and he were the opposite sides of the same coin. He said you'd know what he meant."

"Collins?"

"Know anybody else who makes phone calls like that?"

"Get the plane ready," he said.

An hour later, they lifted off into bad weather, wind currents that shook the single engine's wings and fuselage and quivered all the needles on the instrument panel. Later, down below, Hackberry could see the sharp crystalline peaks known as the Glass Mountains, the columnlike mesas rising red and raw out of volcanic rubble or alluvial floodplain that had gone soft and pliant and undulating, as tan as farmland along the Nile, dotted with green brush, all of it besieged by a windstorm that could sand the paint off a water tower.

Then they were above a great wide fenced area where both domestic and exotic animals roamed among the mesquite and blackjack and cottonwoods, like a replication of a mideastern savannah created by an ecologically minded philanthropist.

"What's your opinion on game farms?" Pam said.

"They're great places for corporation executives, fraternity pissants, and people who like to kill things but can't pull it off without their checkbooks."

"You shock me every time," she said.

Chapter 26

NICK DOLAN HAD stopped thinking of time in terms of calendar units or even twenty-four-hour or twelve-hour periods. Nor did he think in terms of events or old resentments or jealousies or success in business. He no longer indulged in secret fantasies about revenge on his boyhood tormentors, Irish pricks like Artie Rooney in particular. As he watched his bank accounts and stock-and-bond portfolio seep away, and as the IRS focused its bombsights on his past tax returns, Nick remembered his father talking about life in America during the Great Depression, when the Dolinskis first arrived on a boat they had bribed their way onto in Hamburg.

Nick's father had spoken with nostalgia of the era rather than of the privation and harshness the family experienced during the years they lived on the Lower East Side of New York and, later, by the Industrial Canal in New Orleans. When Nick complained about going to a school where bullies shoved him down on line or stole his lunch money, his father spoke with fondness of both the settlement houses in New York and the public schools in New Orleans, because they had been steam-heated and warm and had offered succor and education and opportunity at a time when people were dying in Hitler's concentration camps. Nick had always been envious of his father's experience and emotions.

Now, as his possessions and his money seemed to be departing piecemeal in a hurricane, Nick had begun to understand that his father's fond memories were not a gift but an extension of the personal strength that defined his character. Whether in the Bowery or in a blue-collar school by the Iberville Project, Nick's father must have run up against the same kind of Jew-baiting bullies who had plagued Nick in the Ninth Ward. But his father had not empowered his enemies by carrying their evil into his adult life.

The new measure of time and its passage in Nick's life had become one of mental photographs rather than calendar dates: his children floating on inner tubes down the Comal River, the sunlight slipping wetly off their tanned bodies; Esther's bemused and affectionate glances after his return from Phoenix and his verbal victory over Josef Sholokoff (which he did not tell her of and would never tell anyone else of, lest he lose the newly found sense of pride it had given him); the smiles of his employees, particularly the blacks, who worked in his restaurant; and not least, the unopened carton of cigarettes he soaked in kerosene and set afire in his barbecue pit, saying to the clouds and Whoever lived there, *Guess who just had his last smoke.*

He had even stopped worrying about Hugo Cistranos. Nick had stood up to Josef Sholokoff in front of his goons on his property, with no parachute except a Pakistani cabdriver who shouldn't have been licensed to drive in a demolition derby. Who were the real gladiators? Nondescript, bumbling people with no power who had stood up while the Hugo Cistranos brigade bagassed for the bomb shelter.

Nick had another reason to feel secure. That lunatic called Preacher Collins had thrown his mantle of protection over

Nick's family. True, Esther had bashed him with a cook pot, but one great advantage in having a peckerwood crackbrain on your side was the fact that his motivations had nothing to do with rationality. Collins scared the hell out of the bad guys. What more could you ask for?

As Esther always said, a good deed done by a Cossack was still a good deed.

Nick had begun lifting weights at a gym. After the initial soreness, he was amazed at the resilience his body still possessed. In under two weeks, he could see a difference in the mirror. Or at least he thought he could. His clothes looked good on him. His shoulders were squared, his eyes clear, the fleshy quality starting to disappear from his cheeks. Could it be that easy? Why not? He came from working people. His grandfather had been undaunted by physical labor of any kind and had been ingenious and marvelous with his hands when he'd built his own house and created a thriving vegetable garden amid urban decay. Nick's father had been a short, wiry shoe repairman, but he could slip on a pair of Everlast gloves and turn a speed bag into a leathery blur. Even Nick's rotund compulsive mother, who overfed and protected him and sometimes treated him like a human poodle, scrubbed her floors on her hands and knees twice a week, from the gallery to the back stoop. The Dolan family, as they were called in America, stayed in motion.

As Nick looked at his full-length profile in the mirror, sucking in his stomach, his chin up, his arms pleasantly stiff and tinged with pain from curling a sixty-pound bar, he thought, *Not bad for Mighty Mouse.*

Even though he didn't like to see blood leaking from every orifice in his portfolio, his finances had a formidable degree of solidity at their core. He still owned the restaurant, a wholesome place that served good food and offered mariachi music, and nobody was going to take it away from him, at least not

Josef Sholokoff or Hugo Cistranos. He still had a mortgage on his house in San Antonio, but his weekend home on the Comal in New Braunfels was free and clear, and he was determined for the children's sake to hold on to it. He and Esther had started out with virtually nothing. For the first five years of their marriage, she'd had to give up attending classes at UNO and work full-time as a cashier at the Pearl while Nick ran Didoni Giacano's cardroom until five in the morning, fixing drinks and coffee and making sandwiches for Texas oilmen who told Negro and whorehouse and anti-Semitic jokes in his presence as though he were deaf. Then he would swamp out their piss and puke in the bathroom while the sun rose and a greasy exhaust fan roared above his head.

But those days were all behind him. Esther was his Esther again, and his kids were his kids. They were not just a family. They were friends, and more important, they loved one another and loved being with one another. What he owned he had worked for. Screw the world. Screw the IRS. Nick Dolinski, badass at large, had arrived.

It was Saturday evening, and Nick was relaxing on the terrace of his weekend home on the Comal, reading the newspaper, drinking a gin and tonic. Fireflies were lighting in the trees, and the air was fragrant with the smell of flowers, charcoal lighter flaring on a grill, meat smoke pooling among the heavy green shadows on the river.

Esther had taken the kids to deliver a box of her peanut-butter-and-chocolate brownies to a sick friend in a San Antonio suburb; she had said she would be back no later than six-thirty P.M. with a delicatessen cold supper they would eat on the sunporch. He glanced at his watch. It was after seven. But sometimes she decided on impulse to take the children to an afternoon movie. He flipped open his cell phone to check for missed calls, although he was sure it had not rung that afternoon. He put aside his paper and called her cell number. His call was transferred to her voice mail.

"Esther, where are you?" he said. "I'm starting to think alien abduction here."

He went inside the house and checked the kitchen phone. There were no new calls. He walked in a circle. He went into the living room and walked in another circle. Then he called Esther's cell phone again. "This isn't funny. Where are you? This is Nick, the guy who lives with you."

He tried Jesse's number and was sent to voice mail. But Jesse was one of those rare teenagers who had little interest in computers, cell phones, or technology in general; he sometimes left his cell phone turned off for days. Regarding his son, the more essential question for Nick was: Did Jesse have an interest in anything? It surely wasn't girls or sports. The kid had an IQ of 160 and spent his time listening to old Dave Brubeck records or playing lawn darts by himself in the backyard or hanging out with his four-man chess club.

Nick realized he was inventing other forms of worry to keep his mind off Esther's failure to check in. He went back outside in the twilight and retrieved his gin and tonic from the arm of the redwood chair. He drank it standing up, one hand propped on his hip, crunching the ice on his molars, chewing and swallowing the lime slice, his eyes fixed on the boiling rapids and the whirlpool farther down the river. When he touched his brow, it felt as tight and hard as a washboard.

The phone rang inside. He almost broke a toe on the back step getting to it before the message machine clicked on. "Hello!" he gasped, out of breath.

"Dad?"

"Who'd you expect?" he said, wondering why, of all the times in his life, he chose now to sound impatient and harsh with his son.

"Did Mom call?"

"No. You don't know where she is?"

"She left us at Barnes and Noble. She was going back for something at the deli. That was an hour ago."

"Kate and Ruth are with you? Y'all are still in San Antonio?"

"Yeah, but the deli is only three blocks from here. Where would she go?"

"Did she go back to Mrs. Bernstein's?"

"No, Mrs. Bernstein went to Houston with her daughter. We went all this way to deliver the brownies, and she wasn't there."

"Did you see any strange guys around y'all? Like somebody watching or following y'all?"

"No. What strange guys? I thought all that stuff you were worried about was over. Where's Mom?"

PAM TIBBS AND Hackberry Holland drove in their borrowed cruiser on a winding two-lane road that followed a dry creek bed bordered by cottonwoods that were bending hard in the wind, the torn leaves flying high in the air. To the east they could see irrigated ranchland and a long horizontal limestone formation that resembled a Roman wall traversing the bottom of a hill. The cruiser was shaking in the wind, grit and the needlelike leaves of juniper trees ticking against the windshield. They entered what appeared to be another domain, one that was dry and cluttered with brush and spiked plants and thick tangles of undergrowth, one that seemed abandoned to Darwinian forces, all of it surrounded by huge wire-mesh game fences of the kind one sees along highways in the Canadian Rockies.

"Shit, what was that?" Pam said, her head jerking sideways at something they had just passed.

Hackberry looked through the back window while Pam drove. "I think that's called an oryx or something like that. I've always had a fantasy about these places. What if the patrons were allowed to hunt one another? The fences could be electrified, and the boys could go inside the fences with three-day licenses to blow one another all over the brush. I think there's a lot of merit to that idea." He heard her laughing under her breath. "*What?*" he said.

"God, you're a case," she said.

"I'm supposed to be your administrative superior, Pam. Why is it I can't adequately convey that simple concept to you?"

"Search me, boss."

He gave up and remained silent as they continued down the road, the cottonwoods and pebble-strewn creek bed gone, the terrain one of twisting arroyos, brush-covered hills, and flat expanses of hardpan where trophy animals as diverse as bison, elk, gazelles, and eland grazed. It was a surreal place sealed off by hills that seemed to suck light into shade, lidded by clouds that were as yellow and coarse as sulfur.

"I've got to tell you something," Pam said.

He continued to look out the window and didn't answer.

"I think sometimes you go to a place inside yourself that isn't good. I think that's where you are now. I think that's where you've been all day."

"What place might that be?"

"How can anyone know? You never share it with anyone, least of all me."

He stared at her profile for a long time, somehow thinking he could force her to look him squarely in the eye, to make her admit the nature of her assault on his sensibilities. But she was unrelenting in her concentration on the road, her hands set in the ten-two position on the wheel.

"When this is over—" he said.

"You'll what?"

"Take you out for dinner. Or give you a few days off. Something like that."

She closed her eyes for a second, then opened them as though coming out of a trance. "All I can say is I have never in my life met anyone like you," she said. "Absolutely no one. Never."

They went around a curve and saw an archway over a cattle guard and, at the end of an asphalt driveway, a two-story log building with a peaked green metal roof. The logs in the building had not been debarked and, over the years, had been darkened by rainwater and smoke from wildfires and gave the rustic impression characteristic of roadside casinos and bars along western highways. The American and the Texas state flags flew on separate metal poles at the same height in front of the building. A pile of deer antlers and what looked like cattle bones was stacked like a cairn by the arch, an incongruous strip of red ribbon blowing from the eye socket of a cow's skull. An SUV and two new pickup trucks with extended cabs and oversize tires were parked by the building's front porch, the paint jobs freshly waxed and powdered with dust from the storm. Every detail in the picture seemed to tell a story of some kind. But there were no people in sight, and once again Hackberry was reminded of the paintings of Adolf Hitler, who could draw every detail in an urban setting except human beings.

"Slow down," Hackberry said.

"What is it?"

"Stop."

Pam pressed softly on the brake, her eyes sweeping the front of the building and the terrace on one side and the outdoor tables that had been inset with umbrellas. Hackberry rolled down his window. There was no sound anywhere except the wind. No lights burned in the building except one deep inside the entrance. None of the umbrellas inset in the outdoor tables had been collapsed in advance of the windstorm, and three of them had been blown inside out, the fabric feathering around the aluminum supports. A saddled horse grazed on the back lawn, dragging its reins, its droppings fresh and glistening on the grass. One stirrup was hooked on the pommel as though someone had pulled it out of the way to tighten the cinch and been interrupted in his work.

"Look at the woodpile by the fence," he said. "Somebody was splitting wood and dropped his ax on the ground. That lawn is like a putting green, but somebody is letting his horse download on it."

"It's Sunday. Maybe they're drunk."

"Pull up to the door," he said.

"You want me to call for backup? We can cancel it if we have to."

"No, you go around back. I'll go through the front. Don't come inside until their attention is on me."

"Why?"

"Because I said so."

She cut the ignition and walked around the side of the house, her khaki shirt tucked in her jeans, her right hand resting on the holstered butt of her .357. In that moment, details about her caught his eye in a way they never had before: her rump tight against her wide-ass jeans, the wedges of baby fat on her sides, the thickness of her shoulders and the perfect symmetry of her upper arms, her round breasts pressed against her shirt, the way her mahogany-colored hair with its curly tips lifted in the wind and exposed her cheeks.

Pam, he thought he heard himself say. But if he spoke her name, it was lost in the wind.

The front door was already ajar. He set his hand on his revolver and eased the door back on its hinges. He found himself inside a dark foyer, one lined with brass coat hooks on which there were no coats. Farther on, he could see a large living room with a stone fireplace and hearth and a chimney made from stacked slag, and heavy oak tables and dark leather–covered stuffed chairs. In back were a dining room, a long table set with silverware and plates and glasses, and a kitchen that was filling with smoke and the smell of charred meat.

Off to the right of the foyer was a lounge area, the French doors at the entranceway hanging slightly open. Through the glass, he could see the heads of trophy animals mounted on the walls, the bar top wiped clean and shining, the bottles of whiskey and Scotch and gin and vermouth sparkling with the multicolored reflection of light from an antique Wurlitzer jukebox.

He pushed back one of the French doors and stepped inside the room. Somewhere in the shadows, from one corner of the lounge, he could hear an erratic sound like a hard object on a string knocking against a piece of wood. He removed his .45 from its holster and cocked the hammer, the muzzle still pointed at the floor.

A shaft of light burst through a rear hallway, and Hackberry realized Pam Tibbs had just come through a back door and was walking toward the lounge, gripping her .357 in both hands. He held up his palm so she could see the light reflect off his skin. She stopped and waited, her weapon pointed upward at a forty-five-degree angle.

The smoke from the kitchen was seeping into the lounge, the stench of burned meat different from any he could remember. Then he saw the shell casings on the floor, all .45-caliber, ejected in such profusion they could have come from only one type of weapon.

He pointed his revolver in front of him and walked around the tables and at an angle to the bar, closer and closer to the corner of the room where the erratic knocking sound continued. Now he could see the holes in the vinyl padding of the booths and the divots blown out of the wood trim and more holes stitched across the walls. He could see the glass beer steins and long-necked bottles exploded on top of the tables. He could see the men who had either been caught unawares in the first burst, or those who had been herded up against a wall and mowed down, probably disbelieving and terrified and trying to bargain all the way to the end.

"Sweet God in heaven," Pam said behind him. Her weapon was still pointed with both hands in front of her. She looked to her right and left, then turned in a full circle before putting her pistol back in its holster. "Who *are* these guys?"

"I don't know. Call it in. Tell the dispatcher to send all the medical personnel they can."

Three men had died in a booth. The backs of their heads had burst all over the pine paneling on the wall. Two other men lay behind a poker table. Their chips were still stacked in columns, their five-card-stud hands laid out faceup on the felt. The exit wounds in their backs had streaked the wall five feet from the floor down to where they had fallen.

"What's that knocking sound?" Pam asked.

Hackberry walked to the end of the bar. A man lay on his back in the shadows. There was one hole high up on his thigh, one in his stomach, and one in his neck. His eyes were closed, and his lips were compressed tightly in a cone, as though he were sucking on a piece of candy or trying to deal with a terrible sliver of pain working its way through his viscera. A pool of blood was spreading out from his sides into the wood floor. His face was round and white, in stark contrast to his black hillbilly sideburns and eyes that glinted like obsidian, buried deep inside the folds of his flesh.

He wore pointed ostrich boots, and his left foot was striking the side of the bar spasmodically. Hackberry holstered his revolver and knelt beside him. "Who did this to you, partner?" he said.

The inside of the man's mouth was red with blood, his voice hardly more than a whisper. "Collins. Preacher Collins. Him and Bobby Lee."

"Bobby Lee Motree?"

The man closed and opened his eyes by way of an answer. He said, "Yes, sir."

"What's your name?"

"T-Bone Simmons."

"Why did Collins shoot you?"

"He picked up two hundred grand from Hugo. But he wanted Hugo, too."

Hackberry looked back at where the other bodies lay. "Hugo Cistranos?" he said.

"Yes, sir."

"Collins kidnapped Cistranos?"

T-Bone choked on his own blood and saliva and didn't try to answer.

Pam handed Hackberry a towel she had found behind the bar. Hackberry began to work the towel behind T-Bone's head. "I'm going to turn your head to the side to drain your mouth. Just hang on. An ambulance is on its way. Where did Preacher and Bobby Lee go?"

"Don't know. They had a—"

"Take your time, bud."

"A woman in their car."

"A woman was with Preacher and Bobby Lee?"

"The Jew's wife. We were supposed to pop her. She was supposed to get it in the mouth."

"You're talking about Nick Dolan's wife?"

T-Bone didn't answer. A metallic odor rose from his mouth.

"You're losing a lot of blood," Hackberry said. "I'm going to roll you on your side, and we're going to plug up that hole in your back. You with me on this?"

"My spine is cut. I don't feel anything down there."

"Where did Preacher take Cistranos and Mrs. Dolan?"

"I hope to hell."

"Come on, bub. Don't let Preacher and Bobby Lee get away with this. Where would they go?"

"Preacher can do things nobody else can do."

It was pointless. A strange transformation had begun to take place in T-Bone's eyes, one Hackberry had seen in battalion aid stations and triage situations and in a subfreezing POW shack where men with ice crystals in their beards and death in their throats stared intently at everything around them, as though taking the measure of the world, when in reality they saw nothing, or at least nothing they ever told the world about.

"My roast," T-Bone said.

"Say again?"

"My pot roast is burning. It's addax. It cost five grand to kill it."

"Don't worry about it. We'll handle it," Hackberry said, looking up at Pam Tibbs.

"I'm a good cook. Always was," T-Bone said. Then he closed his eyes and died.

Pam Tibbs walked away, her hands on her hips. She stood still, looking at the floor, her back turned to Hackberry.

"What is it?" he said.

"I saw a security camera mounted on the corner of the building. The lens is pointed at the parking lot," she said.

He glanced at the TV mounted above the bar. Below it was a VCR. "See if it has a tape."

BOBBY LEE MOTREE placed his hand on Hugo Cistranos's shoulder and walked with him to the cliff's edge, like two friends enjoying a panoramic view of topography that seemed as old as the first day of creation. Down below, Hugo Cistranos could see the tops of cottonwood trees along a streambed that had gone dry in late summer and whose banks were flanged with automobile scrap jutting from the soil like pieces of rusted razor blades. Farther out from the cliff was a cluster of trees that still had flowers in the branches. Beyond the streambed and the trees was a long flat plain where the wind was troweling thick curds of yellow dust into the air. The vista that lay before Hugo Cistranos's eyes was like none he had ever seen, as though this place and the events transpiring in it had been invented for this moment only, unfairly, without his consent as a participant. He hawked and spat downwind, leaning away from Bobby Lee, anxious to show his deference and care. "I was just delivering the money," he said.

"You bet, Hugo. We're glad you did that, too," Bobby Lee replied.

The plateau was limestone, topped with a soft carpet of soil and grass that was surprisingly green. The wind was cool, flecked with rain, and smelled of damp leaves and perhaps the beginning of a new season. Twenty yards away, Preacher Collins was talking in Spanish to two Mexican killers who had a great gift for listening while he spoke, absorbing every word, never challenging or advising, their taciturnity an affirmation of his will.

Their pickup truck was parked next to Preacher's Honda, the compact's back window pocked with a hole that looked like a crystalline eye. The Jewish woman sat in the backseat, her expression less one of anger than of thought, her purse and a box of brownies next to her. What did Preacher intend to do with her? Not harm her, certainly. And if Preacher wasn't going to harm her, maybe he would not harm Hugo, at least not in her presence, Hugo told himself.

"Beautiful, isn't it?" Bobby Lee said. "Puts me in mind of the Shenandoah Valley, without the greenery and all."

"Yeah, I know what you mean," Hugo said. He lowered his voice. "Bobby Lee, I'm a soldier just like you. I take orders I don't like sometimes. We've been on a lot of gigs together. You hearing me on this, son?"

Bobby Lee squeezed Hugo's shoulder reassuringly. "Look yonder. See the deer running inside the wind. They're playing. They know fall is in the air. You can smell it. It's like wet leaves. I love it when it's like this."

As Hugo looked into Bobby Lee's face, he knew for the first time in his life the distinction between those who had a firm grasp on the day and the expectation of the morrow and those who did not.

Preacher finished his conversation with the Mexicans and walked toward the cliff. "Let me have Hugo's cell phone," he said to Bobby Lee.

Preacher wore a suit coat and a rumpled fedora and slacks that had no crease, one cuff tucked inside a boot. The wind was blowing his coat as he dialed a number on the cell phone. "When Arthur Rooney answers, you say, 'I did what you told me to, Artie. Everything went fine.' Then you hand the phone back to me."

Hugo said, "Jack, Artie is going to be confused. Why would I say 'Everything went fine'? I was just bringing the money up. Artie could say anything, because he wouldn't know what I meant. And give you the wrong impression. See?"

Preacher took a tin of Altoids from his pocket and snicked open the lid and put one on his tongue. He gave one to Bobby Lee and offered one to Hugo, but Hugo shook his head.

"See those trees down yonder with the flowers inside their branches?" Preacher said. "Some people call them rain trees. Others say they're mimosas. But a lot of people call them Judas trees. Know why?"

"Jack, I'm not up on that crap, you know that." And for just a moment the confidence and sense of familiarity in his own voice almost convinced Hugo that things were as they used to be, that he and Jack Collins were still business partners, even brothers in arms.

"The story is that Judas was in despair after he betrayed Jesus.

Before he hanged himself, he went out on a cliff in the desert and flung his thirty pieces of silver into the darkness. Every place those coins landed, a tree grew. On each tree were these red flowers. Those flowers represent the blood of Jesus. That's the story of how the Judas tree came to be. You cold? You want a coat?"

"Talk to him, Bobby Lee."

"It's out of my hands, Hugo."

Jack winked at Hugo, then pushed the send button with his thumb and placed the phone in Hugo's palm.

Hugo shrugged, his expression neutral, as though he were placating an unreasonable friend. The five rings that he hoped would deliver him to voice mail were the longest rings he had ever heard. When he thought he was home free, Artie Rooney picked up.

"That you, Hugo?" Artie said.

"Yeah, I—"

"Where are you? I heard that crazy sonofabitch kidnapped Nick Dolan's old lady."

"I did what you said. Everything is fine."

Preacher pulled the cell phone from Hugo's hand and pressed it against his ear.

"I hope he went out shivering like a dog passing broken glass," Rooney said. "Tell me Mrs. Dolan was with him. Make my day perfect. Don't hold back on me, Hugo. I want every detail. You parked one in her mouth, right? I'm getting hard thinking about it."

Preacher folded the cell phone in his palm and dropped it in the pocket of his trousers. He stared out at the dust and mist blowing across the canyon, his expression contemplative, his mouth like a surgical wound. He stuck his little finger in one ear and removed something from his ear canal. Then he smiled at Hugo.

"Everything okay?" Hugo said.

"Right as rain," Preacher said.

"Because words can get mixed up over the phone, or people can misunderstand each other."

"No problem, Hugo. Take a walk with me."

"Walk where?"

"A man should always have choices. Ever read Ernest Hemingway? He said death is only bad when it's prolonged and humiliating. When I brood on things like this, I take a walk."

"I don't get what you're saying. Where we going?"

"That's the point. It's for you to choose. Pancho Villa always gave his prisoners a choice. They could stand against a wall with a blindfold over their eyes or take off running. If it was me, I don't think I'd run. I'd say screw that. I'd eat a round from one of those Mausers. Winchesters and Mausers were the standard issue for Villa's troops. Did you know that?"

"Jack, let's talk a minute. I don't know what Artie said, but he gets excited sometimes. I mean, you'd think that two hundred grand I brought you was drained out of his veins. He's always yelling about what you did to his hand, like he didn't bring it on himself, which everybody knows he did. Come on, Jack, slow down here. It's a matter of keeping things in perspective, like the lady in your car there, I know you want to care for her and everybody knows you've always been a gentleman that way and you got a code most people in the life don't have, wait, we don't need to keep walking anywhere, let's just stay right here a second, I mean right here where we're talking, I'm not real big on heights, I never have been, I'm not afraid, I just want to be reasonable and make sure you understand I always thought you and Bobby Lee here were stand-up, and look, man, you got your two hundred large and I'm never gonna breathe a word about this stuff, you got my word, you want me to blow the country, you want my condo in Galveston, you name it, hey, Jack, come on, whoa, I'm telling you the truth, I get vertigo, my heart won't take it."

"Don't fault yourself for this, Hugo. You've made a choice.

Bobby Lee and I respect that," Preacher said. "Keep looking at me. That's right, you're a stand-up guy. See, it's nothing to be afraid of."

Hugo Cistranos stepped backward onto a shelf of air, his eyes closed and his fingers extended in front of him, like a blind man feeling in the dark. Then he plummeted three hundred feet, straight down, through the top of a cottonwood into the streambed filled with rocks that were the color of dirty snow.

Chapter 27

Hᴀᴄᴋʙᴇʀʀʏ ᴅɪᴅ ɴᴏᴛ get back home until almost ten that night. When he tried to sleep, the insides of his eyelids were dry and abrasive, as though there were sand in them or his corneas had been burned by the flash of an arc welder. Each time he thought he was successfully slipping off to sleep, he would feel himself jerked awake by the images of the dead men in the game farm's lounge or, less dramatically, by the banality of an evil man who, when dying, had grieved over the wasted pot roast that had come from the exotic animal he had paid five thousand dollars to kill.

The tape Pam Tibbs had retrieved from the security camera had proved of little help. It had shown the arrival of a Honda and a Ford pickup truck. It had shown the back of a man wearing a fedora and a suit coat and slacks that flattened against his body in the wind. It had shown two tall unshaved men in colorful western shirts and bleached tight-fitting jeans that accentuated their genitalia. One of the tall men carried an elongated object wrapped loosely in a raincoat. The tape also showed a man in a dented and sweat-ringed top hat, his face shadowed, his striped overalls starched and pressed.

But it did not show the license tag on the pickup truck, and it showed only one letter and one number on the Honda: an *S* and the numeral 2. The value of the tape was minimal, other than the fact that the *S* and 2 confirmed that the vehicle Pete Flores had attacked with rocks was being driven by Jack Collins and perhaps was even registered to him, although under an alias.

Maybe the grouping of the letters and the numbers on the plate would narrow down the list provided earlier by the Texas DMV. In the morning Hackberry would call Austin again and start over. In the meantime, he had to sleep. He had learned long ago as a navy corpsman that Morpheus did not bestow his gifts easily or cheaply. The sleep that most people yearned for rarely came this side of the grave, except perhaps to the very innocent or to those willing to mortgage tomorrow for tonight. Tying off a vein, watching the blood rise inside a hypodermic needle, staining a mint-bruised mug of crushed ice with four fingers of Black Jack Daniel's were all guaranteed to work. But the cost meant taking up residence in a country no reasonable person ever wanted to enter.

Throughout the night, he could hear the wind stressing the storm shutters against their hooks and swelling under his house. He saw flashes of lightning in the clouds, the windmill in his south pasture shivering in momentary relief against the darkness, his horses running in the grass, clattering against the railed fence. He heard thunder ripping across the sky like a tin roof being slowly torn asunder by the hands of God. He sat on the side of his bed in his skivvies, his heavy blue-black white-handled revolver clenched in his hand.

He thought of Pam Tibbs and the way she had always covered his back and incessantly brought him food. He thought of the way her rump filled out her jeans and the bold way she carried herself and her mercurial moods that vacillated from a martial flash in the eyes to an invasive warmth that made him step back from her and put his hands in his back pockets.

Why think about her now, at this moment, as he sat on the side of his bed with the coldness of a pistol on his naked thigh, like an old fool who still thought he could be the giver of death rather than its recipient?

Because he was alone and his sons were far away, and because every unused second that clicked on the clock was an act of theft to which he was making himself party.

He went into the office at seven on Monday morning, hung his dove-colored hat on a wood peg on the wall, and pulled from his desk drawer the DMV fax that contained the 173 possible registrants of the Honda driven by Preacher Jack Collins. He flattened the pages on his ink blotter, placed a ruler under the name of the first registrant, and began working his way down the list. He had gotten through six names when the phone rang. The caller was not one he cared to hear from.

"Ethan Riser," Hackberry said, trying to hide the resignation in his voice.

"I heard you had a bad day up at the game farm," Riser said.

"Not as bad as the guys Jack Collins eased into the next world."

"A couple of my colleagues say it was a real mess. They appreciated your help."

"That's funny, I don't remember their saying that."

"So you know about Nick Dolan's wife?"

"No, not the particulars. Just what I got from this guy T-Bone Simmons." Hackberry leaned forward on his desk, his back stiffening. "What about her?"

"She was carjacked or kidnapped, I guess it depends on how you want to put it. Her vehicle was found on a side road off I-10, just east of Segovia."

"When did you know about this?"

"The day it happened, Saturday afternoon. Mr. Dolan is a little distraught. I thought maybe he'd called you by now."

"Tell me this again. You knew Mrs. Dolan was abducted Saturday afternoon, but I have to hear about it from a dying criminal a day later? And you thought I had probably gotten word from the husband of the victim?"

"Or from my colleagues," Riser said wearily. "Look, Sheriff, this is not the reason I called. We have information that indicates you may be giving sanctuary to Vikki Gaddis and Pete Flores."

"I don't know where you got that from, but I don't really care. You know why the right-wing nutcases around here don't trust the government?"

"No, I don't."

"That's the point, sir. You don't know. That's the entire point."

Hackberry hung up. Thirty seconds later, the phone rang again. He glanced at the caller ID, picked up the receiver, and without speaking, hung up a second time, his eyes returning to the list of names on the DMV fax.

Pam Tibbs came into his office and looked over his shoulder. "It sounded like you were talking to Ethan Riser," she said.

"There's no such thing as a conversation with Riser. The two voices you hear are Riser talking and his voice echoing."

"Get enough sleep last night?"

He raised his head. She was silhouetted against the light from the window, the tips of her hair lit by the early sun. Behind her, he could see the silver flagpole and the flag popping hard in the breeze. "I didn't eat breakfast. Let's go down to the café."

"I have a pile of stuff in my intake basket," she said.

"No, you don't," he said, lifting his hat off the wood peg.

At the café, he ordered a steak, three scrambled eggs, grits, hash browns and gravy, fried tomatoes, toast and marmalade and orange juice and coffee.

"Think you can make it to lunch?" she said. Her fingers were knitted on top of the table. Her nails were clean and unpainted and closely clipped. There was a shine in her hair just like the light in polished mahogany. Behind her, tumbleweeds were bouncing through the streets, the tin roof on an old mechanic's shed rattling, forked lightning striking the hills in the south. "You trying to make me uncomfortable?" she said.

"Why do you say that?"

"Looking at me like that."

"Like what?"

Her eyes went away from him and came back. "You think I'm your daughter?"

"No."

"Well—"

"Well, what?" he said.

"God!" she replied.

A calendar hung on a post not far from their booth. No one had folded back a page on it since June. The days in June had been marked off with a black felt-tip pen, up to the twenty-first. He wondered what event in June had been so important that someone had in effect indicated all the previous days were to be gotten past and rid of. Then he wondered why the events after June 21 were so lacking in significance that no one had even bothered to turn the calendar page to the following month.

"Know why people in jail use the term 'stacking time'?" he said.

"It makes a collection of dimwits sound clever?"

"No, it makes them sound normal. The goal for most people is to get time out of the way. I learned that in No Name Valley, under the sewer grate. I counted the threads in my sweater so I wouldn't have to think about the time being stolen from my life."

She turned a University of Houston class ring on her finger. The waitress brought coffee and went away. Pam watched a church bus pass on the street, its headlights on in the mixture of blowing dust and rain. "You're the most unusual man I've ever known, but not for the reasons you might think," she said.

He tried to smile but was disturbed by the tenor in her voice.

"You're blessed with an innate goodness the Communists couldn't take away from you. But I think in your mind, Jack Collins has become the prison guard who tormented you in North Korea. Collins wants to make you over in his image. If you let him do that, he wins, and so does that prison guard in the POW camp."

"You're wrong. Collins is a defective amoeba. He's not worth thinking about."

"Lie to God, lie to your friends, but don't lie to yourself."

"If you're going to talk church-basement psychology to me, would you lower your voice?"

"There's no one sitting around us."

He looked sideways and didn't reply.

"Don't blow me off, Hack." She pushed her right hand across the table and bumped the tips of her stiffened fingers hard against his.

"Do you think I'd do that? Do you think any intelligent man would ever treat a woman like you with disrespect?"

She bit a hangnail on her thumb and looked at him in a peculiar fashion.

IN FRONT OF the office, Hackberry took one glance at the sky and unhooked the chain on the flagpole and lowered the flag in advance of the impending storm. He folded the flag in a tuck and placed it in his desk drawer. Then he went back to work on the list of registrants given to him by the DMV. He went through the entire list twice, his eyes starting to swim. What was the point? If the FBI couldn't locate Collins, how could he? Did Collins actually possess magic? Was he a griffin loosed from the pit, a reminder of the bad seed that obviously existed in the gene pool? It was always easier to think of evil as the work of individuals rather than the successful and well-planned efforts of societies and organizations operating with a mandate. Men like Collins were not created simply by their environments. Auschwitz and the Nanking massacre hadn't happened in a vacuum.

His phone rang again. The caller ID was blocked. "See if that's Ethan Riser," Hackberry called through the doorway. He heard Maydeen take the call in the other room. A moment later, she was standing in the doorway. "Better pick up," she said.

"Who is it?"

"Same asswipe—pardon me—same dude who called yesterday and said you two were the opposite sides of the same coin."

Hackberry lifted the receiver and put it to his ear. "Collins?" he said.

"Good morning," the voice said.

"I'm getting pretty tired of you."

"I watched you through binoculars yesterday afternoon."

"Revisiting our murderous handiwork, are we?"

"I'm afraid your thinking is muddled once again, Sheriff. I didn't murder anybody. They tried to set me up. They also threw down on me first. I wasn't even armed. An associate was carrying my weapon for me."

"An associate? That's a great term. The guy with the raincoat on his arm?"

"The security camera caught that?"

"You left the camera intact deliberately, didn't you?"

"I didn't give it a lot of thought."

"Why'd you kidnap Mrs. Dolan?"

"What makes you think I did?"

"Because you left a witness."

Hackberry heard Collins breathe in, as though sucking air across his teeth while he thought of a clever response.

"I don't think I did," he said.

"You thought wrong. You'll get to meet him at your trial. I have to ask you something, bub."

"'Bub'?"

Hackberry leaned forward in his chair, one elbow on the desk blotter, rubbing one temple with his fingers. Both Maydeen and Pam were watching from his office door. "I don't know you well, but you seem like a man with a code. In your way, maybe you're a man of honor. Why do you want to do so much injury to Mrs. Dolan? She has three children and a husband who need her. Set her free, partner. If you have an issue with me, that's fine. Don't punish the innocent."

"Who are you to lecture me?"

"A drunkard and a whoremonger with no moral authority at all, Mr. Collins. That's the man you're talking to. Let Esther Dolan go. She's not a character out of the Bible. She's flesh and blood and is probably afraid she'll never see her husband or children again. You want that on your conscience?"

"Esther knows she's safe with me."

"Where's Hugo Cistranos?"

"Oh, you'll find him. Just watch the sky. It takes two or three days, but you'll see them circling."

"And you don't think she's afraid?"

There was a long beat.

"Good try. I've always heard the inculcation of guilt is a papist trait."

"I have an envelope filled with photos of the nine terrified women and girls you machine-gunned and buried. Did they scream when they died? Did they beg in a language you couldn't understand? Did they dissolve into a bloody mist while you sprayed them with a Thompson? Am I describing the scene accurately? Correct me if I haven't. Please tell me in your own words what it was like to shoot nine defenseless human beings who were so desperate for a new life they'd allow their stomachs to be filled with balloons of heroin?"

He could hear Collins breathing hard. Then the line went dead.

Maydeen filled a cup with coffee in the other room and brought it to him on a saucer. Both she and Pam watched him without speaking.

"Y'all got something to do?" he said.

"We're going to get him," Pam said.

"I'll believe it when it happens," he said, picking up the fax sheets from his desk blotter again, his thumbs crimping the edges of the paper to the point of tearing them.

As THE MORNING passed, a seemingly insignificant detail from his conversation with Jack Collins had burrowed itself into his memory and wouldn't leave him alone. It was the sound of Collins breathing. No, that wasn't it. It was the way Collins breathed and the image the sound conjured up from the Hollywood of years gone by. Collins seemed to draw his air across his teeth. His mouth became a slit, his speech laconic and clipped, his face without expression, like a man speaking not to other people but to a persona that lived inside him. Perhaps speaking like a man who had a nervous twitch, who was wrapped too tight for his own good, who was at war with the Fates.

A man with dry lips and a voice that rasped as if his larynx had been fried by cigarettes and whiskey or clotted with rust. A man who wore his hair mowed on the sides and combed straight back on top, a man who wore a hat and clothes from another era, his narrow belt hitched tightly into his ribs and his unpressed slacks tucked into western boots, perhaps like a prospector of years past, his whole demeanor that of tarnished frontier gentility.

Hackberry re-sorted the fax sheets and found the third page

in the transmission. He stared at one listing as though seeing it for the first time. How dumb does one lawman get, particularly one who considered himself a student of his own era? "Come in here, Pam," he said.

She stood in the doorway. "What's up?"

"Take a look at the names on this page."

"What about them?"

"Which one of them sticks in your mind?"

"None."

"Look again."

"I'm a blank."

He put his thumb on the edge of one name. She stood behind him, leaning down, one arm propped on his desk, her arm touching his shoulder.

"F. C. Dobbs. What's remarkable about that?" she said.

"You remember the name Fred C. Dobbs?"

"No."

"Did you see *The Treasure of the Sierra Madre*?"

"A long time ago."

"Humphrey Bogart played the role of a totally worthless panhandler and all-around loser whose clothes are in tatters and his lips are so chapped they're about to crack. When he thinks he's about to be slickered, he grimaces at the camera and says, 'Nobody is putting anything over on Fred C. Dobbs.' "

"Collins thinks he's a character in a film?"

"No, Collins is a chameleon and a clown. He's a self-educated guy who believes a library card makes him more intelligent than an MIT graduate. He likes to laugh at the rest of us."

"Maybe F. C. Dobbs is a real person. Maybe it's just coincidence."

"There are no coincidences with a guy like Jack Collins. He's the thing that's wrong with all the rest of us. He just has more of it and nowhere to leave it."

"There's no physical address for Dobbs, just a post office box in Presidio County?" she said.

"So far."

"Give Maydeen and me a few minutes," she said.

But it was almost quitting time before Pam and Maydeen got off the phones. In the meantime, Hackberry had his hands full with Nick Dolan, who had called three times, each time more angry and irrational.

"Mr. Dolan, you have my word. As soon as I learn anything about your wife, I'll call you first," Hackberry said.

"That's what the FBI says. I look like a douche bag? I sound like a douche bag? I *am* a douche bag? I'm stupid here? Tell me which it is," Nick said.

"We'll find her."

"They were following me around. They were bugging my phones. But they couldn't protect my wife."

"You need to take that up with the FBI, sir."

"Where are you?"

"I'm sitting in my office, the place you just called up for the third time."

"No, like where are you on the map?"

"You don't need to be here, Mr. Dolan."

"I'm supposed to play with my joint while this crazoid kidnaps my wife?"

"Stay home, sir."

"I'm getting in my car now. I'm on my way."

"No, you're not. You're—"

Dead connection.

Pam Tibbs tapped on the doorjamb. She had a legal pad folded back in her left hand. "This is what we've got. A man using the name F. C. Dobbs had a Texas driver's license two years ago but doesn't have one now. His rent on his post office box in Presidio has lapsed. Ten years ago a man named Fred Dobbs, no middle initial, bought five hundred acres of land down toward Big Bend at a tax sale. There were four big parcels strung all over the place. He sold them six months later."

Hackberry fiddled with his ear. "Who owned the land before Dobbs?"

Pam looked back at her notes. "A woman named Edna Wilcox. I talked to the sheriff in Brewster. He said the Wilcox woman had been married to a railroad man who died of food poisoning. He said she died of a fall and didn't leave any heirs."

"What happened to Dobbs?"

"The clerk of court didn't know, and neither did the sheriff."

"So we've got a dead end?" Hackberry said.

"The state offices are closing now. We can start in again to-morrow. Was that Nick Dolan calling again?"

"Yeah, he said he's on his way here." Hackberry leaned back in his swivel chair. Rain was blowing against the window, and the hills surrounding the town were disappearing inside the gray-ness of the afternoon. "Who did Fred Dobbs, no middle initial, sell the land to?"

Pam turned the page on her legal pad and studied her notes. "I don't know if I wrote it down. Wait a minute, here it is. The buyer was Bee Travis."

Hackberry knitted his fingers behind his head. "T-R-A-V-I-S, you're sure that's the right spelling?"

"I think so. There was static on the line."

Hackberry clicked his nails on the desk blotter and looked at his watch. "Call the clerk of court again before the courthouse closes."

"Has anyone ever talked to you about OCD problems?" She looked at his expression. "Okay, sorry, I'm on it."

Two minutes later, she came back into his office. "The first name is actually the initial B, not 'Bee' with a double e. The last name is Traven, not Travis. I wrote it down wrong." She glanced away, then looked back at him and held her gaze on his face, her chest rising and falling.

But he wasn't thinking about her chagrin. "Collins sold the land to himself. He laundered his name and laundered the deed."

"I'm not following you at all."

"B. Traven was a mysterious eccentric who wrote the novel *The Treasure of the Sierra Madre.*"

"Sell that one to Ethan Riser."

"I'm not even going to try. Sign out a cruiser and pack your overnight bag."

She went to the door and closed it, then returned to his desk. She leaned on the flats of both her hands, her breasts hanging down heavily inside her shirt. "Think about what you're doing. If anybody could figure out Collins's aliases, it would be someone with your educational background. You don't think he knows that? If he's there now, it's because he wants you to find him."

"Maybe he'll get his wish."

Chapter 28

"THAT'S HAIL," PREACHER said to the woman sitting on the cot across from him. "Hear it? It's early this year. But at this altitude, you cain't ever tell. Here, I'll open the flap. Look outside. See, it looks like mothballs bouncing all over the desert floor. Look at it come down."

The woman's face was gray, her eyes dark and angry, her black hair pulled straight back. In the gloom of the tent, she looked more Andalusian than Semitic. She wore a beige sundress and Roman sandals, and her face and shoulders and underarms were still damp from the wet cloth she had washed herself with.

"A plane will be here tomorrow. The wind is too strong for it to land today," he said. "The pilot has to drop in over those bluffs. It's hard to do when the wind is out of the north."

"You'll have to drug me," she said.

"I just ask you to give me one year. Is that a big price, considering I protected your family and spared your husband's life when Arthur Rooney wanted him dead? You know where Arthur Rooney is today, maybe at this very moment?"

He waited for her to reply, but the only sound in the tent was the clicking of hailstones outside.

"Mr. Rooney is under the waves," he said. "Not quite to the continental shelf, but almost that far."

"I wouldn't give you the parings from my nails. I'll open my veins before I let you touch me. If you fall asleep, I'll cut your throat."

"See, when you speak like that, I know you're the one."

"One what?"

"Like your namesake in the Book of Esther. She was born a queen, but it took Xerxes to make her one."

"You're not only a criminal, you're an idiot. You wouldn't know the Book of Esther from a telephone directory."

Bobby Lee Motree bent inside the open tent flap, wearing a denim jacket, his top hat tied down with a scarf. He held a tin plate in each hand. Both plates contained a single sandwich, a dollop of canned spinach, and another one of fruit cocktail.

"Molo picked up some stuff at the convenience store," Bobby Lee said. "I seasoned the spinach with some bacon bits and Tabasco. Hope y'all like it."

"What the hell is that?" Preacher said, looking down at his plate.

"What it looks like, Jack. Fruit cocktail, spinach, and peanut-butter-and-jelly sandwiches," Bobby Lee said.

Preacher threw his plate outside the tent into the dirt. "Go to town and buy some decent food. You clean that shit out of the icebox and bury it."

"You eat sandwiches every day. You eat in cafés where the kitchen is more unsanitary than the washroom. Why are you always on my case, man?"

"Because I don't like peanut-butter-and-jelly sandwiches. Is that hard to understand?"

"Hey, Molo, Preacher says your food sucks!" Bobby Lee shouted.

"You think this is a joke?" Preacher said.

"No, Jack, I'm just indicating maybe you don't know who your friends are. What do I have to do to prove myself?"

"For starters, don't serve me shit to eat."

"Then get your own damn food. I'm tired of being somebody's nigger."

"I've told you about using language like that in my presence."

Bobby Lee flipped the tent flap shut and walked away without securing it to the tent pole, his hobnailed boots crunching on the hailstones. Preacher heard him talking to the Mexican killers, most of his words lost in the wind. But part of one sentence came through loud and clear: "His Highness the child in there . . ."

At first Esther Dolan had set down her plate on the table, evidently intending not to eat. But as she had listened to the exchange between Bobby Lee and the man they called Preacher, her dark eyes had grown steadily more thoughtful, veiled, turned inward. She picked up the plate and set it in her lap, then used the plastic knife to cut her sandwich into quarters. She bit off a corner of one square and chewed it slowly, gazing into space, as though disconnected from any of the events taking place around her.

Preacher tied the flap to the tent pole and sat down heavily on his cot. He drank the coffee from his cup, his fedora snugged low on his brow, the crown etched with a thin chain of dried salt.

"You should eat something," she said.

"My main meal is always at evening. And it's a half meal at that. Know why that is?"

"You're on a diet?"

"A horse always has a half tank in him. He has enough fuel in his stomach to deal with or elude his enemies, but not too much to slow him down."

She feigned attention to his words but was clearly not listening. Bobby Lee had put a paper napkin under her plate. She slipped it out and set one of the sandwich squares on it. "Take this. It's high in both protein and sugar."

"I don't want it."

"Your mother gave you too many peanut-butter-and-jelly sandwiches when you were little? Maybe that's why you're always out of sorts."

"My mother fixed whatever a gandy dancer brought to the boxcar where we lived. That was where she made her living, too. Behind a blanket hung over a rope."

"What happened to her?"

"She took a fall off some rocks."

When Esther didn't reply, he said, "That was after she poisoned her husband. Or deliberately fed him spoiled food. It took him a while to die."

"You're making that up." Before he could answer, she wrapped the piece of sandwich in the napkin and set it on his knee.

"I've always heard Jewish women are compulsive feeders. Thanks but no thanks," he said, setting the sandwich square on the table.

She continued to eat, her shoulders slightly stooped, a demure quality settling over her that seemed to intrigue and arouse him.

"A woman like you is a once-in-a-lifetime kind of person," he said.

"You're very kind," she said, her eyes lowered.

By dark Hackberry Holland and Pam Tibbs had had no luck finding the residence that might have been occupied by the man using the name B. Traven. On the back roads, in the blowing rain and tumbleweeds and darkness, they could find few mile markers or rural mailboxes with numbers or houses that were lighted. A crew on a utility truck told them there had been a giant power failure from Fort Stockton down to the border. No one, including the sheriff's department, had any knowledge of a man by the name of B. Traven. One deputy who had worked previously at the tax assessor's office volunteered that Traven was an absentee landowner who resided in New Mexico and rented his property to hippies or people who came and went with the season or tended to live off the computer.

At nine-thirty P.M. Hackberry and Pam took adjoining rooms at a motel south of Alpine. The motel had a generator that created enough power to keep the motel functional during the storm, the outside lights glowing with the low intensity and yellow dullness of sodium lamps. A number of revelers had taken refuge there, talking loudly in the parking lot and on the concourse, slamming metal doors so hard the walls shook, carrying twelve-packs and fast food to their rooms. As Hackberry looked out the window at the darkness of the night, at the lightning flashes in the clouds, at the leak of electric sparks from a damaged transformer that was trying to come back on line, he thought of candles flickering in a graveyard.

He closed the curtain and sat on the bed in the dark and called the department. Maydeen Stoltz picked up.

"You're not on duty tonight," he said.

"You and Pam are. Why shouldn't *I* be?"

"So far we haven't gotten any leads on B. Traven or the guy calling himself Fred C. Dobbs. Did you hear anything from Ethan Riser?"

"Nothing. But Nick Dolan was here. Boy, was he here."

"What happened?"

"I put some earplugs in. I mean that literally. That guy has a voice like a herd of pygmies. He went into your office without permission and said he'd wait there until you got back. That's not all."

"What's the rest of it?"

"Did you have the flag folded up in your drawer?"

"Yeah, I did."

"I think he took it. The drawer was open when he left, and the flag wasn't in it."

"What does he want with our flag?"

"Ask him."

"Where is he now?"

"I'm not real sure. He went to your house."

"Don't tell me that."

"What can Dolan do at your house?"

"I gave Vikki Gaddis and Pete Flores an approximate idea where we were going. I thought Collins might have said something to Gaddis that would link him to the properties he's bought and sold under an alias."

"That was the right thing to do, Hack. Don't worry about it."

"Early in the morning, get on the horn to Riser."

"What do you want me to tell him?"

"Give him all the information we have on Collins. Tell him to send the cavalry or stay home. It's his call."

"Hack?"

"What?"

"Pam thinks Collins is trying to steal your soul."

"So?"

"Pam's feelings are not objective."

"What are you telling me?"

"Don't take chances with Collins."

"The man has a hostage."

"In one way or another, they all do. It's what they use most effectively against us. You blow that bastard out of his socks."

"Maydeen, you're a good woman, but you've got a serious character defect. I can never be quite sure where you stand on an issue."

After he closed his cell phone, he continued to sit on the side of the bed in the dark, the long day starting to catch up with him. Someone had left the engine running on a diesel-powered vehicle immediately outside Hackberry's window. The sound vibrated through the wall and floor, staining the air with noxious fumes and a ceaseless hammering that was like a deliberate assault on the sensibilities. It was the signature act of the modern correspondent of the classical Vandal—senseless and stupid and at war with civilization, like someone graffiti-spraying a freshly painted white wall or smearing his feces on someone's furniture.

Nazis were not ideologues. They were bullies and sackers of civilization. Their logos and ethos were that simple. Hackberry felt that he had lived into a time when gangbangers who sold crack to their own people and did drive-bys with automatic weapons were treated as cultural icons. Concurrently, outlaw white bikers muled crystal meth into every city in the United States. When they went down, it was only because they were murdered by their own kind. They were like creatures that had been incarnated from a Mad Max script. And like any form of cognitive dissonance in a society, they existed because they were given sanction and even lionized.

Who was to blame? Maybe no one. Or maybe everyone.

He opened the door and stepped out on the concourse. A bright red oversize pickup truck with an extended cab was parked two feet from him. The sound of the diesel engine was so loud he had to open and close his mouth to clear his ears. He could hear a party roaring two doors down. He walked out onto the lawn by the parking lot and picked up a brick from the border of the flower garden. The brick felt cool and heavy in his hand and smelled faintly of moist soil and chemical fertilizer.

He returned to the pickup truck and broke the driver's window with the brick, setting off the alarm. Then he reached inside and unlocked the door and ripped the wiring from under the dashboard. He tossed the brick into a shrub.

A minute later, the driver, an unshaved man in greasy denims, was at his truck, aghast. "What the fuck?" he said.

"Yeah, too bad," Hackberry said. "I'd file a report if I was you."

"You saw it?"

"A guy with a brick," Hackberry said.

Pam Tibbs had opened the door to her room and was drinking a beer in the doorway. She was dressed in jeans and a maroon Texas Aggie T-shirt. "I saw him running across the lawn," she said.

"Look at my fucking truck."

"The world is really sliding down the bowl," Pam said.

A few minutes later, she tapped on the bolted door that connected her room to Hackberry's. "Are you having a nervous collapse?" she said.

"Not me," he said.

"Can I come in?"

"Help yourself."

"Why are you sitting in the dark?"

"Why waste electrical power?"

"You thinking about Jack Collins?"

"No, I'm thinking about everything." He was sitting at the small wood table against the wall. There was a telephone on it and nothing else. The chair on which he sat was as utilitarian as wood was capable of being. She walked into a blade of light from the window so he could see her face. "You think we're firing in the well?" she said.

"No. Collins is out there. I know it."

"Out where?"

"Someplace we don't suspect. It won't be part of a pattern. It won't be in a place we look for the bad guys. He won't be surrounded by whores or dope or stolen goods or even weapons. He'll be in a place that's as ordinary as rocks and dirt."

"What are you saying, Hack?"

He shrugged and smiled. "Where's your beer?"

"I drank it."

"Open another one. It doesn't bother me."

"I only bought one."

He stood up, towering over her. Her shadow seemed to dissolve against his body. She lowered her head and folded her arms across her breasts. He could hear her breathing in the dark.

"I'm really old," he said.

"You've said that."

"My history is suspect, my judgment poor."

"Not to me."

He cupped his hands on her shoulders. She hooked her thumbs in her back pockets. He could see the gray part in the shine on her hair. He bent over her, his arms circling her back, his hands touching her ribs and sliding up between her shoulder blades into the stiffness of her hair on the nape of her neck. Then he drifted his fingers across her cheek and the corner of her eye, brushing a lock of hair back from her forehead.

He felt her step on top of his feet, and before he knew it, she had raised her mouth inches from his, the yeasty smell of beer touching his lips.

When Preacher unzipped the flap on Bobby Lee's polyethylene tent, the storm had passed and the heavens were ink-black again, bursting with stars that stretched from horizon to horizon, the mesas in the east pink and barely visible against the few distant thunderheads that still flickered with lightning.

Bobby Lee pushed his head out of his sleeping bag, his hair matted, his eyes bleary with sleep. "Is the plane here?"

"Not yet. But I made coffee. Get up. I want to take care of some business," Preacher said.

"It's cold."

"Put your coat and hat on. Take my gloves."

"I've never seen it this cold this time of year."

"I'll get your coffee. Where are your boots?"

"What's going on, Jack?"

Preacher lowered his voice. "I want to give you your money now. Don't wake up Molo and Angel. Nor the woman."

"You're really taking her with us?"

"What did you think I was going to do?"

"Shoot your wad and get it out of your system?"

Preacher was squatting, balancing on his haunches. He looked at the fire curling and then flattening under the tin coffeepot he had set on the refrigerator grille propped across a ring of blackened rocks. His eyes were as empty as glass in the firelight, his shoulders poking through his suit coat. "Coarseness toward women doesn't behoove a man, son."

"You slept in the tent with her?" Bobby Lee said, pulling on his boots.

"No, I wouldn't do that, not unless I was invited."

"She invited us to kidnap her? You're one for the books, Jack." Bobby Lee climbed out of the tent, pulling on a black sheep-lined leather coat that was spiderwebbed with cracks. "Where's the spendolies—"

Preacher placed a finger to his lips and began walking up the compacted footpath to the cave opening in the side of the mountain, his body bent slightly forward into the incline, his right hand hooked through the bail of a battery-powered lantern. He glanced back at the large tent where the two Mexican killers slept, then smiled enigmatically at Bobby Lee. "The freshness of the predawn hour has no equivalent," he said. When he stepped inside the cave, the darkness enveloped him like a cloak.

"Jack?" Bobby Lee said.

"In here," Preacher said, turning on the lantern, which gave off a glow that was gray and dim and created wispy shadows on the cave walls.

Bobby Lee sat down on a rock and watched Preacher pull a suitcase from behind a wood pallet that he sometimes dried his clothes on.

"I promised you ten percent. That's twenty thousand dollars," Preacher said, squatting to unlatch the suitcase. "Looks nice bundled in rubber bands, doesn't it? What are you going to do with all that money, Bobby Lee?"

"I'm thinking about leasing a building in Key West and starting up an interior decorating business there. The place is full of rich fudge-packers building condos."

"I've got a question to ask you," Preacher said. "Remember when you told me you and Liam had been talking about my health, about what I ate and didn't eat, that sort of thing? I just cain't quite get that image out of my head. Why would you two be so concerned about my food intake? It seems a peculiar subject for young fellows to have any investment in. Wouldn't you say so?"

"I don't even remember what we were talking about." Bobby Lee yawned, his eyes going out of focus with fatigue. He turned his face to the cold air puffing through the cave entrance. "The stars are beautiful over those bluffs."

"I don't talk about what you eat and drink, Bobby Lee. It's of no consequence to me. So why would you and Liam be having these discussions about my diet?"

Bobby Lee shook his head. "It's too early in the morning for this stuff."

"You've always been loyal to me, Bobby Lee. You have, haven't you? No temptations, so to speak?"

"I've modeled my life on you."

"Can you see the little crack of light in the east? It's behind those thunderheads. A little rip in all that blackness. Our pilot is going to fly us right through that hole into the sunlight. Then we'll make a wide turn to the south and cross into Mexico and fly all the way to the ocean. This afternoon we'll be eating pineapple and mangoes on a beach and watch people race horses in the surf. But first you have to tell me the truth, or our relationship will remain permanently damaged. We cain't allow that to happen, boy."

"Truth about what? How'd I damage our relationship?"

"You were plotting with Liam to hurt me, Bobby Lee. People are frail. They get scared and betray their friends. I forgive you for it. You thought you'd go where the smart bet was. But you've got to own up to it. Otherwise I can only conclude you think I'm a stupid man. You think I'll abide someone letting on like I'm a stupid man?"

"You're not stupid, Jack."

"Then what am I?"

"Pardon?"

"If I'm not stupid or ignorant, then what am I? Somebody you can deceive and not pay any price for it? Somebody with no honor or self-respect who lets other people wipe their feet on him? Which is it?"

Bobby Lee propped his hands on his thighs. He stared at his feet and at the cave opening and at the landscape starting to gray with the coming of dawn. "Everybody thought you were losing it. I did, too, at least for a while. You're right, though, I was selfish and thinking of myself. Then I realized you were the only guy I admired, that Liam and Artie and Hugo and the others weren't real soldiers, but you were."

"You and Liam were going to pop me?"

"It didn't get that far."

Preacher was smiling. "Come on, Bobby Lee. You've given honest witness about your failure. Don't water the drink now. You'll undo the courage and the principle you've shown me."

"Yeah, we talked about popping you."

"You and Liam?"

"I told Liam that was the order from Artie Rooney and Hugo.

But I decided all of them were a bunch of dirtbags, and I called you up on my cell phone and told you how much I respected you."

"That was just before you decided to let Liam eat a bullet point-blank in the women's restroom? I'll hand it to you. You can slide around and reshape yourself faster than quicksilver."

Bobby Lee started to speak, then realized Preacher had already disengaged from the conversation and was standing in the cave's entrance, his hands on his hips, watching the wind ripple the tents down below, watching the mysterious transformation of the desert from darkness to a pewterlike stillness that resembled a photograph defining itself inside developing fluid. Then Preacher said something Bobby Lee couldn't quite hear.

"Say again?" Bobby Lee asked.

Preacher turned and reached behind the wood pallet. Unconsciously, Bobby Lee fastened the top button on his cracked sheep-lined coat as though protecting himself from a gust of cold air.

"I told you I always wanted you to be a piece of this property," Preacher said. "That sentiment has not changed one iota."

Down below, the Mexican killers and Esther were wakened by a burst of machine-gun fire and a tinkling of brass hulls on stone. But the sounds were absorbed so quickly inside the earth, they each wondered if they had been dreaming.

AT FIRST LIGHT Hackberry Holland and Pam Tibbs talked to an elderly man and a small boy at a dirt crossroads where they were picking up trash out of a ditch. The land was level and hard, marked by little other than fence lines and loading pens that were gray with rot and impacted with tumbleweed. Far to the east, the sun was pale and watery behind a low range of hills that looked coated with frost, ragged like glass along the crests.

"Traven?" the old man said. "No, there's nobody here'bouts by that name."

"How about Fred Dobbs?" Hackberry said.

"No, sir, never heard of him, either." The old man was very large and straight in physique for his age, his hands horned with calluses, his face oblong, as big as a jug, the creases so deep there were shadows in them. He wore strap overalls and a yellow canvas coat and no cap. He studied the departmental logo on the cruiser's door, obviously noting Hackberry was out of his jurisdiction. "It's the frozen shits this morning, ain't it?"

Hackberry showed him photographs of Jack Collins, Liam Eriksson, Bobby Lee Motree, and Hugo Cistranos.

"No, sir, if they live around here, I ain't seen them. What'd these fellows do?"

"Take your choice," Hackberry said from the passenger window. "Did you know a woman by the name of Edna Wilcox?"

"Died of an accident or a fall of some kind?"

"I think she did," Hackberry said.

"She owned a big chunk of land about ten miles up the road and to the east. People have rented there off and on, but the house burned down. There's some Mexicans been working there. Show your pictures to my grandson. Look right at him when you talk. He cain't hear."

"What's his name?"

"Roy Rogers."

Hackberry opened the passenger door and leaned over so he was eye level with the little boy. The boy's hair was jet-black, his skin brown, his eyes filled with a black luminosity sometimes characteristic of people who live inside themselves.

"You know any of these men, Roy?" Hackberry said.

The boy's eyes slid across the photographs that Ethan Riser had sent to Hackberry's office. He remained immobile, the wind tousling his hair, his face as expressionless as clay. In the silence, he wiped at his nose with the back of his wrist. Then he glanced sideways at his grandfather.

"Want to help me out here?" Hackberry said to the grandfather.

"Not much gets by him. Roy's a smart little boy."

"Sir?"

"You wouldn't tell me what these men had done, but now you want me and him to he'p you out. I suspect that seems like a one-sided deal to him."

Hackberry got out of the vehicle and squatted down, suppressing the pain that flared in the small of his back. "These men are criminals, Roy. They've done some very bad things. If I can, I'm going to put them in jail. But I need people like you and your grandfather to tell me where these guys might be. If you've seen one of them, just point your finger."

The boy looked at his grandfather again.

"Go ahead," the grandfather said.

The boy touched one photograph with the end of his finger.

"Where'd you see this fellow?" Hackberry said.

"The store, last spring," the boy said, his words like wood blocks that were rounded on the edges.

"We run a store up at the next crossroads," the grandfather said.

Hackberry patted the boy on the shoulder and stood up. "How many houses are there on the old Wilcox property?" he said to the grandfather.

"A shack here and there, sweat lodges and tepees and such that a bunch of hippies smoke marijuana in."

"You said there was a place that burned down."

"That's the place the Mexicans were cleaning up. That's where the Wilcox woman lived. By the way, y'all are the second people to come by this morning asking about those fellows."

"Who else was here?"

"A little round man in a Cherokee with an American flag flying on it and a young fellow and girl with him. The young fellow had a scar on his face like somebody glued a pink soda straw on it. Y'all grow them a little strange back where you come from?"

"Where'd they go?"

"Up the road. I can tell you how to get there, but the Mexicans will probably run off when they see y'all coming."

"They're illegals?"

"Oh, hell no."

Hackberry got directions and got back in the cruiser. Pam dropped the transmission into gear and drove slowly up the road headed north, waiting for him to speak. A piece of the moon still hung low in the sky, like a carved piece of ice.

"The boy picked out Liam Eriksson, the only guy we know for sure is dead," he said.

"You want to talk to the Mexicans?"

"For all the good it's probably going to do, why not?" he replied.

WITHOUT ANY SENSE of grandiosity, Esther Dolan could say she had never feared mortality. Accepting it in the form it came to most people—in their sleep, in hospitals, or by sudden heart attack—seemed an easy trade-off considering the fact that one did nothing to earn his birth. The stories of violent death told her by her grandparents, who had survived the pogroms in Russia, were another matter.

The word "pogrom" came from an early Russian word that meant "thunder." It meant destruction and death caused by irrational forces. It meant hatred and suffering that descended on helpless people without cause or motivation or reason. And the perpetrators of it were always the same group: those who wished to infect the world with the same self-loathing that had been the three-6 tattoo they had brought with them from the womb.

In the aftermath of the gunfire, she had stood motionless outside the polyethylene tent, the cold leaching the strength from her body, the wind swelling the tent on the support poles, the hillside black against a sky that was fading to dark blue in the east.

She watched the man called Preacher descend from the cave, his submachine gun clenched against his side with one hand, his coat collar pulled up and the brim of his fedora pulled down, smoke leaking from the barrel of his weapon. He watched each step he took on the compacted path as though his own life and safety and well-being were of enormous importance, whereas the man he had just killed was a disappearing memory.

The Mexican killers had also come out of their tent. The smoke from the cook fire contained a dense sweet smell, like burning sage or unopened flowers that had been consumed by the flames. Preacher leaned over the fire and, with his bare hand, picked up the metal pot boiling on the refrigerator grille and poured coffee into a tin cup, never setting down the Thompson. He drank from the coffee, blowing on the cup. He gazed at the frost on the hills. "It's going to be a fine day," he said.

"*¿Donde está Bobby Lee?*" Angel said.

"The boy made his peace. Don't be worried about him."

"*¿Está muerto?*"

"If he's not, I'd better get a refund on this gun."

"*Chingado, hombre.*"

"Molo, can you fix up some huevos rancheros? I could eat a washtub load of those. Just cook it on the coals. I didn't fire the woodstove this morning. A man shouldn't do more work than is required of him. It's a form of greed. For some reason, I could never get those concepts across to Bobby Lee."

While Preacher spoke, he had not looked directly at Esther.

His back was turned toward her, his bone structure as stiff as a scarecrow's inside his coat, the Thompson hanging straight down from his arm. His face lifted toward the sky, his nostrils swelling. Now he turned slowly toward her, taking the measure of her mood, his gaze seeming to reach inside her head. "I've scared you?" he said.

"He was your friend."

"Who?"

"The man in the mine."

"It's not a mine. It's a cave. You know the story of Elijah sleeping outside the cave, waiting to hear the voice of Yahweh? The voice wasn't to be found in the wind or a fire or an earthquake. It was to be found at the entrance to a cave."

As she looked into his face and listened to his words, she believed she had finally come to understand the moral vacuity that lived behind his eyes. "You're going to kill us all, aren't you?"

"No."

"You weren't listening. I said you're going to kill us all."

"What does that mean?"

"You're going to kill yourself, too. That's what this is all about. You have to die. You just haven't found somebody to do it for you yet."

"Suicide is the mark of a coward, madam. I think you should treat me with more respect."

"Don't call me madam. Did the man in the cave have a gun?"

"I didn't ask him. When Molo is done cooking, fix me a plate and one for yourself. The plane will be here by ten."

"Prepare you a plate? Who do you think you are?"

"Your spouse, and that means you'll damn well do what I say. Get in the tent and wait for me."

"Señora, better do what he say," Angel said, wagging an admonishing finger. "Molo already gave him food that makes him real sick. Señor Jack ain't in a very good mood."

She went back inside the tent, her temples pounding. She sat down on the cot and picked up the box of uneaten brownies she had prepared for Mrs. Bernstein. She placed her hand on her chest and waited until her heart had stopped racing. She hadn't eaten since the previous evening, and her head was spinning and gray spots were swimming before her eyes.

She slipped the string off the box and took out one brownie and bit off a corner. She could not be sure, but she believed she might be holding a formidable weapon in her hand, at least if her intuitions about Preacher's refusal to eat the peanut-butter-and-jelly sandwiches were correct. She had learned the recipe from her grandmother, a woman whose life of privation had taught her how to create culinary miracles from the simplest of ingredients. One of the grandmother's great successes had been brownies that were loaded with government-staple peanut butter but were baked with enough chocolate and cocoa powder to disguise their mundane core.

Esther closed her eyes and saw Nick and her son and her twin daughters as clearly as if she were looking out the front window of their home on the Comal River. Nick was cooking a chicken on the barbecue grill, standing downwind, his eyes running, his glossy Hawaiian shirt soaked with smoke, forking the meat as though that would improve the burned mess he was making. In the background, Jesse and Ruth and Kate were turning somersaults on the grass, their tanned bodies netted with the sunlight shining through a tree, the river cold and rock-bottomed and swift-running behind them.

For just a moment she thought she was going to lose it. But this was not a time either to surrender or to accept the terms of one's enemies. How did her grandmother put it? *We didn't give our lives. The Cossacks stole them. A Cossack feeds on weakness, and his bloodlust is energized by his victim's fear.*

That was what her grandmother had taught her. If Esther

Dolan had her way, the man they called Preacher was about to learn a lesson from the southern Siberian plain.

When Preacher opened the tent flap, she caught a glimpse of mesas in the distance, an orange sunrise staining a bank of low-lying rain clouds. He closed the flap behind him and started to fasten the ties to the aluminum tent pole, then became frustrated and flung them from his fingers. He was not carrying his weapon. He sat down on the cot opposite her, his knees splayed, the needle tips of his boots pointed outward like a duck's feet.

"You've been around men who didn't warrant your respect," he said. "So your disrespect toward males has become a learned habit that isn't your fault."

"I grew up not far from the Garden District in New Orleans. I didn't associate with criminals, so I didn't develop attitudes about them one way or another."

"You married one. And you didn't grow up by the Garden District. You grew up on Tchoupitoulas, not far from the welfare project."

"Lillian Hellman's home on Prytania Street was two blocks from us, if it's any of your business."

"You don't think I know who Lillian Hellman was?"

"I'm sure you do. The public library system gives cards to any bum or loafer who wants one."

"You know how many women would pay money to be sitting where you are right now?"

"I'm sure there're many desperate creatures in our midst these days."

She could see the heat building in his face, the whitening along the rims of his nostrils, the stitched, downturned cast of his mouth. She picked up a small piece of brownie with the ends of her fingers and put it in her mouth. She could feel him watching her hungrily. "You haven't eaten?" she asked.

"Molo burned the food."

"I made these for my friend Mrs. Bernstein. I don't guess I'll ever have the opportunity to give them to her. Would you like one?"

"What's in them?"

"Sugar, chocolate, flour, butter, sometimes cocoa powder. You're afraid I put hashish in them? You think I bake narcotic pastries for my friends?"

"I wouldn't mind one."

She held out the box indifferently. He reached inside and lifted out a thick square and raised it to his mouth. Then he paused and studied her face carefully. "You're a beautiful woman. You ever see the painting of Goya's mistress? You look like her, just a little older, more mature, without the sign of profligacy on your mouth."

"Without *what* on my mouth?"

"The sign of a whore."

He bit into the brownie and chewed, then swallowed and bit again, his eyes hazy with either a secret lust or a sexual memory that she suspected gave birth to itself every time he pulled the trigger on one of his victims.

Chapter 29

P AM TIBBS PULLED the cruiser onto the shoulder of the dirt road and stopped between two bluffs that gave onto a breathtaking view of a wide sloping plain and hills and mesas that seemed paradoxically molded by aeons and yet untouched by time. Hackberry got out of the vehicle and focused his binoculars on the base of the hills in the distance, moving the lenses across rockslides and flumes bordered by mesquite trees and huge chunks of stone that had toppled from the ridgeline and looked as hard and jagged as yellow chert. Then his binoculars lit on a large pile of bulldozed house debris, much of it stucco and scorched beams, and four powder-blue polyethylene tents and a chemical outhouse and a woodstove and an elevated metal drum probably containing water. A truck and an SUV were parked amid the tents, their windows dark with shadow, hailstones melting on their metal surfaces.

"What do you see?" Pam asked. She was standing on the driver's side of the cruiser, her arms draped over the open door.

"Tents and vehicles but no people."

"Maybe the Mexican construction guys are living there."

"Could be," he said, lowering the glasses. But he continued to stare at the sloping plain with his naked eyes, at the bareness of the hills, the frost that coated the rocks where the sun hadn't touched them. He looked to the east and the growing orange stain in the sky and wondered if the day would warm, if the unseasonal cold would go out of the wind, if the ground would become less hard under his feet. For just a second he thought he heard the sound of a bugle echoing down an arroyo.

"Did you hear that?" he said.

"Hear what?"

"The old man back there said hippies were living in tepees and smoking dope out here. Maybe some of them are musicians."

"Your hearing must be a lot better than mine. I didn't hear a thing."

He got back in the vehicle and shut the door. "Let's boogie."

"About last night," she said.

"What about it?"

"You haven't said much, that's all."

He looked straight ahead at the hills, at the mesquite ruffling in the wind, at the immensity of the countryside, beveled and scalloped and worn smooth by wind and drought and streaked with salt by receding oceans, a place where people who may have even preceded the Indians had hunted animals with sharpened sticks and crushed one another's skulls over a resource as uncomplicated in its composition as a pool of brown water.

"You bothered by last night?" she said.

"No."

"You think you took advantage of an employee?"

"No."

"You just think you're an old man who shouldn't be messing with a younger woman?"

"The question of my age isn't arguable. I *am* old."

"You could fool me," she said.

"Keep your eyes on the road."

"What you are is a damn Puritan."

"Fundamentalist religion and killing people run in my family," he said.

For the first time that morning, she laughed.

But Hackberry could not shake the depression he was in, and the cause had little to do with the events of the previous night at the motel. After returning from Korea, he had rarely discussed his experiences there, except on one occasion when he was required to testify at the court-martial of a turncoat who, for a warmer shack and a few extra fish heads and balls of rice in the progressive compound, had sold his friends down the drain. Even then his statements were legalistic, nonemotional, and not autobiographical in nature. The six weeks he had spent under a sewer grate in the dead of winter were of little interest to anyone in the room. Nor were his courtroom listeners interested, at least at the moment, in a historical event that had occurred on a frozen dawn in the third week of November in the year 1950.

At first light Hackberry had awakened in a frozen ditch to the roar of jet planes splitting the sky above him, as a lone American F-80 chased two Russian-made MiGs back across the Yalu into China. The American pilot made a wide turn and then a victory roll, all the time staying south of the river, obeying the proscription against entering Red Chinese airspace. During the night, from across a snow-filled rice paddy spiked with brown weeds, the sound of bugles floated down from the hills, from different crests and gullies, some of them blown into megaphones for amplification. No one slept as a result.

At dawn there were rumors that two Chinese prisoners had been brought back by a patrol. Then someone said the Korean translator didn't know pig flop from bean dip about local dialects and that the two prisoners were ignorant rice farmers conscripted by the Communists.

One hour later, a marching barrage began that would forever remain for Hackberry as the one experience that was as close to hell as the earth is capable of producing. It was followed throughout the day by a human-wave frontal assault comprised of division after division of Chinese regulars, pushing civilians ahead of them as human shields, the dead strung for miles across the snow, some of them wearing tennis shoes.

The marines packed snow on the barrels of their .30-caliber machine guns, running the snow up and down the superheated steel with their mittens. When the barrels burned out, they sometimes had to unscrew and change them with their bare hands, leaving their flesh on the metal.

The ditch was littered with shell casings, the BAR man hunting in the snow for his last magazine, the breech of every M-1 around Hack locking open, the empty clip ejecting with a clanging sound. When the marines were out of ammunition, Hackberry remembered the great silence that followed and the hissing of shrapnel from airbursts in the snow and then the bugles blowing again.

Now, as he gazed through the windshield of the cruiser, he was back in the ditch, and the year was 1950, and for a second he thought he heard a series of dull reports like strings of Chinese firecrackers popping. But when he rolled down the window, the only sound he heard was wind. "Stop the car," he said.

"What is it?"

"There's something wrong with that scene. The old man said the Mexicans working here were illegals. But the vehicles are new and expensive. Undocumented workers don't set up a permanent camp where they work, either."

"You think Collins is actually there?"

"He shows up where you least expect him. He doesn't feel guilty. He thinks it's the rest of us who have the problem, not him."

"What do you want to do?"

"Call the locals for backup, then call Ethan Riser."

"I say leave the feds out of it. They've been a cluster-fuck from the jump. Where you going?"

"Just make the calls, Pam," he said.

He walked twenty yards farther up the dirt track. The wind was blowing harder and should have felt colder, but his skin was dead to the touch, his eyes tearing slightly, his palms so stiff and dry that he felt they would crack if he folded them. He could see a haze of white smoke hanging on the ground near the tents. A redheaded turkey vulture flew by immediately over Hackberry's head, gliding so fast on extended wings that its shadow broke apart on a pile of boulders and was gone before Hackberry could blink.

An omen in a valley that could have been a place of bones, the kind of charnel house one associated with dead civilizations? Or was it all just the kind of burned-out useless terrain that no one cared about, one that was disposable in the clash of cultures or imperial societies?

He could feel a pressure band tightening on the side of his head, a cold vapor wrapping around his heart. At what point in a man's life did he no longer have to deal with feelings as base as fear? Didn't acceptance of the grave and the possibility of either oblivion or stepping out among the stars without a map relieve one of the ancestral dread that fouled the blood and reduced men to children who called out their mother's name in their last moments? Why did age purchase no peace?

But he no longer had either the time or luxury of musing upon abstractions. Where were the men who lived in the tents? Who was cooking food inside a fire ring no different from those our ancestors cooked on in this same valley over eleven thousand years ago?

The cave located up the mountainside from the camp looked like a black mouth, no, one that was engorged, strung with flumes of green and orange and gray mine tailings or rock that had simply cracked and fallen away from constant exposure to heat and subfreezing temperatures.

It was the kind of place where something had gone terribly wrong long ago, the kind of place that held on to its dead and the spiritual vestiges of the worst people who had lived inside it.

Hackberry wondered what his grandfather, Old Hack, would have to say about a place like this. As though Old Hack had decided to speak to him inside the wind, he could almost hear the sonorous voice and the cynical humor for which his grandfather was infamous: "I suspect it has its moments, Satchel Ass, but truth be known, it's the kind of shithole a moral imbecile like John Wesley Hardin would have found an absolute delight."

Hackberry smiled to himself and hooked his coat behind the butt of his holstered revolver. He walked back toward the cruiser, where Pam Tibbs was still sitting behind the steering wheel, finishing her call to Ethan Riser.

But something in the door mirror had caught her attention. She put down the phone and turned around in the seat and looked back toward the twin bluffs, then got out of the cruiser with the binoculars and focused them on a vehicle that had come to a stop by the twin bluffs. "Better take a look," she said.

"At what?"

"It's a Grand Cherokee," she said. "It's flying an American flag on a staff attached to the back bumper."

"Nick Dolan?"

"I can't tell. It looks like he's lost."

"Forget him."

"Flores and Gaddis are probably with him."

"We're going in, babe. Under a black flag. You got me?"

"No, I didn't hear that."

"Yes, you did. Collins has killed scores of people in his life. What's in the pump?"

"All double-aught bucks," Pam said.

"Load your pockets with them, too."

PREACHER WAS EATING his second brownie when the first cramp hit him. The sensation, or his perception of its significance, was not instantaneous. At first he felt only a slight spasm, not unlike an irritant unexpectedly striking the stomach lining. Then the pain sharpened and spread down toward the colon, like a sliver of jagged tin seeking release. He clenched his buttocks together, still unsure what was happening, faintly embarrassed in front of the woman, trying to hide the discomfort distorting his face.

The next spasm made his jaw drop and the blood drain from his head. He leaned forward, trying to catch his breath, sweat breaking on his upper lip. His stomach was churning, the interior of the tent going out of focus. He swallowed drily and tried to see the woman clearly.

"Are you sick?" she said.

"You ask if I'm sick? I'm poisoned. What's in this?"

"What I said. Chocolate and flour and—"

A bilious metallic taste surged into his mouth. The constriction in his bowels was spreading upward, into his lower chest, like chains wrapping around his ribs and sternum, squeezing the air out of his lungs. "Don't lie," he said.

"I ate the brownies, too. There's nothing wrong with them."

He coughed violently, as though he had eaten a piece of angle iron. "There must be peanut butter in them."

"You have a problem with peanut butter?"

"You bitch." He pulled open the tent flap to let in the cold air. "You treacherous bitch."

"Look at you. A grown man cursing others because he has a stomachache. A man who kills women and young girls calls other people names because a brownie has upset him. Your mother would be ashamed of you. Where did you grow up? In a barn-yard?"

Preacher got to his feet and held on to the tent pole with one hand until the earth stopped shifting under his feet. "What right do you have to talk of my mother?"

"What right, he asks? I'm the mother you took from her husband and her children. The mother you took to be your concubine, that's who I am, you miserable gangster."

He stumbled out into the wind and cold air, his hair soggy with sweat under his hat, his skin burning as though it had been dipped in acid, one hand clenched on his stomach. He headed for his tent, where the Thompson lay on top of his writing table, the drum fat with cartridges, a second cartridge-packed drum resting beside it. That was when he saw a sheriff's cruiser coming up the dirt track and, in the far distance, a second vehicle that seemed part of an optical illusion brought on by the anaphylactic reaction wrecking his nervous system. The second vehicle was a maroon SUV with an American flag whipping from a staff attached to the back bumper. Who were these people? What gave them the right to come on his land? His anger only exacerbated the fire in his entrails and constricted his lungs as though his chest had been touched by the tendrils of a jellyfish.

"Angel! Molo!" he called hoarsely.

"¿Qué pasa, Señor Collins?"

"¡Maten los!" he said.

"¿Quién?"

"Todos que estan en los dos vehiculos."

The two Mexican killers were standing outside their tent. They turned and saw the approaching cruiser. "¿Nosotros los matamos todos? Hombre, esta es una pila de mierda," Angel said. "Chingado, son of a beech, you sure you ain't a marijuanista, Señor Collins? Oops, siento mucho, solamente estoy bromeando."

But Preacher was not interested in what the Mexicans had to

say. He was already inside his tent, gathering up the Thompson, stuffing the extra ammunition pan under his arm, convinced that the voice he had sought in the wind and in the fire and even in an earthquake would speak to him now, with the Jewish woman, inside the cave.

"A GUY JUST came out of a tent," Pam said, leaning forward on the steering wheel, taking her foot off the gas. "Dammit, I can't see him now. The trash pile is in the way. Wait a second. Two other guys are talking to him."

The visual angle from the passenger seat was bad. Hackberry handed her the binoculars. She fitted them to her eyes and adjusted the focus, breathing audibly, her chest rising and falling irregularly. "They look Hispanic," she said. "Maybe they're construction workers, Hack."

"Where's the other guy?"

"I don't know. He's gone. He must have gone back in one of the tents. We need to dial it down."

"No, it's Collins."

She removed the binoculars from her eyes and looked hard and long at him. "You thought you heard a bugle. I think you're seeing and hearing things that aren't there. We can't be wrong on this."

He dropped open the glove box and removed a Beretta nine-millimeter. He pulled back the slide and chambered a round and set the butterfly safety. "I'm not wrong. Pull to the back of the trash pile. We get out simultaneously on each side of the vehicle and stay spread apart. If you see Collins, you kill him."

"Listen to me, Hack—"

"No, Collins doesn't get a chance to use his Thompson. You've never seen anyone shot with a weapon that has that kind of firepower. We kill him on sight and worry about legalities later."

"I can't accept an order like that."

"Yes, you can."

"I know you, Hack. I know the thoughts you have before you think them. You want me to protect myself at all costs, but you've got your own agenda with this guy."

"We left Dr. Freud back there on the road," he said. He stepped out on the hardpan just as the sun broke over the hill, splintering like gold needles, the bottom of the hill still deep in shadow.

He and Pam Tibbs walked toward the pile of house debris, dividing around it, their eyes fixed on the four tents, their eyes watering in the wind and the smoke blowing from a fire that smelled of burning food or garbage.

But because of the angle, they had lost sight of the two Hispanic men, who had gone back in their tent or were behind the vehicles. As Hackberry walked deeper into the shadows, the sunlight that had fractured on the ridgeline disappeared, and he could see the tents and the pickup truck and the SUV and the mountainside in detail, and he realized the mistake he had made: You never allow your enemy to become what is known as a barricaded suspect. Even more important, you never allow your enemy to become a barricaded suspect with a hostage.

Pam Tibbs was to his left, the stock of her cut-down pump Remington twelve-gauge snugged against her shoulder, her eyes sweeping from right to left, left to right, never blinking, her face dilated as though she were staring into an ice storm. He heard her footsteps pause and knew she had just seen Collins at the same moment he had, pushing a woman ahead of him up a footpath that led to the opening in the mountainside.

Collins had knotted his left fist in the fabric of the woman's dress and was holding the Thompson by the pistol grip with his right hand, the barrel at a downward angle. He looked back once at Pam and Hackberry, his face white and small and tight under his hat, then he shoved the woman ahead of him into the cave and disappeared behind her.

"He's got the high ground. We've got to get one of the vehicles between us and him," Hackberry said.

The tent that the two Hispanic men had been using was the largest of the four. The SUV was parked not far from the tent flap; the pickup truck was parked between two other tents. The only sounds were the ruffling of the wind on the polyethylene surfaces of the tents and a rock toppling from the ridgeline and the engine of the maroon SUV coming up the dirt track from the bluffs.

Hackberry turned around and raised one fist in the air, hoping that Pete Flores would recognize the universal military signal to stop. But either Flores did not see him, or the driver, who was undoubtedly Nick Dolan, chose to keep coming.

Hackberry shifted his direction, crossing behind Pam Tibbs, his .45 revolver on full cock, the Beretta stuffed through the back of his gun belt. "I'm going to clear the first tent. Cover me," he said.

He opened his Queen pocketknife with his teeth and walked quickly to the back of the tent, taking long strides, watching the other tents and the two parked vehicles, both of which had tinted windows. The blade of his knife could shave hair off his arm. He sliced the cords that were tied to the tent's support poles and steel ground pins and watched the shape go out of the tent as it collapsed in a pile.

Nothing moved under its folds. He crossed behind Pam Tibbs, lifting his eyes to the cave entrance on the mountainside. The pile of building debris was behind them now, the bulldozed stucco powdering, the broken asbestos feathering in the wind. If Collins opened up on them, the only cover available would be the pickup truck or the SUV, and he could not be sure either of them was unoccupied.

He felt naked in the way a person feels naked in a dream, in a public place, before a large audience. But the sense of nakedness in his and Pam's circumstances went beyond that. It was the kind of sensation a forward artillery observer experiences when the first round he has called in for effect strikes home and his position is exposed. It was the kind of nakedness a navy corpsman feels when he runs through automatic-weapons fire to reach a wounded marine. The sensation was akin to having one's skin pulled off in strips with a pair of pliers.

Then he realized that regardless of the criminal background of his antagonists, at least one of them had made the mistake of all amateurs: His vanity or his libido or whatever megalomaniacal passion defined him was more important to him than the utilitarian simplicity of a stone killer and survivor like Jack Collins.

One man was wearing lizard-skin cowboy boots, chrome-plated on the heels and toes. They flashed with a dull silvery light beneath the running board on the far side of the pickup truck.

"Three o'clock, Pam!" Hackberry said.

At the same moment the man behind the truck fired an Uzi or a MAC-10 across the hood, then moved back quickly behind the cab. But his one-handed aim was sloppy, and the bullets hit the trash pile and stitched the water drum and cut a line across the hardpan, flicking dirt into the air and ricocheting off rocks and whining into the distance with the diminished sound of a broken bedspring.

Hackberry aimed his .45 with both hands and fired through the tinted window on the driver's side, cascading glass onto the seats and blowing out the opposite window. He fired two more rounds, one through the window on the extended cab, one through the back door, leaving a clean-edged, polished indentation and hole the size of a quarter. But the three rounds he had let off did no good. The man with the automatic weapon moved behind the back of the cab and sprayed the whole area blindly, probably as masking fire for either the other Hispanic man, who was nowhere in sight, or Jack Collins up in the cave.

The shooting stopped. Hackberry had pulled back to the edge of the trash pile, and Pam was somewhere off to his left, in the shadows or behind the concrete foundation of the destroyed house. In all probability, the shooter was changing magazines. Hackberry got down on his hands and knees, then on his stomach. He heard a metallic click, like a latching steel mechanism being inserted into a socket. He extended his .45, gripping it with both hands, his elbows propped in the dirt, the pain along his spine flaring into his ribs.

Hackberry saw the chrome-sheathed lizard-skin boots of the shooter move from behind the back tire. He sighted down the long barrel of his .45 at the place where the blue-jean cuff of the shooter's right pants leg met the top of his foot. He pulled the trigger.

The shooter screamed when the 230-grain round tore through his boot. He fell to the ground and yelled out again, holding his destroyed foot and ankle, blood welling through his fingers, his other hand still gripping his weapon.

Pam Tibbs ran toward the truck, her pump shotgun held in front of her, the safety off, lifting the barrel, stepping sideways in an arc around the hood of the truck, almost like an erratic dancer, coming into position so that she stood in full view of the shooter. All the time she was yelling, as though to a man with neither sight nor hearing, "Give it up! Give it up! Give it up! Do it now! Do it now! Throw it away! Hands straight out on the ground! You must do it now! No, you do not do that! Both hands in the dirt! Did you hear me?"

Then she squeezed the trigger. Five feet away, the man who would not release his weapon ate a pattern of buckshot as wide as his hand and watched his brains splatter across the side panel of his truck.

When Hackberry got to her, she had already jacked the spent shell from the chamber and was shoving another one into the magazine with her thumb, her hands still trembling.

"Did you see the other guy?" he said.

"No, where is he?" she said. Her eyes were as round as marbles, jittering in their sockets.

"I didn't see him. We're exposed. Get behind the truck."

"Where's Collins?"

"In the cave. Get behind the truck. Did you hear me?"

"What's that sound?"

"What sound?" he said. But the .45 rounds he had fired had left his ears ringing, and he couldn't make out her words.

"It's that idiot Dolan," she said.

They couldn't believe what they saw next. Nick Dolan's SUV had veered off the dirt track, swinging wide of the concrete slab on which the stucco house had once stood, and was now coming full-bore across the hardpan, rocks and mud flying up into the undercarriage, the frame jolting on the springs.

"Has he lost his mind?" Pam said.

Nick Dolan plowed through the tent closest to the mountain, ripping it loose from its steel pins, wrapping the polyethylene material and destroyed aluminum poles across the grille and hood. But inside the sounds of the tent tearing and the tie ropes breaking and the steel pins whipping back against the SUV, Hackberry had heard a solid weight impact sickeningly against the SUV's hood.

Nick slammed on his brakes, and the tangle of material and tent poles and a broken cot rolled off his vehicle into the dirt, with the body of the second Hispanic man inside.

"I saw him go into the tent. He had a gun," Nick said from the window. A pair of binoculars hung from his neck.

"Your wife could have been in there," Pam said.

"No, we saw Collins take her into the hole in the mountain. Let's get up there," Nick said.

Vikki Gaddis sat in the passenger seat, and Pete Flores sat in back, leaning forward against the front seat.

"Y'all stay where you are," Hackberry said.

"I'm going up there with you," Nick said.

"No, you're not," Hackberry said.

"That's my wife," Nick said, opening the door.

"You're about to find yourself in handcuffs, Mr. Dolan," Pam said.

Hackberry dumped the spent shells from the cylinder of his revolver into his palm and reloaded the empty chambers. He motioned to Pam Tibbs and began walking with her toward the mountain, ignoring the three new arrivals, hoping his last words to them had stuck.

"You don't want to wait for the locals?" she said.

"Wrong move. I'm going straight up the path. I want you to come in from the side and stay just outside the cave."

"Why?"

"Collins won't shoot if he thinks I'm alone."

"Why not?"

"He has too much pride. With Collins, it's not about money or sex. He thinks it's the twilight of the gods and he's at center stage."

Nick Dolan and Vikki Gaddis and Pete Flores were all getting out of the SUV.

"You three get right back in your vehicle and drive back toward the road and stay there," Hackberry said.

"To hell with that," Nick said.

"Sheriff, give me a weapon and let me go up there with you," Pete said.

"Can't do it, partner. End of discussion," Hackberry said. "Ms. Gaddis, you keep these two guys here. If you want to see Mrs. Dolan come out of that cave alive, don't mess in what's about to happen."

Hackberry began walking up the path alone, while Pam Tibbs cut across the green and orange and gray tailings that were strung down the incline, carrying her shotgun at port arms.

Hackberry paused at the cave's entrance, his .45 holstered, the Beretta still tucked inside the back of his gun belt. He smelled a dank odor like mouse droppings or bat guano and water pooled in stone. He felt the wind coursing over his skin, flowing into the cave. "Can you hear me, Collins?" he said.

There was no answer. Hackberry stepped inside the darkness of the cave as though slipping from the world of light into one of perpetual shade.

The body of a man lay behind a boulder. The wounds in his chest and stomach and legs were egregious. The amount of blood that had pooled around him and soaked into his sheep-lined leather coat and bradded orange work pants seemed more than his body could have contained.

"You can do a good deed here, Jack," Hackberry called out.

After the echo died, he thought he heard a rattling sound in the dark, farther back in the cave.

"Did you hear me, Jack?"

"You're backlit, Sheriff," a voice said from deep in the cave's interior.

"That's right. You can pop me any time you want." Hackberry paused. "You're not above doing a good deed, are you?"

"What might that be?"

"Mrs. Dolan has children. They want her back. How about it?"

"I'll take it under advisement."

"I don't think you're a man who hides behind a woman."

"I don't have to hide behind anyone. You hear that sound? Why don't you come toward me a little more and check out your environment?"

"Rattlers are holed up in here?"

"Probably not more than a couple of dozen. Just flatten yourself out against the wall."

"Your voice sounds a little strange, Jack."

"He's had an anaphylactic reaction to peanut butter. It may be fatal," a woman's voice said.

"You shut up," Collins said.

"Is that right, Jack? You want to go to a hospital?" Hackberry said.

But there was no answer.

"I was a navy corpsman," Hackberry said. "Severe anaphylaxis can bring on respiratory and coronary arrest, partner. It's a bad way to go, strangling in your spit, your sphincter letting go, that sort of thing."

"I can squeeze this trigger, and you'll be a petroglyph."

"But that's not what this is about, is it? You're haunted by the women and girls you killed because your act was that of a coward, not because you robbed them of their lives. You don't want redemption, Jack. You want validation, justification for an act you know is indefensible."

"Sheriff Holland, don't bait this man or try to reason with him. Kill him so he doesn't kill others. I'm not afraid," the woman said.

Hackberry gritted his teeth in his frustration with Esther Dolan. "That's not why I'm here, Jack. I'm not your executioner. I'm not worthy of you. You already said it—I'm a drunk and the sexual exploiter of poor third-world women. I've got to hand it to you, for good or bad, you're the kind of guy who belongs to the ages. You screwed up behind the church, but I think the order for the mass shooting came from Hugo Cistranos and wasn't your idea. That's important to remember, Jack. You're not a coward. You can prove that this morning. Turn Mrs. Dolan loose and take your chances with me. That's what real cojones are about, right? You say full throttle and fuck it and sail out over the abyss."

There was a long silence. Hackberry could feel the wind puffing around him, blowing coldly on his neck and the backs of his ears. Again he heard a rattling sound, like the wispy rattling of seeds inside a dried poppy husk.

"I've got to know something," Collins said.

"Ask me."

"That night I went inside your house, you said my mother wanted me aborted, that I was despised in the womb. Why would you treat me with such contempt and odium?"

"My remark wasn't aimed at you."

"Then who?"

Hackberry paused. "We don't get to choose our parents."

"My mother wasn't like that, like what you said. She wasn't like that at all."

"Maybe she wasn't, sir. Maybe I was all wrong."

"Then say that."

"I just did."

"You think your words will make me merciful now?"

"Probably not. Maybe I've just been firing in the well."

"Get out of here, Mrs. Dolan. Go back to your family."

Unbelievingly, Hackberry saw Esther Dolan running out of the darkness, her shoulder close to the right wall, her arms gathered across her chest, her face averted from something on the left side of the cave.

Hackberry grabbed her and pushed her behind him out into the light. He turned and went back into the cave, lifting his revolver from his holster. "You still there, Jack?"

"I'm at your disposal."

"Do I have to come in after you?"

"You could wait me out. The fact that you've chosen otherwise tells me it's you who's looking for salvation, Sheriff, not me. Something happen in Korea you don't tell a lot of people about?"

"Could be."

"I'll be glad to oblige. I've got fifty rounds in my pan. Do you know what you'll look like when I get finished?"

"Who cares? I'm old. I've had a good life. Fuck you, Jack."

But nothing happened. Inside the darkness, Hackberry could hear the rilling sound of small rocks, as though they were slipping down a grade.

"Maybe I'll see you down the road, Sheriff," Collins said.

Suddenly, a truck flare burst into flame far back in the cave. Collins hurled it end over end onto a rock shelf where diamondbacks as thick as Hack's wrists writhed among one another, their rattlers buzzing like maracas.

Hackberry emptied his .45 down the cave shaft, then pulled the Beretta from the back of his belt and let off all fourteen rounds, the bullets sparking on the cave walls, thudding into layers of bat guano and mold, ricocheting deep underground.

When he finished firing, he was almost deaf, his eardrums as insensate as lumps of cauliflower. The air was dense with smoke and the smell of cordite and animal feces and the musky odor of disturbed birds' and rats' nests. He could see the snakes looping and coiling on the shelf, their eyes bright pinpoints in the hot red glare of the truck flare. Tarantulas the diameter of baseballs, with black furry legs, were crawling down the sides of the shelf onto the cave floor. Hackberry opened and closed his mouth and swallowed and forced air through his ears. "I get you, Jack?" he called out.

He listened for an answer, his head slightly bowed. All he heard in response were feet moving farther down the shaft, deeper into the mountain, and the voice of an impaired man saying, "Ma, is that you? It's Jack, your son. Ma?"

Epilogue

THE WEEKS PASSED, then months, and Hackberry Holland's life slipped back into routine. Search teams and spelunkers crawled deep into the tunnel where Jack Collins had disappeared. A geologist borrowed from the University of Texas, with a flair for the poetic in his report, described the tunnel as "serpentine in pattern, in places as narrow as a birth canal, the floor and ceiling ridged with sharp projections that lacerate the palms, knees, and back simultaneously, the air akin in its foulness to a water well with a dead cow in it."

Everyone who went into the cave conceded that somewhere on the other side of the mountain there was an air source, perhaps a small one hidden behind brush growing out of the rock, but an opening of some kind that allowed water and light and small animals into the mountain's interior, because on the far side of the spot where the tunnel bottomed and then rose at a forty-five-degree angle, there were seeds from piñon trees that had drifted down from above, and on a flat rock a hollowed-out depression that had probably been used as an Indian grinding bowl.

The official statement from a government spokesman indicated that Jack Collins had probably been wounded by gunfire and died inside the mountain, and his remains would probably never be found. But local residents began to report sightings of an emaciated man who foraged in landfills and Dumpsters and wore rags that were black with grime and a rope for a belt and whose beard grew in a point to the middle of his chest. The emaciated man also wore cowboy boots whose soles were held on with duct tape, and a fedora with holes in the creases.

When a reporter asked Hackberry Holland about his speculations on the fate of Jack Collins, he thought for a moment and said, "What difference does it make?"

"Sir?" the reporter said.

"Preacher's kind don't go away easily. If Jack isn't out there now, his successor is."

"You sound like y'all had a personal relationship," the reporter said.

"I guess you could say I got to know him in North Korea."

"I'm confused," the reporter said. "Korea? You're saying the guy's a terrorist or something?"

"How about I buy you coffee up at the café?" Hackberry said.

No charges were ever filed against Pete Flores, in large part because the perpetrators of the massacre behind the church were thought to be dead and no local or federal official wanted to see a basically innocent and decent man inserted into a process that, once started, becomes irreversible and eventually destroys lives for no practical purpose. If there was any drama at all in the aftermath of the events that took place on the mountainside above Jack Collins's burned and bulldozed cottage, it occurred in an idle moment when Vikki Gaddis was sorting through her purse at the kitchen table and found a business card she had put away and forgotten about.

"What's that?" Pete said. He was drying the dishes, glancing back at her from the kitchen counter.

"A guy from the Nitty Gritty Dirt Band left it at the steak house. He liked my music."

"Did you call him?"

"No."

"Why not?"

"Why should I?"

He didn't have an answer. A few minutes later, he picked up the card from the table and walked outside and over a bare knoll dotted with clusters of prickly-pear cactus. From the top of the knoll, he could see a half-dozen oil wells methodically pumping up and down on a rolling plain that seemed to bleed into the sunset. The air smelled of natural gas and creosote and a stack of old tires someone had burned. Behind him, the ever-present dust gusted off the road and floated in a gray cloud over the clapboard house he and Vikki rented. He opened his cell phone and dialed the number on the business card.

Six weeks later, Vikki Gaddis cut her first record at Martina and John McBride's Blackbird Studio in Nashville.

For Hackberry Holland, the end of the story lay not in the fate of Jack Collins or Hugo Cistranos and Arthur Rooney or any of their minions. By the same token, it did not lie in the fact that justice was done for Pete Flores and that the talent of his wife, Vikki Gaddis, was recognized by her fellow artists, or even in the fact that Vikki and Pete later bought a ranch at the foot of the blue Canadian Rockies. Instead, the conclusion of Hackberry's odyssey from Camp Five in No Name Valley to an alluvial floodplain north of the Chisos Mountains was represented by a bizarre event that remained, at least for him, as an emblematic moment larger than the narrative about it.

It involved the unexpected arrival of Nick Dolan, the former operator of a skin joint, on Collins's property, driving an SUV that had the lacquered brilliance of a maroon lollipop, a stolen American flag with a broomstick for a staff mounted on the rear bumper, his passengers a blue-collar community-college student who thought it perfectly natural to sing Carter Family spirituals in a beer joint and a former American soldier who was so brave he had forgotten to be afraid.

The three of them made for an improbable cast of heroes. Perhaps like an ancient Roman watching a Vesuvian mountain grow red and translucent until it exploded and rained its sparks on a dark sea, they did not recognize the importance of the events taking place around them or the fact that they were players in a great historical drama. They would be the last to claim they had planned the charge across the hardpan into Jack Collins's camp. But that was the key to understanding them: Their humility, the disparity in their backgrounds, the courage they didn't acknowledge in themselves, the choices they made out of instinct rather than intellect, these characteristics constituted the glue that held them together as individuals and as a people. Empires came and went. The indomitable nature of the human spirit did not.

Or at least these were the lessons that Hackberry Holland and Pam Tibbs tried to take from their own story.